NO ONE ELSE FEELS LIKE THIS

Henry Bonham-Carter

Copyright © Henry Bonham-Carter 2024

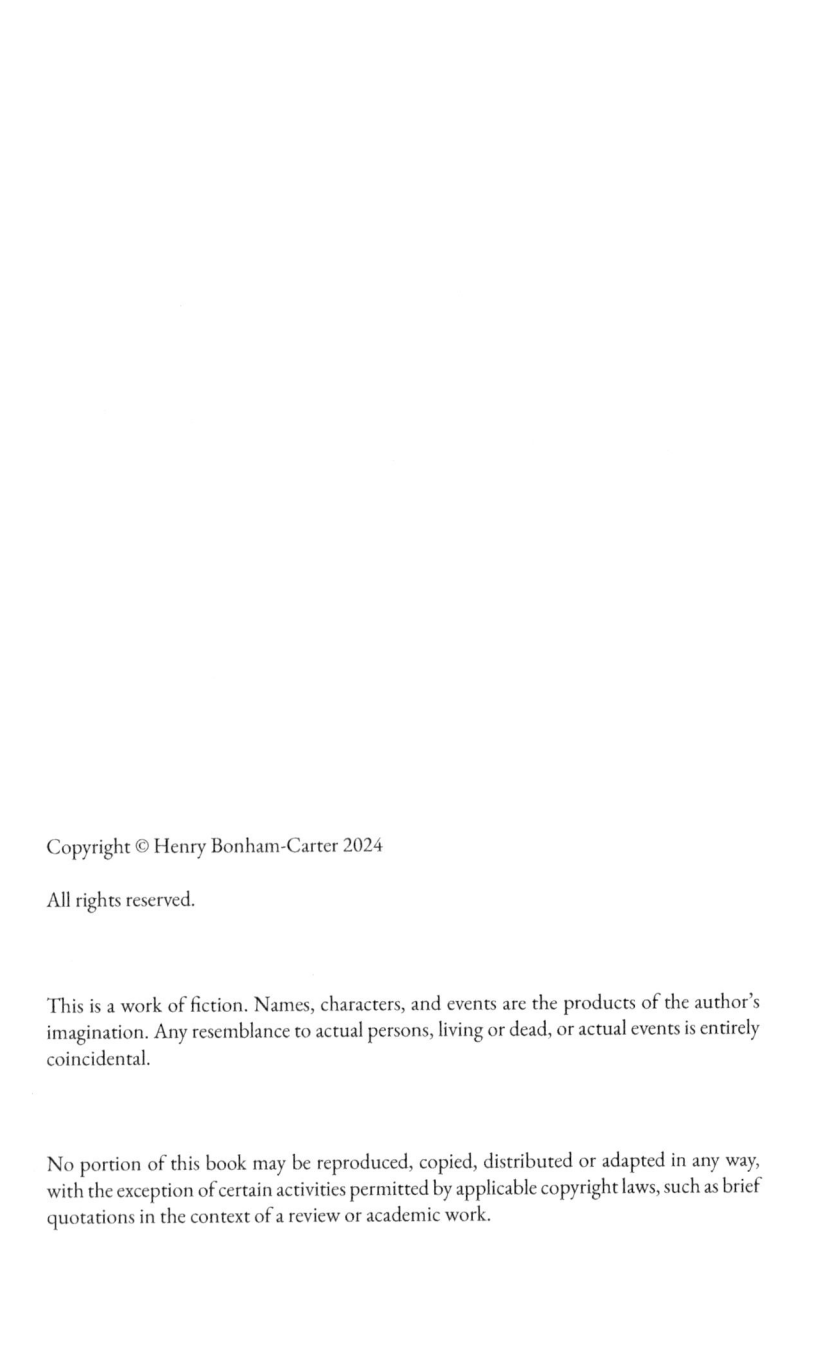

All rights reserved.

This is a work of fiction. Names, characters, and events are the products of the author's imagination. Any resemblance to actual persons, living or dead, or actual events is entirely coincidental.

No portion of this book may be reproduced, copied, distributed or adapted in any way, with the exception of certain activities permitted by applicable copyright laws, such as brief quotations in the context of a review or academic work.

For all those who are struggling: You are not alone. Please talk to someone and get help. It can make all the difference.
For all those who are helping: It's worth it.

With special thanks to my beloved family.
Thanks for keeping me afloat.

Chapter One

"Jump, jump, jump." There's just one voice at first, coming from outside the Boathouse pub below, but it is soon joined by three, then four more, finally settling on a chorus of about ten, mainly male, drunk, laughing voices: no harmonies, no malice, just no idea what they're doing.

You know this pub, this stretch of the River Thames and this bridge like you know your own unhappiness. You stare down at the water below, as ominous and inhospitable as the gloomy early evening June sky above, wondering if it will wash away the pain. It's not meant to be like this. It's the Summer Solstice, the longest day of the year, the day when light should reign. Tomorrow the days will start getting darker. They won't get any darker for you.

And you jump.

Though just one person jumps, the ripples as you hit the water will engulf countless others for years to come. Desperate people can do tragic things. And many people are desperate people. It's just not always obvious which ones they are.

So why did you jump? Who are you? Where do we start?

"You've got crazy pipes, you know? When you sing it's like you're opening a window into your whole fucking soul and I can't look anywhere else. Know what I mean?"

Martha James doesn't reply. She isn't paying much attention to the words. She's heard similar from her ex many times before. She is carefully watching the knife he is scraping up and down the strings of his guitar, producing a screeching sound which slices through her attempts at composure with alarming ease.

"Music gives the world its colour, Mar. And we can give the world music."

"I hope so, Dan." Martha smiles weakly this time and keeps her eyes fixed on the moving blade. She catches a brief glimpse of her reflection off its shiny surface and notices the nose ring bearing her mother's initial, 'N', gleaming in the light. She looks calmer than she feels.

"But this world will never listen, Mar. This world is screwed. It only recognises fucking loudmouths and mediocrity. It's screwed and we're screwed because of it."

Martha can see Dan's getting agitated now. He's pulled the knife away from the guitar and is slowly running it between the thumb and forefinger of his left hand, as someone might do if they were trying to straighten out a slightly crumpled piece of paper. His head is staring down, so Martha can only see the top of the long blond hair, which she had once pictured as a sign of his beautiful rebellion, but now merely acts as a serene facade for the turmoil beneath it.

"It's OK, Dan. It takes time. Like all we can do is keep writing our stuff and keep playing. It's still early days. Everything can change in an instant."

She knows that phrase well. Her dad used to say it to her when she was young and feeling sad, so that she would know things would soon get better.

He doesn't say it any more.

"Nothing's going to change for us while we're on this fucked-up break. We both know that. We've got to be together… you know… properly together, for our music to work. We're soul mates, Mar. We're different from the losers in this suburban shithole. We know what it's like to live in big cities… we know what it's like to live."

Martha can hear the desperate cracks in Dan's voice, betraying the fractures which started in his heart but now splinter his whole being. She knows she mustn't pity him though because, if she did, she'd have to pity herself too.

He's right about one thing, and one thing only. They do both feel like outsiders in this town. Dan moved from London eight years ago, after his parents read an article about how the Sonnley AllRays Academy was going to be one of the best state schools in the country. That's almost half his life ago. When does it become too long to be an excuse?

As for Martha, five years ago, she would never have imagined herself here in Berkshire, only 55 minutes from central London (as the slogan on the Welcome to Sonnley sign smugly advises all visitors); five years ago, Martha was still in Los Angeles with her brother and her parents; five years ago, Martha had a mother.

Everything can change in an instant. And when it does, all that's left is nostalgia for a future which never happened.

"It's not a break, Dan. We won't be a couple again." Martha tries to speak as gently and kindly as she can. She moves to put a consoling hand on his shoulder before thinking better of it. "Come on, Dan, chill. I'm only sixteen, you're only eighteen! There's no point looking back. Focus on the future... and music is our future. That's where we're best together. You know that really."

Martha wasn't meant to be here this evening. She was meant to be at school watching her dad speaking at some dull event to open the new Performing Arts Centre. But she missed it because Dan sounded excited about a new song for the band. At least that's what she told herself. She doesn't like letting her dad down without a reason.

Her ex doesn't say anything. He just tugs the sleeve of his shirt up, stops running his fingers up and down the blade, and slowly presses it into his forearm until the blood starts to well up, adding another line to those of differing prominence which cover it.

"No, Dan. Don't... it doesn't help. It won't change anything."

"It does help. You used to know that."

Martha looks at the fading scars on her own forearm. She's changed. That's what she knows now.

And she wishes that she'd gone to support her dad at the boring school event.

People notice Finn James. He can still turn heads with his passing resemblance to a youngish Barack Obama, which many years ago almost landed him the film role which might have changed his life. Though he's never seen the similarity himself, even more so now that he is in his early forties and all he sees in the mirror is what he's been through. He stands on the stage and surveys the audience. He can feel the same buzz of nervous excitement he used to get in his acting days. But it feels more valuable now, and the words are his own.

"Marsh Park means so much to most of the students here today: they sat on a swing for the first time there; they played with other toddlers for the first time there; they kicked their first football or climbed their first tree there." Finn throws his arms out towards the audience, imploring them to join him. "We can't just sit back and let another supermarket destroy all that. We've only got three weeks. Think about that... three weeks, and then Marsh Park will no longer be ours. It's going to be tight, but we can do it, we have to do it. This isn't just about a few do-gooders fighting for a worthy cause, this is about all of us." Finn pauses, slowly glances round the audience, and absent-mindedly strokes the scar on his left cheek, which always seems to fascinate other people. But it's the invisible scars which matter more to Finn. He waits six seconds for dramatic effect, before lowering his left hand from his face, pointing directly at random people and slamming his right fist down on the lectern in front of him to the same beat as his next sentence. "It's about you... you... you... me... all of us. Do the people of Sonnley have a voice? Do the people of Sonnley make a difference? Do the people of Sonnley matter?... I say we do."

When your mum is Norwegian, your dad Antiguan, you were brought up in Ireland, and then spent years trying to launch an acting career in America, it's difficult to believe you fully belong anywhere. And Finn James wants to belong. He knows he's missed out, and he knows that little things like parks can help people belong. So he's going to fight to save them with a strength reserved for only the most precious things in life; a strength he needs a lot these days; a strength he should have shown five years ago.

He skims his eyes round the audience again, looking for his daughter this time. He wants Martha to be proud of him on stage, commanding an audience, showing her that dreams really can come true. And if they don't, you dust yourself down and dream and dream again until you find one that does. That's what Finn has done, and that's why he's standing on the stage of the newly-opened Ray Hope Centre for Performing Arts as a drama teacher, announcing a fund-raising play to save Marsh Park and trying to inspire as many teenagers as he can to become the best versions of themselves. He knows his beloved wife, Niamh, would have been so proud of him. And he knows he's only here because she's gone.

But there is no sign of Martha. She isn't there. Why would she be? This isn't her dream and she's not ready to dream again yet.

Art Mann is not sure if he is stupid or not. He hopes not. He knows his teachers think he is, and his mum says he isn't. But she would say that, wouldn't she? She's his mum. He's not that stupid.

Of course, his teachers don't use the word stupid, they are too smart for that. They just give him bad marks. And Art knows that there are only two types of people who get bad marks: the ones they call "underachievers", who get told off and the teachers spend loads of time with; and the ones who have "found their level", so no one bothers about. Those are the stupid ones, and Art is usually one of those. Usually, but not always, as he does also get told off sometimes.

So it's not easy for him to know if he is stupid or not. And Art doesn't like uncertainty. His mum says that he sees everything as black or white, and always says what he thinks, whatever the impact on others, but he knows she's wrong. When Art looks in the mirror, he can't even see if he is black or white himself. It's easy for her, she hasn't got that uncertainty. But his skin is the light brown of the moths he sometimes sees when he leaves his bedroom window open in summer, circling his bedside light as though it will give them all the answers they need. And he doesn't know where it comes from. And he has never asked.

There is no uncertainty in what he sees now. Why did his mum force him to waste a Friday evening at AllRays Academy watching adults gush about another school building, which he hopes he'll never see again? He had almost managed to get them to the exit unscathed and now this.

"Good evening, Miss Mann." A teacher is speaking to his mum. That doesn't usually end well.

"Ms." Art's mum knows that it is no one else's business whether or not she is married. She also knows that most of the teachers don't like her because she is younger and more attractive than they are. At least that's what she tells Art, but he thinks it is because she gives them grief for thinking he is stupid. But he doesn't say so. You see, he can think about the impact before he speaks.

"I need to warn you that Art is a million miles away from passing his History GCSE."

"Maybe he needs a better teacher?"

The corners of Art's mum's mouth have a natural slight lilt upwards, as though she is always smiling about something that others don't know about. Maybe she is? Either way it's certainly an effective way to irritate a history teacher who badmouths her son.

"Or maybe he needs to spend more time in the real world and less in a little dreamworld?"

"Why?"

"Because he's going to have to live in the real world when he leaves this place?"

"All the more reason to stay out of it as long as he can then."

Art closes his eyes. He knows what this will mean. In his next history lesson he will get a detention simply for asking why the Romans built roads but didn't bother to build cars and be told to keep his smart-arsed comments for home where no one cares about his future.

But Art's mum does care. She cares about him more than anyone could ever care about anything. If it weren't for him she wouldn't even be alive any more. So she'll defend him against anyone, right or wrong.

"Art... Art... Ms Mann. Can I have a quick word please?" A second teacher has delayed their escape. Mr James is a little out of breath as he's run straight from the stage to catch them up. The slight breathlessness and the gentle Irish lilt in his voice give the words both an urgency and a kindness which demand attention. As a drama teacher, he should be proud of his delivery.

Art doesn't notice the kindness. He just notices another teacher wanting to speak to them.

"Hi Finn. How are you?" His mum smiles. She doesn't do that to teachers often. And how does she know his first name? It sounds a bit creepy to be honest. Why would she do it?

"I'm good ta, Ms Mann... so sorry to bother you." He pauses for a few seconds and takes some deep breaths. "Whoah... I'm not as fit as I once was. Sorry." Art's mum smiles again and waits for him to continue. "I just wanted a quick word if I can. Did you hear what we were saying up there about putting on a play to raise funds to save Marsh Park?"

Art hadn't heard. He hadn't been listening to the teachers on stage. He had been staring at a fire extinguisher and a defibrillator pinned to the wall next to each other at the side of the auditorium, wondering which would be the correct order to use them in if someone carrying a candle were to collapse with a cardiac arrest and start a fire.

"Yes. Lovely idea, Finn. I've taken Art there since he was a baby. We don't need another nondescript supermarket."

"Exactly, Ms Mann... It's more than just a park, it's the place where most of these kids have learnt to live and have fun." This really does seem to matter to him.

But it doesn't matter to Art. OK, he used to go to Marsh Park a lot when he was a kid, so maybe that's why his mum is all sentimental about it. He still goes there two or three times a week, in fact, when it is dark and no one is around, and just sits on the swings and thinks. It is still a dump though... might as well be a supermarket.

"I couldn't agree more, Finn." Art doesn't like his mum repeating his teacher's first name so often. She sounds like someone who has suddenly remembered a name she had forgotten and is saying it as often as possible to prove that she knows it. Embarrassing. Art looks down at his feet.

"Aww, thanks, Ms Mann. You're a star... Well, I need a favour from you, Art."

Art doesn't like those words. Favours usually mean someone wants you to do something you don't want to do. He keeps looking at his feet. His left foot looks bigger than his right, but it's not. Why is that, he wonders?

"I really want... no, I would absolutely love it if we could use one of your stories as our play, Art."

"Wow! Exciting! That's amazing, Finn!" Art's mum prods him in the arm, and nods at him wide-eyed. He's learned that this means he has to say something.

"What?" says Art. Maybe it's the lighting in the hall that is making his left foot seem more prominent.

"Just that, Art. One of your stories would be perfect."

"What stories?"

"The ones you've written in history... I'm sorry, I probably shouldn't say this, but I've heard about them in the staff room, and I love them."

"They're not stories, they're history essays."

"Yeah, yeah, yeah... of course... sorry... and they're great."

"They're not. They're rubbish. That's why I'm a million miles away from my history GCSE."

"Ah no, I'm sure you're not... I guess, well, maybe they're not quite classic history essays, and that's why I love them. They'd make fantastic plays. They've got drama, humour, emotion... real impact, Art."

Art's mum makes one of those embarrassing whooping noises, and pats Art on the shoulder with one hand and Mr James on the arm with the other.

"Wonderful. Thanks, Finn. That would be amazing!" She turns to Art and hugs him. "I've always told you your stories were special." It's true. She has. She's got a big box at home where she has kept all Art's writing since he was at Primary school and wrote a story about how Julius Ceezar (sic) had a cat called Dennis. Dennis was very big and all the other cats were scared of him. If the other cats wanted his food he would bite them and kill them, but if Dennis wanted their food he just took it. Then, one day, another cat called Bluetooth, who had a strange ability to read everyone's minds, bit him first with his special blue tooth and Dennis never stole anyone's food again.

"What do you say, Art?... it could be a fantastic opportunity for you... everyone will see one of your stories come to life." Mr James sounds like his voice is dancing with excitement.

Art scratches anxiously at the small, rounded nose he unmistakeably inherited from his mother, but which looks lost in his long angular face, as opposed to being the alluring, jaunty centrepiece of her smaller, softer features.

"Uh... OK, I guess." Art doesn't look up. He feels like a cat with a full food bowl who has just spotted Dennis before Bluetooth has appeared on the scene. He doesn't want everyone to see his stories come to life; he doesn't want to be the centre of attention; he doesn't want his history essays to be seen as stories. But Art does want his mum to be proud of him for something he's done at school. It doesn't happen often.

"Thanks, Finn, that's wonderful." Charley Mann playfully taps her son on the back of the head. If he were the sort of person who looks into people's eyes, he would notice hers are sparkling at the moment. But he's not.

And if he were the sort of person who notices when something happens which will change the course of their life radically, he would have said no.

But he's not.

Priya Moore heads for the only table at the front of the auditorium with two empty seats. She had spotted it earlier and hoped that Tommy was just late, but it was no more than hope. She glances at their names printed on pieces of folded cardboard alongside the *AllRays Software* logo of a world map with lightbulbs igniting all round it, and sighs inwardly at the spelling of her name. Preeanker. How difficult can it be to get Priyanka right? She's seen so many spellings over the years that it only slightly irritates her these days.

She takes a deep breath, and absent-mindedly runs her left hand through the long hair, which Tommy once said was as beautiful, shiny and black as finely polished obsidian, before joking that he hoped it hadn't needed a volcanic eruption to form it. That was a long time ago though, before their own ash clouds had formed.

Priya takes her seat on the table with four of Tommy's work colleagues and their partners and helps herself to a glass of red wine to help with the small talk. They're all ahead of her, having made the most of the free alcohol whilst she was on stage with Finn James trying to summon up interest in the fundraising play to save

Marsh Park prior to the *All Rays Software* awards ceremony, but she's missed the food, so it won't take long to catch up.

Priya glances at her phone, wondering if her husband tried to call while she'd put it on mute earlier. He hadn't. But there's a message. *Sorry xxx.* That's all it says. She drains her glass and nods appreciatively as the man next to her, whose name card is annoyingly slanted away from her so that she can't thank him by name, lifts the bottle to offer her more. She notices this time that it's Chilean Merlot. It hadn't mattered before, but it's fine anyway. He empties the contents into her glass, then raises his left arm and clicks his fingers in the direction of one of the waiting staff, whilst waving the empty bottle in his right hand and pointing at it to make his requirement clear. Priya winces.

"There you go, sir." The waitress places another bottle of red wine on the table next to him. She is a slim, middle-aged woman whose age and beauty are only betrayed by a few lines creeping up from her neck and down from her forehead as if in a race to the nose. Only she knows if the lines tell a story of joy and a life well lived, or of guilt, sadness and grief. Or maybe a combination of both?

"Hi Mel. What are you doing here? How's Rosa?" Priya doesn't know why she asks the questions. Maybe it's just a reaction to the awkwardness of the situation. But she knows the answers already. Mel had been the co-owner of Sonnley's best restaurant; she and Rosa had babysat Tommy (and years later his and Priya's children), always refusing payment; they had thrown the best parties in Sonnley. They should be relishing retirement and their future together. But they are not. Mel is waiting tables at company functions to keep them alive.

"She's... you know... she's only going to get worse."

Priya pats her friend on the arm. "Can we take her out in the next few days?"

"Thanks, that's kind, but we're OK."

"We'd like to, Mel. We've not seen her this week."

"Thanks, Pri... It was a long time ago... Different times."

"They don't have to be, Tommy. You're a good man. I wish you could see that."

He doesn't reply, so she carries on. "You should have come, you know."

"Yeah... sorry."

"How are the kids? I guess you've not had to save them from stabbing each other with a kitchen knife in an argument over the last brownie or put out an unexpected chip fan fire or protect them from a masked intruder who..." The sarcasm arrows down the line more clearly than the words themselves. Priya hadn't intended to say any of it, but sometimes frustration finds a way out, especially with a few glasses of wine to ease its path. But getting angry doesn't help. She knows that.

"OK, Pri, I get it... Sorry."

"No... I'm sorry."

Chapter Two

"I don't do forgiveness. Forgiveness is for weak people; forgiveness is for those who have no self-respect; forgiveness is for life's losers, who will continue to be hurt and let down until the end of their sad, miserable existences. It's quite simple really. If someone lets me down, I crush them, and they don't do it again. I don't do forgiveness."

Martha James slams her fist on the table and stares directly at her dad.

He's heard those words spoken countless times today, but never with the same conviction as he's hearing now.

"Fantastic. Thanks, Martha. That's great. We've got a couple more to hear, and then we'll decide." Priya Moore smiles, leans towards her co-director and whispers "I think we may have found our Mrs Thatcher, Finn. She's clearly got the family acting gene!"

"I hope not... mine never did me any good!" Finn James laughs not altogether convincingly and changes the subject. "I think we've got a couple of girls over from Sonnley Ladies to hear now, haven't we?"

To use its formal title, Sonnley College for Young Ladies is a private school renowned for its academic achievements, sporting and theatrical excellence, and most of all its cost. It does not generally collaborate with Sonnley AllRays Academy on anything, nor encourage its pupils to do so either. Nonetheless a few of them have turned up for the open audition. After all, Marsh Park is for everyone. It doesn't discriminate on any grounds. Sonnley Ladies pupils are just as entitled to use it and want to save it... or at least to want the lead role in a fund-raising play which the whole town knows about.

"Those are the posh slags, aren't they?" As he stands at the side of the room watching the auditions, the voice drills into Art's ear with a volume which makes him wince and tense his body with fear. Or, more accurately, it's not the volume but the realisation of who owns the voice which is actually responsible.

Michael Enzo Kinane doesn't speak to the likes of Art. That's the way it's always been, and that's the way Art likes it.

"Er... er... yeah, I guess, Mek." Art turns round slowly so that his eyebrows are at the same level as Mek's grinning mouth. Size makes a massive difference when people are young. From an early age, the tallest, strongest children are more likely to get picked in the school sports teams, identified as leaders by teachers and feared by fellow pupils. As they get older, some of these children stop growing early and lose their advantage, which can be hard to handle as their place in the school pecking order correspondingly shifts. But other children continue to grow, until they have a physical dominance over not just the other pupils, but the teachers also. Mek is one of those. And he is well aware of it, and absolutely comfortable with using it to his advantage at every opportunity.

He leans over Art and smiles down at him. It doesn't feel like a smile to Art. It feels like a threat.

"You wrote this shit, didn't you?"

"Well sort of... it's based on one of my..."

"Yeah, yeah, whatever." Mek doesn't want the finer details. "Good. So you can get me the lead role then, yeah?" It sounds like a question, but it isn't. "Those posh slags will love all that, won't they?" Again, it isn't a question.

"Um... well, you see, it's not really up to me, Mek."

The smile gets wider so that the jagged teeth are on full display, like staring into a shark's mouth.

"But I'm sure you can sort it, can't you?"

"Um... er... And the lead role is Mrs Thatcher. She's a woman."

"Not in this play she's not, is she?"

Art looks down at his feet.

"I'll have a word with Mr James and Mrs Moore and see what I can do."

"I'm sure you'll sort it, won't you?"

This is just the sort of reason why Art doesn't like being the centre of attention. The more visible you are, the more likely you are to get shot at.

He wanders slowly over to the two teachers running the show.

"Er... Mrs Moore... er... Mr James... er... can I have a quick word?"

"Of course, Art. Have you been watching? It's going brilliantly. So many people want to be involved. It's fantastic!" The excitement in Priya Moore's voice is matched only by the glow in her deep brown eyes. Art doesn't see it though. He's looking at his feet.

"Erm... I've just been chatting to Mek. He wants to be Mrs Thatcher."

"But..." Mrs Moore sees the slight quivering in Art's lip and checks her reply. She looks across the room and sees Mek staring intently over at them, his grin seemingly getting broader by the second.

"What do you think, Finn? This could be interesting! A comment on what it meant to be the UK's first female Prime Minister in a man's world!"

Mr James follows her eyes as they flicker in the direction of Art's terrified face.

"Yeah... maybe there's something in that... we'll definitely give him an audition... and maybe we should get one of the girls to play Ronald Reagan too? It could really get the audience thinking... fit in with the almost chaotic theme of the story."

Art doesn't like his essay about the history of the early 1980s being called a story. And he certainly doesn't like it being called chaotic. But he'll put up with it if it gets Mek off his back.

"Sorry, Art... I didn't mean chaotic in a bad way. It's part of the brilliance of the story. You're challenging all the accepted wisdom about historical events and making us all think. You've got a real gift, you know. You can see things in a different way to the rest of us." Mr James is trying to be kind.

It doesn't feel kind to Art. He doesn't want to see things differently to everyone else. He looks at his feet. There's a tiny spider walking across his left shoe making the laces look like a ready-made web. He's never noticed that before.

Art's mum is in her dressing gown, sipping coffee and looking out at the steady stream of boats heading down the Thames in the direction of the lock. The view from the first floor balcony of this riverfront property is stunning. No wonder it's Sonnley's most expensive.

"You are lucky, you know, Ray. This is stunning. It gets me every time." She turns to face the man walking out to join her carrying a cafetière. He is very slightly smaller than her and looks more than the twelve years older which he is. Maybe it's the bald pate surrounded by the tufts of silver-flecked brown hair, which make his head look like it could work just as well the other way up? Maybe it's the strange combination of mismatched features which give his face a distinctly worn look from a bygone era? Or maybe it's the air of experience and self-confidence which exudes from someone who is the biggest employer and richest person in the town?

Whatever it is, Ray is an unusual-looking man, who must have been at the back of the queue when they were dishing out facial features, leaving him with an unsettling mixture of contradictions: his eyes are small and narrow, like they are squinting in a bid to see better; his cheeks are sharp and angular, and his mouth is a tiny 'o' shape, as if trying desperately to ensure that he will never be mistaken for a wide mouthed frog; none of which seems to fit in with him having the unfortunate honour of a boxer's nose despite never having boxed.

"It's not luck, Charlotte. It's a lot of graft, a lot of sacrifice, and a reasonable amount of talent. By the time you've got all that, luck makes very little difference." The words don't sound quite as blunt as they look in print, and he smiles as he leans over and tops up their coffees from the cafetière.

Art's mum likes the fact he makes her coffee; she likes the way he calls her Charlotte, when everyone else she knows calls her Charley; she likes the way they can chat about anything and he listens to her points of view; she likes the way he treats her with respect. Not everyone does that.

"Thanks, Ray. Don't you ever get lonely having all this, but no one to share it with?"

Charley waves her arms extravagantly in the directions of the grounds which surround the property and the beautiful views of the Thames and the countryside beyond.

"Charlotte! I hope you're not suggesting...'

"No way, Ray. Not me! Come on! You know me better than that... but someone? Surely sometimes it would be nice to have someone you can share it all with?"

"Phew... you had me worried for a second there, Charlotte!" Ray chuckles softly and gently puts his arm on her shoulder before continuing in a more serious tone. "If there's one thing I learnt growing up, it's don't get too close to people. They will only let you down." He is facing Charley directly and staring intently into her soft blue eyes. There is a steel and determination in him, which she has not witnessed before. "My parents taught me that. From what I remember of it, I was happy for my first six years, then my parents split up when my mum found out about all my dad's affairs, and everything changed. As a small child I had thought we would be a family forever... that we would have this happy bubble, just the three of us. But the world's not like that, Charlotte, is it?... And then I idolised my father for the rest of my childhood, even forgave him for what he'd done to my mum, what he'd done to our family. Did everything I could to make him proud of me. That's why I started making money fixing PCs and building websites when I was twelve. I wanted him to see I was good at things. I wanted him to boast to his friends about me. I wanted him to know that I could be someone... and you know what happened?" Ray is not looking for a response. "I'll tell you what happened, Charlotte. The day after my seventeenth birthday, he left me... he died... he was gone. Call it what you want. It doesn't matter. What matters is that he was out of my life, I was heartbroken, lost. And I vowed then that I would never risk that pain again, that I would never let anyone too close again... and it's served me well."

Charley knows the pain of losing a father. Not via death maybe, but of losing him nonetheless. She had reacted differently though. She had a son to love.

"I'm so sorry, Ray." She moves towards him with arms outstretched to hug, but he pulls away, and starts looking out along the river.

"I'm fine, Charlotte. Absolutely fine. I've got everything I need."

Charley isn't so sure, but just lets the words hang in the air for a few seconds before trying to cheer up the mood.

"You've done a great job with the new Performing Arts Centre. It looks amazing!"

"Yeah, it's turned out alright... Not down to me, though. It's not like I designed it or anything. I only gave them the money."

"They couldn't have done it without the money, Ray!"

"Yeah, true, I guess. But what else am I going to do with it?"

"Well... er... Ray, I was..." Charley hesitates just enough for the richest person in Sonnley to take his cue to interrupt.

"I know what you're thinking, Charlotte." He turns back towards her and looks directly in her eyes. His gaze is gentler and more relaxed than previously. "You're wondering why I didn't just give them the money they need to buy that park off the council and keep the supermarket out, right?"

Charley Mann nods. She doesn't like being that easy to read.

"Well, Charlotte, it's simple really. If people really do want to save the park, they need to show how much they want it, do something for themselves. It's no good if they've just got someone who will bail them out as soon as they come up with another thing for the wishlist. They need to work for it themselves. It'll mean so much more that way. That's why this play is great. I'm sure it'll be crap, but it's what it means that matters."

"My son, Art, wrote the story for the play." Charley's offended tone is only half-joking.

"Wowzer! Sorry, Charlotte. No offence. I'm sure it won't be crap then. Well done him. You must be very proud."

"Too right, Ray. I can't begin to tell you how proud I am and how happy it makes me." Charley pauses for a second to let it sink in, then lets a mischievous smile light up her face and winks at him. "There are benefits to being close to people you know."

Ray Hope laughs loudly and looks at his watch.

"Brilliant, Charlotte! That's what I like about you. You challenge me. You won't just accept what I say. I like that. It doesn't happen enough when you're rich or you're the boss. You won't change me, but you make me think." He strokes her gently on the arm and gives her a light kiss on the top of her head. Her straight, shoulder-length hair is the same alluring, reddish-brown colour as the fruit of the sweet chestnut tree and it glistens in the morning sunlight. She smells so good that Ray could happily stand there for hours just breathing in the fragrance. But he's not a weirdo. He doesn't do things like that. He just backs away a little and continues talking. "Thanks... I'm afraid I'd better be off now though. Got to nip into the office before the flight back to Monaco this evening. You OK to let yourself out? The cleaners will be in this evening, so feel free to stay as long as you want." He goes back inside and grabs a very full envelope off the kitchen table before coming back on to the balcony and giving Charley a little kiss on the side of her head. "Thanks,

Charlotte. I always hate this bit... feels so awkward. It's been fun as ever. I'll let you know when I'm over next. Bye for now."

He places the envelope in Charley's left hand and heads back inside.

"Thanks, Ray. See you next time."

Priya Moore hates wasting time. She likes to keep herself busy. Or maybe she just needs to keep herself busy. It's easier than the alternative. Either way she knows she's going to have to leave the auditions soon. They've gone better than she'd hoped so far, and it's all beginning to feel a bit more real now, more possible, more exciting. But there's no time to dwell. She needs to be at football practice, coaching a bunch of fourteen-year-olds for the biggest game of their young lives.

The coaching was never meant to be her thing really. She'd got involved eight years ago when Nina was six and had decided that she wanted to play football. There were two options really: go along to Sonnley Town with the multiple teams at every age group, trophy cabinet stuffed with numerous regional trophies and Berkshire Cups; or sign Nina up with Marsh Park Rovers, formed the previous year by a group of disgruntled parents whose children had been at Sonnley Town but were not good enough players to get more than the occasional five minutes on as a substitute at the end of the game, and only then if the victory was already secured.

It was an easy choice really. Not because Nina was no good at football, but because sport needs to be open to all children, not just the biggest or fastest or most talented. Tommy had agreed with her, and they had both offered themselves up to help out with the coaching too. It was meant to be something they could do together, supporting their eldest child, and getting Tommy out doing something he loved, which football would probably have topped any list of. She only mentioned the first part of that of course. It seemed like a win-win, and the plan was that Priya would gradually reduce her involvement to support the younger children in whatever activities they showed an interest in, while Tommy and Nina would cement their father-daughter relationship over passing drills and penalty practice.

But it didn't quite work out like that. Tommy turned up for a few sessions early on, even completed the FA level one coaching badge on the same course as Priya. As time wore on, however, he started missing training sessions, making excuses, being too tired, having too much work that needed doing immediately, whatever he could think of really. It wasn't that he didn't want to be involved, he just couldn't face it. Priya knew that, but she couldn't understand it.

So, these days, she is the main coach of Nina's Marsh Park Rovers under fifteen team, assisted by a couple of the other parents and, on a rare good day, by Tommy. They wouldn't usually still be training at this time of year, what with the season finished, but bad weather had prevented the biggest game of the season being played in April, so it had been rescheduled as part of the entertainment at the upcoming Marsh Park Fair.

Local rivalries always mean more than other games, but when one of the teams has been formed by the rejects of the other, that adds an extra dimension. Every year since the formation of Marsh Park Rovers the two clubs have played four fixtures against each other on the same day for the AllRays Sonnley Cup, with the boys' and girls' teams competing at under fifteen and under sixteen level. And every year, Sonnley Town have won every game easily, with a four-one defeat having led for nine minutes being the closest scoreline on record.

But...

Nina's age group is the first which was not formed by players not good enough for Sonnley Town; the first set of players who chose Marsh Park Rovers above their rivals, as opposed to having no option if they wanted to play; the first set of players who will be in the same division as their local opponents next season, after working their way up through the league structure with promotion after promotion. They could be the ones to break the sequence, the first team to win against their hated rivals; the players who inspire all those after them to chase their dreams.

That may sound like a ridiculous overstatement. It's only a game of football between two teams of youngsters, some of whom will have drifted away from the game within a few years, won over by the competing charms of partying, music, romance, other sports even. So it's just a small thing, it doesn't matter.

But small things are important. Sometimes the things which don't matter, matter the most.

Priya knows this. That's why she's put on the extra training sessions. That's why she needs to leave the auditions as soon as possible. That's why she wishes Tommy hadn't cried off again this evening.

Not to mention that it may be the last ever football match played in Marsh Park.

Art doesn't want to be at the auditions any more either. In truth, he hadn't wanted to come in the first place, but Mr James and Mrs Moore had said they wanted him to be there. Supposedly they wanted to discuss how they could rewrite his work as a play and let him see people "bringing his ideas to life." Whatever that means?

Mrs Moore had briefly mentioned something about how they are planning to open the play with an empty stage and a large screen showing a map of the UK with the beautiful Falkland Islands positioned just off the south coast of Wales. Apparently they've signed up some of the Art A level students to put it all together and depict how a fleet of Argentinian warships arrive in the dark of night and try to tow away the Falkland Islands and take them back to Argentina. There's then going to be a tug of war scene, in which a single British boat manages to attach a rope to the Islands and stop them getting stolen.

It's fairly true to the start of his history essay, so Art doesn't add much. He just knows that the essay was marked as a failure and he got given a detention.

"You're Art, aren't you? You wrote this crazy shit, didn't you? I love it! I'm like fucking blown to be playing Reagan."

Martha James has tapped Art on the shoulder and scuppered his attempts to be as unnoticeable as possible. As he turns round, she spots a few wispy hairs beginning to sprout above his lip, like the first tentative steps of a daffodil making its entrance in the outside world, unsure what is going to be waiting for it. He looks down at his feet and mumbles a question as though he would rather be anywhere else than here, which he would.

"Are you American?"

"Kind of, I guess. My dad's family were from Antigua, but he grew up in Ireland. That's where he met my mum. Her family was like Irish through and through though. But I was born and brought up in America until we moved here, so yeah, I guess I'm American if anything."

"I've never met an American... well apart from the tourists who are only here because they're on a boat trip to Windsor to see the Castle and they've stopped here for a break. But I don't count them as I've only ever spoken to them to give directions to a 'quaint coffee shop' or a 'traditional pub'."

Martha laughs. "You're funny, Art. I like that."

Art wonders what was funny, but he doesn't ask. He looks up from his feet and, through the long wavy dark hair tumbling over Martha's shoulders, he can see Mek walking towards them.

"I'd better go now."

"See you around, Art."

He doesn't hear. Art heads out of the main hall and glances around for somewhere to disappear into. He sees what looks like a broom cupboard and opens the door. It's a lot bigger than expected, and seems to be full of tables, chairs and serious sporting equipment. There are footballs, various different racquets, a rounders bat (although Art wonders if Martha would call it a baseball bat or if they are different), some cricket stuff, various mats, and those ridiculous medicine balls which are clearly too heavy to kick and serve no obvious medicinal purpose. The new Performing Arts Centre is clearly already being used to cover up for other space shortfalls at the school too.

Art closes the door behind him.

"You're not hiding from me, are you?" The door opens and Mek is staring down at him with the same unfriendly smile as before. Art doesn't like to lie, so he doesn't answer and keeps his stare fixed intensely on his own feet until Mek carries on.

"Well, you don't need to, do you? Look at me, I'm smiling, ain't I?"

Art doesn't look up. In fact, he doesn't look at all. He keeps his head pointing down and closes his eyes. He doesn't want to see what Mek will do next. But all he misses is a shrug before the bigger boy starts talking again.

"Please yourself... Just wanted to let you know that I got the part of the Thatcher geezer. Those Sonnley Ladies slags are all over me already, aren't they?"

"Er... right."

"Yeah. Well done Art. I won't forget this. I always thought you were one of those weird geeky twats, but you're alright. I guess it must be tough when your mum's a whore, right?"

"What d'you say?"

"Come on, everyone knows your mum's a whore. Don't worry, man. I'm on your side. I feel sorry..."

Mek doesn't finish his sentence. Art picks up the rounders/baseball bat and swings it at him with all his force several times until the bigger boy lies motionless and silent on the floor in the cupboard.

Art leaps out and closes the door behind him.

Some things can make people behave in a way that they didn't know they were capable of. Maybe everyone has a tipping point?

Art doesn't know if he is pleased or disgusted with what he has done.

But he knows he is terrified.

Chapter Three

Tommy:

Everyone thinks you're lazy, but you're not.
They don't know the effort it takes you to do anything: to get up; to speak to people; to make it look like everything is fine. It's the hardest work you've ever done, and it drains every ounce of energy out of you. All you want to do is stay in bed, close your eyes, hopefully fall asleep, and get some brief respite from your mind sniping at you, creating imaginary dangers, terrifying you, and sucking every last drop of joy and vitality out of you. Yet somehow you go out into the world and try to be normal.
For now. But you are so, so tired of being tired. You can't keep on doing this forever. One day you will just go to sleep and stay asleep, and no one will ever know how hard you tried for so long.
And everyone will still think you were lazy, but you were not.

Receiving no response to her cheery "Hi' as she arrives home to change for football practice, Priya pauses to watch her husband from the living room door for a few seconds. Where once his brown hair would tone in well against the pale green sofa like the stone in an avocado, the emergence of grey makes them an awkward match, like he no longer belongs there. His shoulders are slumped, as if he is carrying a rucksack full of all the world's woes on his back. Maybe he is? He is staring at the television where two football teams Priya doesn't recognise seem to be battling out a goalless draw after seventy-two minutes.

"Who's playing love?"

"Uh... oh hi, Pri... It's an Italian cup match I think."

Tommy turns his head towards his wife and she looks into his eyes where a trace of a tear is battling to escape. No one else would notice it, but she does. She always does. If it were to fight free, an avalanche would surely follow. But that isn't what grabs her attention. She looks for the eyes she fell in love with all those years ago: full of joy, excitement and anticipation of love. Yet now the glow is gone. All she can see is a man overwhelmed by sadness, fear and desperation.

The eyes can't lie in the way that the rest of a person can.

"I've got something for you, Tommy... I hope you don't mind... I just... I just didn't know what else to do."

Priya walks over to the sofa, takes his right hand in her left, gives it a lingering squeeze, then places a small credit card sized laminated piece of paper in it. She has evidently made this herself, with an immaculate precision that she seems to bring to everything. The corners of the laminated paper have even been rounded off and the writing is neat, beautifully crafted and, above all, clear, as though she were writing something for one of her students for whom English is not the first language.

Tommy glances down at it, and sees a photo of him, Priya and the kids smiling in Corfu two years ago. His smile looks genuine. She did well to find it. There aren't many photos like that these days. Above the photo in deep blue handwritten letters is the word *Please* and underneath Priya has written *For all of us*.

Tommy turns the card over and reads the other side.

"Thanks, Pri." She knows he doesn't mean it.

"Sorry love... I couldn't think what else to do, and just thought maybe you could keep it in your wallet, and one day, when you're ready... well... you know."

"Thanks... yeah, I will."

Priya leans over, puts a hand on each of her husband's shoulders and kisses him tenderly on the forehead.

"I love you, Tommy... we all do... but..."

She doesn't get time to finish, as Tommy wraps his arms round her and squeezes tightly as if it will somehow draw some of her energy and joy into him.

"Thanks, Pri... I know it probably doesn't seem like it, but I love you too, all of you. So much. More than you will ever know. I'm sorry."

"Don't be sorry, Tommy. I just wish you could see the good things in your life, and stop being so hard on yourself. You're a wonderful person, you're a great dad, an amazing, caring person. That's why you've got so many friends... that's why they want to see you, want you to stop making excuses and go out with them. You're a good man, Tommy, I just wish you..."

This time it isn't her husband who interrupts Priya, but a sudden increase in volume from the television behind her, which causes him to pull away to look past her and watch the celebrations after the goal which her body had blocked him from seeing.

"Typical."

Art has never tried to kill someone before. He doesn't even know if he did try to kill Mek. Or if he succeeded.

He sits on a swing looking across Marsh Park. A few people are walking their dogs, kicking footballs, sitting on benches chatting over cups of something or other, but the playground bit is empty, apart from Art. He likes it like that. He swings back and forward, tucking his legs under the swing seat as he leans ahead on the backswing, and kicking them out as far in front of him as he can while he throws his body back on the forward upswing. It took him a long while to learn that manoeuvre when he was little, and he still can't execute it perfectly, but he concentrates and tries as best he can. The concentration makes the swing go higher, and momentarily helps him forget what he's just done.

Art has never even hit anyone before. His mum doesn't like violence. But she didn't hear what Mek said, did she? She'll be proud of him for sticking up for her.

He wonders if Mek is dead. He's never seen a dead body before, so he doesn't know what one would look like. He knows that Mek was still and silent, which are presumably two of the criteria used when assessing death. He doesn't know if he had a pulse or not. Art had had no intention of checking that at the time.

In fact, he doesn't even know if he hopes Mek is dead or not. If he is dead, then Art will be caught and go to prison, and his mum will be ashamed of him. If Mek is not dead, then Art probably soon will be. He tries to propel the swing as high as he can. Maybe he could get such a momentum going that he could let go and it would hurl him skywards with such force that he would never come down, and would float around in space for ever, safe from the lose-lose scenario that awaits him on earth.

He hears the creak of the gate into the playground and glances over. An old woman with long straggly hair is slowly rattling the bar which is intended to keep the gate closed and make it harder for toddlers to escape. Then she bangs the gate closed and open again a few times before wandering into the playground. She looks around and stares at Art for a few seconds, but the expression on her face doesn't change. Or, more accurately, the lack of expression on her face doesn't change. She looks odd to Art. She's wearing a smart-looking cardigan buttoned up all the way to the top, coupled with some tatty old grey tracksuit bottoms and is walking barefoot.

Art doesn't usually look at people, but he can't help watching the old woman. He feels a bit angry with her. She's far too old for the playground. This is meant for young children, not for old women who don't even dress properly. He watches as she wanders over to the little playground roundabout, which he once fell off as a young child because his mum didn't remind him to hold on to the bars. He sees her crouch and start to pull her tracksuit bottoms down. Before they are fully down, she is weeing partly on the roundabout, but mainly on her tracksuit.

Why would anyone do that? Art knows right from wrong. He's had that drilled into him all his life. He knows you treat people kindly and with respect. And he knows that you don't wee in children's playgrounds, unless you are a toddler who hasn't learnt proper bladder control yet. So he knows that what the old woman has done is disgusting. Young children use that roundabout. Art used to use that roundabout. He watches as she gets slowly to her feet, and tugs at her tracksuit bottoms so that they are up to her waist at the front and not covering much at the back. She trundles in the direction of the baby swings. Art wonders what she's going to do to them, but he doesn't have time to find out.

He hears some shouting, then sees two other women running towards the playground. One of them is crying and looks old, but not as old as the woman in the tracksuit bottoms. The other woman is Mrs Moore.

Art doesn't want Mrs Moore to see him. He'll be in trouble. She'll know what he's done to Mek. She'll probably even blame him for what the dirty old woman has done. He jumps off the swing as soon as it is low enough to do so, and climbs over the low fence behind, rather than use the entrance gate. That way he can escape before they spot him. They seem to be more interested in the old woman in truth. Hopefully they will perform a citizen's arrest and drag her away in handcuffs. He runs away as fast as he can, which isn't very fast in reality, but is good enough on this occasion.

Art doesn't like running. He never has. But he may have to do so more and more now.

Priya wonders for a second who the teenage boy was whom she had seen running awkwardly away from the playground. It was probably one of her students, but she doesn't dwell on it. She's got more important things on her mind. She can see the stains on the front of her friend's grey track pants, and the look of bewilderment and desperate fear, which no one could mistake for expressionless, on her face.

"It's OK, Rosa. Everything's OK." Priya speaks as softly as she can and reaches out a hand to support Rosa's arm.

"Fuck you. I can walk myself." Momentarily the older woman's face contorts in anger, as she bats the hand away. Rosa has always had a temper, but it used to be part of her charm in a strange sort of way, as it always preceded a calming down, an apology and impromptu acts of kindness and generosity. Now it seems to have lost its purpose.

"It's alright, my little Rosa. I'm here too." Mel walks forward, wipes her eyes, and smiles as convincingly as she can, as she takes her wife's left hand in her own right one, and gives it a gentle squeeze.

Rosa is calmer now but looks scared again.

"Where's Mel?"

"I'm here, my little Rosa... like I have been for 38 wonderful years and always will be." She squeezes her hand again, a little longer this time, and looks straight into the green eyes she fell in love with all those years ago. She sees a flicker of the sparkle that used to light up every room Rosa entered and made her a friend to everyone other than the foolish few who would always regret making her a lifelong enemy. But it's only a flicker, and Mel wonders if she imagined it anyway. She runs the fingers of her left hand through the wild black hair which seems to erupt out of Rosa's head with all the menacing beauty of lava pouring out of a volcano, and which used to wow everyone and mirror her beautiful, crazy personality. Now it looks out of place: the only part of her beloved wife not to have aged, and now more messy and unmanageable than instantly endearing.

"How will I get home?"

"It's OK, my little Rosa. I'm here. So's Priya. We'll take you home. We were worried about you." Mel smiles reassuringly, then leans her head forward and rests her chin on her wife's shoulder, so that Rosa can't see the tears rolling down her face.

Priya points over to the bandstand on the other side of the park. It looks different, like someone has splashed paint over it. She starts leading the others towards it, to see what's happened. She's got time now. She's not going to make the football training session. Hopefully the other parent coaches will understand that looking for her neighbour with dementia has to take priority. And hopefully enough of them will have turned up to make the session viable. Tommy won't be one of them.

"That bandstand was where you put on the best party Sonnley has ever seen... Rosa's Party in the Park. People still talk about it. Your amazing cooking, the music, the laughter, and most of all you in that amazing, colourful dress which you'd made yourself, singing *My Way* with the band not once, not twice, but three times in a row at three AM! Like you always said 'Life's a party. Keep going until the music stops'. And the music didn't stop that night!" Priya laughs at the memory and smiles at her friend in the stained track pants.

As they get nearer to the bandstand, Priya can see what the splashed paint actually is. One of the supporting pillars of the bandstand is covered in graffiti of a little girl sitting on a sofa staring glumly at a slim woman in a beautiful red ball gown alongside a plump, balding, middle-aged man, who bears more than a passing resemblance to Sonnley's own MP and is wearing a tuxedo and black bow tie. The adults are screaming at each other, their faces contorted with unconfined rage, whilst wild drops of spittle fly from their furious mouths. Behind the couple is a large television displaying a war scene as a bomb explodes in a busy city centre and, on the arm of the sofa next to the little girl, the front page of a folded newspaper shows a still image of a crowd of young men kicking another figure on the ground. On one of the steps below the graffiti is written the accompanying caption *When all you see is hatred, how do you learn to love?* The artwork looks very professional, is signed by *Neola*, and its impact startles Priya. She wonders who did it. She thinks of her brother. He loved street art. She glances at Mel, who is gently supporting her wife's left arm and stroking her hand as they walk. Her eyes are red, but the tears have stopped. This isn't the time for a graffiti discussion, though Priya knows how much the old Rosa would have loved it. She had always adored anything which challenged the established order and wound up the knee-jerk "it's disgusting" brigade, and this ticks both those boxes.

"They're trying to get rid of this park now, Rosa. Turn it into a supermarket... But it's never going to happen. We won't let it... I mean, where else could you do your next Party in the Park? Where else can we keep going until the music stops?!" Priya doesn't laugh this time. She just looks at Rosa and thinks how no one would ever have tried to get rid of Marsh Park if Rosa had been leading the opposition.

"Where's Mel?... How am I getting home?"

The music is stopping now.

Art is talking to Llama. He likes to do that when he's got things on his mind. As usual Llama doesn't reply. Art likes that. Llama just keeps swimming round and round the bowl, like most goldfish do, but Llama is definitely listening. If it had been up to Art, Llama would have actually been a llama, not a goldfish, but Art's mum had said that llamas were not practical pets for a small house with a courtyard garden and, besides, she had no idea where to get one. Art had said that she hadn't tried hard enough to find out, but she hadn't changed her mind, and had just spoilt his fun as usual. She had got him a goldfish instead. So he called the goldfish Llama.

Art had been eight then and, seven years later, this is actually his second goldfish called Llama. The first one had sadly died unexpectedly when it was three. Art had been hysterical and inconsolable for two hours, had asked his mum to give it mouth-to-mouth resuscitation (she refused as usual), had buried Llama in the garden, and then asked his mum for another goldfish, which he called Llama, and everything went back to normal.

Today Art is telling Llama about the no-win position he's in. He ran straight up to his room when he got in from Marsh Park, and has been chatting to Llama ever since, until a knock on the door interrupts.

"Art, love... are you OK? Is something wrong?" Why does she always know?

"Leave me alone."

"Come on love, let me in. I might be able to help." Art doubts that very much.

"No. You won't. Go away."

"I'm not going anywhere. What's happened? I'm sure I can help." Art is sure she can't.

He doesn't reply, so his mum opens the door and sits down next to him on the bed.

"This is my room. You can't..."

"Sorry... I was worried about you, that's all." Art's mum stares straight into his eyes for a split second before he turns away and looks at Llama. "What is it, Art? It can't be that bad. I can help, you know."

Art says nothing and keeps watching Llama go round and round the bowl. If only life were that simple.

After exactly nine seconds, Art's mum speaks again.

"Come on Art, speak to me. I can help you sort it, whatever it is."

He breathes in deeply then stands up and shouts at the wall, so as not to alarm Llama.

"Only if you've killed someone."

"What do you mean, Art?"

"I hit a boy with a baseball bat."

"OK. Why do you think he's dead?" Why isn't she screaming at him? This is far worse than when he has a shower, leaves his towel in a heap and doesn't dry the water off the bathroom floor. She screams at him then and says he's got to start taking more care of the place.

"Because he didn't move."

"For how long?"

"I don't know, do I? I ran off?"

"OK. So firstly... he's probably fine. Maybe winded or knocked out or something. Where is he? We can check it easily."

"No... no way. I'm not going back there."

"Back where Art? What happened?... You're not a violent person? Why? Was he bullying you?" Art's mum stands up, leans over and tries to hug him, but he pulls away and keeps looking at the wall.

"No."

"Well, what then? Come on, Art. You can tell me anything. You know that."

"He said something terrible."

"What?"

"About you. He said you are..." Art can't finish the sentence.

"Go on, Art. This is important." Art's mum's voice is louder now. Why is she more angry with Mek saying something than with Art possibly killing him?

"He said you're a whore. There, I've said it. You wanted to know. It's not my fault, is it? I had to hit him when he said that, didn't I?"

Art's mum sits back down on the bed, and puts her head in her hands, then taps the space beside her, and speaks in the voice like the one she used when she confirmed that the first Llama was dead. Except for this time she is crying.

"OK, Art. Come and sit here. I need to explain some things about my life... I've wanted to for years, but the right moment has never cropped up, and now it's the wrong moment." Art doesn't move, so she taps the bed again. "Please Art, this is important." He stays where he is, watching Llama go round and round, but she continues anyway.

"Firstly, Art, I need you to know, I'm not ashamed of who I am, and I don't want anyone ever to make you think I should be. Got it?"

Art nods towards Llama.

"To be honest, Art, I've often wondered why you've never asked more questions about my life? Most kids know if their parents are teachers, gardeners, bricklayers or whatever, but you've never once asked me." In truth, Art has never cared if his mum is a teacher or a gardener or a bricklayer. She is his mum.

"When I was a couple of years younger than you are now, Art, everything was fine. I guess you'd say we were an old-school middle class family. Dad was quite high up in the army, Mum stayed at home and looked after Uncle James, Aunt Amanda and me... to be honest, I was my dad's favourite. I was the youngest, and, in some ways, I guess I had the temperament he'd kept suppressed for years in the army... you know, I was a bit cheeky, a bit of a rebel. Nothing serious, but always on the lookout for the fun option."

Art's mum gets up from the bed, and stands next to Art, raising her hand round his shoulders. He lets it stay there.

"My dad was the only man I had ever loved, until you came along, Art... but it all changed... By the time I was your age, I'd become very wild, and had become an alcoholic and a junkie."

"Do you mean drugs?" Art looks away from Llama and looks at his mum's feet. She's not wearing shoes. Does she usually wear shoes indoors? He does. "But... but you've always told me drugs are bad... and you can't be an alcoholic at fifteen. You can't even drink at that age."

Art's mum lets out a strange, snorting laugh he's never heard before. This is no laughing matter.

"Yeah... I wish I hadn't... actually I don't wish I hadn't because if I hadn't, I'd have never had you." Art's mum tries to squeeze the top of his arm with the hand draped over this shoulder, but he flinches so she stops. Of course Art flinched if she only wanted to have him because she was a drunken junkie. What does that say about how much he means to her? He looks back at Llama and stays as silent as the goldfish.

"Anyway, my parents... no, my dad... was strict and he kicked me out as soon as I turned sixteen... told me that if I was old enough to drink and take drugs then I was old enough to fend for myself and go and clean myself up... Of course that was the last thing I was able to do... all I knew was that I needed the drugs, so I became a street prostitute.... It was only about a year or so... the other girls were the ones who looked after me, and your Aunt Amanda of course, who was at Uni at the time. It taught me a lot really... other women, some of them troubled like me, looking after a frightened sixteen-year-old like she was their own child, while my own parents had disowned me.... I got beaten up a few times, one time really badly... but nothing hurt like being rejected by those I loved most... and then I got pregnant with you, and I knew instantly that I would do whatever I had to do for you, that I would always be there for you whatever happened... it wasn't easy, but I haven't touched drink or drugs since that day I found out I was pregnant. I know I'm lucky, because it's not easy... no, it's much harder than not easy, it's the hardest thing I've ever done... but Aunt Amanda was amazing. She got me all the help and support I needed and that's what stopped me relapsing... and you, of course, Art. You saved my life. I begged my parents to have me back, told them I was cleaning myself up, but they refused." Art can feel a teardrop falling off his mum's face onto his left shoulder. He winces.

"Why?"

"Why what?"

"Why did they refuse to take you back?"

"Oh, you know, it's... it's complicated."

"What do you mean?"

"Yeah, you're right, Art. I need to be honest with you." Art hadn't actually said that his mum needed to be honest with him, so he isn't technically right, but he decides not to point that out because he can think about the impact on others of what he says before he speaks.

And, besides, his mum has raised her voice again now, so he wouldn't be heard if he did point it out.

"OK, Art... They said they would take me back if I had an abortion."

Art looks away from Llama and shouts at the wall again, louder than his mum this time. "They wanted me dead?!"

"I'm sorry, Art. It wasn't quite like that, they didn't know it was you of course, they just didn't want me having a baby on my own so young, without a father. But yes, I guess, the impact is the same, so yeah, ok, you're right." Art really is right this time, but he doesn't feel like celebrating.

"So who is my dad? Where is he?" Art shouts even louder than before and the words bounce back off the wall and reverberate round the room.

"I'm sorry, love. I don't know... I really don't know. I swear I would tell you if I did, but I don't... and we don't need anyone else anyway, do we? We've got each other." Art's mum tries to pull him in closer, but he doesn't let her. He just stares at the wall until she starts talking again.

"Can I ask you something, Art?"

"What?"

"Why have you never asked about your father before?" Maybe it wasn't important when he thought they had each other.

"Dunno." Art's mum doesn't seem that interested in the answer. She tries to hug him again and carries on talking about herself.

"Now I've started, I've got to tell you the whole story, Art. Aunt Amanda was amazing. She put me up in her tiny flat whilst I was pregnant and when you were born, but once you were nearly two, I was feeling a lot stronger and healthier and needed to do something for myself, give her some space, and get us a life of our own. But when you're nineteen, with a small child, a wasted education, drugs convictions and no money, there aren't many employers desperate to give you a chance, believe me... Then I saw an advert for escorts for wealthy businessmen, and I put on my best middle class voice, and got the job. The money was good, it was much safer than I was used to, I could work largely when I wanted, and I was always at home with you in the day... And Aunt Amanda would always babysit if I needed to be working... so it fitted in perfectly, and still does, to be honest... and listen, Art, this is really important. I am not ashamed of what I do, and you mustn't be either. I have four or five regular clients now. They are all kind men, older than me, and they treat me well. Maybe I'm lucky, I don't know. But I'm happy with it, and proud that I've managed to put a life and home together for us both."

Art is now rocking back and forward screaming loudly at the wall. "NOOOOOOO."

"Calm down, Art love. It's OK"

"SO MEK WAS RIGHT! AND I KILLED HIM."

"No love, he was not right. And you haven't killed him... I'm sure he'll be fine."

"YOU DON'T KNOW THAT. YOU DON'T KNOW ANYTHING. YOU DON'T EVEN CARE ABOUT YOUR OWN SON."

"I do Art. I care about you more than anything in this whole world. You know that. Please." Art's mum has positioned herself between him and the wall and is crying uncontrollably now. Art saw an interview with an actress once, who explained how there are techniques to make yourself cry on demand.

"Please Art, I'm so sorry. I really am. I know I should have told you all this before, but it never seemed like the right moment, and I was scared if I'm honest. I was worried you'd think less of me or something... I know you wouldn't really, of course, and you're not like that, but... I don't know, I'm so used to people being so disgusting and judgmental and stuff, so I guess I lost sight of reality... I was just scared ... I couldn't risk losing you. You're the best, most important thing that has ever happened to me."

"NOOOOOO." Art opens his bedroom door and starts running as best he can down the stairs. His mum follows.

"Please Art. Listen to me.... You know I love you more than anything... please Art. We're a team, you and me. Always have been... Please Art. Don't abandon me. Please."

Art runs out of the front door slamming it behind him before his mum can get out. He knocks the black rubbish bin over so that it blocks the door further and delays her exit. He's seen that trick in foot chases on films, where it seems to work every time. In reality, it barely delays his mum's pursuit by more than a fraction of a second.

By rights, at five foot eleven and a quarter inches tall and being fifteen years old, he should be able to outrun his mum. She's three and a quarter inches shorter, and older of course. But she's still quicker. So he has to try a different approach.

He stands in the middle of the street, turns back to his mum and shouts as loud as he can.

"LEAVE ME ALONE, WHORE." Then he runs.

Art's mum sits down on the edge of the pavement, her head in her hands and her feet dangling out into the road.

She cries, and cries, and cries.

But Art doesn't notice. He is running again.

Chapter Four

"Call these goddamn muffins?! You're kidding me. Taste more like goddamn cardboard! Are they Russian or something?"

Johnson James looks at his little sister prodding the breakfast on her plate and shouting in an exaggerated American accent, nothing like her fading natural one. He shakes his head and laughs.

"I'm already wishing you hadn't got the Reagan part! It's only been, what, 16 hours, and I'm sick of it already."

"It's called method acting I think you'll find." Martha laughs too, and takes a bite of one of the muffins... "Actually, they're almost edible. You're getting better, JJ."

Her brother smiles and prods her gently in the arm. "I bloody should be. I get enough practice round here!" It's true. Johnson has been cooking breakfast for his sister ever since, well, ever since their mother stopped being around. Neither of them knows how it started really. Maybe she needed someone to look after her? Maybe he needed something to occupy him? Or maybe a bit of both?

"Where's dad, JJ?"

"He's gone in early... something to do with sorting out stuff after that fight at your rehearsals yesterday, and that kid going missing?"

Martha spits a piece of muffin out of her mouth onto the table. She's got so much to ask, but Johnson gets in first.

"Urgh, that's disgusting, sis! Come on. They're not that bad! Surely?!"

"What fight? Who's missing?" Martha says the words so quickly the two questions almost overlap.

"C'mon sis, you're shitting me, right? It's your play, your school... I left last summer, remember?! You were there. You know what happened!" Martha had been there, but she had got the Ronald Reagan part and immediately come straight home. For the first time since she was old enough to remember, she had stayed off social media for the rest of the afternoon and just read, re-read and re-re-read the script. This part means a lot to her.

"Please Johnson, this is serious. What fight?"

"Between the weird kid who wrote the play and that big guy? Mex, is it?"

Martha feels a sickening in her stomach that she doesn't recognise.

"Art had a fight with Mek? Is he OK?" There is a panic in her voice which takes them both aback.

"He's still in hospital, I think. He was out cold for a few seconds apparently, so they've kept him in for checks but, last I saw, he's going to be OK it seems."

"Art's in hospital! Please no..." Martha leaps out of her chair and starts towards the door before her brother stands directly in front of her, with both palms out towards her, splayed fingers pointing up, blocking her way.

"Whoah sis... what's got into you? Calm down? It's the Mex guy who's in hospital."

A mixture of incredulity and relief surges through Martha's body as Johnson ushers her back to her seat.

"What do you mean Mek's in hospital?... What happened?"

"Like I said, it sounds like they had a fight, and the Mex guy was knocked out sparko by your boy."

"He's not my boy!" Martha's blushes may be confusing her, but not Johnson.

"Course not, sis. Now calm down and finish your breakfast. It's no big deal. The Mex guy says there was no fight, and he just slipped, but no one believes it. He's got to say that, hasn't he? Got a reputation to protect! Apparently your... I mean the Art guy... was seen running away from some storage room by one of the Sonnley High girls, who then found poor Mex out cold inside."

"But... but... Art wouldn't hurt anyone. He certainly couldn't knock Mek out cold." Martha feels a rush of guilty pride threaten to engulf her and tries to suppress it.

"Well, it sounds like the Mex guy is saying the same thing... nasty slip he had, mind!" Johnson laughs and points at the muffin on the breakfast table to get his sister eating again.

"So how's Art? He's OK, isn't he?"

Johnson shrugs. "Well yeah, I guess. He was anyway."

"What do you mean he *was* OK? What's happened to him? C'mon Johnson, please!"

"Woah, calm down sis! It's no big deal... a couple of guys have a fight. Everyone's OK, then one of them disappears for a while... probably just waiting for things to calm down a bit."

"What do you mean 'disappears'? Where is he?"

"Well, if I knew that he wouldn't be disappeared, would he, dumbo?!... can you say 'be disappeared'? It doesn't sound right." Johnson points at Martha's plate again and carries on "You going to eat that muffin or not? I'll..."

"Shut up, Johnson, this is serious. I need to know every detail. We've got to find Art. He could be in danger."

"Why would he be in danger? He's just had a little fight and gone off on his own till it all blows over. We've all been there." Martha hasn't been there, and she doesn't remember her brother going there either. She gets up from the table, grabs a coat and heads for the door.

"Where're you going, sis?"

"Out... just out... and it's Mek, not Mex, right!"

Johnson shakes his head, pops the unfinished muffin in his mouth, and nods approvingly. His breakfasts are getting better.

"You OK to get the kids off to school, love?" Priya Moore is walking round the kitchen, munching on a piece of dry, brown toast.

"Of course." The words are fine, but the slightest of sighs betrays them. Priya just wishes Tommy would actively enjoy these moments with their children.

"I'm off to see Art's mum. See if I can do anything to help."

"Good idea."

Priya stops munching on the dried toast, wanders over to the kitchen table where her husband is sitting with a bowl of cereal and reading the news on his iPad. She leans over and gives him a quick kiss on the top of his head.

"Sorry to abandon you, Tommy. Love you."

"It's fine, love." He picks up his Best Implementation of AllRays Software award, which is still on the kitchen table, "I'll probably get better conversation from Ray's statue anyway!"

"Yeah, probably." Priya doesn't laugh. She still loves Tommy, she really does. But she doesn't recognise when he's joking any more. Because he hasn't joked much at home in the last fourteen years. She shoves the last piece of toast in her mouth and rushes out of the room.

Tommy closes his eyes and takes a deep breath. How can he successfully manage a programme of sixty-four people (if he includes himself) in a software implementation and win an award for it, but he can't even tell if his wife knows when he's joking or not any more? Who's he kidding? Not himself. He knows he only won the award because of his relationship with Ray. When someone feels indebted to you for saving their life when they were young, they might not want to get close to you, but they may well keep repaying you in the ways they think they can.

Tommy bites his lip as hard as he can, till the pain distracts him and stops his mind in its tracks. He doesn't want the children to see him crying. And he doesn't want it to feel so difficult to manage his kids having breakfast. It should just be a routine part of daily life. He knows it should be fun. He knows it should be rewarding. Yet "fun" and "rewarding" are two words which don't seem to fit with Tommy's daily life these days. He hears Priya shout "come on you three, get down here. Make it easy for dad please. I'm off. Love y'all."

Tommy doesn't feel hungry any more. He's messed up again, without meaning to. He's good at that. If they had awards for that, he would have a cabinet stuffed full of them. He can turn anyone in his household against him within seconds. It's a remarkable skill, and he wishes he didn't have it. But he probably deserves it.

He gets up and scrapes the contents of his bowl into the food waste bin. As he does so, he thinks about Art and he thinks about Art's mum. Or, more precisely, he thinks about how he would feel if he were having to go through what she must be.

He's trodden this ground many times before, imagining what it would be like if Nina or Mia or Kian disappeared. The horrors of not knowing where your child might be and being helpless to protect them. He's seen them all being abducted or murdered or running off with a convicted child molester having being lured in by unfounded promises of unlimited access to whatever their current toy/tv show/band of choice may be.

And it's real now. Not for Tommy thankfully, though he feels guilty for being thankful about that. Then guilty for feeling guilty that he is thankful that his kids are not missing. He puts his bowl in the dishwasher, closes his eyes again and imagines the pain and horror that Art's poor mum must be going through. Except, it doesn't feel like imagining it. The pain feels very real. He knows he's got to do something to help.

"What are you doing, dad?" Nina has wandered into the kitchen and is staring at her father, as he stands by the dishwasher with his eyes closed mumbling to himself.

"Uh... oh, sorry, just, you know, thinking." Nina doesn't know, but she doesn't dwell on it. She is pretty much used to it by now.

"You coming to football training tonight, dad?"

He won't be. "I hope so, but it's looking a bit tricky." He doesn't look up. He doesn't want to see his daughter's reaction.

"Mum reckons we're going to beat them, you know. Do you really think we can?"

"I hope so." He hates his answer. Why doesn't he boost his daughter's confidence? Why isn't he more positive about it? Why isn't he more positive about anything?

"I'm off now."

"What about breakfast?"

"Nah... don't fancy any today."

"But breakfast is the most imp..."

"Leave it dad. You're embarrassing yourself."

Tommy was just trying to get his daughter to have something to eat to start the day. It doesn't seem like an unreasonable request. But Nina is right. She raises her eyebrows towards the ceiling and shakes her head in pity. He definitely feels embarrassed and humiliated now. Fourteen-year-olds know exactly how to do that to their parents. She heads out of the room without a goodbye.

"Nina, don't forget to walk Mia and Kian in with you."

Too late.

Tommy hears the front door slam. He wanders over to the jacket which he's left draped over the back of one of the kitchen chairs instead of hanging up on the coat rack like he's supposed to, takes out his wallet and stares at the writing on the back of the laminated card which Priya had given him. He knows she is right, but that doesn't make it easy. He puts it back in his jacket, then closes his eyes, takes a deep breath, pops two pieces of bread in the toaster, walks to the bottom of the stairs and calls up in a calm friendly voice.

"Hurry up kids. Toast is on. Two-minute warning to get down here. Good news: I'm walking you in today."

"Don't scream! I'm on my way... You're not walking me to school! How old d'you think I am?" shouts twelve-year-old Mia.

"Where's mum?" shouts nine-year-old Kian.

Charley Mann isn't eating breakfast. She's sitting on the sofa in her front room, with the box of Art's stories on her lap, and a few of them neatly placed on the sofa beside her.

She's not slept since Art ran away. She had given him half an hour to come home, but he hadn't. So she had searched all the places she thought he might have gone: Marsh Park; the spot on the river by the Boathouse pub where they used to throw bread to the ducks until someone told them that it was bad for ducks to feed them bread, and Art got angry with her; the cafe on Sonnley High Street which serves the best hot chocolate in the world according to Art. But she hadn't found him.

As evening had approached, she had called her sister, Amanda, in a panic, and Amanda had tried to help as she always does. They had rung the school, the hospitals, the climbing centre which Art goes to every Thursday evening in the summer term, and had contacted the police to report him missing. Charley can't remember the exact figures, but apparently the number of children who go missing is appallingly high, much higher than Charley had ever imagined, and most of them return safely within twenty-four hours. The policewoman had been very polite and kind and had tried to reassure Charley with that fact. But it hadn't worked. Art isn't like other kids. His mum knows that and had explained it. The policewoman had nodded and smiled kindly. She'd heard it all before. Everyone's child is special. But she hadn't said that. She had nodded again, and taken some details about Art. The fact that he is five foot eleven and a quarter inches tall (though Art insists that it is actually five sixteenths of an inch) and turning sixteen next month hadn't made him a top priority. The policewoman hadn't said that either, but Charley could tell.

So she had left the police station and continued walking round Sonnley with her sister until two AM, when Amanda had said they should both get some rest, and had taken Charley home, saying she would be back after she'd dropped her kids at school in the morning, and making Charley promise she wouldn't do anything stupid.

Once home, she had known she wouldn't sleep, so she had fed Llama and told him not to worry. Art would have liked that. Then she had got the box of Art's stories down from on top of the wardrobe in her bedroom and had sat on the sofa reading every single one, until she could cry no more, and decided to go out to the all-night garage and buy a bottle of vodka to see if that would help.

So now, Charley is back on the sofa, re-reading Art's stories and gently tapping at the lid on the bottle of vodka. She thinks about how good the alcohol had been at numbing the pain when she had been kicked out of home and was living on the streets; she thinks about how she hasn't touched alcohol since the day she found out she was pregnant with Art; she thinks about all the pain she is in now.

But, most of all, she thinks about Art. He's out there on his own somewhere. He's never been on his own before. He's got no father. Charley is all he's got and now he feels he hasn't got her anymore. The pain of knowing that Art is suffering is unbearable. Maybe Ray is right? Maybe it's best not to let people get too close, as they'll only end up hurting you? She admonishes herself. No, don't think like that, that's not going to help Art.

Charley plays with the top of the unopened vodka bottle again. Screw tops are so easy: one little twist and they are open. She's had a call from the school. They're sending round one of the teachers to offer support. Only if it's Mrs Moore or Mr James, she'd told them. The woman on the phone had said she'd see what she could do, but she sounded like she thought that beggars can't be choosers and she'll get who she gets.

There's probably about half an hour until the teacher turns up. They won't get through the door if it's not Mrs Moore or Finn. Charley knows that. She's tired, she's terrified and she's sick of people judging her.

She gives the screw top a little tweak and the seal gives easily with an almost imperceptible crack.

Art's missing. She doesn't know what to do. She just wants him home.

She removes the lid, lifts the bottle to her nose and breathes in the smell of the vodka. It's over sixteen years since she last felt that odour so close to her, and her first reaction is it smells bitter and unpleasant. She thinks of the alternatives; she thinks of the reality.

Where's Art?

Chapter Five

Dan:

You've never heard the expression that hurt people hurt people. Maybe if you had, it would ring a bell. You've been hurt all your life: belittled by those who were meant to take care of you; mocked by those who you hoped would be your friends; sent links to videos of how to kill yourself by online accounts you don't recognise, but whose true owners you would. So it's not your fault. It's all you know. But it certainly feels like your fault.

And hurt people hurt themselves too.

Sonnley High Street is a buzz of activity this morning: coffee shops full of young parents with prams and pushchairs nattering about how well little Sophie is sleeping these days; gift shops heaving with tourists buying Windsor Castle tea towels and T-shirts; frustrated drivers sitting angrily in cars waiting for the traffic to ease, so that they can get on with whatever they actually need to be doing today.

In short, Sonnley High Street is much the same as on any other summer's day. And Martha doesn't like that. There's a fifteen-year-old boy gone missing. These people should be out looking for him. She knows it's ridiculous, but she still resents them as she peers in through each shop window, hoping for a sighting of

Art. Most of these people probably don't even know him, let alone that he's missing. And, for those that do, it's not important because they've got their own busy lives to get on with. Those are the ones that Martha resents the most.

"Hey Mar! Why aren't you at school?"

Martha knows the voice of course, but she doesn't want to hear it. Not now, especially, though barely at all these days if she's honest. She turns round to see its owner jogging towards her grinning.

"Oh, hi Dan... what about you? Why aren't you at school?"

"Same reason as you I imagine! Waste of time. There's nothing there for the likes of you and me."

Martha cringes inside. She hates the way Dan still links the two of them together so casually. She tries to think how to get rid of him without upsetting him. He needs help. She's not the one who can give him it.

"No Dan. Not the same reason at all. Stuff to do."

"Tell you what... I've got an idea." Dan's face lights up. He brushes a few strands of his long blond hair back behind the left ear which sticks out a little bit further than the right, as though it were tweaked too many times in his childhood. It's so slight that no one else would ever notice, but to him it is all he can see when he looks in the mirror, and he hates it. Then he trains his dark blue eyes directly on Martha. She can still see why she was attracted to him. Physically he's got a lot going for him, and that's what she'd noticed first.

"No Dan, Sorry. I can't."

"I haven't even told you yet, Mar!" Dan laughs and carries on with the air of someone who's not used to the answer being no, "I've got a new song. You'll love it. It's perfect for your amazing voice. You've got to hear it. This could be the one. Let's go try it out." He puts his right arm on Martha's left to guide her in the direction he wants to go.

"I can't, Dan. No." She pulls her arm away as gently as she can.

"Come on, Mar, don't be stupid. We've got to do this. You'll love it. I really believe this is the one... when you've got a talent like yours,

Mar, you've got to use it!" His eyes are pleading now, in a way that Martha once found appealing, but now looks pathetic.

"No, I can't. I'm sorry Dan."

"What, so you're just going to spend all day looking round these shit shops that you've seen a million times before?"

"No, Dan, I'm looking for someone."

"Well, I'm here! Soul mates, right?"

Martha doesn't want to look at her ex any more. She turns her head and looks in the nearest shop window. It's a charity shop selling once expensive clothes of Sonnley residents to raise money to save cats or something. No sign of Art in there. She wonders if Art even likes cats.

"No, Dan. I've got to find someone who's gone missing."

"Typical you, Mar! Always caring about other people. That's why you're so special. I'll come with you. I can help... wait, hang on... it's not that stupid loser from school who took on Mek, is it?"

Martha says nothing, so he carries on regardless, his tone changed as quickly as a flick of a switch turns a room from light to dark. "It is, isn't it? You're not... no way, Mar... you wouldn't... not with that weirdo loser... no way. You're sick, Mar. You know that. I knew you were fucked up, but... You're fucking sick! How could you?! What about me?" Dan shakes his head and tries to grab Martha's arm again. The pleading in his eyes has been replaced by anger. She pulls away. She has said nothing.

"What the fuck's up with you, Dan?! Just fucking listen to yourself! Someone's gone missing and I'm trying to find them. That's all! Like it's not always about you!"

Martha turns away and runs down Sonnley High Street. Dan follows for a few metres, screams "don't mess with me, Mar!", then stops and kicks a bin, causing a discarded coffee cup to tumble out of the top in full view of a couple of ageing, disapproving tourists. Dan picks the coffee cup up, places it back in the bin and walks off in the opposite direction to his ex-girlfriend.

Martha doesn't really know which direction she is going in. She just knows she needs to find Art.

Sadness comes in many different forms: sharp, stabbing jabs that pierce the heart; wave after wave which engulf you every time you're free and coming up for air; or sudden all-encompassing clouds which remove all traces of light in an instant. But, however it comes, sadness never comes alone. It brings with it a legacy which means that things can never be quite as they were before.

Charley Mann knows that, she's experienced it before. She had always believed that sadness could never be more painful and overpowering than it had been then. She knows now she was wrong. By a long way. She looks down at the piece of paper on her lap and reads it again.

King Alfred the Great had run away. Bad things were happening so he had to run away. A kind old woman saw him looking sad and said she would give him some food and keep him safe. He went into her tiny, little house and she gave him some food, which was very nice. Then she went out, so he thought he would make her some cakes as a nice surprise to say thank you. When she came back, King Alfred was asleep on the sofa, all the cakes were burnt and the tiny house was full of smoke. The old woman wasn't kind any more, she was very angry and shouted at Alfred and told him he was stupid and useless. This made Alfred sad because he had only been trying to help. But the old woman was not as kind as she had seemed, and he couldn't trust her any more, so Alfred ran away.

Charley Mann has read this story more than any others over the last few hours. She guesses that Art had been about eight when he wrote it. In neat red handwriting just below the text a teacher had written 'lovely story, Art' accompanied by a smiley face and three stars. At that age, the teachers had liked his historical stories, regardless of their accuracy.

A tear rolls gently down Charley's nose and splatters on the paper, slightly smudging the teacher's red comments. She tries to wipe it away with her thumb, but it only makes the smudge worse. So she gets up and walks to the hall where she knows there is a box of tissues on the side and grabs one of the tissues, but is interrupted by a knock at the door before she can get back to dab at the blurred red ink.

"Who is it?"

"It's Priya Moore... from Art's school."

Charley doesn't say anything. She wipes her face with the tissue instead and looks at herself in the mirror in the hall. She looks a terrible, drawn mess. She hasn't looked this bad for sixteen years.

"Hi Ms Mann... would it be OK if I come in, please? I just want to chat, see if there's anything we can do to help."

Charley tries to force a smile, but fails, so she stares at the door and grits her teeth.

"Come in... thanks... do you want a cup of..." She can barely muster the energy both to open the door and to finish the sentence, so she just does the former.

"Thanks, Ms Mann... you sit down. Let me make it. Tea or coffee?" Priya smiles kindly at Charley and follows her into the kitchen where there's a small table with two chairs. There's no response, so she puts the kettle on and spots some fruit tea bags on the side. That's a relief, as Priya thinks she's the only person in the world who doesn't know how to make proper coffee. She hates the stuff.

She glances at the kitchen table. It is empty except for the clay salt and pepper pots which have lived there since Art made them in a Junior School art lesson. They worked for about a month until the holes became sticky and bunged up, so that nothing could ever escape from them, despite all efforts to clear them out. But they still live on the kitchen table, a permanent reminder that unconditional love is blind. Priya doesn't need to ask who made them.

"I can't begin to imagine what you're going through, Ms Mann, but I want you to know that the whole school is with you, and we're going to do whatever we can to help you find Art. He's such a lovely, special lad." Priya wishes she hadn't phrased it like that. She would want to help find him even if he weren't a lovely lad, and "special" isn't always the kindest description to use. A bit like "interesting" or "different". But Art is special, and she's said it now.

"Thanks, Mrs Moore." Charley struggles to get the words out. She knows Art is special. It's good others know it too. She wishes she were stronger. She used to be. She had to be.

Maybe the body can only find the unexpected reserves to drag us back up from the bottom of the well once in our lives. When they are gone, they are gone.

"Please... Call me Priya."

"Er yeah. Thanks, Priya." Charley knows she has to see if any reserves have been left behind. "Coffee please."

"Sure."

"Actually, I'll do it, Priya. I'm very particular about my coffee... that's probably where Art gets it from." Charley doesn't say what "it" is, but they both know what she means. She's trying to be normal again, trying to be strong. That's what Art needs her to be. That's what Art has always needed her to be.

Priya and Charley sip their drinks and exchange pleasantries for a couple of minutes, neither of them really sure how to steer the conversation in the direction it should be going, until it's hard to think of many more pleasant things to say at such an unpleasant time.

"Look, Ms Mann, like I say, we all want to do anything we can to help you find Art. He's not in trouble. The other boy, Michael Kinane, is going to be fine, and he swears that he fell anyway, so Art has nothing to worry about. He's done nothing wrong."

"Art wouldn't hurt a fly, you know?"

Priya nods. She does know. "He's going to be fine, Ms Mann. Everything will be back to normal in no time." Charley nods, unconvinced.

Things will never be back to normal. They can't be after what Art's done and what she's told Art. But that's for another day. Now she just wants Art back. Normal can come later.

"Thanks, Priya. Do you know where he is?"

"No. Not yet, but there's a lot we can do. I'll come out with you, help you search, help you put posters up."

Charley closes her eyes. Why hasn't she put any posters up yet? Sitting around reading Art's stories isn't going to get him back.

"Thanks, Priya." It's all been too overwhelming, she hasn't known where to start.

"My husband works in IT. He's good at all that sort of stuff. I'll get him to run off some really eye-catching posters if it would help?" Maybe it would help Tommy too?

"Thanks, Priya." Knowing people care is probably as good a starting point as many. It can certainly help release inner strength.

"Listen, how about we go for a walk round the places Art might go? You can give me a few details of anything you'd like on the poster and I can get them sorted straight away."

Charley knows she went to those places last night, so what's the point? She also knows that she's got to keep trying. For Art. For herself.

"Yeah. Thanks, Priya. Let's go!" Charley's sudden energy takes Priya aback almost as much as it does herself. One second she feels helpless, alone, lost and completely incapacitated by fear and worry; the next second she's got the energy and drive to be positive and really believe that she can find Art.

The two of them head out of the door into the cool Sonnley morning air. Several people stare at them and immediately turn away when they look back. It's a new feeling for Priya. She doesn't like it. It feels like people are talking about them, judging them. Or, more accurately, it feels like people are talking about Charley, judging her, blaming her.

Charley doesn't even think about it. She's used to it.

"Can I ask you one thing, Priya?" she asks. In her mind she can hear Art saying 'you just have, that's your one thing.' She wishes he were here saying it now, and looking perplexed when she calls him a pedant.

"Of course, Ms Mann."

"You will still put on Art's play, won't you?"

"Of course we will... if you're sure."

Charley nods slowly and releases a faint, genuine smile.

"I'm sure, Priya. Thanks. Art would like that... we both would."

Art read once that the best place to hide is in plain sight. He doesn't understand why, because it makes no sense really. If you are in plain sight, then you are going to be easy to see, and if you are easy to see, then you are not hiding well. He tries to make sense of it. What other hiding place options had been considered by the person who recommended hiding in plain sight? And how bad must they have been? Or maybe the person actually wanted to be found?

Still, in present circumstances, Art hasn't managed to come up with the perfect hiding place himself, so is loosely following the advice. Maybe not in plain sight, exactly, but not in some dark, hidden cave where no one would look either.

Currently, he is cramped in next to a selection of rusting almost-empty paint pots, a box of matches, a toolbox, some firelighters and a foldable ladder in the tiny shed in his garden. He is keeping his head down most of the time, but peers up every now and then to see if his mum and Mrs Moore are still at the table in the kitchen. He has seen them chatting and drinking hot drinks instead of trying to find him. If Art had a child and the child went missing, he would do everything he could to find them. But then again, he wouldn't have to be a junkie and an alcoholic to have a child. He would have the child because he wanted it, so maybe that's the difference. Though he doesn't think he would want a child anyway.

He just wants to be back in his home with his mum and Llama like it used to be.

He sees them leave the kitchen and hears the sound of the front door closing, then waits a few minutes, keeping an eye on the kitchen, until the lack of movement in the house seems to confirm they have gone out. They probably wanted to try one of Sonnley's far-too-many coffee shops. Why does a high street need more than one coffee shop? You can only ever sit drinking coffee in one place. Or more than one charity shop or bakery or estate agent or pub for that matter? It's one of Art's bugbears. Every shop should have to sell different things. Then the high street would be much more diverse, interesting and worthwhile.

He leaves the shed and takes the five steps required to pass the fire pit and the two plastic garden chairs and reach the back door. Art has told his mum many times about the risk of having plastic garden chairs next to a fire pit, but she has ignored him. They were free from someone who was throwing them out apparently. He glances into the house through the kitchen window, and all looks quiet. He can see more clearly from this distance, and it's clear that the front room is empty too. So there's no one downstairs. He turns his key in the backdoor lock as silently as possible and slowly pulls down the handle. He knows exactly what he'll do if he hears anyone in there. He's already planned his escape and has deliberately left the gate open at the bottom of the garden, so he can be off down the alley behind the house before anyone sees him.

He goes upstairs and listens outside the bathroom and his mum's bedroom for any noises for a few seconds, before looking round the doors to confirm they're empty. Then he does the same with his own room, leaving him secure in the knowledge that no one else is in the house.

He picks up some fish food from by the goldfish bowl and sprinkles it liberally into the water.

"Sorry, Llama. You must be starving. I bet mum's not been feeding you, has she?... I'm afraid I've got some bad news. I've got to go away for a bit, but I'll pop back whenever I can. I would take you with me, but it's too dangerous. You wouldn't like it... but I'm not abandoning you, right. You hear me?"

Art opens the little cupboard by the side of the bed and pulls out a small green rucksack which his mum had bought him a few years ago for the end of Primary School trip away to a sports activity centre. It had been fun to get away and there had been a good climbing wall there, but he had hated the other sports, and it had been nice to get home on the Friday.

"What would you do, Llama?" He keeps talking as he starts stuffing a few random items of clothing into the bag. "I mean, I've got no choice really, have I? I'm not wanted here. Mum always lies to me... She doesn't care what happens to me... so why would I stay? You wouldn't, would you?... And what would you do if you'd killed Mek? You'd have to run away or you'd be arrested and sent to prison, wouldn't you?... if they have prisons for goldfish, which I don't suppose they do actually... so you'd be OK. But I won't be... and if I haven't killed Mek, he'll be after me, and that'll be worse than going to prison, so I've got to go... you understand, don't you?" Llama keeps pecking at the food in the water above him. It's been a good day for food so far.

"If it hadn't been for that stupid play, none of this would have happened, Llama. I wouldn't have had to hit Mek. I wouldn't have had to find out about mum's lies and how she only wanted to keep me because she was a drunken junkie. And I wouldn't have known that my grandad tried to kill me. I hate that stupid play. I knew I shouldn't have let them use my essay..." He throws a couple of pairs of the dark blue socks, which he always wears, into his bag, and leans over conspiratorially to the goldfish bowl. "I've got a plan though... wait here." Llama is going nowhere.

Art picks up a pen and the little notebook which his mum had given him when he was eight, so that he could write down what he was feeling when she did selfish things like saying they were going out without discussing it in advance or making something new for dinner without asking him first. She thought he might prefer to write down how he felt instead of getting angry and screaming. She was wrong. The notebook is still empty.

He looks at the big poster on his wall, which he got for Christmas when he was eleven, and which lists out the greatest inventions of all time chronologically. He knows them all by heart, but there is something comforting in reading them anyway. László József Bíró invented the ballpoint pen in 1931. There is no information on when notebooks or paper were invented on the poster, which has always felt like a serious oversight, as a pen without paper is no use, surely? So you either include both on the list or neither. And it would have been much more useful to invent the ballpoint pen before the typewriter which was invented by Christopher Latham Sholes in 1868. Writing is a lot easier than typing.

Art walks into his mum's bedroom and opens the drawer in the small table beside her bed. He knows what he's looking for because he stumbled across it once when he was looking for one of her red lipsticks so that he could write 'Happy Birthday to the World's Best Mum' on a big piece of white card, and wanted it to stand out more than if written in pen. He hadn't really understood what it was then, but he knows now. And there it is, tucked away at the back of the drawer: a small, white postcard on which Aunt Amanda has written "I know it's not what you're looking for now but, just in case you do ever want to see them again, here's their new address. All my love forever. A xxxxx'.

Art copies the address into his notebook and puts the postcard back in its place, before returning to his bedroom. He waves the notebook triumphantly in the direction of Llama, then places it carefully in his little rucksack.

"Wish me luck, Llama... Sorry to leave you. I'll pop back whenever I can... Sorry."

Art throws the rucksack onto his back, runs down the stairs much more noisily than he climbed up them, and glances into the front room. He sees a bottle of vodka on the small coffee table and some of his stories laid out on the sofa, next to the box which holds the rest of them. They are his stories. She has no right to look at them without asking. And the vodka bottle is empty.

So, when she's not been chatting to Mrs Moore, his mum has been getting drunk and reading his stories without permission. She wouldn't do that if she cared even the slightest bit about Art. She'd be worrying about him, trying to find him, reporting him missing.

Art puts all his stories back in the cardboard box where they belong and carries them out to the garden. He knows what he's going to do. He locks the back door, goes back in the shed and picks up the firelighters and the box of matches, and carefully places three firelighters in the cardboard box. Then he puts the box into the fire pit, moves the two plastic chairs a safe distance away, and strikes a match. The wind puts it out before he can light the firelighter, so he tries again with the same result. Finally, on the third match, one of the firelighters catches.

Art stares at the fire pit as the flickering flame catches the second firelighter, then the third, and then starts to catch on the pieces of paper and the cardboard box itself. He sees a few tiny, blackened wisps of paper fly up in the air and get carried away in the wind, and he watches as the mesmerising flames get larger and louder, before disappearing almost as quickly as they came, and taking his lifetime of stories with them.

He puts the matches back in the shed, walks out of the back gate into the alley behind, and looks back into the garden to check that the fire is safely out. A small scrap of the cooling ash flutters onto his cheek in the wind. Art wipes it off, closes the gate, and heads off to hide in plain sight.

Chapter Six

Mel:

What do you do when you lose your reason for living? It sounds simple, doesn't it, when it's put as bluntly as that? But it's not. Nothing ever is. You can try to find another reason for living; you can carry on in pain, making the most of what remains and cherishing the memories; or you can give up.

And sometimes giving up feels like the answer. There is something missing from your life: the most important thing. And it's not coming back. You know that. Every day you wake up dreaming of what you used to have, knowing that it's gone forever now.

But there are moments of relief too: the occasional mischievous glance, which Rosa has always reserved for you, and only you will ever notice; the smile which can still illuminate your darkness with hope; even the sudden, opinionated outbursts which seem to come from nowhere but still make you laugh. They always have.

You try to be strong, but being strong has never been your strength. So you stumble through most days as best you can, longing for the time you can close your eyes, drift off to sleep, and get some respite. You think how much simpler it would be if you could stop the pain by never having to wake up again. Just go to sleep and stay asleep forever.

But it's not just about the pain and it's not just about you. You know that. There is hope too, however fleeting, and there is someone who needs you more than ever.

So it's not that simple. Nothing ever is.

"You OK?"

"Yeah... yeah, I'm fine, Tommy... just a bit tired." Mel Jarvis looks at her neighbour, who she has seen grow from the age of seven to forty-three with children of his own now, and thinks about how time changes everything. She's looked up Shakespeare's seven ages speech from As You Like it recently, and also chanced upon an article about how some people are like a fine wine and seem to get better and better with age. It didn't mention that even fine wine eventually gets too old and loses all the traits which made it so special in the first place.

Mel ushers Tommy through the front door and into the living room, where her wife is sitting up and sleeping on the sofa, with an upside-down plate beside her concealing a half-eaten piece of cheese on toast.

"Rosa's having a nap at the moment, Tommy. You OK to wait till she wakes up? I don't really want to wake her if we don't have to...you know, she looks so peaceful." Mel doesn't know if she said the last few words to justify the chance of a few minutes respite to Tommy or herself.

"Sure... no rush at all for me."

Mel carefully picks up the plate and the toast, and they head towards the large kitchen, where she tips the toast into the food waste bin and puts the plate in the dishwasher. Tommy spots a piece of paper drop out of her pocket and leans over to pick it up.

"Leave it!" The force in Mel's voice is something he has never heard before. Rosa was the one who shouted.

"Sorry, Mel."

She bends over, picks up the paper and puts it back in her pocket. She's been reading it over and over since she found it in a box of Rosa's old photographs in the attic last night. She was just trying to find some happy pictures that they could look at together, but she found this letter which made her re-evaluate everything. And she doesn't know what to do about it.

"No... I'm sorry, Tommy... it's been one of those days... Drink?" Mel is back to her usual calm self now or, more accurately, her usual calm, tired, sad self.

"I'm fine, Mel. Just had a cuppa at home." Tommy wonders what was on the paper. He can't ask though, and watches as she pours herself a glass of white wine, and they sit down at the beautiful oak dining table.

"This'll be the only one, Tommy... honest... I don't get the chance often." She looks guilty, as though drinking a glass of wine is somehow betraying her sleeping wife.

"Mel, it's fine... honestly, please... are you sure you're OK? I, well both of us, are really worried about you."

"I'm fine, Tommy... thanks." Mel doesn't want to catch Tommy's eye as she knows it will be obvious she's not. She looks at the wall, covered in certificates, awards and newspaper cuttings: *'Rosa's Kitchen - Berkshire's Best Restaurant'*; *'Ten best places to eat in the UK - Rosa's Kitchen'*; *'Twenty places you must eat before you die - Number 3, Rosa's Kitchen'*; *'Lucky Sonnley residents find food and a welcome which the London elite can only dream of at unbeatable Rosa's Kitchen'*.

The restaurant may be boarded up these days, but Mel is sitting in Rosa's actual kitchen now, and is surrounded by reminders of a life so loved and so missed. This has been Mel and Rosa's home for thirty six years, but the kitchen was always Rosa's kitchen, and the restaurant could never have been called anything else.

"I've got the paper." Tommy puts a *Mirror* on the kitchen table, and gently asks "Do you still want us to..."

"Yes" Mel interrupts loudly before abruptly composing herself. "Sorry, yes please. I know she doesn't read it any more, but it... I don't know how to say it really... I guess it makes things feel a bit more normal... a bit more like they used to be." Rosa had never let another newspaper in the house. They either hated her for being an immigrant or they didn't hate her, but they didn't have enough gossip in them. So they had bought the *Mirror* every day since they first moved to Sonnley all those years ago.

"Sure... of course... Look, Mel, you do know we're always here for you, me and Priya, don't you? We're very happy to help out whenever you want. Anytime, night or day."

Mel looks down from the wall and smiles kindly, revealing the wonderful dimples which utterly outshine the few lines which have begun to creep up her face while her wife's dementia has been changing their lives. She looks far younger than her sixty-two years: still the slim, beautiful, immaculate woman to whom Rosa had said on their first meeting at a party in Earl's Court 'I may be a crazy, loud, foul-mouthed Lebanese woman who dresses like a tramp and washes up for a living, whilst you are clearly beautiful, talented and successful. But you are my soul mate. I'm sorry. It's probably not what you wanted, and definitely not what your family wanted, but you are my soul mate.'

"Thanks, Tommy. You both do more than enough already. I can't tell you how much I appreciate it. I really do. But I'm OK. She's my Rosa. I'll always look after her."

Tommy stretches his arm across the kitchen table and gently squeezes Mel's right hand. As a child, he had never appreciated the sacrifice involved in Rosa and Mel giving up rare evenings away from the restaurant to babysit him and his little brother, and allow his mother a rare break. As an adult, he still hadn't really, until now. Somehow nothing Rosa and Mel did had ever seemed like a sacrifice to them. But he can see Mel's pain now.

"Come on, Mel. I'm here if you want to talk." He gives her hand another gentle squeeze and smiles as openly as he can.

"Thanks, Tommy." Mel pauses for a moment, takes a deep breath, then continues. "OK then... you're right. I will... if you're sure?"

Tommy nods and lets Mel carry on.

"Do you know what it feels like to never look forward to anything, Tommy?" 'Yes', he thinks. "Sounds awful", he says.

"And, even more than that, imagine dreading everything... absolutely hating the thought of every potentially fun outing, every seemingly exciting party, all the things you know you should love."

Tommy doesn't have to imagine it. He knows it.

"Terrible" he says sympathetically.

"Well, that was me, Tommy. Before I met Rosa. She changed everything. She saved me.... she became my best friend, my confidante, my informal therapist, my lover, my everything. She gave me my happiness and my life back. I'm one hundred percent certain that everyone can be saved by something, Tommy, they just need to find the right help which works for them."

Tommy wonders if this is directed at him. What has Priya told Mel or has she just noticed herself? Or is he just being selfish and thinking it's all about him? He tries to tell his mind to shut up and keeps listening as Mel continues.

"And Rosa was my help, the perfect help I needed... and now she needs my help, and I don't know if I can cope with it... I resent it, Tommy. I hate seeing Rosa, my lovely little Rosa, like this: not knowing how to dress herself; not able to leave the house without immediately asking 'how will I get home?'; taking a swig from a bottle of vinegar on the side in the same way that she used to from a wine bottle in the kitchen, and not even noticing it tastes wrong... I resent it, Tommy. I resent having to wipe her arse for her. I resent her walking out of the room when friends are round because she doesn't understand why they're there. I resent her shrieking 'don't go' when I nip into the garden. I resent her saying 'where's Mel?' to me. And, most of all, I resent myself for resenting."

Tommy gives Mel's hand a reassuring stroke.

"I'm sorry, Tommy. I shouldn't have said all that. I don't mean to burden you. It's..."

She doesn't get the chance to finish, as a voice screams out from the front room in a Lebanese accent which is far stronger than you would expect of someone who has lived in England for fifty-one years. The voice is not happy.

"Fucking fuck."

Mel gets up immediately and heads to the front room.

"Are you OK, my little Rosa?"

Mel sees her wife's face break out in the warm, loving smile of welcome reserved only for her, but which she has seen less and less of recently. Rosa's green eyes dazzle and the flawless teeth which no dentist has ever had the chance to look at ("no stranger is going to stick metal rods in my mouth unless they want their hand bitten off") still glint with a beauty that belies their neglect. The tears which Mel had been struggling to hold back in the kitchen come tumbling out now, but for a happier reason.

"I love you, Rosa." Mel gently strokes her wife's wild black hair, pulling it away from in front of her eyes, where it had tumbled whilst she was asleep. "Look who's here to see you?"

Rosa looks up blankly at Tommy.

"Hi Rosa. I need your help." Tommy sees a flicker of the old Rosa in her eyes: the Rosa who would do anything to help anyone, as long as they weren't one of the few people she hated. So he carries on quickly, trying to reignite it. "A poor fifteen-year-old lad from Priya's school has gone missing. I've put together some posters. I need you to help me put them up round town. Is that OK?"

Rosa says nothing, and Mel gently helps her up from the sofa.

"Wow! That's right up your street, my little Rosa... Do you need a wee first?"

She sees the damp stain on the sofa where her wife had been sitting, and knows the answer.

"Let's get you into something more suitable to wear outside, my lovely little Rosa, eh?"

"OK everyone. Before we start, I've got a few updates: firstly, this play is definitely happening. Mrs Moore has spoken to Art's mum and it's what she wants, and what Art would want." For some reason, Finn James had almost said 'what Art would have wanted'. He doesn't know why and corrects himself just in time before the words come out. "Secondly, which you probably know already, there's a consultation meeting with the council this evening at the sports centre about the future of Marsh Park. Please go along if you can and encourage your parents and friends to as well. The more we get, the better... And finally, good news about Mek. He's out of hospital after his fall." Finn ignores the barely-suppressed laughs which echo round the Performing Arts Centre and re-emphasises the point. "Yes fall... No long-term damage, just a bit of mild concussion and he'll be back with us in a few days."

"I already am, aren't I?" Mek swaggers onto the stage from the wings on the left, towers over Finn, and addresses the rest of the cast. "I recover quicker than normal people, don't I?... And I fell, right?" He knows what everyone's thinking, and they now know that they mustn't talk about it.

"Er... thanks, Mek. Great to have you back." Finn's acting training pays off in that last sentence. He claps his hands together, announces "let's get to work then everyone", and calls over to his daughter, who looks distracted in one of the seats at the front of the hall. "Martha, could you get a teapot, a cricket bat and the Union Jack flag from the store room please? We're going to need them for the scene where Thatcher lectures Reagan about what put the Great into Britain."

Martha doesn't say anything, but nods back at her dad, and walks in the direction of Mek, who is jumping down off the stage and heading towards a couple of the Sonnley High girls. Martha has spent most of the day searching for Art without success, and has only turned up for the after-school rehearsal because her brother as good as forced her to. She intercepts Mek before he reaches his destination, and prods him in his chest, which is at her eye level.

"What did you say to Art?"

"Eh?"

"You heard me. What did you say to Art? No one's seen him since he beat you up. You must have said some..."

Mek interrupts with a short, joyless laugh filled with menace. "You deaf or something? I fell, didn't I? And I didn't say anything to that weirdo, did I? Wouldn't waste my time talking to a nut job like him, would I?... You want to be careful what you say, don't you?"

Martha has never been careful what she says, and she's not going to start now.

"So where is he? Did you threaten him?"

"Are you fucking thick as well as deaf? Don't ask me, why not ask someone who gives a fuck like his whore of a mum?"

"You're a fucking sick bastard, Mek!"

"Thanks. You're learning, aren't you?" He laughs, with more joy this time, and walks off towards the Sonnley High girls.

Martha stares after him, shaking her head with rage. "Pathetic" she shouts, ensuring it's loud enough for everyone to hear, and for Mek to know he can't frighten her.

Finn only captures this final part of the exchange, and doesn't like it. He gestures at his daughter to go to the store room. He wants her away from Mek. A parent never gets the chance to stop worrying about their children.

Martha skulks off to the store room, seething. She opens the door, then closes it behind her so that no one can see what she does next. She punches the wall inside the room repeatedly until the knuckles on her right hand are throbbing and beginning to swell, and a little trickle of blood starts to ooze across her middle finger. She doesn't feel better, worse if anything. She takes a deep breath and starts to look for the objects she's been sent to collect.

The room is a mess, much like it was when Art went in the day before: full of tables, chairs and various bits of junk and sporting equipment. She picks up a cricket bat and wonders if it is what Art used to hit Mek with. She doesn't like cricket. Nothing ever happens in it. She wouldn't be searching for cricket bats in a store room if she were still in LA.

Martha places the cricket bat on one of the tables next to the teapot which is already there. She doesn't like this room. It's dark and chaotic: all a bit too familiar. She wants to get out as soon as possible.

The Union Jack is easy to spot. It's enormous and draped over one of the other tables, so that it trails down to the floor. She gives it a tug and leaps back in horror. Underneath the table she can see a shoe. But it's not just a shoe. It's a shoe with a leg in it. Martha wants to run. Has she stumbled over some gruesome murder scene? In a matter of a few seconds her mind imagines several horrific scenarios: multiple bodies piled on top of each other with one pleading for help as it gasps its last agonised breath in front of her; a murderer slamming the door behind her, and whispering ominously in her ear 'well, well, well, who have we got here then?'; a severed leg under the table, a bit of torso on one of the chairs, and a head with eyes gouged out and a mad grinning smile nailed up on the wall.

Martha leans slowly forward and peers under the table. There is no blood and only one body, and she can just hear the gentle sounds of its rhythmic breathing. That's a good start. Carefully she edges closer and can see that the body is male, reasonably tall, slim in a non-athletic way, with rich brown skin slightly lighter than her own, and is lying down resting its head on a small green rucksack. Her heart beats faster than when she thought she'd uncovered an horrific murder scene.

"Art?! What are you doing here?"

"Shh... be quiet." Art is disappointed in himself. He didn't need to say 'be quiet', as 'Shh' had already covered it. But he has only just woken up.

Martha crawls under the table and lies down next to him, so that she can talk to him in a whisper.

"Are you OK, Art? What happened? Why are you here?"

"I'm OK. I ran away. What was the third question?"

"Why are you here?"

"I'm hiding and I was tired, so I needed somewhere to sleep."

Martha laughs. "Well, this is a shit place to hide!"

Art doesn't like swearing. His mum always says it's a sign of an inability to express yourself properly and it offends her. So he never swears. He doesn't tell Martha this, because he said it once to a boy in the year above who had sworn, and the boy punched him. It's better to stay quiet than to get punched.

"Why?"

"Because I found you!"

"Were you looking for me?"

"Well, no, not this time, but I was earlier."

"Why were you looking for me earlier?" Art is lying on his back, staring up at the table above him, and Martha is on her side next to him. She raises her head so that it is directly above his and looks into his eyes. They are an unremarkable brown, but she doesn't have time to read much into them before he turns away.

"I don't know... you were missing, weren't you? I was worried about you, I guess."

"Why?"

"Because I wanted you to be OK, you dick!" Martha really does seem to have trouble expressing herself.

"Why would you care?"

"Because... I don't know... I want everyone to be OK... and I like you. You're funny."

"I don't mean to be funny."

"Well you are! Anyone who thinks that a store cupboard in a busy school is a good to place to hide is either funny or stupid!" Martha twists her head further over Art's body to try and engage his eyes again. The floor prevents him turning his head any further and Martha's head above him blocks him from turning it back. He closes his eyes.

"I'm probably just stupid then." He knows he shouldn't have fallen for the hiding in plain sight argument.

"No Art. You're not stupid." Martha pats him on the head kindly. His black hair is untidy, not in a deliberate way, but in the manner of someone who has never thought it important to think about looking good.

"Thanks."

"Did you want someone to find you, Art? Is that why you came here? Do you want to go home?"

"No." Art opens his eyes momentarily and answers with a force which Martha has not seen in him before. She instinctively juts her head back away from him.

"Woah... OK... Listen. I've got an idea. I can help you. I know where you can go. A much safer place than this."

"Why would you want to help me?"

"Because you need help." Art can't argue with that. He knows he needs help. "Thanks."

"And I'm sure you'd do the same the other way round."

Art has never thought about it. "I've never thought about it."

Martha laughs again. "Thanks, Art!... You do want help, right?"

Art wants everything to be like it was yesterday morning. He wants to be at home with Llama and a mum who cares about him.

"Yeah. I suppose."

"Good. I know just the place, near my brother Johnson's tennis club..."

"Your brother owns a tennis club?"

Martha laughs. "I told you you were funny, Art! No, he plays there." Is it really Johnson's tennis club if he doesn't own it? Art wouldn't say 'that's my pen' just because he was using someone else's pen. He doesn't get the chance to point that out, however, because Martha is talking again.

"So, wait until the rehearsal has finished, and everyone has left, then get out of here and go down to that row of old shops by Johnson's tennis club." She says it deliberately this time. "I'll meet you at the bottom of the alley at the back of the tennis club. Know where I mean? The tennis club just the other side of Sonnley Bridge, right? Six thirty?"

"OK."

"Be careful though. Make sure you wait till everyone's gone and no one sees you... especially Mek!"

Art looks straight at Martha for a split second. "Is he alive?"

"Of course he is! He's fine... well, not fine. Like he's still a wanker, but he's not hurt!" She contradicts herself and swears in the same sentence. Martha's ability to express herself clearly needs a lot of work. It's surprising really given that her dad is a teacher, but Art is beginning to get used to surprises.

"Oh. OK." He is relieved. He is terrified. He is confused.

Martha leans over, gives Art a quick kiss on the forehead, and gets up. She gathers the Union Jack, the teapot and the cricket bat, and heads to the door.

"See you at six thirty, Art. Be careful."

"Yes." Most of all Art is now confused.

Martha heads back out to join the rehearsal, feeling a bit confused herself. If she were to turn to her right, she would notice a figure enter the hall and take a seat at the back, as far from the stage as is possible, where the lights are still off. But she doesn't. She strides towards the stage carrying the kettle, the cricket bat and the Union Jack.

"What took you so long? We were about to send out a search party!" shouts her dad. He instantly wishes he'd phrased it differently.

"Where's Mel?"

Tommy and Rosa have been walking for about fifteen minutes now, roughly the same number of times which she has asked that question, and several more than the number of missing posters they have so far put up.

"She's fine, Rosa. She's at home, looking forward to seeing you when you get back."

"How will I get home?"

"You'll walk back with me, I hope... Unless you get a better offer!" Tommy laughs, hoping it will help Rosa relax. She says nothing, so he carries on talking and reminds her of their mission.

"A poor boy from Priya's school has gone missing, Rosa. He's only fifteen. We need to find him, get him home. So we're putting up these posters round town." He shows Rosa one of the posters he's made. Underneath the word *Missing*, there's a picture of Art in his room, smiling. He isn't looking at the camera, but other than that (or maybe because of that), it gives a very good impression of what he looks like. The unkempt black hair, the small nose, the slight build, the not-so-slight awkwardness. They are all clearly visible. He's looking at Llama.

Below the picture are a few words about when Art went missing, a brief description, the relevant contact numbers for the police and for Priya (she volunteered to take the calls to stop Art's mum having to deal with weirdos and crank callers) and the words *please find him and please bring him home safely*. They are a direct quotation from a story Art once wrote when the history topic was the role of aircraft in the Second World War. The story had focused on a pilot who had been shot down and gone missing, and whose distraught mother was trying to find him. It didn't mention much about the actual role of aircraft in the Second World War. It didn't get many marks, just a detention for Art.

Rosa looks at the poster for a few seconds and reads the word *Missing* out loud, as Tommy stops to put another one up on a lamppost in the leafy road leading up to Marsh Park.

They walk on very slowly with Tommy pointing out to Rosa all the good features he can think of in the houses they pass. 'Wow, that one's enormous, it must have at least six bedrooms'; 'look at those stained glass windows. They're beautiful, the colours are amazing in this early evening light'; 'there must be space for at least three cars on that drive, Rosa'.

"My car's been stolen."

"Are you sure, Rosa? I think you sold it a few years ago."

"Where's Mel?"

"She's at home. She's fine, Rosa."

They reach the park and go in via one of the side entrances, on a small street which separates the park from St Luke's Church. Tommy gets out another poster and carefully attaches it to the gates of the park. He's seen posters for missing cats there before and has momentarily thought 'ah that's sad' before forgetting all about them. He hopes that his poster for Art doesn't get the same response. But he doubts it.

Rosa is agitated. She starts to turn round to head back out of the gate, so Tommy gently catches her arm.

"What's up, Rosa? It's OK. We're just going to have a bit more of a walk and put some more of these up."

"Mel's missing. I've got to find her." Rosa shakes Tommy's hand off her arm and starts trying to pull the gate towards her. It doesn't open that way, but she keeps trying.

"It's OK, Rosa. Mel's fine. She's at home. It's this poor lad who's missing. He's run away from home." He shows Rosa a poster, which momentarily seems to reassure her, and they turn back and start walking through the park.

"I've run away from home."

"Have you, Rosa? When?"

"I need to find a new home, so I've come to England. But I haven't told my parents. They'll worry." Tommy knows the story of how Rosa ended up in England. He heard a very different version several times before Rosa was ill: she left Beirut when she was seventeen to come to England, as she thought it would be more fun and exciting, and that people would be more accepting of her sexuality. On the whole they weren't, but she certainly had a lot of fun and excitement. She'd never mentioned anything about not telling her parents though. Tommy doesn't know if it's true, but he thinks about the torture his life would be if he were to go fifty-one years with one of his children missing, and never even knowing if they were dead, alive, suffering, happy, injured, healthy or even if they had left of their own choice.

"It's OK, Rosa..." he tries to reassure her again, but doesn't get the chance to finish.

"It's not OK. I must tell them where I am. I'll call them at home."

"Yeah. Good idea." Tommy doesn't know what else to say. They walk on in silence for a minute, Tommy flicking his eyes around the various teenagers in the park, hoping to catch a sighting of the boy on his posters.

"Where's Mel?"

"She's at home, Rosa. She's fine."

"She's missing."

"It's OK, Rosa. Mel's fine. It's a boy from Priya's school who's missing" He waves one of the posters at her which she stares at without a hint of recognition as he continues. "Hopefully these will help find him very soon."

The last word triggers an unstoppable reaction in Rosa, like the involuntary knee-jerk of someone who has been lightly tapped on the right place on their leg. She starts slowly, but gathers pace as she continues the quotation.

"Soon, eh? ... *No sooner met but they looked, no sooner looked but they loved, no sooner loved but they sighed, no sooner sighed but they asked one another the reason, no sooner knew the reason but they sought the remedy; and in these degrees have they made a pair of stairs to marriage.*"

"Wow Rosa! That's amazing? It's *As You Like It*, isn't it?" Tommy only knows it's a quotation from *As You Like It*, because he's heard Rosa recite it countless times before, and Mel has told him where it comes from. Apparently it was part of their wedding vows, and now it stubbornly clings on to its place in Rosa's mind whilst so many other words and memories relinquish theirs.

"Is it?"

He spots a small crowd of people gathered round a side wall of the small cafe in the park where he has bought many overpriced ice creams for the children over the years, and hopes fleetingly that it's something to do with Art. He hasn't put a poster up there yet, so it can't be that.

"Look, I wonder what's happening there, Rosa." He points at the cafe and gently leads her in the direction of the side wall.

The gathering is not what he'd hoped for. It's just a few people looking at a new piece of graffiti which has popped up on the cafe wall. In this picture, a young man in a white T-shirt is holding a gun against his head and has evidently just pulled the trigger. His eyes are popping out and his brains are exploding out of his head in a manner which reminds Tommy of cartoons from his childhood, when everything would be back to normal in the next scene. But there is no suggestion that everything will return to normal for this poor young man. At his side, a group of identical-looking chubby, balding middle-aged men in tuxedos and black bow ties are looking at him and laughing.

The reaction amongst the assembled park audience is decidedly mixed. Tommy overhears 'disgusting', 'vandals' and 'that's cruel mummy', interspersed with 'that's great', 'fantastic' and some enthusiastic murmurs of appreciation. He stares at the shocking artwork for a few seconds, then reads the words written below, just above the artist's *Neola* signature: *No one else feels like this.* Tommy thinks of the young man's pain. He thinks that maybe he does feel like that.

"Where's Mel?'

"She's fine, Rosa. She's at home. Let's go back and see her, shall we?"

"Thanks, everyone. Great session on the whole, but Martha you do need to learn your lines please. It's not fair on everyone else. We're up against the clock as it is." Finn James doesn't like calling out his daughter in front of the rest of the cast, but he can't give her special treatment just because of who she is. It's not like her and it worries him. She seems distracted.

Martha ignores him, so he carries on speaking to the whole cast.

"Let's call it a day there then. Can you all put your chairs away and tidy the place up please?" Finn would normally stick around and watch to ensure the students leave the hall as it was when the rehearsal started. But something, or more accurately someone, has caught his eye, and that requires immediate action. He leaps down off the stage and walks as quickly as he can without attracting attention in the direction of the back of the hall. As he does so, he sees the figure get out of their seat, and head towards the exit, so he abandons all pretence and runs after them calling "wait... hang on a minute, can I have a quick word?" But the figure is not waiting for anyone.

As Finn reaches the exit at the back of the hall, he sees the figure moving quickly towards the car park, and sprints after them. He sees them climb into a small red car (no idea what make, he's got no interest in cars other than as A-to-B machines), and switch on the engine just as he catches up. Without thinking, Finn stands in front of the car to block its exit calling "please, wait, I just want a word." He's unsuccessfully auditioned for too many parts where a car has driven off at high speed with someone trapped against its windscreen to think that it's a good idea to stand in front of a car with a running engine and a driver keen to get away. But sometimes, instinct and curiosity outweigh good ideas.

The car doesn't move, the engine switches off and Finn sees who he is dealing with. Breathing heavily after all the running, he manoeuvres himself round to the driver's side of the car, just as the window winds down.

"Finn... I'm sorry... I didn't, you know, want anyone to see me."

"No... I'm sorry... Ms Mann... I didn't know it was you... I'm so sorry... you must think I'm the world's unfittest man.... Every time you see me, I'm out of breath."

Charley hasn't laughed since yesterday morning, and she doesn't now, but she smiles. It's a start.

"Can I get you a coffee or something, Ms Mann?"

"No... no, Finn, thanks... I just wanted... I don't know... I just wanted... needed something to remind me of Art." Charley rubs her hands up and down over her face and sobs.

"Of course... you're bound to... it's OK. Let it out."

"Sorry... I just... I don't know. I just... where is he, Finn?" Charley takes her hands off her face and stares out of the window directly at Finn. The fear in her eyes is partially obscured by the tears, as a coin is hard to find if you drop it in a moving stream. But you know it's there. He wishes he could answer, make everything right for her. But he can't. He never has been able to, not even for his own children.

"I don't know, Ms Mann. But, believe me, he'll be fine. He really will... here, come on, you can't drive like this, can you? Come and have a cuppa inside, eh?"

Charley winds up the window and gets out of the car. She wipes her face, looks around to check no one is watching and follows Finn in silence into a different part of the building from the one they have just left. In truth, he needs the silence. It gives him a couple of minutes to regain his breath.

Once inside, they head to a small room with four armchairs, a sink, a cupboard and a kettle.

"This is where we teachers can escape to if we need a bit of a break" explains Finn without being asked.

After they've been through the niceties of sorting out the drinks, he hands Charley her coffee and sits down in the armchair facing the one she's in.

"Thanks, Finn. I've never been offered so much coffee as I have today. Not sure I'll ever sleep again." It sounds like a joke, but there is no smile, no hint of happiness.

Finn smiles sympathetically. If there's one thing Charley looks like she needs, it's sleep. Well, one thing apart from Art coming back that it is.

"Yeah... I bet... we're none of us much good at knowing what to do and say, I guess. Sorry... but we care you know?"

"Thanks... Who was that big bloke playing Mrs Thatcher?" Charley had been watching the swirls of water settle in her stirred coffee, but she looks up as she asks. Finn hadn't expected that question.

"Er... he's called Michael Kinane."

"Is his nickname Mek?"

"Yeah." He wonders what direction this is heading.

"He's a good actor."

"Yeah... thanks... surprised us all if I'm honest." This certainly wasn't a direction he'd considered.

"He seems so confident and angry, but you can tell he's hiding something."

"Yeah... thanks." Finn doesn't know why he keeps thanking her for complimenting Mek's acting. Maybe these are the words he wished he'd heard more often about his own performances.

"He's the one Art hit, you know?"

"So they say, Ms Mann, so they say... Mek says he fell though."

"Do you know why Art hit him, Finn?"

"No."

"He was defending me... and now he's run away, and he hates me, and he's terrified of Mek... it's all my fault, Finn. Can you see that?"

"It's not Ms Mann, it's really not." He looks into Charley's eyes. The tears have stopped for now, and the pain is more visible. "Things aren't always someone's fault. I've been told that a lot over the last few years, and I believe it... I have to."

"Why? Why do you have to believe it?"

"Because the alternative is unbearable."

Charley looks down at her coffee again. The liquid is still now, like a whirlpool that has finally stopped rotating. She feels like it's already taken her down with it. She wonders what happened to Finn, but she hasn't got the energy to ask today. Maybe one day, when things are back to normal, if they ever can be. She stirs the coffee with her finger, and the whirlpool starts up again.

"You know, I haven't had a drink since I got pregnant with Art?... alcohol I mean."

"Wow, good on yer. I can't say the same I'm afraid." Finn starts stirring his coffee with his finger too. He doesn't notice.

"It's not choice... well it is sort of, I guess... I mean. I can't. I can't have one drink."

"Oh, I get it. Sorry. I didn't mean to be in..."

"No, don't worry. I'm OK with it... well I am usually. But as soon as Art went missing, do you know what one of the first things I did was, Finn?" She doesn't wait for him to answer. "I went out and bought a bottle of vodka... my son's missing and I go and buy myself a bottle of vodka! What's wrong with me?!"

"Don't be hard on yourself, please. There's no right way to react, Ms Mann." Finn notices his finger in his cup, takes it out and wipes it on his trousers, then holds both his hands face up in the direction of Charley almost in a pleading gesture. "You mustn't torture yourself... believe me... you mustn't." His voice trails off as he finishes the sentence.

"Thanks, Finn. I looked at that bottle for hours, wondering what to do, but something, I don't know what, but something stopped me... maybe I knew it wouldn't help Art, I don't know. So I poured it down the sink... but it shouldn't have even come to that."

"Please Ms Mann, don't be hard on yourself. You're the best mother Art could wish for... I've often heard him telling people how great you are." Finn places his hands gently on either of Charley's arms and gives a gentle squeeze of reassurance.

"Have you?" He hasn't.

"Of course... And we're going to find him. He'll be back."

"Will he though, Finn? Are you sure?" He's not sure.

"Of course I am. Trust me."

Chapter Seven

The person who jumps:

With some people it's not what they say that really needs listening to, it's what they don't say. And you are one of those people. Maybe if people had tried harder to understand what is going on in your head, they could have stopped you? Maybe they still can? It's not the longest day of the year yet, so there's still time.

But they won't. They've got their own issues to keep them busy; their own problems to worry about; their own reasons for not wanting to go looking for someone else's pain, when it hasn't been thrust in their faces where they can't ignore it.

So you go on as you are, living your life and living your lie. Until the longest day of the year at least.

In the garden of the Boathouse pub there is a wooden bench, which bears a small bronze plaque inscribed with the words *Priyesh Mishra: best son and brother. Gone far too early. You never realised how much you were loved, but you were happy here x.* There used to be flowers beside it, but a pub garden is not the best place for flowers to stay. A few drinks and some making up to do at home can make them irresistible.

Priya has bought herself a rhubarb gin and tonic and is heading out of the pub towards the bench at the back of the garden. It's been a long day, as they often are. It's a rare treat to get a bit of time on her own, with just her memories for company. It doesn't feel like eleven years ago that it happened. But the bench is a fitting tribute and it's in a beautiful spot, facing away from the pub, overlooking the river, with Sonnley bridge above, just a few yards to the right. It's a place where you can stare into the flowing water and forget everything. If you can block the noise from the traffic on the bridge and other drinkers behind you, that is.

She walks past a few tables of people enjoying after-work drinks in the sunshine and spots a group of youngsters in their late teens. She recognises them as ex-pupils of AllRays Academy and smiles politely at them. One of the group has a bag beside him, out of which four tennis rackets are poking, and he's still in full tennis kit. He gestures toward Priya and calls out.

"Evening Mrs Moore. How are you? Want to join us?" It could have been a joke, an ex-student mocking his former teacher now that they're on a level playing field, but it clearly isn't. She feels a surge of pride that she's had that impact.

"Thanks, Johnson. I've got something to do. Another time maybe?" Priya smiles, then nods at the bag of rackets and asks "How's the tennis going? Still on course for Wimbledon?"

"Probably wouldn't be doing this if I was." He laughs and points at the full pint glass and the several empty ones on the table in front of him.

"Pity." It is a pity. Johnson James is a very talented tennis player. So talented, in fact, that in the year after they had moved over from America, he had been UK national champion in his age group. It hadn't gone down well with some of the other players who resented this outsider taking the crown they'd been seeking for years. But he won them over. Johnson always did. He's one of those people. However much you want to hate him, you can't.

"Nah... it's just how it goes. I haven't got the dedication. It's fine when the alternative to tennis training is school, but... well you know... it's different when you get older, isn't it?" He laughs and nods down towards his glass again, then gestures at the group of young men and women he's with.

"I know what you mean." Priya does know. She loved her late teens and early twenties when everything was an adventure and, for a brief period in her life, she didn't have to think about or answer to other people. "Still" she continues, "pity not to use a talent like that when you've got it." She instantly wishes she hadn't said that. Once a teacher always a teacher.

"Yeah, you may well be right, Mrs Moore." Johnson's too polite to say she's wrong. "I did think about it... but reality is that being in the top few junior players in England means nothing when you start playing the big boys. I saw so many players win everything at youth level, then move up to adult tennis, and realise they weren't quite good enough to make it. It wasn't good for them, believe me... destroyed them. I was lucky really. I realised I wasn't quite good enough before the public humiliation!" Johnson laughs again and takes a sip of his pint.

"Er sorry, Johnson, I wasn't trying to... you know..."

"Nah, it's fine, Mrs Moore. You're good. A bit of tennis coaching here and there, a few drinks with my mates, maybe a bit of travelling sometime, and off to Uni in September. It's all good."

"Actually, Johnson, you've given me a thought... I don't suppose you'd be up for giving my daughter's football team a few tips. We've got the game against Sonnley Town coming up, and I reckon we can win."

He raises his eyebrows and pulls his head back in surprise. "Er... yeah, sure... But you do know I've lived most of my life in America, right? I've not played much soccer at all."

"No, no, that's fine. I'm just talking about the mental aspect. Help them get the belief they can win, that sort of thing."

"Sure, my pleasure... like I say though, dedication was my problem, so I'm not sure they'll learn a lot from me!" He takes another sip from his pint and laughs.

"I'm not looking for them to be world-beaters... just anything to help make them believe they really can win that game. They've got a bit of a mental block, always been told that Sonnley Town are better than them... You've got to have some sort of mental strength to have been national champion, surely?!"

"I don't know about that, but kind of you to say so!... of course, I'm happy to come along if you really want. Can't promise I'll be any help though!"

"Thanks, Johnson."

"My pleasure, Mrs Moore... be good to see if I'm any better at it than I am at tennis coaching. Won't take much!" He empties his pint and waves it temptingly in his ex-teacher's direction. "Sure you won't join us?"

"No... really. Thanks. I've got something to do." She gestures towards the bench at the bottom of the garden.

"Oh, I'm sorry, Mrs Moore. Was that someone you knew?" Everyone knows about the bench. Not everyone is old enough to remember the Boathouse regular to whom it is dedicated.

"Yeah, you could say that."

"So sorry. I hadn't realised."

"Please, Johnson, don't worry about it at all. Really lovely to see you all. Makes my job worthwhile when I see you lot turning out this well!" She knows that was cheesy and a bit embarrassing, but it is true and she needs to move on.

"Thanks, Mrs Moore. Take care." Johnson raises his pint glass in the air, as do the rest of his group, and makes a toast "to your friend. May he rest in peace."

"Thanks." Priya smiles and walks on towards the back of the pub garden.

She reads the inscription, which she could recite with her eyes closed if she needed to, and lifts her glass in the air. "Cheers P." It's a routine she's been through ten times before on the anniversary of her twin brother's death. She takes a sip of her drink and sits down on the bench. There's no one else within earshot if she whispers, which is the way she prefers it. It saves having to explain the situation or convince people who think that she's talking to herself, that she's not mad. Or maybe she is. She doesn't care on this day.

"I'm not sure about this rhubarb gin, to be honest, P. I had a nice pink grapefruit and pomelo one the other day, whatever pomelo is. Probably should have just got that again. Still, got to try these things, I guess... Where shall I start? Mum and Dad are good. They miss you as much as ever and pray for you every day. Do you hear them? But they're good really... guess what dad's up to these days? Wait for it... he's the Network Architect at AllRays Software!" Priya chuckles to herself and carries on in her whisper. "Shock horror, eh?! How long's he been doing that now? Seems like forever! He's managed to find yet another excuse to put off his retirement. Mum's delighted!... I reckon AllRays can't have spotted he's still there!" Priya chuckles again, takes another sip of her gin, winces and starts talking to her brother again.

"I wish you could see the kids grow up, P. They'd love you. Nina's fourteen now and Mia's twelve. Fourteen and twelve! Can you believe it? They were babies when you last saw them. They're lovely, bright girls... well I would say that, wouldn't I? But they really are... some of the time! Nina seems to think she owns the place these days and clashes with Tommy sometimes, and Mia's a teenager before her time. So they have their moments, but they're so wonderful, P, they really are. Nina's got the game against Sonnley Town coming up. I can't wait. They can win it. I know they can, P. I so wish you could be there, it's going to be special, I'm really sure they can do it... And little Kian's nine now! I can't believe it. He's naughty in that funny way you can't get angry with, just like his uncle P... I so, so wish you'd met him. You would have loved each other... would have been impossible to control the two of you, mind." Priya hears her voice beginning to crack, so pauses and has another taste of her drink before carrying on.

"Actually, this rhubarb gin gets a bit better, the more you have of it, P. I might get another when we've finished chatting... where was I? Oh yeah, the kids. They are so wonderful. They're everything to me now, P, they really are... I know what you're thinking, P, what about Tommy? I didn't mean it like that, I really didn't. He's... I don't know what the right word is... he's struggling, I guess. Yeah, still struggling. No one else sees it, because he hides it so well, but I know. I still love him to bits, P, but it's different now. Sometimes I feel like his carer more than his wife. Sorry, I know I shouldn't say that... I've told him so many times that there's help out there, that it might really help him if he spoke to someone, but he won't. He says he can deal with it, but he can't, can he, P? It's gone on too long now, it's chronic. He's been depressed for years now, pretty much since Nina was born. I got him some leaflets on paternal depression, but he didn't want to read them... says he'll do it his way, whatever that means. I know you'd be able to get through to him better than me, of course you would... and he still misses you more than you could ever have guessed, P. You were his best friend... you were my best friend. Oh P, why you?! I'm so angry with you sometimes for leaving us... I'm sorry, I know I shouldn't be, it wasn't your fault, but that fucking cancer couldn't care less if I'm angry. But I know you will, and I need someone to care that I'm angry... does that make sense? No, probably not. And it's selfish, I know. Sorry. I just wish you were still here ... I miss you so fucking much!"

Priya stops talking and lets the tears flow out. She knows she's supposed to be the strong, happy one. She's been told as much. At her brother's funeral, her dad gave a speech in which he said 'it must be, with twins, that there is a limited amount of health, joy and strength to be shared round. The joy was evenly split, but Priyesh got smaller slices of the strength and the health than Priyanka.' It had hopefully just been clumsy phrasing, as Priya and her dad are close, and he's a good, kind man. But there will always be that thought jabbing away at her mind that he blames her for her brother's death. She is generally very positive, very strong and happy, and can block it out. But, on a day like today, the jab gets through the defence, and she needs an outlet like everyone else. She wipes her eyes, takes another drink and returns to her brother.

"Sorry, P. I didn't mean to explode like that... I just miss you, that's all. And I love you so, so, so much. We're the other half of each other, remember that!... but I'm good, really good. We all are... Tommy won an award the other day... best something or other, I don't know, something he's done brilliantly at work anyway, so he's buzzing from that." Priya doesn't want to burden her brother further with the truth. He'll care too much and take her worries on as his own. He's so sensitive and kind. It's what makes him so wonderful. It wasn't enough to keep him here though.

"Anyway, P. You're probably sick of me prattling on, so I'll let you go. Thanks for listening. You're always such a great listener. I love you, P. Bye for now."

Priya raises her glass up to the sky and looks up. Is her brother up there? Is he happy? She drains her drink, and sits on the bench for several more minutes, staring at the relentless, intoxicating movement of the river in front of her. As one body of water rolls gently away down the river, the next one moves in to replace it and the cycle goes on. It's how it always has been. And how it always will be she supposes.

Some people do all they can to help others; others do all they can to help themselves. No one could fit as neatly into the first category as Councillor Faith Roberts, but today she is sitting in a packed sports hall, flanked by a couple of more experienced councillors facing an audience who can best be described as hostile and not prepared to listen. Doing all you can to help others doesn't always lead to appreciation.

Not that Faith wants appreciation. She never has. And she doesn't want to be a councillor. She's got more than enough to do as a mother, grandmother, choir singer, part time charity shop manager, and lay preacher at St Luke's. Not to mention the volunteer work and the time she spends visiting her ninety-two-year-old father and helping with her dear old friend and neighbour, Rosa Angelina. And Faith certainly would never dream of mentioning any of that. She doesn't want praise, she just wants to help.

But a councillor she is. It happened more by accident than anything else, when the council announced that cuts in funding from central government meant that they were going to close the day centre for autistic adults, which her youngest son, Marshall, attends. Faith campaigned passionately and respectfully with other parents, but to no avail, until someone (Faith doesn't remember who now) suggested that if they had some representation on the council it might help their case. And as a well-known, much-loved member of the community, it had to be Faith. It sounded sensible at the time and would have flattered the ego of most people. But not Faith. She doesn't do ego. She just does what she thinks is right, and standing for the council seemed right at the time. It doesn't feel so right now. She looks up at the waves of people staring at her, the collection of 'Save Marsh Park' and 'People before Profit' banners fluttering in front of her, and momentarily wonders how she is helping people now.

Faith wasn't even meant to be here this evening. But, one by one, other councillors had dropped out of the event citing prior engagements, illness, even an emergency vet appointment. So she has turned up, because she knows it's important to listen, and the council needs to listen. She also knows she can't change anything by herself. She was one of the few councillors who had voted against the proposal to accept the supermarket offer for the park in a bid to reduce the deficit in the council's coffers after years of underfunding, so she knows that her voice only has limited influence. But she did manage to get them to agree to a two-month delay to give the community the chance to raise the money themselves for a counter offer.

"I know you... you're the one who wants to use all our money saving that centre for those mentally handicapped people, aren't you?" The question is shouted by a middle-aged man sitting a couple of rows back. His face is contorted with anger, and if steam were pouring out of his ears, no one could really be surprised.

"They are actually autistic..." As Faith starts her reply, the hall lights glint off the silver-rimmed glasses, which match the flicks of grey in her black hair. But the man doesn't want to listen.

"Mentally handicapped, autistic, whatever... that's not the point. The point is there's, what, twenty or thirty of them use that centre? There's thousands of us use Marsh Park. What about us? Who cares about us? We'll have nothing." Faith knows about no-one caring. Her parents arrived from Barbuda three months before she was born, and there certainly wasn't much care going around for them. Her father has talked to her many times about the hatred they experienced when they first arrived in the UK. But he also taught her not to be bitter. Bitterness doesn't help anyone, love does. Even when her mother died from breast cancer when Faith was just twelve, her father helped her to move forward. 'Without suffering, you can not appreciate joy' he had told her. He gave her her name and he gave her her faith.

The serenity in Faith's voice cuts through the tension in the room.

"Thank you, sir. This is not an either-or situation. I would like us to save both the autism day centre, and Marsh Park, but the council have decided that the only way they can make up the shortfall in funds caused by reduced central government funding is to sell Marsh Park. And I very much hope that we, as a community, manage to find a way to bring it into community ownership. I know that there are already a significant number of fund-raising activities in progress, including a sponsored walk, the AllRays Academy play, the..."

The man interrupts again.

"A poxy play's not going to make enough money to buy the park... and I've done my research you know, you can't pull the wool over my eyes. You've got a bloody conflict of interest, haven't you? Your kid's one of the mentally handicapped ones who uses that centre, isn't he? So no wonder you're more interested in saving that. You're corrupt! You're all the bloody same you lot." The final sentence hangs in the air, its true meaning ominously ambiguous to everyone in the room. Faith glances at the two councillors on either side of her. They are both shuffling papers on the table in front of them, and staring down at them, as though they have got something critically important hidden in their papers if only they could locate it.

Finn James watches the scene in horror from five rows behind the middle-aged man. He recognises him as a parent at the school. Worse than that, he recognises him as the father of his daughter's ex-boyfriend, Dan Slaw. He's glad that she's moved on, though she's still in a band with Dan, and maybe he's not like his father anyway. He hopes so. That much anger and hatred can only lead one way, but it hasn't ended yet.

"And what are you doing to catch the vandals who are defacing our town with their mindless whingeing graffiti? This is Sonnley, not some bloody rundown American hood crawling with brain-dead gangsters!" Judging by Dan's dad's face, all the blood from the rest of his body has now congregated in it, so that it's redder than an horrific case of sunburn. But it's not caused by embarrassment.

"With respect, sir, that is an issue for the police, and this evening's meeting is purely intended to discuss the future of Marsh Park."

"'With respect!!' What do you mean 'respect'?! You lot don't show any respect for us good, law-abiding citizens! Another bloody cop out! Don't worry, I've told the police, and those vandals better hope they catch them before I do!"

Finn puts his hand up, and Faith smiles patiently at him, and nods to let him know he's good to speak. He hasn't planned what he's going to say, but he knows he needs to say something.

"Thanks, Councillor Roberts. I'm Finn James, a teacher at AllRays Academy. I know how much this park means to you and all the efforts you've put in for us even to have this chance to save it, so I want to put on record my thanks for that." He does know. Priya is a neighbour of Faith Roberts and has told him how hard she fought just to get the two month delay in the sale of the park. He wishes Priya were here this evening, but she had to be somewhere else apparently. It must have been something important for her to miss this. Finn gets to his feet and turns slowly round in a full circle so that every person in the hall can see the passion in his face as he says the words. "I just want to put out an appeal to every person in this room to support our play, to support every fund-raising activity, to come up with new ones even... please, please, please... We can save Marsh Park. We really can. If we all work together, we can do this." He can see the rage five rows in front of him. Tough.

The consultation meeting continues for another fifteen minutes or so in a generally polite tone as if no one really knows what to make of what's gone before. As it winds up and people flood out of the hall, some mumbling, some laughing, some moaning about the waste of their time, Finn waits behind for Faith to head towards the exit. He notices that she walks with a stick and slight limp, but it doesn't affect her pace.

"I'm so sorry, Councillor Roberts..."

"Call me Faith, please."

"I'm so sorry, Faith. You shouldn't have to put up with that. Most of us know what you've done to try to save the park."

"Thanks er..."

"Finn."

"Thanks, Finn. No need for anyone to apologise. People have strong feelings."

They turn left out of the hall together and start walking between the hall and the five-a-side football pitch which adjoins it.

"Are you a religious man, Finn?" There is no judgment in the question.

"Well, I'm Irish, so I guess I should be... but no, no, I'm not really. Sorry." Finn feels strangely embarrassed, as though he has let Faith down.

"No more sorries, please, Finn! Do you mind if I tell you a bible quote I love though?"

"Course not."

"Thanks, Finn. I'm not preaching... for once!" Faith chuckles warmly and carries on. "But I love these words. They're from the First Epistle of Peter, Chapter three, Verses eight and the start of nine: *Finally, all of you be like-minded, compassionate, loving as brothers, tenderhearted, courteous, not rendering evil for evil or insult for insult; but instead blessing.*" Faith smiles at Finn and continues. "I suppose that did sound a bit like preaching really! But I hope it makes sense. It certainly does to me!"

"Yeah... kind of. Not sure I've got it in me though!" He smiles back at her.

"Of course, I could have quoted you Proverbs Chapter eighteen, Verse two, but that would have been cruel!" Faith chuckles naughtily, like someone who is about to swear in front of their grandmother for the first time, but can't help themselves.

"Go on... you've got me now!"

"*A fool has no delight in understanding, but only in revealing his own opinion.*"

"That fits better for me!" They both laugh, whilst Faith slaps herself lightly on the back of her left hand with her right palm and winks.

As they reach the end of the Sports Centre, Finn makes a gesture with his hand to indicate that he is going to be turning left again round the back of the building, and questioning if she is also heading in that direction.

"No, the other way for me." She props her stick against her left leg, leans forward and clasps his hand firmly but gently between both of hers. "It has been a great, great pleasure to meet you, Finn, and thank you for your help and support. I will pray for the success of your play. I do hope we meet again."

"Thanks, Faith. Me too."

As she lets go of Finn's hand, she accidentally knocks her stick to the ground, and he quickly retrieves it for her.

"Thank you, Finn. Damn thing, I'm always dropping it!"

He nods towards her right leg, unsure how to phrase the question.

"Nothing serious I hope?"

"No... it's nothing... just a nuisance, that's all. It's been twenty years, I should be used to it by now." She chuckles, but it doesn't sound like the chuckle of someone who is used to it by now. "And besides, it was my own fault."

"Oh, sorry..."

"Don't be Finn. I'm not." Faith waves her stick theatrically in the air as if trying to reassure one or the other of them, smiles, says another farewell, then places her stick on the ground and hurries off at an unnaturally quick pace.

Finn watches for a few seconds trying to take it in, before heading round the back of the Sports Centre with a calmness he's not felt in a while. There's a quality in Faith Roberts that he's not noticed in anyone else. He can't put his finger on it. Serenity? Acceptance? Peace maybe? He's not sure exactly, but he knows that she has left him feeling less stressed than he was a few minutes ago, even if it is unlikely to last. Out of the corner of his eye something catches his attention on the wall of the Sports Centre. He's never seen it before, and it doesn't look like a commissioned mural, but it certainly looks freshly done. It's signed by Neola. Finn wonders if he knows Neola. An ex-pupil maybe?

In this picture, a noose has been drawn and the body of a skinny teenage girl in a simple white dress hangs limply down, her defeated expression shocking Finn so much that he instinctively glances away to avoid the desperate pain and fear in the girl's eyes. Next to the body is drawn a plump, middle-aged man in a tuxedo and black bow tie and with a resemblance to Sonnley's MP. He looks sad and tears are streaming down his face.

Finn stares at the picture of the man, trying to work out if the tears are genuine or not. It is difficult to tell. Deliberately so. Whoever did this has got talent.

Below the artwork is the caption *It's never too early to start caring, but it is often too late.* Finn reads it slowly, then looks back up at the girl hanging from the noose. Her desolation and helplessness are captured with heartbreaking honesty and expertise. He doesn't glance away this time.

Art stands at the bottom of the alley at the back of the tennis club which Martha's brother does not own. He looks at the little bedside travel clock, which he had thrown into his small green rucksack when Llama was watching. He hadn't realised at the time how useful it would be, what with not being able to use his phone because his mum might contact him or someone might track him. So the travel clock is his only way of knowing the time. And it is six thirty now, but Martha is not here. She's not coming. He waits until the clock clicks over to six thirty-one, just in case, then starts to walk off back down the alley, not knowing where to go now.

He hears some footsteps running down the alley behind him and darts behind an industrial bin, which presumably belongs to the tennis club.

"What are you doing, Art? It's me!" Martha catches Art up and pauses for a second to catch her breath.

"I thought you weren't coming."

Martha looks at her phone and laughs. "It's six thirty-one! Come on, Art. Are you for real?"

Exactly. She's proved his point. It's six thirty-one and they agreed six thirty. He doesn't have time to say this though. Martha leans over and gives him a hug and a little kiss on his cheek.

"I'm sorry, Art! Forgive me... please!" Martha pulls a mock unhappy face and opens her eyes as wide as she can in a pleading expression. Art doesn't notice.

She grabs his arm, and starts leading him back down the alley, towards a small side road, which hosts a few houses, a newsagent and a boarded-up building. The road is as dreary as the high street is vibrant, as though they belong in different towns. Before they turn into it, Martha puts her hand over his eyes, and giggles.

"Close your eyes."

"Why?"

"Because I want to see your face when you see where we're going!... You're going to love this place, Art." He doesn't like surprises, let alone love them, so he doesn't close his eyes. But he can't see anyway with her hands over them. They turn the corner and Martha pulls away her hands and triumphantly announces "Voila." He wonders if she speaks French fluently or that is just a word she's picked up from TV.

"It's a boarded-up building."

"It's not any old boarded-up building, Art. It's your boarded-up building. You'll be much better off in here."

Art looks at the building suspiciously. Above the boards at the front, he can see a sign saying *Rosa's Kitchen*.

"It's someone's kitchen. What good's that to me?"

"It's some shit old restaurant I think." Martha laughs and leads him by the hand round to the back of the building. Art stays quiet about the swearing, and she carries on. "No wonder it's boarded up. A restaurant is never going to work in a backstreet dump like this! Like even I know that." But Martha doesn't know how wrong she is.

Round the back the windows are boarded up, but there's a rickety door, which has clearly been kicked open by someone at some stage since the restaurant closed, and then pushed closed later to pretend that nothing has ever happened. Martha pushes the door gently, and it creaks open far enough for the two of them to sneak through the gap before it shudders to a halt against an enormous rusting saucepan jammed between the door and the wall behind. In the commotion, a tiny spider scurries out of the pan in the opposite direction to the two intruders. Still holding his hand, Martha leads Art down the hall past the kitchen on the right into what must have been the dining area of the restaurant. It's got the highest ceilings that either of them has ever seen in a room, where the floor above has been ripped out to make the space larger and more impressive, leaving an enormous, tall single-story building. There are no tables or chairs in there any more, but a few tell-tale signs indicate that something used to go on here: a once-beautiful mural of a woman with wild black hair adorns one side of the room, whilst the opposite wall is covered in scrawled testimonies of the restaurant's customers, written in a variety of colours and with as much variety of legibility. Martha nods towards them, and laughs "a few things for you to read when you're bored, Art... though they'll probably make you more bored!"

"What's all this?" Art points at the floor on which some blankets have been neatly laid out with one as a base and two others on top. Beside the blankets there is a torch, a couple of packets of crisps, a bar of chocolate and some baby wipes.

"Oh, it's nothing. Just thought you might need a few things to make you comfortable and keep you clean... I didn't have much time, as you can see!"

"Thank you." Art smiles. Martha smiles back and squeezes his hand.

"You going to be OK here?" She takes hold of his other hand too and faces Art directly, looking into his eyes for the answer. For once, he doesn't turn away instantly, and Martha is sure she can see a frightened soul waiting to be rescued. She knows it well.

"Yeah. I'll be fine. Thanks," Art looks down at the floor now, and Martha engulfs him in a tight warm embrace. No one has ever cuddled him before except his mother. It feels good.

"What are we going to do with you, Arty boy?"

"I'll be fine. I've got a plan." He doesn't sound fine.

"Ooh, sounds exciting! What is it?" Martha relaxes the embrace and looks for an answer in Art's face, but nothing is obvious.

"I'm going to see someone. They will give me some money to keep me going.'

"Who?"

"I won't say." Martha likes the way he says 'won't' instead of 'can't', because 'can't' wouldn't have been accurate. It makes her smile inside.

"Why not?"

"I don't want to risk being let down again."

"Oh Art... that is so sad... I won't let you down." She gives him another hug and a kiss on the back of the neck, then sees her phone light up with a new message and notices the time on the screen. "Shit, I'm sorry, Art. I'm going to have to shoot. I'm supposed to be cooking this evening, and dad'll be back from some meeting he's been at soon. I don't want him getting suspicious."

"That's fine. Thanks for your help." Art smiles, and momentarily looks at Martha. Maybe there's a hint of happiness there. It's difficult to tell. He follows her back down the corridor towards the door, and she points at an old black wheelie bin which has been discarded in the former kitchen of *Rosa's Kitchen*.

"When I leave, jam that in front of the door, so it won't open from the outside... keep you safe in here. And when I come back I'll do three short knocks, then a pause, then two short knocks, and you'll know it's me... don't want you letting any old fucker in!" Martha laughs loudly this time. Perhaps a little too loudly to convince. But Art doesn't notice. He doesn't even notice the swearing. He goes over to drag the wheelie bin out of the kitchen until he is standing in the corridor with the door and Martha on one side of the bin and him on the other.

Martha leans over the bin, takes Art's head in between her hands and gives him a short, sharp kiss on the lips.

"I've never met anyone like you before, Art... I really haven't... and I like you."

"Thanks. I like you too."

"I'll be back tomorrow as early as I can."

"It's my birthday tomorrow."

"Oh... I'm sorry... no... I don't mean sorry... I don't know what I mean... that's great!" Martha leans back over the bin and kisses Art on the lips again, but much longer this time and is met with an enthusiastic response.

"Happy Birthday!" she says as she eventually pulls away, smiling.

"It's tomorrow." He says.

Martha laughs loudly and blows a kiss at Art as she looks back one last time. When she laughs, her nostrils twitch and flare very gently in time to her laughter, making her 'N' nose ring look almost like a hologram as it changes colour with the light. If he noticed, Art would probably find it fascinating. But he doesn't notice. "You're so funny, Art! I love it! See you in the morning!" She closes the door behind her and heads back out into the early evening.

Art blocks the door with the black wheelie bin, and goes back into the main dining area, where his makeshift bed is. When he was younger, he used to struggle to get to sleep on the night before his birthday, dreaming of the excitement and the presents to come the next day. He wonders if he'll sleep better tonight.

Chapter Eight

Song:

*I listen to my mind
But my mind is unkind.
And it hates me all the time
And makes me scared.*

*I'm standing on a wall,
Where I have stood many times before.
And I know that I might fall,
But I don't care.
No, I don't care.... Care, care, care, care*

*And I'm walking through a storm
And it's just like that.
And this pain is now my norm
Yes, it's just like that, like that.*

*I know I should walk tall,
If I had any self-respect at all.
But I can barely even crawl
In my self-centred slump.*

I'm waiting for a train
Oh no, not this again.
My mind always says the same
And tells me to jump.
Yes it tells me to jump... Jump, jump, jump, jump

And I'm walking through a storm
And it's just like that.
And this pain is now my norm
Yes, it's just like that, like that.

I can't stop the noise,
And the noise just destroys
All the hope of the joys
For which I yearn.

My mind is not my friend
And my friends can't comprehend
How my pain will never end
Until I burn
Yes, until I burn ... Burn, burn, burn. burn

And I'm walking through a storm
And it's just like that.
And this pain is now my norm
Yes it's just like that, like that.

I can't stop the dread
Because the voice in my head
Repeats what it's always said
It wants me dead... It wants me dead... It wants me dead.

Dan doesn't like having to rehearse at eight o'clock on a Saturday morning. They usually don't start until late morning or early afternoon. But Martha had insisted. They either do it at eight o'clock in the morning today or not at all. So he had no choice. And Dan doesn't like having no choice. He strums the chords with an anger and unhappiness which suits the mood of the song perfectly. They've played this same song eight times so far this morning, and on each occasion his mood has blackened further.

Martha sings the final lines of the song in a desperate, yet somehow tuneful, howl. She watches intently as Dan plays the closing notes, then leans over and presses the button on her phone to stop recording.

"I reckon that's the one" she says, her face radiating in a joy totally at odds with what she's just been singing.

"We fucking nailed it, Mar! Your voice is made for that song. It's perfect." Dan's anger has transformed almost instantly into an elation, which Martha hasn't seen in him since the early days of their relationship when anything had seemed possible. It's good to see him happy, though she knows it won't last.

"Thanks, Dan... guitar's on a different level too!" That's true inasmuch as Dan's guitar playing has definitely improved dramatically in the last few months, though it was a pretty low starting point. Music is not really his natural habitat as much as he wants it to be. But Martha isn't going to be the one to tell him that.

"If anyone had the slightest taste, that'd be fucking number one all over the world. It's amazing... we're amazing, Mar. You can't make the magic we've got. It's either there or it's not." Martha knows that it is not. She wonders if it is somewhere else though.

"The songs are definitely beginning to work much better, Dan." She tries to sound as neutral as she can, pouring the bucket of water on the flames before they get out of control. She knows where this is heading.

"It's more than that, Mar! We've got it all. This is the one! We need to get gigging... need to let the world see what we've got." Dan has put down his guitar and is taking some tobacco from a small pouch and placing it into a green Rizla to roll. He's not meant to smoke in the house, but his room is at the top of the house, the window is open, and his parents only come up here if he's in trouble already, so he's got nothing to lose.

Martha glances at her phone. It's nine o'clock.

"I need to get off now, Dan. Great session!"

"You can't go now! We're on a roll." Dan puts the cigarette in his mouth, wipes a loose bit of tobacco off his lower lip, and clicks on his black disposable lighter. They may be disposable, but they are always black. It's his thing.

"Best to leave on a high then!" Martha tries to make light of it. She needs to change the direction of travel.

"We could do a few more songs, have a few drinks, spend the day together having fun, like we used to... I've got some vodka over there." He takes a drag on the cigarette and blows the smoke in the direction of a few bottles on the floor by his bed.

"I can't, Dan. I've got stuff to do..."

"Or rum... or whiskey? Come on, Mar. Lighten up... we've just made the perfect song. Let's celebrate!"

"I can't. I told you. I'm sorry." Martha puts down the microphone she was using on his bed, picks up the small holdall she brought with her, and starts to walk towards the door.

"Go on then. You give up... you just walk out again... you're selfish, you know that, Mar? It's all about you. What about me, eh? You need to grow up, start thinking of others." Martha is thinking of others, or more precisely one other, at the moment, and that's who she wants to see. She stops next to Dan and stares straight into his eyes, the ones which had once drawn her in so readily. She can still see the deep intensity, which had once been so appealing, slightly dangerous even, but now just looks misplaced and pathetic.

"I'm not going to listen to this, Dan. I'm off." Martha moves her head away as he blows a cloud of smoke straight at her, then she walks towards the door and turns back one more time to address her ex.

"It doesn't have to be like this, Dan."

"No, it doesn't."

She watches as Dan takes another drag on his cigarette, then slowly grinds it into his forearm to put it out. She sees a few embers sparkle brightly on his arm before turning grey as they flutter off towards the floor. And she sees him bite his lip in a vain effort to disguise the pain.

"Don't Dan. Please. Don't torture yourself."

He says nothing. He just stares at the burn on his arm and tosses the extinguished cigarette butt out of the window.

Martha thinks about going back into the room to talk further, but she knows what will happen. She's tried it before.

"Take care, Dan. I'm not the answer… I can't help you. But someone can."

She closes the door gently behind her and hears his response on the other side.

"You can. You will one day. You're just scared of how you feel now."

Finn doesn't know if this is a good idea or not. He looks at the doorbell for a few seconds wondering if he should or shouldn't. For some strange reason, Martha had got up very early this morning to go to band practice with Dan. That always made Finn feel a bit anxious. He doesn't trust Dan, and wonders if he's like his dad. But Martha is sixteen. She'll do what she wants to do, so Finn knows better than to argue with her about it. It won't work, it'll just drive a wedge between them. And that's the last thing either of them need. She's got no mother, and he's got no wife. So he said nothing, didn't even argue with the unlikely "I just woke up early" answer to his gentle probing about her being up at seven thirty on a Saturday morning for the first time since she was about eight and would watch a Disney film with her mum whilst he had a lie in.

But Martha had mentioned that today is apparently Art's birthday, so here Finn is.

He presses the doorbell. No going back now. After about twenty seconds, a sad voice answers from the other side of the closed door.

"Who is it?... Art, is it you?"

Finn feels terrible for providing the brief glimmer of torturous hope and replies as quickly as he can.

"Er no, I'm sorry Ms Mann. It's Finn James... I er... I don't know really... I just heard it's Art's birthday today, so thought... I don't know... maybe you might want a bit of company or something... sorry, probably a stupid thing to think... I just thought..."

"It's OK, Finn, thanks." Charley opens the door, smiles weakly and waves him inside. She is still wearing the same beige vest top and white skirt that she was wearing at the play rehearsal yesterday. Maybe all those coffees did stop her sleeping. Though it was more likely something else of course.

They both walk into the small front room, where Charley gestures for Finn to sit down on the sofa, and then sits down beside him. There are no other seating options. None have ever been needed. A sofa big enough for Charley, Art and occasionally her sister has always been enough. Though now that Amanda is married with two children of her own, it can get a bit of a squash if they all come round.

"Thanks, Finn. It's nice to know someone cares. Means a lot." It really does mean a lot. Seemingly small gestures can make a big difference.

"No worries. I wasn't sure if I should come to be honest... didn't want to... I don't know... intrude I guess." Finn raises an awkward hand to his face as if he's trying to hide the fading, but still noticeable, scar on his left cheek, which he blames for many of the roles he's missed out on over the years.

"You're not intruding." Charley pauses for a couple of seconds to look out towards the window and the world outside where Art is hiding somewhere, then looks back at Finn with a faint, awkward smile. "Like I said, it's nice to know someone cares." She stops again momentarily, conjuring up the strength to continue, and fixes her stare directly at Finn with an openness which makes him fleetingly look away. "You know what I do, don't you, Finn?"

"Well, er... no... not really." He doesn't know how to answer, but he knows he should have done better than that. Charley smiles. It's difficult to tell what the smile means.

"You don't have to lie, Finn. It's OK. Everyone knows... even Art knows now."

"Er... sorry... I didn't mean to..."

"I don't do anything wrong, Finn. You know that? Everything I do is entirely consensual, and I don't hurt anyone. Not like those people who slag me off, but go to work and happily cut costs by sacking their low paid cleaners; or make money by beating down the costs from factories whose workers can't even afford their next meal; or invest heavily in companies who value profit above people... I don't hurt anyone, Finn, but everyone judges me. Do you get it?"

"Yeah... sorry... course I do. It's terrible." Finn finds himself thinking of Faith Roberts. She wouldn't be judging Charley.

"And you know what, Finn? One of my clients rang me today... he's going to pay for a private detective to help find Art. How's that, eh? Doesn't want anything in return. Just wants to help me, because... well he wants to help, that's all... because he's not a bad person, I'm not a bad person. But the way people look at me, the way they talk about me behind my back, you'd never know it, would you?"

"Er... I know... I'm sorry."

"And I never really cared, Finn, if I'm honest. Let them think what they like. I know the truth... but now Art thinks I'm a bad person, and the truth doesn't seem to matter any more. Do you know what I mean?"

Finn can see a strange mix of strength, pain and honesty in Charley's face. The three emotions are clearly battling each other and it's hard to tell which is winning. It's the honesty which strikes him most though. He's not heard that sort of openness since he first met Niamh all those years ago. It's an amazing, unsettling quality. He nods.

"I do... you're a good person. You don't deserve that." He wishes he could improvise better than that.

"He's been back here you know, Finn?"

"Art has?" Momentarily, all Charley can think of is how Art would have deemed that an unnecessary question and a waste of words. She wishes she had never told him to stop being so pedantic. She would love to hear him pointing out the redundancy of the question now.

"Yes. He came back yesterday."

"Did you see him?"

"No." Charley releases a laugh which Finn recognises as being a 'stupid question' laugh rather than one of joy.

"Oh sorry, Ms Mann. I didn't mean to..."

"No, no, no, it's fine, Finn... Do you always call me Ms Mann?"

"Sorry... er have I got that wrong?"

"No, no... I just hadn't noticed. Call me Charley." She laughs again, this time with a brief hint of pleasure.

"So how do you know?"

"I'll show you."

Charley picks up a half-scorched piece of paper off the sofa next to her and leads Finn through the kitchen into the courtyard garden. They both stare at the remaining ashes in the firepit.

"I kept all his stories in a box, Finn. I got them out when he left. They gave me some comfort. But they're gone now. This is all that's left." She waves the burnt remains of the piece of paper she had picked up off the sofa.

"Oh Charley I'm so sorry. Why would...."

"He's angry with me, Finn. That's why... he hates me!"

"No, Charley... I'm sure he doesn't. He's just..."

"It's OK, Finn. I'm a big girl. I can face the truth... well I can't, but I have to... would you like to read it?" She passes him the last remnant of Art's stories. It was another one about the Second World War.

Marie Antoinette De La Belle knew she had to run. The Nazis were after her. They had found out that she had been hiding Jewish people in a hidden cellar under her house, and helping them escape to safety.

She ran as fast as she could, but could hear the sounds of the chasing Nazis gaining on her with every step. She was tired. She couldn't run for ever. She would have to hide and she knew the perfect place.

She ran through the cemetery into the ninth century church which was barely visible amongst the modern shops and houses which now surrounded it. She climbed the shaky narrow staircase up to a platform overlooking the inside of the church, then darted under the old pew, which had been placed there many centuries ago to allow selected people to feel they were nearer to heaven when they prayed. She knew that there was a secret door here covered in old stones, which no one would notice, and could only be opened by pressing on the stones in a particular sequence.

Marie Antoinette De La Belle knew the sequence. She opened the door, squeezed through the gap, closed the door behind her, and found herself in an enormous room covering the whole loft area of the church. She...

This is as far as the story now goes, with the rest residing in the pile of ashes in the fire pit.

"Do you know what happens, Charley? Do they find her?"

"No, they don't."

"That's good."

"So they just burn the church to the ground with her inside, destroying everything."

"Oh... sorry."

"You're never safe, Finn. Something can always destroy everything, just like that."

Finn nods. He knows. Everything can change in an instant.

Charley takes back the piece of paper and leads them back into the kitchen.

"Would you like a piece of birthday cake, Finn? I always make it the same every year. Art wouldn't have it any other way. I made it yesterday... you know... just in case... It's a chocolate sponge with a caramel icing."

She points at the cake on the side. It looks tasty but not exactly professional, in the shape of an animal.

"Does Art like horses then?"

"It's a llama."

Art considers the knocks on the back door of Rosa's Kitchen for several seconds. Was there a pause between the first three knocks and the final two? It's difficult to say really. There was possibly a slightly longer gap than between the other knocks, but was it enough to make a pause? Probably better to be safe than sorry, so he ignores it.

"Art... it's me, Martha. Let me in!" The voice on the other side of the door is a strange combination of a whisper and a shout, which must be difficult to master.

"That wasn't much of a pause. We agreed there would be a pause." He moves towards the back door, but doesn't open it.

Martha knocks again, leaving a long gap between the first three knocks and the following two.

"Better?"

"That was too long to be a pause."

"Just open the fucking door, Art!" The voice is not whispering now, but laughter has joined the shouting.

Art pulls the wheelie bin away from the back of the door, and Martha bursts in before he can open it. She pushes the bin back in place, drops her holdall on the floor and gently places her hands either side of his face. She can feel a few loose strands of hair pushing their way through, but he clearly doesn't need to shave much yet. It makes him seem younger than the sixteen-year-old that he now is.

"Happy Birthday Art!" Martha moves straight in to give him a tender kiss. She can feel a slight quiver on Art's lips as they connect with hers. In some ways it is a meeting of two opposites. Their faces reflect their characters: hers is a bubbling mix of soft, welcoming curves and loud open mischief; his is the sort of face which a caricaturist would struggle to find the feature to focus on. It is neither obviously attractive nor unattractive, neither fat nor thin, neither long nor short. Nothing particularly to love nor hate about it for most people.

But Martha can see something in it, which maybe others don't. She can see where the two apparent opposites actually coincide: the rich, complicated racial heritage, which she can trace, but he only knows on his mother's side; the deep, black hair, which she carefully controls to ensure its free running look, but he really does let go where it pleases; the vulnerability, which she hides and he doesn't even know exists.

They enjoy the kiss for what Art estimates is about ten seconds, before Martha runs her right hand through his hair, pushing it away from his forehead and gently leans her head back to look straight at him. For a moment he looks back at her, then looks away and speaks.

"Thanks."

"No need to thank me, birthday boy! The pleasure is all mine!" Martha laughs, picks up her holdall, clutches Art's left hand and leads him back into his makeshift bedroom in the main restaurant. "How was your first night here, birthday boy?"

"OK... not as comfortable as being at home though."

"You can go home, Art? You know that, don't you?"

"I can't." They sit down beside each other on the blanket on the floor which had served as his mattress, and Martha strokes her fingers up and down the hand she is still holding.

"There's no shame in going home now, you know. You've made your point."

"I can't... you don't understand."

"I understand what it's like to lose a mum, Art... and I don't want you to. It's too important."

"I've got no choice."

"You have, Art. You've got a choice. I didn't."

He doesn't reply, so Martha gently carries on caressing his hand and asks another question.

"Do you want to know what happened to my mum? I've never talked about it with anyone, not even the counsellor I was forced to see after she died."

"Sorry she died."

"I was eleven when it happened. We were close, real close. At least I thought we were." Martha's voice trails off for a moment, before she gives Art's hand a squeeze and carries on. "Sorry... they moved to LA before Johnson and I were born. Dad had been in a daytime soap in Ireland when he was a teenager... it was crap, believe me, he's made us watch it sometimes!... and he thought he could make it as an actor or film writer or something, so they went to LA, where we were born. But he never made it... OK, the odd ad or corporate video or shit like that, but not enough to keep us going. And mum was a teacher, but she only managed to pick up the odd bits of supply teaching work, so she used to have to do other crap stuff she hated like working as a cleaner or in bars or whatever to get some money in... I know it's a cliche but, fuck it, it's true! ... we didn't have much, but we were happy... At least I thought we were happy, but mum can't have been, or she wouldn't have..." Martha's voice trails off again, and Art leans over and kisses her on the side of the neck. It's hard to tell which of the two is more surprised by the move, but it gives her a strength to carry on.

"Then one day she wasn't there when we got back from school. I was eleven... dad had found her, and he found the pills too... don't know what they were, I've never asked... does that sound weird?"

"I don't know" Art replies honestly. Martha releases a short snorting laugh.

"You're funny, Art. You never say what I think you're going to say." Art wonders what she thought he was going to say. He didn't know if what she had said sounded weird or not, so he couldn't say anything else. He knows that now is not the time to point that out though, so he says nothing and lets her carry on.

"I never saw her body, nor did Johnson... dad didn't think it would be a good idea... he was trying to protect us I guess, but I did see the note she wrote... dad doesn't know I saw it, but I found it when I was looking through some drawers in their room a week or so later."

"Why were you looking through their drawers?" Art is not judging. He's not in a position to, having done something similar himself of course and found something which is now central to his plan for survival on his own. He's just curious. And he doubts Martha was looking for lipstick to write a happy birthday message with.

"You've done it again!" Martha smiles again and squeezes his hand tightly, as if the harder she grips, the less the pain of the memory will be.

"What?"

"Said the unexpected!"

"Oh, sorry."

"No... it's fine... I just did... I guess I like wanted to find something which smelled of mum, and breathe it in... make it feel like she was still there. Does that make sense?... no don't answer that!"

So Art doesn't answer and carries on listening.

"But I found the note. I took a photo of it, and put the note back just where I found it... I've never told anyone about this, you know, Art... Not even dad or Johnson. Do you want to know what it said?" Martha lets go of his hand and picks up her phone.

"Do you want me to?" Art knows that this is a better response than 'no.'

"Yeah... I mean you don't have to, but yeah... I'd like to show you, Art, if that's OK."

"OK."

Martha hands her phone to Art and he reads the message to himself. The handwriting is scratchy and untidy, but he deciphers it as best he can.

Sorry Finn. Sorry JJ. Sorry Martha. I know you'll never understand. I don't even understand myself. But I can't go on. It's all too much. Every day I want so much to feel better but every day I just feel worse. And I can't do this any more. I can't keep pretending. You'll never know how much I love you all. I am so, so, so sorry to do this. You don't deserve this. You deserve laughter and joy and happiness and I can't give you any of that. I will miss you so, so much. I'm so sorry. xxxxxx

Art hands the phone back to Martha and rubs her hand gently but awkwardly. It is based on how she stroked his hand earlier, but misses the indefinable quality which separates a work of art from a copy.

"But the crazy thing is she did give us laughter and joy and happiness, Art. Right up until the day she died... she just didn't know it... and that's our fault."

"Sorry."

"Come here... I need a hug." Martha almost collapses forward and clings on to Art like someone who has climbed to the top of a tree, only to look down and see all the branches they had used to ascend have now been cut off, so they have to hold on for dear life as tightly as they can to stop them falling. It would be very easy for Martha to fall.

They keep the snug embrace going for a couple of minutes in a silence punctuated only by her occasional sniffle. Then she pulls away, wipes her eyes with the back of her right hand and smiles broadly.

"Thanks, Art... I needed that... sorry, it's your birthday. I like hadn't intended all that... sorry, it just came out... the point is, I just don't want you losing your mum... whatever it is, it's not worth it."

"It's not that simple."

"It never is... but it's ever harder when it's too late."

"Maybe, but..."

"OK, Art. How about this? I won't go on about it today, but have a think about it, eh?... maybe you could at least let her know you're OK? She'll be worried shitless... can you maybe get a message to her or something first?"

"I'll think about it." Art doesn't mention the swearing, but knows there are better ways of making worry sound more extreme. He hasn't really thought much about how his mum might be feeling. It's her fault. She forced him out, so why would she be worried? But Martha sounds like she may know something, so maybe she is. He doesn't want his mum to be worried.

"Thanks... Now let's get on with the fun stuff. It's your fucking birthday!!" Martha leans forward and kisses him on the forehead, then sits upright on the blanket and starts to unzip the holdall on the floor next to them. Her face erupts into a mischievous smile and her eyes sparkle with excitement. It's a coping mechanism she has tried to use since her mum's suicide to stop her dwelling on the tragedy and its aftermath. Just block it out, for now at least. Sometimes it works, often it doesn't.

Art doesn't notice the glint in Martha's eyes, but he spots the few rays of sunlight, which have broken through the cracks in the boards on the windows, glinting on her nose.

"Have you always had that thing in your nose since I met you?" Martha likes the way that he clarifies the context of always.

"The nose ring, you mean? Yep... do you like it?"

"I don't know. Not really thought about it yet." He moves his face in a bit closer to study it. "Is that a letter N?"

"Yes... it was my mum's initial."

"That's nice. Have you got any others?"

"Why? Don't you like it?"

"I do. It's nice like I said. I just wondered."

"Well yeah... loads of others! Might have another one with me if you want to see?"

"OK." Martha leans over to reach her jacket discarded on the floor next to her, and flicks through a couple of pockets before pulling out a little stud with a heart on it.

"How about this one? Do you like it?"

"Yes. I like them both." Art decides it's best to avoid any confusion this time.

"This feels more appropriate today." Martha laughs and gently removes the ring with the 'N' on, puts it on the floor beside them and replaces it with the heart stud, whilst Art watches in fascination. He's never seen this sort of operation before.

"Does it hurt?"

"No."

"I think it would hurt me."

"Yeah, probably!" Martha chuckles and gives him a loving peck on the cheek, before dipping her hand into the holdall. "Now birthday boy, if you could have any present you want, what would you chose?" Art knows that he would just like to be at home with everything exactly the same as it was just a few days ago. But he doesn't say so. There's no point. Martha can't give him that.

"A llama." He also knows it's extremely unlikely that she would give him that, and certainly impossible to fit one in the holdall she is carrying, not to mention the cruelty involved were she to try.

"A what?"

"A llama?"

"What the fuck..."

"It's a four-legged mammal usually found in South America, related to the camel, but without the hump. It's usually..."

"I know what a fucking llama is! You're one of a kind, Arty boy! I guess I shouldn't have asked!" Leaving her hand inside the holdall, she laughs and leans over to give Art a quick kiss on the nose. "Well,

I couldn't fit one of those in here I'm afraid, but let's see if these will do! Close your eyes, birthday boy!" Art doesn't close his eyes, but Martha carries on anyway, pulls a sports bottle out of the bag and takes a long swig.

"Here, have some of this, Art." She hands him the bottle, which he looks at suspiciously.

"What is it?"

"It's just orange juice... with maybe just a little bit of vodka."

"We're not allowed to drink alcohol. We're too young."

Martha tries unsuccessfully to stop herself spitting out some of her drink as she laughs, though maybe he might like the angry llama impression. "You're so cute, Art!"

"It's true though."

Martha pulls two bags of crisps out of her bag and dangles them in front of Art so he can choose. He opts for the salt and vinegar, leaving cheese and onion for her. "I think you'll find it's all legal, birthday boy. We're allowed to drink alcohol with a meal in a restaurant, aren't we? And where are we?" She gestures triumphantly round the boarded up remains of Rosa's Kitchen to prove her point, and laughs again.

Art smiles. Two bags of crisps don't really constitute a meal, and this is not technically a restaurant any more, but Martha has been quite funny. He is still not old enough to drink alcohol though, so he passes the bottle back to her.

"Not for me thanks."

"Spoilsport!" Martha sticks her tongue out, takes another deep slug from the bottle and dips her hand back into the holdall to grab a plastic bag containing milk, bread, margarine, cheese, chocolate and a half-eaten packet of Frosties. "Not much I know, but a few more things to stop you starving I hope!"

"Thanks. That's really kind." Art smiles again.

"It's nothing, honestly" Martha worries if she's blushing. Not that Art would notice. She watches as he opens the Frosties packet and eats several handfuls with barely time to swallow. He likes eating with his hands. Cutlery has never been natural to him, but he's learned to use it because that's what you're meant to do apparently.

"Thanks, Martha. They're lovely."

"But this is the best one, birthday boy! I've got another present in here. I hope you love it! You're definitely old enough!" She covers his eyes with her left hand and places a small, neatly-wrapped package in his right one.

"Why did you need to cover my eyes if it's wrapped up anyway?"

"Hmm, yeah, good point!... go on, open it."

Martha takes another long drink and stares intently at Art as he tears off the wrapping and looks down at the present in his hand. "Do you like it?"

"It's a packet of condoms."

"I know what it is, Arty boy, I wrapped it up, remember?!" She waits for him to say something, but he doesn't. It feels like hours, but is only a couple of seconds when she breaks the silence "... er... do you want to?... sorry... I really like you, you know, Art."

"I really like you too, Martha."

"Is that a yes?"

Art nods and they both lie down on the blanket.

"Have you done it before, Art?"

"I've only turned sixteen today, remember, so it's only allowed today?" He says it as if it answers the question which, in his case, it does. Martha laughs uncontrollably and snuggles her face up against his neck.

"I wish we could lie here like this forever, Art. You make me laugh. I love it."

"It would probably get a bit uncomfortable on this floor if we were here forever." This time he laughs with her. She lifts her head up and presses her lips against his. He feels warmer now.

Some moments can make people forget everything else that is happening in their lives and in their minds. There is no past; there is no present. There is just the present moment.

This is one of those moments.

Chapter Nine

Priya:

You are strong, which is just as well, because you have to be. Countless people need you for love, friendship, guidance and support, so you are strong. You have to be. You have no choice.

Or, more accurately, you do have a choice and you know you are lucky. Some people's minds wouldn't give them that choice. So you choose to be strong and you choose to be happy. You know what the alternative is, and you are able to reject it. And hopefully always will be.

But it's not always easy.

"How long does this barbecue go on for then?"

"Don't you remember? I told you yesterday."

Tommy wouldn't have asked if he'd remembered. The answer has told him nothing other than that he knows how to forget things he doesn't want to remember. He stays silent and just keeps looking at the road ahead, gripping the steering wheel slightly tighter than a few seconds ago.

"OK. Sorry. It said midday to four on the invite." Priya can see her husband is sulking. She didn't mean to say sorry. She just does it instinctively these days. It sometimes helps.

"Four hours!? We don't have to stay till the end of course."

"I'd like to, Tommy... it's supposed to be fun. They're your friends too." She gives the top of his leg a reassuring squeeze. It's true. They are Tommy's friends too. He likes them. He's known most of them for years, and there are lots of good memories. But he doesn't want to see them today. It's not their fault. He just can't face the effort, the pretending to be having fun, when he feels unable to. And he knows Priya can't understand. How could she? He sighs quietly to himself. If he weren't driving, he'd have probably closed his eyes too.

"It'll be fun, Tommy, it will... come on, give it a go." Priya squeezes his leg again and smiles. He doesn't see because he's watching the car in front turn right without indicating, and he starts cursing inwardly.

"Yeah." He doesn't convince either of them. He wishes that he would want to go as much as Priya. He really does. He used to love these sorts of events. But he doesn't any more, and he can't force himself to. He knows Priya deserves better.

Her phone rings. Maybe it's going to be an excuse to get them out of it? That would be good. As Priya rummages about in her bag, Tommy thinks of the possibilities. They all include the kids and would certainly not be good: Nina could have been hit by a car whilst crossing the road and looking at her phone; Mia could have been violently attacked by a psychopath embarking on a violence spree in Sonnley; Kian could have been killed in a house fire when he tried to cook his own lunch whilst his parents were out.

Tommy is wrong. He usually is.

"Shit." Priya has finally located her phone at the bottom of her bag, and it's stopped ringing.

"What is it? What's happened?"

"It's OK, Tommy. Calm down. I just didn't get there in time." She can sense the disproportionate panic in his voice. "It's just Mel. I'll call her back."

"I bet something's happened to the kids."

"Calm down, Tommy. Please! It's nothing to do with the kids. It's just Mel." Priya clicks her phone to return the call. How can she know it's nothing to do with the kids? Mel's a neighbour. She'd be the first to find out if something goes wrong while they're out.

"What did she say?"

"Engaged now."

"Probably calling the police or the ambulance."

"Tommy... stop it!" There is an irritation in Priya's voice which makes Tommy wonder why she can't see what he sees. He wishes he couldn't either. He longs for a life without seeing imagined horrors, without suffering the relentless battering of catastrophic thoughts, without their crippling legacy of anxiety and fear which leave him permanently scared. So scared. No one else seems to see what he does. Priya certainly doesn't. Once, when he had told her he was anxious about Nina starting to walk to school on her own, Priya had innocently asked him "what's the worst that can happen?" So he had told her. And she's never asked that question since.

Priya's phone pings again. There's a voicemail. She picks it up and listens.

"Oh shit. Poor thing."

"What? What's happening?"

"It's OK, Tommy. Please calm down. Everyone's fine... it's just poor Mel needs a break. Sounds like she's at the end of her tether... just wondered if we could pop round and sit with Rosa for a few minutes, so she can get out... do you think we should go back?"

He pulls the car over to the side of the road.

"I guess that's a 'yes' then, Tommy?"

"We'd better get back. We can't let Mel down. She's our friend."

"So are the people you don't want to see."

"I never said that."

"You didn't need to."

Martha is nuzzling the top of her head into Art's neck. She can feel a pulse gently ruffling her hair and is slowly making little circles on his naked chest with the index finger of her left hand.

"What are you doing?" He sounds happy. He's still in the present moment.

"I'm just thinking."

"Thinking what?"

"I'm thinking how good we are together... how I love being with you... and how your skin is smoother than a pool ball!" She resists the temptation to get too intense.

"I once read, Martha, that if you reduced the size of the earth to the size of a snooker ball, then the earth would be smoother than the snooker ball, and I guess it's much the same for pool balls. And we know that the earth isn't smooth with all those mountains and valleys. So that means my skin is not smooth then."

"You're great, Art." Martha laughs and reverses the direction of the circles she is drawing.

"So are you."

"Do you mean that, Art?"

"Yes... I wouldn't say it otherwise."

"True."

"Does this mean we're going out with each other, Martha?"

She lifts her head so her face is directly above Art's as he lies on his back.

"Do you want it to?"

"Yes please."

"'Yes please!'... You're so sweet, Art... sweetest boyfriend I could ever have!" She lowers her face and they kiss again, entwining their naked bodies in a happy embrace. The present moment is still winning.

Martha lifts her left hand and slowly runs her fingers through the unkempt mess of his hair, gently untangling the knots she encounters on the way.

"What are those?"

"What?" Martha knows what he's looking at. Her left arm is directly above his eyes as she strokes his hair.

"Those scars on your arm... were you in an accident."

"No, Art. I did them... I used to cut myself sometimes."

"Why?"

"I don't know... it's hard to explain... lots of reasons... it's like... some people do it because they think they deserve it, they need to punish themselves... some people do it just to release all the stress and tension when it builds up and they feel like they're going to explode... some people do it as a cry for help or because they need to be noticed... I've like looked into it. There are all sorts of reasons apparently."

"You're not some people though. You're you. Why did you do it?"

"It could be any of those reasons, really... or all of them even... I don't know exactly. I just know I had to do it. I had no choice.... I know that sounds crazy, but it's true. I had no choice... Sometimes I felt like I was going to explode if I didn't do it, so I had to... it made me feel I could cope somehow, I suppose... Can you see that, Art?"

"No... sorry." He places his right index finger on her back and starts drawing similar circles on her skin to those she had gently outlined on his chest. "Do you still feel like that?"

"Who knows, Art?... Not when I'm with you!" Martha tries to invoke her coping mechanism again. "We're two of kind, you know, you and me.... We don't fit in... We're different from everyone else." She regrets the words immediately. They sound eerily similar to those Dan has said to her many times before. But they ring true when she's with Art.

"Thanks." He changes the direction of the circles, just as Martha had, before their presence is disturbed by a noise.

"Someone's trying to get in" whispers Martha.

"What do we do?"

"Just lie here quietly until they go. They can't get in."

They hear a woman's voice trying to persuade the door to open, as if it would respond to a bit of gentle cajoling, interspersed with some loud thuds as she tries to force it. After a few minutes, the noise lessens to just a few barely audible sobs, and finally a few footsteps moving away from the building.

"Shit. That was close." Martha points at the bedding, and the supplies she's brought in. "When we go out, we'd better hide these. Don't want to leave a trace."

"We could put them in the wheelie bin."

"You're smarter than you look, Art!"

"Don't I look smart?"

"Course you do!" She leans over and kisses him again. "We'd best get out before she comes back though. Meet back here about six maybe?"

"Six is good for me. I've got to go and see someone."

"Be careful, Art. Don't do anything stupid." Art still doesn't know if he's stupid or not, or even if he looks smart.

"I hope not."

"That doesn't sound very convincing!... well take care. I don't want anything happening to you."

"Well, something is bound to happen. Something always happens."

"OK... I don't want something bad happening to you." Martha laughs and shakes her head. They both get up and get dressed.

"Happy Birthday, Art."

"Thanks." He certainly hadn't expected it to start like this.

Martha gets to the door first, and peers out to check the woman has gone, before giving Art a final hug and another long kiss.

"And remember I said meet back here about six, Art... 'About' being the key word."

"'Six' is probably more key actually... as are 'meet' and 'here'."

"Well God bless you both! What a lovely surprise to see you. Please come in." Faith Roberts waves her walking stick at her neighbours to beckon them through the front door, but only Tommy starts to go in. Priya waits on the doorstep, trying to find out what's going on.

"Thanks, Faith... sorry, we hadn't realised you were here, we just got a message from Mel asking us to help out with Rosa."

"Me too, Priya! It's not like my old body to get somewhere first!" She pats her stomach by way of explanation. "Please do come in... have a cup of tea with us, it'll make our day. You've timed it perfectly. It'll make quite a little party of us!"

"Well, it's just, Tommy and I were meant to be at..." Her voice trails off. She can see her husband disappearing down the hall and turning into the front room. "No actually, thanks, Faith. That would be lovely."

They walk into the house to join the others. Rosa Angelina is sitting up, asleep on the sofa, with Tommy next to her, and Faith's twenty-five-year-old son, Marshall, is sitting in an armchair playing a game on a phone. He doesn't look up.

"Hi Marshall, lovely to see you." He still doesn't look up. Priya smiles at Faith and follows her into Mel and Rosa's kitchen where some freshly-baked brownies are laid out on a plate on the table.

"Even you can't have made that since you got here, Faith, surely!?"

"I wish I could!" she laughs, "Marshall and I were making them when Mel called, so we thought we'd finish them off here. They're his favourite... and I've just made a nice pot of tea, well maybe not nice, but a pot of tea anyway! You timed it perfectly like I said... do you mind taking these please?" She adds a couple of cups to a tray already holding three, and passes it to Priya.

"Is Mel OK, Faith? She sounded desperate in the message."

Faith momentarily stops smiling and peers up through the top of her glasses to catch her friend's eye. There aren't many people a full five inches shorter than Priya, but what Faith lacks in height, she makes up for in presence. "I'm worried about her, Priya. Something's happened. I know this is all so hard for her, and it must seem too much at times, but today she just seemed different, more agitated, more upset than I've seen her. I'm worried about her, I can't lie." If ever anyone didn't need to say those last three words, then it would be Faith Roberts.

"Did she say anything?"

"Not really. As soon as we got here, she just grabbed her coat, thanked us and said she needed a bit of space or something."

"Hopefully that'll help, I guess. Poor Mel... I can't imagine what it must be like when someone you love with all your heart loses the traits you fell in love with." Priya doesn't have to imagine. She knows.

A lot of people are hanging by a thread from a cliff. If the thread gets cut, they fall. It all just depends on what it takes to cut their thread.

Mel needs to get into Rosa's Kitchen. She needs to breathe in the happy memories, close her eyes and picture the amazing times they had there, and she needs to talk to the old Rosa.

Finding the back door to Rosa's Kitchen blocked had felt like the last few strands of Mel's thread were threatening to break. She had realised it was probably a homeless person, who had managed to find a safe shelter for the night, and she was pleased to see their beloved restaurant still being used as a force for good. But she needed to get in.

Unable to do so, she had taken the fifteen-minute stroll back over Sonnley Bridge towards Marsh Park, via the grey, rundown homes near the restaurant through to the leafier, larger houses in the streets on the town side of the bridge leading up to the park. It was a pretty typical early summer's day: beautiful warm sunshine without being too hot one minute, then a sudden intrusion of clouds and light drizzle bringing an immediate temperature drop. Mel hadn't noticed any of it. She had been thinking how to get into the restaurant.

She had briefly glanced at the Neola graffiti on the cafe wall in the park, and thought back to the days when they had first started the restaurant in the cheapest premises they could find, and would be greeted most mornings by abusive slogans painted on the wall. Some of them were aimed at the two of them and their sexuality, but most were directed squarely at Rosa, instructing her to 'go home'. Mel would cry and say they should give up, that they'd been mad to think that the restaurant would ever work here. But Rosa wouldn't say anything. She would just repaint the wall, usually in a new, more vibrant colour, and get back to her kitchen. With time, she had had to paint the wall less and less often, until the offensive graffiti stopped altogether, and everyone knew that Sonnley was Rosa's home.

After half an hour or so in the park, Mel had decided to try the restaurant again. Maybe the person inside had heard her trying to get in, and had decided to get out, if only for the day. She had to try.

So now she is turning the handle on the back door again, more in hope than expectation. She uses her shoulder to try to force past the expected barrier on the other side, and tumbles to the floor as the door flies open. She gets up quickly and walks slowly towards the main restaurant area, popping her head round the kitchen door first to check that no one is there.

She finds no sign of anyone having been in the building, and wonders if she somehow turned the handle the wrong way earlier or just didn't push hard enough. She had been in a bad state, but surely not bad enough that she couldn't open a door.

She reads a few of the customer testimonies scrawled on one wall, then sits down in the middle of the room facing the other wall, with the enormous fading mural of Rosa staring down at her. She's seen the mural thousands of times before, yet she still gasps in wonder at how a painting can bring a person so vividly to life, or more accurately, their former life. The wondrous dark green eyes, which Rosa had always claimed were that colour so that she could hide unnoticed in a pile of empty red wine bottles, seem to be looking only at Mel. They always had done. They had only ever been interested in Mel. And that, in some ways, is what makes this so much harder.

Mel closes her eyes for the time she needs to take four deep, long breaths, then opens them and looks straight back at her wife, her best friend, her happiness on the wall in front of her. She can hear Rosa's deep, cackling laugh echoing round her head, followed by the laughter of a packed restaurant unable to resist its infectious spread.

"I'm so, so sorry, my little Rosa... It's a bit different today. I need to talk to you about something I should have told you about years ago."

Mel puts her hand in her bag and pulls out the letter which she had found in the box of Rosa's old photos in the attic.

"So you've known all along, but you never said anything?... I'm so, so sorry... I... I didn't know... I don't know how to explain." She stops talking so that she can bite her lip and look down at the letter in her hand. It's addressed to Rosa from a man, who was quite a famous, posh, old-school actor thirty or so years ago, and had been to a party at Rosa's Kitchen after the completion of filming on a new TV series he was in, which was being shot in Windsor. Mel remembers the evening both well and barely at all. She's thought about it almost every day of the twenty-nine years which have passed since it happened, but never been able to find the words to explain it to Rosa.

Mel had spent the evening, as so many others in the restaurant, mingling with the customers, ensuring that everything was exactly to their liking, whilst Rosa had been in the kitchen conjuring up her Lebanese culinary magic, until the service ended and she joined the party out front. On this particular occasion, what with it being an end of filming celebration, the champagne had been flowing as quickly as Mel and the other staff could open it, and she had tried to hide her nervousness in front of the celebrity guests, by keeping pace with their drinking. In the years which followed, she got used to celebrities relishing the wonders of Rosa's Kitchen, but in those distant days, it was a novelty.

Mel looks down at the letter again. She doesn't really need to. She's read it so many times in the last few days that she knows every venomous, sarcastic word by heart.

Dear Rosa Angelina,

On behalf of myself and the other crew members, may I extend the warmest of thank yous for the most amazing food and wondrous hospitality it has been our delight to encounter at our wrap party. It was a wonderful, happy unforgettable evening for almost all involved.

I say 'almost all involved', because unfortunately the hospitality was somewhat too all-embracing for my own, possibly too conservative, taste.

After a very pleasant evening, I returned to my hotel for a final malt with a couple of the other stragglers, and then stumbled back to my bedroom to by greeted by the rather unpleasant, shocking sight of my wife in bed with your girlfriend. Now, call me old-fashioned, which I probably am, but that is not quite the extra service I was expecting from your restaurant.

Yours Regretfully

William Pemberton

Mel hates the tone of the letter, its fake politeness and mocking pleasantries. But she can't blame him.

She shakes the letter in the direction of Rosa on the wall.

"I'm so, so sorry, Rosa... I was drunk... it was a one off, I swear... I'll never know why I did it... I was drunk, maybe I was flattered by the attention of someone famous... I don't know... either way, it's no excuse, I know, and I haven't got one... I never, ever wanted anyone except you, my little Rosa... please, please believe me, I beg you. I love you... I've always loved you... no one else.... Ever... I'm so sorry."

Mel can't bear the reaction in Rosa's eyes any more. She ducks her head down into her hands and wails like she has never had to since she met Rosa. After a couple of minutes she stops, wipes her eyes, and looks back at her wife.

"I've thought about it every day, my love... regretted it with all my heart, and I so wanted to tell you but... well I didn't know how... I was scared... scared you'd leave me... and that would be the end of me... I just... I just... I just love you so, so much and I am so, so sorry, my little Rosa... and so sorry that I never spoke to you about... that you had to find out from someone else... that you've spent all these years knowing, but not judging me... I love you with all my heart, my little Rosa. I really do. I swear... I'm so sorry."

Mel tucks the letter back in her bag and looks at Rosa's mural. She can still hear her laughing, encouraging everyone else to laugh along with her. But there is a sadness in those beautiful green eyes now. No one else would notice it, but Mel does.

She knows how Rosa would have reacted if she'd told her at the time... No, she's almost sure she knows. Rosa would have forgiven her, because Rosa loved her, and Rosa always forgave those she loved. But Mel can never be absolutely certain about that now. There will always be a lingering doubt. All she can be sure of is that Rosa will never be able to forgive her face-to-face now.

Why hadn't Mel told her? She's asked herself that so many times over the years, and even more so in the last few days. Was it shame? Was it fear? Was it her own attempt to pretend that it had never happened. She'll never know why. She just knows that she let the secret loom over their lives for far too long and it's too late now.

Everyone has secrets. Some people don't think about them, others try to forget, and some just let the secret torture them until the pain is worse than the secret.

Chapter Ten

"How can I help you?" The woman asks the question as she opens the large cream door, which is painted at least annually to prevent any appearance of shabbiness. She hasn't set eyes on her visitor yet, and her voice is friendly if a little suspicious. She is in her mid-sixties, obviously spends a lot of time at the hairdresser's ensuring an immaculate appearance and eliminating the grey tidal wave, and looks like an avid member of the local slimming club, who clearly never quite manages to resist the overwhelming lure of an extra slice of cake at her ladies' coffee mornings, which might enable her to relinquish her membership. She is wearing a smart, short-sleeved flowery blouse and her bare forearms are pale, as though the sun hasn't shone on her in years. And maybe it hasn't?

Art doesn't see any of that. He looks at her feet, and could be noticing that she is wearing only socks; that two pairs of shoes are positioned neatly on a shoe rack next to an umbrella in a stand; and that the otherwise-empty porch clearly gets hoovered at least twice per week and is entirely tidy and shipshape. But he doesn't notice any of that either.

"I'm Art." The woman's mouth drops open so that her chin almost comes to rest on her chest, and her pupils dilate so that both eyes appear momentarily completely black. She tries to say something, but the sound that comes out more resembles someone gargling mouthwash than speaking. Art notices that she hasn't said anything, so continues. "I'm your grandson."

"Yes, yes, I know that." Gillian Mann rapidly reclaims her composure. It's important never to be seen to be flustered. She peers out of the front door to see if the neighbours are watching. "Would you like to come in, Art?"

"OK."

She leads them into a spotless living room, with two large sofas covered in matching beige wipe-clean covers with assorted neat homemade cushions. The centrepiece of the room is a large fireplace holding a coal-effect gas fire and captured within a smart oak surround, which tones in exactly with the wooden bookcase and shelves which run along the walls beside it. A selection of not-easily-identifiable pottery objects and family photographs adorn the mantlepiece and the shelves. It's clearly the home of someone who has a lot of time on their own to indulge their crafting hobbies.

Art walks over to look at the photographs. Most of them seem to be of Aunt Amanda and her kids, but there are a few older ones of a man in army uniform marrying a beaming woman in a long white dress, and the same couple looking slightly older accompanied by three smiling children. He picks up one of these. "Which one's my mum?"

"That's Charlotte. She was seven then." Gillian Mann points at the girl, who is sitting on her father's lap and laughing like her world is the happiest place anyone could ever live in. Maybe it was then. "Would you like a cup..."

"Why did you kick her out?" Art interrupts.

His grandmother sits down on the bigger of the two sofas, and instinctively plumps up one of the cushions.

"It wasn't quite like that, Arthur."

"Art."

"Sorry. I always think of you as Arthur, you know, like your grandfather."

"No. I don't know. No one calls me Arthur except mum when she's angry with me." Art knows nothing of his grandfather, let alone his name. But maybe that explains why his mum only uses Art's full name when she's angry.

"Does she still get angry a lot?"

"No. Only when she thinks I'm being bad."

"And are you bad often, Art?"

"No. She's always wrong when she thinks I am."

His grandmother smiles. She recognises that trait.

"I hear all about you, Art... Amanda keeps us, well me, up-to-date. It's your birthday today, isn't it? Sixteen."

"Yes."

"Happy Birthday." A silence reverberates round the room, noisier than if someone were sitting on the other sofa beating a drum. "I always get you a birthday card, you know."

"No. I don't know."

"No, I don't suppose you do. I'm sorry. I've never sent them... Believe me, I wanted to, Art, more than I can say, but I couldn't."

"Why not?"

"It's complicated, Art... I just couldn't."

"But you could kick your daughter out of the house when she was pregnant."

Gillian Mann shakes her head and looks up at the grandson who is still standing by the mantlepiece, looking down at the photograph of his seven-year-old mother.

"That's not how it happened, Art."

"What do you mean?"

"Well, Charlotte... your mother... was going through a very difficult time. She had got herself mixed up with the wrong sort of people and was doing things she shouldn't have done. It was so out of character. She wasn't the lovely, beautiful girl she had always been. We had to do something or she would have died."

"How do you know that?"

"We could see it with our own eyes, Arthur... Art. She was drinking, taking drugs, getting into trouble, hanging around with bad people. There's never a happy ending when people continue down that path."

"So how was kicking her out going to help?"

Gillian snorts a semi-laugh which makes Art wonder why she thinks it's so funny. Maybe that's why she was able to kick her own daughter out onto the streets.

"You remind me of her, Art. You really do. You've got that... what's the word?... that feistiness that Charlotte always had. She couldn't be reasoned with. Once she'd decided to do something, there was no stopping her."

"So you kicked her out?"

Gillian shakes her head at her grandson. "No... it wasn't quite like that."

"So what was it like then?"

"When Charlotte got... got pregnant, she was in a very bad way. The drugs were controlling her life, she was stealing, she was losing weight she was... well... doing things that were quite frankly dangerous and degrading, so that she could get money for more drugs. She was killing herself."

"So she needed your help."

"You're right, Art, she needed our help. And we did everything we could... We tried to get her into a rehabilitation unit, we paid for counsellors to talk to her, we even tried locking her in the house to keep her away from the bad influences and drugs. But nothing worked. She didn't think she needed help. So she wouldn't let us help. ... she was on a downward spiral, and to cap it all she was pregnant."

"That doesn't mean you had to kick her out."

Gillian takes a deep breath and closes her eyes momentarily.

"OK. So you want to know what happened, do you?"

"Yes."

"Well, when your mother told us about the unfortunate pregnancy, your grandfather offered to help her sort it out." Art doesn't like the word 'unfortunate' here.

"What do you mean 'sort it out'?"

"Pay for a termination... it probably sounds much more clinical, more cruel than it was... surely you must see that it's not going to be good for anyone if a chaotic, drug-addicted teenage girl has a baby?"

"Not good for anyone or not good for you?"

"No Art." Her volume increases for those two words before levelling off back to its previous calm. She shakes her head again. "Not good for anyone: not good for Charlotte, and certainly not good for the poor baby." Art thinks his life would have been a lot poorer if it had been stopped before he'd been born.

"So you wanted me dead? You wanted to kill me?"

"Don't think of it like that, please Art. We just wanted what was best for Charlotte... your mother." Art doesn't need reminding who his mother is.

"Well, it wouldn't have been best for mum or for me, if you'd killed me."

"We didn't think Charlotte was in a place where she could be a good mother."

"Well, she is. She's a great mum."

Gillian Mann smiles.

"Good, I'm pleased. I really am... do you mind me asking why you ran away then?"

"Yes, I do mind. That's different... Nothing to do with her being a good mum or not. She's the best mum. And she saved my life, stopped you killing me like you wanted to."

"No... it wasn't... er... we didn't... er... I need a glass of water. Can I get you one?"

"No thanks." His mother has instilled manners in him. Gillian is pleased.

She gets up off the sofa and walks out into the hall towards the kitchen. This is not how she had imagined meeting her eldest grandchild for the first time, and she has imagined it many, many times. When she returns with her water, Art is holding another photo in which his mum is probably in her early teens. She is playing table football with her dad against her brother, her sister and her mum.

"They always used to be on each other's side, Charlotte and her father, you know?"

"No, I don't." How could Art possibly know that?

"I know parents aren't supposed to have favourites, and Arthur has always been a very fair man, so he wouldn't admit it himself. But there was a special bond between your mother and him from the moment she was born. He would do anything for her."

"Like try to kill her son."

"Oh come on... that's nonsense. He was trying to save Charlotte's life. We both were."

"By kicking her out, you mean?"

"It was her choice, Art."

"What do you mean?"

"Well, your grandfather was... is... very much a man of his word. It's important to him. Something instilled into him in all his time in the army I imagine... and Charlotte knew that as well as anyone. And when she decided not to... you know, terminate the pregnancy, they had a few... what's the polite way of saying this?... strong words with each other."

"What words?"

"Charlotte said that she was leaving and didn't want to see us ever again."

"And what did he say?"

"He said... he said that was her choice, and that if she walked out of the door, she would be walking out of our lives forever."

"And what happened?"

"She walked out of the door."

Art can understand the logic. He can see that his mum made a choice. If someone is presented with clear options and chooses one of them, then there is no denying that they have made a choice. It is a line of argument he has pursued with his mum on several occasions when she has gone back on what they have agreed. However, she has told him that circumstances can change, which can mean that people can change their minds, and that sometimes people say things when they are angry which they don't mean. Neither claim has entirely convinced him previously, but he can see now that both may have applied to his mum when she left.

"But people can change their minds."

"Yes Art, I agree." There is a sadness in his grandmother's voice, which Art does not notice. "But your grandfather doesn't see it like that. People make their choices and live with the consequences."

Again, he finds the argument compelling. If he didn't hate his grandfather for trying to kill him, they might have got along.

"But if you don't see it like that, why didn't you ever try to get in touch with mum?"

"It's not that simple, Art... think about it... I couldn't win, could I? If I contact Charlotte, I lose your grandfather and if I don't contact her, I lose her. What could I do?... I had to decide who needed me more, my husband or my daughter? It's a choice no one should ever have to make, but I couldn't have them both. They had made that clear to me."

"So you chose your husband? How could you do that?" Art's mum has always told him that a mother's love for a child is stronger than any other tie that anyone will ever experience.

"I knew it was the harder option... it wasn't even what I wanted. But he needed me more." She's told herself that so many times over the years that she almost believes it herself now. The alternative is too painful to bear.

"What about mum?"

"Your mother is strong. I knew your aunt and uncle would always look after her... I wasn't so sure they would look after their father."

"So you've never once tried to contact mum?"

"Believe me, Art. I've wanted to every day... more than anything... but she's never tried to contact us either of course."

"That's different."

"Why?"

"You are her parents."

"She's an adult, Art. Just like we are."

"She's still your daughter."

"You are right, Art. She is still my daughter, and I think of her every hour of every day... I cry myself to sleep wondering about her... wondering about you, but..." her voice trails off, before coming back on a different thread, "Can I show you something, Art?"

"What?"

"Wait here." His grandmother leaves the room and heads upstairs. He hears the sound of a door being opened and what sounds like footsteps on metal, before the door is slammed shut and she returns to the room carrying a full black bin liner.

"What's that?"

"I have written a letter to your mother every week since the day she left, Art. And they are all in here along with the birthday cards I've bought over the years for both of you, including yours for today. I keep them in the loft as your grandfather doesn't know about them. Each week, I think that this is the one I'm going to send, but..." her voice disappears again.

"So why don't you?"

"I don't know... it's complicated... it's just... no, maybe you're right, Art." She sounds emboldened. "Would you do me a favour, Art?... do us all a favour hopefully... would you give all these to your mother for me?" She hands the bin bag to her grandson.

"OK. I guess. I could drop them round when she's out."

"You should go home, Art. Your mum will be missing you. She needs you."

"You didn't need her."

"I did... I still do, it's just..." Gillian leaves the words hanging, before starting off again on a different topic. She seems to like doing that. It is a habit which irritates Art. If you start a sentence, you should finish it. "I am so pleased you came, Art. I really am. Thank you... but your grandfather will be back from the golf club lunch soon, and it's probably best if you're... well, you know..."

Art does know this time. He doesn't want to be around when his would-be-murderer of a grandfather gets home. But he still needs to get what he came for.

"Yes."

"Will you come again, Art? I would love that. Wednesdays and Saturdays, your grandfather is always out at the golf club, so they're good. I've got commitments on Tuesdays, Thursdays and Sunday mornings, so not then." It's not clear if the 'morning' refers just to the Sunday or the other days too. That is irritating and could so easily be avoided without clumsy use of language. She ought to know better.

"Can I have some money please?"

Gillian Mann smiles outwardly only. She hadn't asked Art why he had come. She had hoped that he wanted to meet her. She should have known better. It makes sense now. It also makes him more likely to come back.

"Of course." She leaves the room and returns with a neat black handbag, and pulls out a cream purse, from which she takes a handful of notes and places them in Art's hand, giving it a gentle squeeze as she does so.

"Thank you."

"No, thank you, Art. I am so, so happy to have finally met you."

They walk out of the living back to the hall and on towards the front door. In the porch Gillian holds out her arms towards her grandson. "May I?"

"May you what?"

"May I hug you, Art?"

"Er I guess." People seem to want to hug him these days.

Gillian folds her arms round her grandson's back and squeezes as though the harder she does, the more easily the pain of the last sixteen years will disappear. After a few seconds, Art wriggles clear.

"Bye then. Thanks for the money."

"Thank you so much for coming. Give those to your mother, won't you?" She points at the black bin bag of letters and cards which he is carrying, "and please, please come back very soon."

Gillian Mann watches as her grandson walks awkwardly off down the road, struggling to find a comfortable way of carrying the bin bag. Then she goes back into the living room, kisses the photo of the family playing table football, which Art had been holding, and lies face down on the sofa with her head buried in a floral cushion she has made.

She cries until she hears her husband's car pulling into the driveway, then gets up, wipes her face with a clean tea towel from the drawer in the kitchen, puts the kettle on, and washes up the glass from which she had been drinking water. She knows it's for the best for everything to appear normal and fine.

"This woman is the best, Charlotte. Believe me. She's done lots of work for me. She'll find your boy in no time." It's a long while since Ray Hope has been in a home as small as this. It takes him back to his childhood, and he's not sure he likes going back there.

"Thanks, Ray. I hope so."

"Trust me, Charlotte. She will." Ray passes Charley a mug of coffee. He could only find instant in the kitchen, but it's better than nothing. He's only ever seen her looking immaculately dressed and bubbling with energy and fun before, so it's a bit of a shock witnessing the change first hand. But not a total shock. He knows it's what happens when you get too close to someone. It will go wrong at some time.

"Thanks." Charley takes a sip of the coffee and wipes a loose strand of hair off her forehead.

"What did you make of her?"

"You know what, Ray. I've only ever seen Private Investigators on TV or in films. I thought they all wore long macs and fedoras and stuff like that."

Ray laughs. "Well Laura's certainly not like that!"

"No, she's definitely not. She looks just like any other unremarkable middle-aged woman... In fact, I can't remember a single thing about her come to think about it... no idea if she was fat, thin, short, tall, anything. Is that rude?" Charley speaks the words slowly without a trace of humour, then shakes her head and furrows her brow trying to remember.

"Well, she's probably not going to thank you on a personal level, Charlotte, but it's a pretty good trait to have in her job!" She can still make him feel happy and relaxed even when she's at her lowest ebb. He likes that.

"She will find him, won't she, Ray?"

"Laura's the best there is. Trust me." He leans forward and gives her hand not holding the coffee cup a short squeeze.

"Thanks, Ray." Charley looks up and stares straight at him. His eyes are the sort which never reveal what he's really thinking, whereas hers reveal everything. He can see the pain. That's why he's there. She continues "can I ask you something, Ray?"

"Sure."

"Were you coming back to Sonnley today for work anyway?"

"There's always work for me to do in Sonnley, Charlotte. The company won't run itself." He doesn't answer the question and, in so doing, he does answer it.

"Thanks, Ray. That's very kind of you."

"It's nothing... I'm in a position to help a friend. Why wouldn't I?"

Charley nods slowly. "Thanks, Ray." He makes it sound the most natural thing in the world. Maybe it is. Or maybe it should be.

"Can I tell you something, Charlotte?... a little story from my childhood." He likes using anecdotes to make his point. Charley knows that. She's heard loads of them over the years they've been in contact.

"Go on then, if you must!" It's the first time he's seen her smile since he got here with the Private Investigator a couple of hours ago. He sat in silence whilst Charley handed over a selection of photographs and answered lots of questions about her missing son, who sounds like a strange, lost lad. Not that Ray said that of course. He just listened and remembered every word. He can do that. It's the one skill he had which the others didn't have when he was growing up. Not that he appreciated it then. He would have preferred to have been strong, funny, popular, sporty. But he had been none of those things.

"When I was twelve, some of the other kids used to pick on me... bully me, you know. One day a group of them were waiting for me after school... probably five or six of them, I didn't get the chance to count exactly. Anyway, they started pushing me, spitting at me, hitting me... even knocked my glasses off and stamped on them."

"I'm sorry.... I didn't know, Ray."

"No reason you would know, Charlotte. You've never seen me wear glasses. Contact lenses only these days!"

"That's not what I meant!" She laughs briefly for the first time in ages. It's a laugh which has always surprised Ray: more of a short high-pitched cackle than the elegant birdsong of joy which would fit in so much better with the rest of her. Still, it's good to hear it again, even if it lasts no more than a second.

"I know, just trying to lighten it up a bit." He squeezes her hand again. "Anyway, these boys were giving me a right going over, when another lad came over and started pulling them off and telling them to stop... and in the confusion I took the chance to run... no idea where I was a going, I just knew I had to run. But the boys soon started chasing after me, and it was only a matter of time before they would catch me."

Charley raises her eyebrows in surprise. She knows Ray has recently notched up his one hundred and twelfth marathon, so wouldn't expect him to be caught when running.

He knows what she's thinking. "I could always run for a long time, but never fast, Charlotte. I still can't. That's why I never tell you my times!" He laughs again, then continues with his story. He tells it as though he is talking about someone else, without a hint of the discomfort that might be expected when reopening an old wound like that. It's a trick he's taught himself through necessity. He's a very different person these days. "After a few minutes I was running along the pavement next to the road heading out to Windsor. It was different in those days. It wasn't back-to-back cars stuck in traffic like now. It was still busy, but the cars would shoot along there at sixty or seventy miles an hour, way over the speed limit. I could hear the running footsteps behind me, and I knew I had to take a chance. I couldn't see a thing without my glasses, so I just turned and started running across the road to escape."

"Did it work?"

"Not exactly... There were cars racing down the road as usual. I can still remember the noise of the tyres as the brakes were slammed, but it was never going to stop in time. I can still see the yellow blur as I turned my head towards the noise... imagine not noticing a bright yellow car, Charlotte! How stupid was I?!" He laughs again.

"So it hit you?"

"It would have done, Charlotte, it would have done. And I wouldn't have been here telling you about it now, believe me! I'd have been roadkill... but the same boy who had stopped the guys beating me up outside school, had dived and rugby tackled me so that I would fall back onto the pavement instead of being obliterated by a yellow car."

"Wow!"

"Wow indeed, Charlotte! We both got a few bumps and bruises as we came crashing down, but nothing else. He saved my life."

"Who was he? Was he a friend?"

Ray shakes his head. "Tommy? No, he wasn't then. I hardly knew him, in fact, but he is now. He works for me. His wife is a teacher at your boy's school, I think."

"So... why did he do it?"

"I asked him that once, Charlotte, and all he said was 'why wouldn't I?'"

"That's amazing, Ray. That really is." It's Charley's turn to squeeze his hand this time.

"Yeah... and the other boys left me alone after that too... never really found out if it was because they were shaken up by what they'd witnessed or if Tommy had had a word. But they left me alone, and that's what mattered."

"Thanks for sharing that, Ray. It means a lot."

"It certainly meant a lot to me!" He glances at his watch. It's the sort of watch which Charley has seen on adverts costing ridiculous amounts of money, and which looks far too big on his slender wrist. "I'd best at least show my face at the office!" He laughs, gets up, then leans over again and gives her a kiss on the cheek.

"Stay strong, Charlotte. Laura will find him. Goodbye for now, but I'll be in touch, and please, please call if there's anything you need."

"Thanks, Ray. I really do appreciate this you know."

"It's really nothing, Charlotte." He holds out a palm to let her know not to get up, and he lets himself out.

It's the first time he has ever said goodbye to Charley without giving her money.

This feels like the right location for this picture. It's risky to be doing it in daylight of course, but no one really comes to this road behind the tennis club. Even the newsagent shop is closed today whilst the owners go on holiday. It's surely only a matter of time until it goes the same way as the boarded-up restaurant next door.

The figure has a quick scan round to check that no one is nearby, then starts unpacking their materials from the large sports bag they're carrying. It's important to work fast, just in case. They've visited this site several times over the past week, so they know exactly what they're going to do.

They don't want to get caught. This is what keeps them alive; this is what gives them that surge of adrenaline which makes life bearable; this is the only thing that is theirs and theirs alone. No one watches them and criticises while they are doing this. Sure, some people will moan about it when it's done and they see it, but that's exactly the point. The artist wants those people to moan. They need to have their arrogant, complacent, one-eyed views of the world threatened; they are the people that the artist hates. But others will love it. And the artist needs that validation; the artist needs that respect; the artist needs that love. It's the only time they get it.

They put the stencils up on the boards on the side of Rosa's Kitchen, and set to work on the spray painting. Everything has been meticulously planned with a precision and dedication that they have been repeatedly told they lack, so the operation goes as smoothly as they knew it would.

Once finished, they pack their tools away back in the bag, and step back to look briefly at their work. But only briefly. It's important to get away just in case. Without noticing, they start tapping the fingers of their left hand restlessly on the side of their bag, as if they're not allowed to relax and switch off for a single moment.

They look at the picture of the contented chubby, balding middle-aged man in a tuxedo and bow tie, sitting at a table with his napkin neatly tucked in, and gorging himself with his hands on a gourmet meal served on a silver platter. There is far too much food for a banquet of fifty people, let alone one overfed man. At the side of the table, five scrawny children in rags are looking up longingly at the food. The children are painfully thin, drooling and holding their hands palms up, pleading for the food they are not being given.

Underneath the table is the caption *Need before greed* followed by the customary Neola signature.

The artist looks at their creation. They are happy. They know that a lot of people won't be, but some will. That makes them even happier.

Art has been giving some thought to what 'around six' actually means and has decided to turn up back at Rosa's Kitchen at five past six. Arriving before six would risk a long wait for Martha to turn up, whilst turning up on the dot of six would make the word 'around' redundant and ruin the whole point. So five past feels like a good compromise.

As he walks down the road behind the tennis club, he can see Martha outside the restaurant staring at the boards which cover the old front windows. She doesn't even notice him approaching until he's barely three metres away, when she grins, walks over and embraces him with as much passion as when they had last been together. It feels good.

"What do you think of it?" Martha is still cuddling Art, but has turned her face back to look at the newly-sprayed cartoon on the boards.

"It's illegal, isn't it?"

"You and your legal shit!" She laughs. "Forget all that. Do you like it?"

"Yeah, it's not bad. Makes its point, I suppose."

"I wonder who Neola is? Might be someone we know… it might be you, Art!" Martha pulls a teasing grin, revealing a flashing set of white teeth, which he can almost see his reflection in. He wonders if she brushes them for the full two minutes twice a day to get them like that. He's never managed it because he hates the sensation of teeth brushing. Maybe not as much as when he was younger, but definitely enough to make two minutes an impossibility.

"No, it's not me. I can't draw."

"Pity. If would be so cool if my boyfriend was a graffiti artist." She playfully pats him on the cheek. "But you're not too bad just as you are, Arty boy." She leans her head back towards him and kisses him again, before continuing.

"What the hell's in that bag?" She reaches out to grab the black bin bag from his right hand, but he pulls it away.

"Oh, nothing... just some old rubbish... I need to put it in that big bin by the tennis club."

"Intrigued! What old rubbish, Art?"

"It's nothing... just rubbish."

He starts walking down the road towards the alley at the back of the tennis club. He would run, but he hates running, is very slow, and the weight of the bag would make it tricky anyway.

"Let me see!" Martha follows him down towards the alley, trying again to grab the bag.

"No... leave it. It's just rubbish, right."

"Woah, sorry, I'm just like playing, Arty boy! What you got in there? A dead body or something?" Martha laughs, trying to break the tension which she can sense developing.

"No. Nothing like that. Just rubbish, like I say." They reach the large industrial bin behind the tennis club, which he opens and hurls the black bin bag inside. If his grandmother had been so bothered about his mum seeing the letters, she would have sent them when she wrote them.

"OK. I get it. You don't want to tell me!" Martha pouts at Art with her lower lip sticking out and curled down at the corners.

"It's just some old family rubbish I had to get rid of. It's private, right?"

"Yeah, I get it! Calm down. I'm not going to crawl in there and get it out, am I?"

"Good. Please don't."

"I won't!"

They walk back in silence towards Rosa's Kitchen, where they push open the back door, retrieve the stuff they'd put in the wheelie bin in the kitchen, and sit on top of the blankets on the main restaurant room floor.

"Was that our first argument?"

"Dunno. Was it?"

"Well, I don't remember another one!"

"No. Was it an argument?"

"I hope so."

"Why?"

"Because making up after an argument is my favourite bit!"

Martha places her hands behind Art's head and pulls him towards her for a long, intense kiss.

Art has never made up after an argument before. He has never needed to. It has never been his fault.

Chapter Eleven

Art:

Why do you get in trouble for telling the truth and doing the right thing, yet others can talk in riddles and lie all they want, and be called "sensitive" or "thoughtful" or "clever". It makes no sense. You always say what you mean, why doesn't everyone? They should. Everything would be so much easier then.

Why do people tell you to look at them when they're talking to you? You don't need to see them, you need to hear them when they're talking to you. It's obvious.

Why do some people call you "weirdo" and worse? You're not weird, they are. And they're rude too.

"Do you think you've made your point now? Maybe it's time to go home?" Martha has been thinking how best to say this and isn't confident she's got it right. She is lying on her side now, facing her boyfriend, who is on his back, staring up at the ceiling while she talks to him. Without realising, she marks out a question mark on his chest with her right index finger.

"What point?"

"The point that you're angry with your mum... the point that made you run away."

"But nothing's changed."

Martha thinks about this in silence for a while before trying a different tack.

"My dad saw your mum the other day. She's really suffering... that's not what you want, is it?"

It's not what Art wants. But it's not his fault. It wasn't him who had deliberately led a secret life for so long; it wasn't his behaviour which led to Mek calling his mother a whore, and Art having to hit him with a baseball bat; it wasn't his actions which left him with no choice but to run away. It was a consequence of his mum's behaviour. But he still doesn't want her to be suffering.

"Of course I don't, but I had no choice."

"You always have a choice, Art... we all do."

"I'm not going home, Martha."

"Well, at least let her know that you're OK. That would be a start."

"She'll know by now. I went to see her mum earlier."

"What? Why?"

"I needed some money... I figured she'd give me some, and she did."

"Oh, that's good... that you saw her, I mean. She can reassure your mum."

"She won't do that, but she'll have told Aunt Amanda who will have told mum." Art proceeds to give Martha a few more details of his mum's split from her parents, and how they wanted him dead. When he has finished, she lays her head down on his chest, where her left ear can hear the constant pounding of his heart. She wonders if it is broken. It doesn't sound like it.

They lie in silence for a few minutes, until Martha tries something else.

"Are you happy, Art?"

"Why?"

"I'm just wondering if you're happy, that's all."

"I don't know. How could I? There's no independent standard, is there? So I can't know what happiness is or unhappiness is. I just know how I feel, that's all."

"And how do you feel?"

Art thinks about this for a moment.

"Let down."

Still with her head on his chest, Martha stretches her right arm out and squeezes Art's left hand tightly.

"I won't let you down, I promise."

"Thanks."

"But you shouldn't be angry with her, Art."

"Why not?"

"She was just like doing the best she could to give you a good life."

"Well, she failed."

"Did she?"

"Yes."

"You had a good life until you found out what she does, didn't you?"

"Yeah, I guess."

"So you still can... nothing's changed other than you've found out how she earns her money. So what?!" Everything has changed for Art actually. He is about to say as much, but Martha doesn't let him, as she carries on before he gets the chance.

"So why are you angry with her then?"

Art pauses for a moment to consider the question. The lost expression on his face indicates sadness more than anger.

"Because she never really wanted to have me. I was only born because she was a drunken junkie."

"She did want you, Art.... She still does. She loves you and she's there for you. That's too precious to let go of. When it's gone, it doesn't come back. I should know." Martha's voice falters as she thinks of her own mother, but she doesn't spell it out and Art doesn't pick up on it. His mind is focused on explaining his anger.

"And my dad is some horrible monster who enjoys paying vulnerable, drunken junkies for sex. No wonder I'm angry."

Martha slightly turns her head to plant a light kiss on Art's chest, then squeezes his hand again, trying to reassure one, or maybe both, of them.

"So, if you're angry with anyone, it should be your dad and all the other men who have paid her for sex."

Art sits straight up with the urgency of a jack in the box being opened for the first time, whilst the mechanism still works. He hadn't thought of that. And he hadn't meant for Martha's head to get pushed off his chest by the sudden movement.

"Sorry Martha."

"It's fine, Art." She rubs her neck for effect only and winks, though both actions go unnoticed.

"You're right. If it hadn't been for them, she would never have done it, and we'd have been fine as we were." Martha can spot the flaws in his logic, but now is not the time to point them out. She can see Art is agitated. She wishes she hadn't mentioned the men.

"It's OK, Art." She puts her hands on his back and starts massaging his shoulders to relax him, but it doesn't work. "You look to me like you a need a good swear, Art."

"What?"

"You just look like you need to scream, swear, say whatever you want... unload it all!"

"I don't swear."

"I've noticed. Why not?"

"Mum always says that swearing is for people who don't know how to express themselves, and I do know."

"Fucking charming!" Martha laughs. It doesn't break the tension, so she tries again. "Go on, Art, just this once, let it all out. Swear all you like. I won't tell anyone."

He thinks about it for a few seconds, then unloads in more spectacular style than she had expected.

"Fucking, fucking bastard wankers... you fucked with the wrong bastard fucker this time, you arsehole bastard shithead wankers. I'll fucking make you regret it, you wank-brained fuckfaces!"

Martha laughs and pats him on the back.

"Nice one, Arty boy!"

"Sorry."

"Feel better?"

"No."

He does seem more relaxed, however, and there are no more signs of anger in the next few minutes as they dress, leave the restaurant and step back out onto the pavement.

"I'm going to get something from home if mum's out... I'm not going home properly though, right? Just getting something." Art speaks matter-of-factly, as it is a matter of fact.

"What are you going to get?"

"I won't say. It's better for you not to know."

Martha has been here before. There is no point arguing.

She gives Art a long goodbye kiss, arranges when they will meet next, then watches as he heads down the road. Once he is out of sight, Martha heads down the alley at the back of the tennis club and opens the big industrial bin. It's quite full, so the black bin bag is still easy to reach near the top. She leans in and pulls it out. It's heavy. No wonder Art was struggling to lift it.

She tries to make carrying the heavy bin bag seem as natural as it can be. She doesn't want anyone questioning her about it. She checks that Art has long gone, then walks back past Rosa's Kitchen with the bin bag casually slung over her shoulder.

An unremarkable middle-aged woman is standing outside the boarded-up restaurant and watches expressionless as she walks past. Martha notices her briefly, but remembers nothing about her, other than that she doesn't appear to think that dragging a heavy bin bag over the shoulder is an odd thing to be doing.

Priya stands at the side of the pitch, with another parent-coach, watching Johnson in action. She wishes Tommy hadn't said he was too tired to make it. He might have enjoyed this. Or if not enjoyed it, at least this might have helped him in some way.

Johnson has split the players into groups of two and lined them up so that each pair faces each other on the Marsh Park pitch. Half the girls are standing on the halfway line blindfolded, while their partners are about a metre away throwing tennis balls over the shoulders of the unseeing girls into buckets placed on the pitch behind them.

At first there is lot of nervous giggling and concern from the girls with the blindfolds on that they are about to be hit in the face by a flying tennis ball. Some of the throwers are being overly careful, pitching their tennis balls too far away from the partner's face so that they miss the bucket behind them. But, with time and practice, they settle into it. The buckets start to fill, the throws get more accurate, and the giggling is replaced by encouragement and determination to be the team with the most balls in the bucket. Every minute, Johnson blows a whistle and the two girls in each partnership change places, and every other minute the thrower takes a step back so they are further away from the bucket and the challenge is harder.

After four two-minute cycles, Johnson ends the routine. No one is hurt. A few have taken glancing blows to the face from gently lobbed tennis balls, but nothing to stop their enjoyment or cause any damage. And that's the point. Johnson gathers the girls round him in a semicircle and debriefs them on the purpose of the exercise.

"Why do you think we did that then?"

"Because you know nothing about football?" "Coz we're rubbish at throw ins?" "Something about trust?"

Johnson laughs politely at the first answers and focuses on the last one.

"Exactly... when you started doing that, some of you were worried. You didn't care if they got it in the bucket or not, you were just worried they would hit you in the face. You didn't trust your partners not to... or maybe you did trust them, you just didn't have faith in their ability not to hit you. But the longer it went on, the more you believed in them and the more you started concentrating on the main task of getting the balls in the buckets, and the more you wanted to win it, right?"

The murmurs of agreement may not be overwhelming, but are enough to encourage him to continue.

"And that's what this is all about... the more you trust each other, the more you believe in each other, the more you have absolute faith in your team members, then the more you can focus on winning. Because you know that you're in it together and you know none of you is going to let anyone else down... and when you've got that belief, you win. Simple as that. You are a team and you believe in every single one of you... that's an unstoppable combination. Believe me." He pounds his right hand repeatedly into his left palm to emphasise his point.

They do believe him. They know his track record. He knows how to win.

Priya watches from the sidelines as he carries on the theme with an exercise in which the girls have to complete a course as quickly as possible by walking backwards and avoiding the tennis balls scattered liberally on the floor, guided only by the instructions given from their partner. To avoid the risk of potential injury caused by stepping on the ball, only one pair goes at a time, and Johnson jogs alongside them with a stopwatch, ready to kick any tennis balls out of the way when the instructions aren't working and someone is about to step on one. That hadn't been his plan, but Priya had insisted on it. She doesn't want to have to explain to an angry parent how their daughter has broken her ankle. But most of all, she doesn't want any players getting injured before the AllRays Cup match.

She hopes they can win. She believes they will too now.

"I'm so sorry, my little Rosa. It was a terrible mistake, the worst I could ever make, and I have regretted it every single moment of every single day since... I'm so sorry, I wanted to tell you, I really did, but I just didn't know how... I hated myself for it, I still do, but I didn't want you to hate me too... I love you with all my heart. I always have and I always will."

Mel is not speaking to a mural this time, she is speaking to her wife on the sofa next to her. She leans across to cuddle Rosa, who pulls away instinctively in horror. Is that how she would have reacted if Mel had told her the truth all those years ago? She doubts it, but she will never know.

"Get off... where's Mel?"

"I'm here, my little Rosa. It's me." She looks into her wife's eyes, once so bright and mischievous, looking for a sign that the old Rosa is still there. All she can see is uncertainty.

Mel knows that it was never meant to come to this. She remembers the two of them having a discussion once over a few bottles of wine whilst watching a documentary on TV about a choir of dementia sufferers for whom music was providing an invaluable link to their former lives. Mel picks up her phone and scans her playlists. She chooses *Rosa's Party in the Park*, and puts it on, so that it fills the front room with life and joyous memories. Rosa's expression doesn't change at first, but on the third song, she suddenly pulls herself off the sofa, smiles and starts singing loudly along with chorus. She throws her arms up and down in a slower, toned-down version of the dancing style that only Rosa would ever have the lack of inhibitions to do.

It's like witnessing the explosion of light when a professional firework display illuminates the darkness to greet a New Year: exhilarating, intoxicating and momentarily all-consuming, yet it will soon be over and the reality of time marching on will have sharpened its focus.

Rosa is having fun. That's all Mel has ever wanted and it's the mantra Rosa lived her life by. Mel smiles at her wife. If only this moment would last forever. But it won't.

She thinks back to something Rosa had said when they had watched the programme. They had both found it inspiring and hopeful even, but what Mel remembers most is the closing credits rolling and Rosa announcing "if I ever end up like that, you will shoot me, won't you, Mel?!" It wasn't the most sensitive reaction, but it wasn't meant cruelly. It was just honest, and Rosa was always honest.

Mel studies her wife's face looking for signs of how she feels about it now. She looks happy at the moment, caught up in the music, flailing her arms with an abandon that is very reminiscent of the past. Mel has assumed that because Rosa is no longer the same person she once was, she must be unhappy. But that may not be true. It certainly doesn't look it now.

Mel leaps off the sofa and starts dancing with her wife, imitating Rosa's wild uncontrolled style in a way that she had always been too self-conscious to do in the past. For the next couple of minutes she feels liberated, lost in a time where only the two of them exist, and the world is all theirs.

As the song reaches its end, Mel leans forward and hugs her wife with a warmth that only love can supply. She wishes the moment could last for the rest of time. But it doesn't. The next song starts and Rosa pulls away and sits back down.

"This is a shit song."

"It's your playlist, Rosa!"

"No, it's not. It's shit."

Mel laughs, sits back down on the sofa again and starts stroking her wife's left hand.

Would Rosa really want Mel to shoot her now? Not that she could. She hasn't got a gun for starters. But there are other ways. She knows that. She thinks about it a lot. She's even stockpiled over-the-counter painkillers just in case. They could go together, and end their pain together. Or would it just be Mel's pain. She will never know.

"What the fuck's that, sis?" Johnson James arrives home just in time to see his sister struggling through the door dragging a big black bin bag behind her.

"It's a bin bag." She sticks her tongue out at him and grins inanely.

"Ha fuckin ha! What's in it?" He moves towards her as she hauls the bag towards the bottom of the stairs and motions to take it off her.

"Leave it, JJ!" Martha understands now how Art must have felt when she was pestering him about what was in the bag. It doesn't feel such fun on the other end of it.

"Woah! What's with you, sis? Just interested, that's all!" He holds his hands up in surrender and starts to back off.

"It's nothing, just some old shit I've got to sort through for the play."

"Well good luck with that!" He doesn't move. He just stands in the hallway watching her fight to heave the bag up the stairs.

"What are you fucking doing, JJ?"

"Come on, sis. This is comedy and drama all in one!... Will she fall down the stairs? Will the bag split? I've gotta see this!" He laughs again, and loses interest when there's no sign of either happening as she reaches the top of the stairs.

Martha lugs the bin bag into her room and closes the door behind her. There's a note from her dad on her bed saying 'don't forget to learn your lines, please!!' with a hand-drawn smiley face at the end of it. He shouldn't be coming in her room uninvited. It's her room.

She dips her hand into the bag and pulls out a letter at random. It's from November the fourteenth, twelve and a half years ago. She starts to read.

My darling Charlotte,

I hope you and Arthur are coping with this cold spell as well as you can. I'm finding this beastly weather a bit of chore if I'm honest, and your father thinks it's causing his knee to play up again. Personally, I think he's just making a fuss about nothing, like men do, but don't tell him I said that please!

This is probably going to be the first Christmas that your Arthur will understand what is happening I imagine. That must be so exciting for you both. I so wish I could spend it with you. Three and a half is such a wonderful age when children are so enthusiastic and full of the joys of life that it makes your heart melt. I remember when you were that age and we had to spend hours convincing you that Amanda had been lying when she told you that Santa doesn't exist, though I'm not sure you ever really believed us. Did you?

I'm looking forward to Christmas as we've got Amanda, Matt and the boys coming round on Christmas Day, though sadly your brother James has got other plans this year, so won't be able to join us. I desperately wish with all my heart that you and Arthur would be with us too.

I think that Amanda is finding it quite hard working full time with the boys so young, but I guess you know all about that anyway. In my day, she would have probably stopped working by now, though in my day she probably wouldn't have been a doctor in the first place! I wonder if things would have been different if I had kept working once the three of you came along? I wonder if I would have been different? These modern women seem to be so much more assertive than I ever was. I suppose we are all a product of our times to a certain extent, but I do often wonder if I could have been the mother you needed in a different era.

Anyway, you don't want to hear me rambling on any more, I would imagine. I'm sure you've got a lot more fun things to do with young Arthur. I think about you both all the time, you know. I hope with all my heart that one day we can be reconciled and be the loving family that I have always longed for us to be. I am so sorry for the part I have played in our estrangement. It is a constant source of pain to me, and I hope that one day we will all forgive each other and let our love bring us back together.

Your father is well apart from his blasted knee.

Will all my love.

Mum xx

Martha puts the letter down on her bed. She's never heard anyone speak like that, not even since they moved to England. Is Art's gran stuck in a Jane Austen novel? She pulls out another one. It was written four years later, but the handwriting is identical and the content much the same: a slightly strange mix of formal pleasantries, cheery news updates, barely-concealed heartbreak, and pleas for both forgiveness and apologies. The more letters she reads, the more the themes are confirmed.

Martha feels like she has intruded directly on a deeply personal, intimate conversation which she has no right to read. And she is right, of course. Except, if she hadn't retrieved the letters from the bin, they would have been gone forever. Maybe she could use them to help Art's family get back together? She wonders if she should tell Art; she wonders if she should deliver them to his mum herself; she wonders if she should just put them back in the bin. Martha knows Art well enough by now to have a good idea what the consequence of each choice is likely to be.

As she starts on about the fifteenth letter, she hears the front door open downstairs, and can hear the conversation.

"Hiya JJ. How's your day been?"

"Yeah. Good thanks, dad... bit of tennis... a couple of beers... even helped out with a bit of coaching for Marsh Park Rovers! You?"

"Fine thanks... Is Martha back yet?"

It's not like her dad to let JJ's last bit of news go without digging deeper. He must have something else on his mind, and it sounds like it's Martha. That's not what she wants to hear.

"Yeah, she's in her room?" She was right. He does.

"How did she seem? I'm a bit worried about her, JJ. She doesn't seem herself."

"In what way?"

"It's difficult to pinpoint exactly, but she's just acting a bit strangely... not learning her lines for example, which is so unlike her, never mind putting me in a tricky position, as I'm going have to get someone else to take her part if it carries on and I don't want to have to do that, JJ, I really don't... but it's not just that... not sure what it is really... like she's holding something back."

"She seemed fine to me, dad... and she's definitely still up for the play. She brought some massive bin bag full of stuff back to look through for it."

"Eh?"

Martha doesn't need to see the expression on her dad's face. She can picture it. She hears the footsteps coming upstairs, followed by the knock on the door and the handle beginning to turn.

"Wait! I didn't say come in! This is my room, remember?!"

"Woah, sorry Martha. I just wanted to have a bit of a chat... you know, like we used to." Finn stays on the outside of the room, talking through the door to his daughter. They have always got on so well, always been able to talk to each other about anything. He knows it's a role he has to fulfil when he's covering for both mother and father. And he knows it's something he needs to.

"What is it?"

"JJ mentioned you're going through a bag of stuff for the play. That's great. What is it?"

"Oh, nothing important... just some stuff."

"What stuff?"

"Like I said it's nothing important!" Finn knows it's not worth pursuing. It doesn't take a parent's intuition to know that she is lying.

"Are you OK, Martha? Can I come in?"

"I'm fine... I just need some time on my own. Is that a crime?!" Finn looks at the door he's talking to. It might as well be a ten feet thick wall given the distance he feels from his daughter at this moment. He hates the feeling. He doesn't know what to say.

"Oh, OK... don't forget to learn your lines, eh?"

The silence says it all. If the door had been open, it would have been slammed shut now, but the silence has exactly the same impact.

Chapter Twelve

Charley:

People judge you by what you do, yet most of them know nothing about what you do, let alone who you are and what you've been through. But that doesn't matter to them, it doesn't fit the easy narrative, they're much more comfortable making simple snap judgments, which fit the world views they've developed or, in some cases, have been given to them.

So you are wary. You don't want people to judge you, but they do. Even those you should be able to rely on whatever happens.

"Before we start, I want to make one thing very clear. I'm only here for Art. Nothing else. Understand?" This place has changed since Charley was last here. In those days it was a traditional old-style cafe, all fry ups and big mugs of tea. Now it's packed with thirty-somethings and a few groups of well-dressed older people, and they all seem to be eating poached eggs and crushed avocado or drinking unappealingly-coloured health drinks based on kale or spinach or blueberry, but always containing ginger.

Charley takes a seat at the table and looks straight at her mother for the first time in over sixteen years. The immaculately-coiffured hair bounces on her mother's head in uniform, though no longer natural, reddish-brown waves, which look like they are trying just a little too hard to recapture the look of her youth. She hasn't aged well though she's clearly fighting it. But, however many face masks she's tried, however much anti-aging cream or moisturiser she has applied, it hasn't worked. The lines are winning, and her attempt to smile is overwhelmed by the permanent frown of someone who thinks all the troubles of the world are their own.

"Of course, Charlotte. I understand. I would just like to say..."

"Amanda says he came to see you. What did he say?" Charley doesn't want to hear what her mother would just like to say. She agreed with her sister that she could arrange the meeting as long as it was in a neutral venue and it would only be about helping her find Art.

Gillian Mann pauses. What did Art say? He said he wanted money. He said they should have helped Charlotte more. He said she should have chosen Charlotte ahead of her father.

"He said that you are a good mother."

Charley can't help but raise her eyebrows slightly. She hadn't expected that. She hopes her mother hasn't noticed.

"He's a good son too... the best." Charley sticks her left hand out to pick up a menu off the table. She doesn't want anything to eat or drink, she just needs somewhere else to look. Her mother reaches out to place her own right hand on top, but Charley pulls away just in time.

"I'm sure he is, Charlotte... he reminds me of you. He knows his own mind."

"You must have hated that then." She fakes a laugh, the sort of bitter laugh that comes after you've not seen your parents for sixteen years.

"Charlotte! No need for that. Let's keep things civil."

"Civil! You're telling me to be civil!" If Charley hadn't been entirely sure how she would react to seeing her mother, she is now. She spits the words with an anger that causes her mother to look around and notice several disapproving glances from other tables.

"Please Charlotte. This isn't going to help Art."

"OK. So where did he go?" Charley reminds herself why she has come and tries to compose herself.

"I'm so sorry, Charlotte. I wish I could tell you, but he didn't say... he said he would come back though?"

"Why?... in fact, why did he go to see you in the first place?"

Charley's mum shrugs. She doesn't want to admit it. She looks at her daughter intently. When you haven't seen someone for a long time, it's easy for your mind to snapshot their appearance as being exactly as it was when you last saw them, forgetting how they looked before or how they might have changed since. It's a problem which has tarnished the memories of so many people who have seen their loved ones' failing bodies ravaged by illness before they die, and forever hold on to that picture above the memories of how they looked when they were healthy.

Gillian's snapshot of her daughter is as a thin, sick, drug-addled young woman with blotchy skin, straggly hair and hollow, blank eyes. She is pleased to have a new snapshot to hang on to. It rekindles buried memories of how effortlessly beautiful Charlotte had looked when she was younger, even if it's slightly tempered by the pain she can see in the deep blue eyes she got from her father. It's harder to say who she inherited the pain from, and she wonders if it's just a new addition since Art disappeared anyway.

"I think he just needed some money, Charlotte."

"And you gave him some, right?" The way she snorts the question makes it very clear what she thinks of her mother: that the only reason her grandson would want to see her is to get money. Pitiful. She didn't need to make it clear though. Her mother was fully aware already.

"Yes. I didn't know what... I just... well I couldn't let him starve, could I? What else could I do?"

"You could have told him to come home."

"I did." Charley raises her eyebrows again.

"And what did dad say?"

"He wasn't there." Charley notices her mother look down at the table. She knows what that means.

"You haven't told him, have you?"

"Well... it's just that... you know what he can be like... I didn't want to rock the boat unnecessarily." It's a bit late for that. The boat was rocked sixteen years ago until it capsized and sank to the bottom of the ocean.

"Pathetic... nothing's changed." Charley mutters the words quietly but with enough volume and contempt that her mother can feel the full impact.

"I'm sorry, Charlotte. It's not easy being stuck in the middle, you know."

"Stuck in the middle!" Charley raises her voice again. This time her mother doesn't check the reaction of the other diners.

"Yes... Stuck in the middle between you and your father. It's not easy."

"You're not in the middle! You're so far over to one side, the whole thing tipped over, remember?"

"No, Charlotte. It's not like that." She inhales deeply before continuing. "Let's calm down a bit... I think about you both all the time, you know. I've written you letters every week and bought you both birthday cards every year."

"Of course you have, and I've read them all. I just seem to have forgotten all about them... stupid me!" Charley doesn't recall feeling so angry and sarcastic since, well, since she last saw her parents in fact.

"It's true, Charlotte. I just... I just never felt the strength to send them... until now. I gave them all to Art to give to you."

"He's not at home at the moment, remember?!"

"He said he'd drop them round when you're out... and I thought maybe, just maybe, it might help... might give him an excuse to go home."

"He doesn't need an 'excuse' to come home. He lives there. He's happy there."

It's Charley's mother's turn to raise her eyebrows this time, though she doesn't ask the obvious question she wants to ask.

"I'm sure he is." She takes another deep breath, puts her elbows on the table and covers her face with both hands. "Look, I know this isn't going as we'd hoped, Charlotte. It's been a long time... far too long. I know I've made some terrible mistakes and it's cost me the most precious thing in my life. I just don't want you making the same mistakes." She removes her hands from her face and stares into her daughter's eyes. She can't read her this time.

"I won't. Believe me."

"I hope this can be a new start for us, Charlotte. I really do... I know it'll take time, but..." She doesn't get to finish her sentence, as a young woman in a yellow t-shirt and matching apron has sidled up to the table and asks them if they're ready to order.

Charley's mum sits up straight, picks up a menu, and smiles politely as though she has just been discussing the weather with her daughter. "I'll have an Americano please. No sugar." She pulls a small container of sweeteners out of her pocket by way of explanation. "How about you, Charlotte?"

Charley pushes her chair back and stands up.

"No. Not for me. I've got to go." She looks at her mother, shakes her head and waves a finger in her direction. "And you ring Amanda the second Art comes back to see you, OK?... the second he arrives, right?" The young woman in the apron shuffles off. She's been doing this long enough to know when to leave the customers to it.

"Of course, of course. I will... And Charlotte, please let's meet again. I... I do love you, you know."

Charley has almost reached the door by the time those words come out.

Art is getting quite good at knowing when the house is empty. After a few minutes peering round from behind the shed in the back garden, he is now looking through the kitchen window and can see there is no movement downstairs and all the lights are off. His mum always turns all the lights off when she goes out. He knows that because she has got unreasonably angry with him when he hasn't done it. Apparently he'll understand when he has to pay the bills, but he doubts it. He will never get angry with someone for leaving a light on. He's not unreasonable.

He gets the key out of his pocket, and opens the backdoor as quietly as he can, ready to flee through the open back gate if he gets interrupted. But he doesn't. So he walks slowly upstairs, listening for any sounds and still ready to turn and escape if needs be. But there is no need. He checks that the bathroom and both bedrooms are empty, then sets to work. He needs to be quick, just in case.

He knows his mum. She likes to write things down. She often tells him how she's forgotten to do her diary today, as if it's the most important thing in the world. Who cares? It's only a stupid diary and no one else is interested anyway. Art certainly isn't. Not usually anyway. But today it might be useful. It might help him find out who the men are, the ones who pay her for... Art doesn't like to think about what they pay her for. She's his mum.

The diary is easier to find than he'd expected. It is lying open on her bedside table. That's a good start. It's open on yesterday's date with just a short entry written: *Still no sign of Art. I can't cope with this much longer. Please, please come home Art.* What was the point in writing that? She didn't know that he was going to come back and read it. In fact, she had told him before that he wasn't allowed to read her diary, which itself was an odd thing to say, because he had never had any intention of reading it. Until today, that is.

He flicks through a few pages, skim reading as he has no interest in finding out about his mum's life. He just wants names and contact details. He notices the name Ray coming up a few times as he's flicking through, without a surname unfortunately. There can't be that many Rays in Sonnley or the world for that matter, can there? It's a terrible name, almost as old-fashioned as Arthur, but without the option to shorten it to something less obviously embarrassing. In fact, Ray is probably already the shortened name, but is just as bad as Raymond or Rayford or Rainier or whatever the full name is.

Finally, he stumbles on an entry for that horrible evening when she dragged him to school for the opening of the Performing Arts Centre and kicked off the chain of events which led to him having to run away. He doesn't read it all, but a couple of sentences leap out at him: *so funny to see Ray on stage cutting the ribbon to open the Performing Arts Centre! He looked a lot smarter and more serious than when he's with me!*

Art doesn't like the two exclamation marks. It makes it seem like the whole thing is a joke. This is not a joke. And he knows which Ray he is dealing with now. Ray Hope. So the richest man in Sonnley doesn't just spend his money on building schools and pretending to care about the community. He also spends it on paying Art's mum for... Art doesn't complete the sentence again.

He puts the diary back on the bedside table, open on the same page it had been when he found it, then walks into his own bedroom. It looks exactly as it did when he left it. At least she is not renting it out to a lodger or anything like that yet. He walks over to the goldfish bowl, picks up some fish food and sprinkles it into the water.

"There you go, Llama. A bit more than usual... keep you going until mum feeds you, if she ever does." The goldfish looks healthy and as big as ever, but is still happy to eat the unexpected meal thrown its way.

"How are you doing? I'm sorry I've not been able to come back more, but I haven't forgotten you, honest. I've got a place of my own now, sort of, but it's still probably not safe to take you with me. Sorry. I will do soon though. As soon as I've got somewhere more permanent, I'll be back for you. So don't fret."

Art knows that he can't stay too long. He has no idea when his mum will be back.

"Sorry Llama, but I'd better go. You take care of yourself until I'm next back." He heads for the bedroom door, before glancing back at Llama one more time, "and look after mum, please."

He might have run downstairs to hasten his escape, but he knows it's dangerous. His mum told him that when he was young. So he walks carefully, then speeds up a bit on the way to the kitchen. Before leaving through the backdoor and the garden, he opens one of the kitchen drawers, and pulls out a bread knife. That will teach Ray Hope not to mess with him.

"OK, everyone, just over a week to the opening night, so we really need to kick on." Finn James thinks he can sense an air of nervous energy in the room, as the realisation sinks in that the actual performance is now so close. It's going to be the closing night too, what with it being a one-off performance, but opening night sounds much better.

He waves Martha and Mek on to stage and takes a seat in the front row next to Priya.

"First time we've tried this scene. Fingers crossed, eh?" he whispers.

Priya nods but says nothing. That's not like her. She's usually bubbling with enthusiasm, but today she looks like all her natural excitement has been drained out of her so that everyone else in the room can have it.

The stage is split in two by a full-length curtain hanging down from the ceiling. Mek, as Mrs Thatcher, sits at a desk on one side with a Union Jack flying above him and a phone in his hand. Martha, as President Reagan, is on the other side with the Stars and Stripes waving proudly above the desk and a phone in her hand. It's not subtle, but this is not the West End. It doesn't need to be.

In this scene the two leaders are meant to be discussing options for ending the dispute with Argentina over the Falklands. Maybe they could offer somewhere else instead?

"I've been thinking, Ronald," says Mek, in his best strident and confident Mrs Thatcher voice. "I've got the perfect place to give them." Mek proudly flicks away a piece of imaginary fluff on the lapel of his blue jacket. It's the first time they've actually tried a scene in costume, and Finn is pleased with how well it seems to work with the two leads playing characters of a different gender. The costumes really help the impact.

"Go aaan, Maggie." The American accent should be easy for Martha of course, but she seems to be affecting a strange, possibly Southern, drawl and is clearly ad-libbing here. It's not what it says in the script, but the meaning is much the same, so Finn lets it go.

"Well, think about it. The Argentinians love football, don't they? And I hate it... ghastly game followed entirely by thugs. But, apparently, we currently have the best team in Europe here in the UK, and they come from a terrible rundown city which has no oil and where the people are rioting troublemakers and never vote for me anyway... so it's win-win!" Mrs Thatcher laughs and waits for Reagan's response. She doesn't get one, so Mek decides to carry on anyway.

"I have already put in place plans to cut Liverpool adrift and offer it in exchange for the Falklands Islands." Again, it is time for Mr Reagan to say something, but he doesn't. Finn looks at Martha. He didn't want it to come to this, but he can't treat her differently just because she's his daughter. He gets up from his seat and walks towards the stage, but is stopped in his tracks by Mek holding up both hands and speaking in his usual voice.

"Sorry everyone, I feel crap, can we call it a day please?"

"What's up, Mek?" Finn wasn't expecting this. No one was.

"I don't know, must be something I ate, mustn't it? Sorry. I'm sure I'll be fine tomorrow, won't I?"

Finn looks at Priya. She shrugs.

"OK.... You'd best get off home, I guess. We'll work on a different scene today then." He rubs his chin for a thinking moment. He needs a scene without Martha either. "OK, let's do the scene where the Argentinians celebrate winning the World Cup with a team full of Liverpool players and Diego Maradona."

Mek and Martha exit the stage and head towards what is generously described as a changing room. It's actually just an area to the side of the stage which has been sectioned off with dividers and into a few separate parts.

"Thanks, Mek."

"Eh?"

"Thanks for covering up for me not knowing my lines."

"Did I?"

"Well why else would you suddenly say you weren't feeling well?"

"Well maybe I wasn't feeling well, was I?" Mek walks off into another changing area. There's nothing more to say.

Martha pulls the oily wig off her head and runs her left hand through her hair to let it reform its natural shape. She knows she needs to learn her lines. It's not that she hasn't wanted to. It's just there's been too much else going on. She heads into a different changing area, hoping her dad won't get on her case.

He's not going to at the moment anyway. He's busy working through the next scene without her and, when that finishes, he knows there's something else he needs to do. He lets the cast disappear until it's just him and Priya left in the big hall putting the final props and chairs away.

"How did you think it went today?... other than the Mek and Martha scene of course!"

"Yeah... all seemed fine, Finn."

"Are you OK, Priya?" He didn't need to ask really. He can see she's not.

"Yeah, fine... sorry Finn... just got a few things on my mind."

"Wanna talk?" He sits back down on the chair he is carrying, and she does the same with hers.

"Thanks.... It's nothing really... just a few problems with Tommy." Finn doesn't really know Priya's husband. He's always seemed a good friendly bloke on the few occasions they've met, but he never really comes to any of the nights out with staff members and their partners. He's always assumed it's just a childcare thing.

"Oh dear... want someone to listen?"

Priya smiles wearily. "It'll be fine, Finn, I'm sure... it's just it's gone on so long now." She stops talking as though she's said too much already. But she's barely started.

"What has?"

"He's struggling, Finn, really struggling. It started when the kids came along... I think maybe some sort of paternal depression or something, but he tries to hide it. To everyone else he seems fine, and he can put on a show with the best of them when he wants, and sometimes it feels like the real Tommy is back... or is it the old Tommy, and the real Tommy is now the depressed shell of his old self which only I really see, I don't know anymore?... and that's the problem. He can only enjoy himself as an act, and he's a great actor when he needs to be. He hates going out, he hates parties, he hates doing anything really... I think he even hates himself to be honest. He doesn't see all the good things he does: the quick wit and laughter he can bring to any room when he's in the mood; his love for the kids which shines through so, so strongly when he talks about them; the way he'll do anything to help anyone else who needs it. But he won't help himself and he won't tell anyone else he needs it, so his friends all think he's good old kind, funny Tommy." Priya pauses for a moment, looks away and pulls slowly at her mouth with her left hand, as though she is trying to pull the next words out against their will. Then she looks directly back at Finn, her quivering bottom lip betraying all attempts to conceal the pain, and continues. "And I don't know what to do about it. I don't know how much longer I can go on like this, Finn, I really don't... he needs help, proper professional help, and I can't give him that... And I'm so, so worried about him, worried that one day it'll all be too much for him and he'll give up and... you know." Priya's voice trails away and she takes a tissue out of her jacket pocket to wipe her eyes. "Sorry Finn. I shouldn't have..."

"Of course you should! I asked, didn't I?" He tries unsuccessfully to lighten the mood, then puts his right arm round Priya's shoulders and gives her a hug. He knows how she feels. He doesn't want it ending like it did for him. Though it never really has ended for him of course, even after five years and a change of country. It never does end.

"Sorry, Finn. I didn't mean to burden you with all this. I just needed to offload somewhere before I burst." Priya stands up and smiles. If it's not a genuine smile, then she too is a great actor.

"I'm always here you know... I may not be able to fix anything, but I can listen, that's one thing I am good at!" He laughs quietly, embarrassed at how bad that sounded.

"Thanks, Finn. I know that. I appreciate it, I really do, but honestly I feel a lot better now just for telling someone about it, you know, just talking about it."

Finn doesn't know. He's never talked about it.

―――◆―――

Mel looks at everything she has laid out on the bed. There's the black skirt and the white blouse, which the agency has insisted on for all waiting staff at the wedding reception she's working at this evening. She doesn't want to go; she doesn't want to be working for other people like she did all those years ago; she wants to be running her own restaurant with Rosa like they did in the happy days. But the happy days are gone, and they still need money to survive, so she has no choice. Unless...

She looks at the other choice, laid out neatly on the bed next to the clothes. She has always been neat, so unlike crazy, untidy Rosa, but it was never a problem for them. Mel would tidy things up, her wife would mess them up, and Mel would tidy them up again. It worked well.

On the bed there is a large selection of unopened packets of paracetamol, ibuprofen, aspirin and codeine laid out in precise rows by type, as though she were preparing the stock for her own chemist shop with a very limited product selection. Mel picks up one of the paracetamol packets and stares at the label. She's done some research, and she knows what she would need to take.

But she couldn't leave Rosa alone. That's not an option. It would have to be both of them, but how could she make her wife take enough pills anyway? Rosa may not be well, but she's still as stubborn as ever, and she's not going to do anything she doesn't want to.

Mel picks up all the boxes and puts them tidily away in the cupboard. She hates herself for thinking about it. How could she even consider harming her beloved wife? She's not thinking straight. It's not just the sufferers themselves whose minds get scrambled.

She puts on the waiting outfit and wanders downstairs. Faith is going to stay in with Rosa this evening while Mel works, and is already there listening patiently to Rosa.

"Mel's got some people staying at the moment. I don't know them. I wish they'd go. They're not rude, but they're in the way... do you know them? They've got a restaurant... I cook better than them though... my mother taught me, and she loves my food. I'm going to cook for her now."

Mel stands outside the door listening. There are no people staying. She's heard similar mingling of memories and imagined happenings so many times recently, but it doesn't get any easier. She walks into the room to say goodbye.

"See... that's one of them. Where's Mel?" Rosa points at her wife, who leans over to give her a goodbye kiss. Rosa ducks her head out of the way. "Go away."

"Please, my little Rosa, it's me. I'm Mel. Please!" She hadn't meant to sound so exasperated, but sometimes she can't stop it.

Faith smiles at Mel and pats her left arm reassuringly. "It's OK. You get off. We're fine here, we've got a great evening planned, haven't we Rosa?"

"Have we?"

Mel steps out of the door and stands outside for a few seconds listening to the conversation develop.

"Sure! ... first, we're going to do a bit of gardening before it gets dark."

"I hate gardening." It's true. If the garden had been left to Rosa over the years, it would now be a wild, uninhabitable, overgrown shambles. But it wasn't. Mel had kept it beautiful and tidy.

"Well, we'll find something you do like... I need to do some singing practice for the choir, but I need some help. Will you help me?"

Rosa shrugs. She seems a bit happier with that idea.

"Where's Mel?"

"Mel's got to go out to work... you don't get all this luxury for nothing, you know!" Faith chuckles and pulls a song sheet out of her bag.

"She's always going out having fun."

On the other side of the door, Mel is not having fun. She looks at herself in the hallway mirror and straightens her blouse. She hardly recognises herself now, let alone her wife.

Chapter Thirteen

Finn:

You know how to be the life and soul of any party; you know how to chat, listen, joke, politely offer opinions on a wide range of topics; you know how to put people at ease, smile and seem happy. But you're not, at least not in the way you once were. You still catch glimpses of joy and try to hang onto them and, as time passes, you're getting better at it. That's a good sign. But you are not happy yet. And maybe you never can be again after what happened? You still think about it every day, and the more you think about it the more you blame yourself.

Most people think you're calm, confident and easygoing. But you're rarely any of those things these days. You just know how to act. And you're good at acting. It hasn't always felt that way, but you must be, because no one notices the agonising burden you struggle to carry at all times: the unbearable weight of guilt which drags you down and overshadows your natural positivity and urge to keep moving forward.

But you keep trying to push on, find a new happiness. You have to. For yourself, but more importantly for others. You can't let anyone down. Not again.

There is an urgency in Finn's voice as he answers his phone, which makes his daughter stop trying to learn her lines and come out of her room to get close enough to hear clearly. It's been a long day for them both already with school and the play rehearsal afterwards. It's about to get even longer.

"Of course I will, Charley... that's great... where is he? ... Rosa's Kitchen, I thought that was gone... yep, sure... where do you want to meet?... I'm on my way. See you in a minute." He really is on his way. He's grabbed a light jacket off the coat rack and shouts back into the house at anyone who is listening. "Some private eye has found where Art's hiding. I'm off with his mum to get him. Won't be long."

Martha is listening. She hears the door close behind her dad. She needs to be on her way too. She knows Art. He won't like being found until he's ready. She's got to warn him. She runs downstairs, throws on some shoes, grabs a couple of plastic shopping bags to pack things in, and races out of the door. She hates running, but she knows she has no choice this time. It's a familiar route to Rosa's Kitchen these days, and she knows all the roads and sights she will pass on her way very well by now: the house with the crack in the upstairs window which she romantically imagined had been caused by a besotted person trying to wake their lover in the middle of the night by throwing a stone, but hurling it too hard; the rusty car in a front drive with brightly coloured flowers growing out of the missing doors in what was presumably meant to be some sort of artistic statement; the bike with no wheels chained to a lamppost waiting to be rescued and restored to full functionality.

By the time Martha crosses Sonnley Bridge and reaches Rosa's Kitchen, she feels like the person who ran from Marathon to Athens to deliver some sort of message, blissfully unaware that, hundreds of years later, thousands of people would be putting themselves through the same torture in the name of fun. She can't remember the full details of why he did it, but she hopes she doesn't suffer the same fate that he did.

She knocks on the back door, pauses, then follows up with two further knocks as agreed. She's not going to wait for Art to assess the knocks this time though. She hasn't got time, and nor has he.

"Art... quick, let me in. It's me, Martha. Quick... please!" Her words are barely audible through the desperate gulps for breath as she tries to recover from her exertions, but they seem to do the trick, as she hears the bin being moved and the door is pulled open.

Art looks different somehow, more serious maybe, which is not easy seeing as he looks serious most of the time. She gives him a quick kiss on the lips, then grabs his hand and drags him into the main restaurant area. She starts gathering up the blankets and Art's clothes from the floor and squeezing them into the plastic bags she brought with her. She's almost ready to speak again, the air is slowly returning to her lungs.

"What is it, Martha? What's going on?"

"They know where you are, Art. Some detective has tracked you down."

"What detective?"

"I don't know, does it matter?"

Art thinks about it for a second. Yes, it does matter. If it's a police detective, it may indicate that he is in trouble for something and about to get arrested. Whereas if it is a private detective hired to find him, then at least it would mean that he is not about to be arrested. So it matters quite a lot in truth.

"Yes, it does."

"Just fucking pack your stuff up, Art! We need to get out. Your mum must have like hired someone to find you, I guess... I don't know the details, I just know they've found you and they're coming to get you." At least that means it's not the police, so he's not about to be arrested. It would have been simpler if she had just added that detail in the first place.

"Who's coming?"

"Your mum and my dad... she rang him." Art has started helping with the emergency packing now and is putting things in his little green rucksack, but he doesn't understand what it's got to do with Martha's dad. He is about to ask, but Martha has grabbed his arm again and is dragging him back towards the door. She stops for a moment and looks straight at him with a look which suggests that she's just thought of something. Art doesn't see it, but he wouldn't have recognised it anyway.

"Hang on... unless you want them to find you, Art?... you could go home." Martha feels a surge of guilty disappointment at the thought. She hadn't realised quite how much she is enjoying being part of a secret, risky relationship. She wants what's best for Art, but she doesn't want to lose something that is theirs and theirs alone. Once he goes home, everything is out in the open, it's not just theirs anymore. Their families will know about them and want to get involved. They will be quizzed by their friends. Or her friends at least, she's not sure if Art has friends, he certainly hasn't mentioned anyone. Either way, it won't be the same. She can only hope it will still be special.

"No. I can't go back yet. I've got stuff I need to do."

Martha smiles. It can be special for a bit longer at least, but she did notice the 'yet'. They hurry out of the back door and she leads them down the alley by the tennis club. Her dad won't be coming that way. As they pass the large bin where she found the bag of letters, she thinks she hears voices back at Rosa's Kitchen, so she holds her finger over her mouth in a hushing motion and pulls out her phone to place it on silent just in case. Her dad would recognise her ring tone without a doubt. They say nothing until they are safely past the back of the tennis club and heading in the direction of Marsh Park.

"I've got an idea, Art... we can go to the graveyard behind St Luke's... it's massive. It's easy to hide there."

St Luke's Church is just beyond Marsh Park, and they reach it without noticing anyone they know. It looks like there's been a wedding there recently as a few loose strands of confetti are blowing about in the early summer breeze. The church is big and traditional-looking with a large spire, a cross over the front entrance, and beautiful colourful stained-glass windows depicting intricate scenes from the bible. It has been used as the setting for weddings in two films and a television series in the last five years, and its only concession to the modern world is the collection of 'protected by SmartWater' signs which litter its exterior, in an attempt to warn off prospective lead thieves. They head past the church into the large graveyard beyond.

"It's not long-term obviously, Art, but you'll be able to hide here till we come up with a better plan."

"Thanks." He puts the rucksack on the ground, then leans over to Martha and gives her a cuddle and a long kiss. It's the first time he's initiated it, and that makes her happy.

"It's kinda romantic here in a weird sort of way!" Martha laughs awkwardly. That probably sounded a bit creepy.

"Don't know about that!" Art laughs too and strengthens the cuddle. They both feel safe for a moment.

"I wish we could just stay like this forever, Art."

"It would probably get a bit uncomfortable after a while. It's not good to stay in the same position for too long, you need to keep moving."

"Typical!" Martha laughs.

"What's typical?"

"You... squashing my romantic ideas with boring practicalities." She doesn't want it to get uncomfortable. Why does life always have to?

"Sorry."

"It's fine, Art... how did you get on when you went home? Did you get what you were looking for?" Martha knows he is plotting something. She needs to know what it is.

"Yeah... I got it thanks." Art wriggles from the cuddle he had started. He's ready to start moving.

"What was it?"

"I'm sorry, but it's still better for you that you don't know."

"I want to help, Art. No secrets, right?"

"Everyone has secrets... I found that out and that's why I'm here."

"Oh Art... come on. I may be able to help."

"Alright then, if you really want to know, I was getting the name of one of the men who ... you know... took advantage of my mum."

"Who was it?"

"Ray Hope"

"Nooo!" Martha doesn't mean to sound so excited by the revelation.

"Yes. I'm going to see him now."

"Please don't, Art. That's not a good idea. You must know that, surely?" Art does know that, but he also knows he has to do it. And Martha knows that she won't change his mind.

"Maybe not. We'll see."

"Don't do anything stupid, Art. Please, promise me. What are you going to say to him?"

"I'm not going to say anything." He picks up his rucksack and slings it over his left shoulder, leaving the two plastic bags with Martha. "Can we meet back here at six thirty?"

"Sure... six thirtyish!" Martha laughs, but she feels only impending dread at the moment. "Please listen to me, Art... don't do anything stupid. It won't help your mum, and it won't help you... believe me."

Art doesn't reply. He leans forward and kisses Martha again, then waves as he walks back across the graveyard and past the church. She considers going after him, reasoning with him, trying to stop him going. But she knows it won't work, and it's not up to her anyway. She's made her point, but if Art wants to do something stupid, he'll do it. And she also knows that when someone does something stupid, they are never the only ones affected.

And then she sees it. Protruding out of the side pocket of the rucksack and glinting in the late afternoon light. A knife.

"How do we get in?" Charley Mann is pulling at the front door of the boarded-up restaurant, but it's not budging. There's an anticipation in her voice, which Finn hasn't seen since he asked about using Art's story for the play. It's infectious, the sort of excitement which would make her a great teacher or actor for that matter. It's never come quite as naturally to him and he suspects that explains a lot.

"Maybe round the back?" He catches her eye and can see the mixture of eager anticipation and nervous uncertainty shining back at him in radiant blue. Just as they did when he saw her in her darkest moments, her eyes reveal everything. It's an astonishing sight, and hard to let go of. They head round to the back of the Rosa's Kitchen, push the door and rush in as it opens easily.

"Art! Art! Where are you?" Charley's words fleetingly remind Finn of Shakespeare as she calls out and rushes into the kitchen, before running back out to join him in the main restaurant dining area. There are empty crisp packets and chocolate wrappers strewn across the floor.

"He's clearly been here... I'll check the toilets." Finn can see the excitement draining away from Charley before his eyes. It's a harrowing sight. Maybe shattered hopes can be worse than no hope at all? He's never thought that before. He's always tried to cling on to hope. He has no choice. He's got two children who need his hope.

There are only two doors out of the room. One is the front door which they failed to open on arrival, and the other is the toilet, which he heads towards. On the outside of the door are a couple of fading pictures: one is of a wild-haired woman crouching over a toilet laughing and the other is a quickly-scribbled drawing of a boy urinating into a basin, like someone has tried to draw the Mannekin Pis from memory. He remembers them now from the one time he managed to get a table at the restaurant in its heyday. It made him smile then.

There's not much in the room other than a basin and a toilet cubicle with no inner door any more. It's dirty and there is a strong smell of damp in the room, but clearly no sign of anyone having been in there for a long time. He steps back out.

"I'm sorry, Charley." He sees the last vestiges of hope drain from her face, and instinctively moves over to hug her. There is nowhere else in the building to look, what with the first floor having been removed to leave the incredible single-story airy space, in which they are standing.

"It's OK, Finn, at least we know he's been here." Charley tries to sound upbeat, but her sobs betray here.

"It's only a matter of time, it really is. Hang in there." Sometimes hanging in there is all you can do.

"Thanks, Finn.... Wait, what's that?" She pulls away and bends down to pick something off the floor from beside the discarded food wrapper debris.

"What is it?"

"Looks like a nose ring to me. It's certainly not Art's!" There is a lightness and hope returning to her voice. Maybe he's with someone? Maybe there's a lead. She waves the nose ring in Finn's direction. He closes his eyes and exhales.

"Shit... sorry." This is one of those times when he really doesn't know how to express himself. Charley can excuse it this once.

"What, Finn?"

He looks at the tiny little 'N' on the end of the nose ring. His daughter's lasting reminder of her lost mother. "That's Martha's. I'm sorry."

"No, Finn, no... that's good... she'll know where he is then, won't she?" The excitement is coming back to Charley's voice.

"Yeah... I guess... sorry." He bows his head, puts his hands on top and looks down at the floor.

"You ok, Finn?"

"Yeah, sorry, I'm fine... I'll call her, find out what's going on."

"You don't sound fine. What is it?"

"Nah, it's nothing... just... nah, nothing." It's not a very convincing nothing act.

"Come on, Finn. You can let it out, you know? That's what you told me, remember? It does help. The 'N' means something doesn't it?" Charley places a reassuring hand on his shoulder.

"Niamh... that was my wife's name... Martha's mother, you know."

"I'm sorry, Finn. What happened?... I'm not prying, just, you know if you want..."

"No, you're alright. You don't want to hear me moaning on." He lets out a weird short grunting chuckle which Charley interprets as a sign he wants to talk.

"Why wouldn't I? You've listened to me enough."

He raises his head and smiles weakly. "You don't have to."

"I'd like to. Go on... it might even help."

"Thanks, Charley. Maybe another time, eh? We need to find Art now, don't we? I'll ring Martha." He starts pressing icons on his phone, but she leans over and gently pulls his hand away.

"Come on, Finn. We can wait five minutes. We've waited long enough, five minutes more won't make a difference to finding him, but it might make a difference to you. Who knows?" He doesn't say anything, just smiles weakly and looks at Charley as though no one has ever really asked him how he feels since it happened, and he doesn't know how to say it. Everyone has concentrated on the children, including Finn, and that's fine. That's the way he wanted it. But...

After a few seconds, Charley breaks the silence. "Seriously Finn, the main thing is we know Art's OK now, and we know he's seen Martha, so we know we can find him. I feel like... I don't know... like the darkness is ending and I can see the sun beginning to break through again!" It's true, Charley feels like the fears and pressures of the days since Art left are in sight of lifting completely. She knows he's alive. She knows he's with Martha. It's going to be OK. But she can see that the sun isn't breaking through for Finn. She squeezes the hand she pulled away from the phone. "Go on, see if I can listen as well as I talk!"

"You're kind, Charley, very kind... but I'm not very good at talking about this sort of stuff, you know."

Charley smiles. "Well, give it a go, eh?"

For someone who is not very good at talking about this sort of stuff, Finn proceeds to put on a very good show. It's as if he's spent the five years since Niamh died perfecting a soliloquy and is now performing it in public for the first time.

"We met when we were both nineteen in Dublin. I had always felt a bit different there in truth. There weren't many other black kids in Dublin in those days. It was fine on the whole, don't get me wrong. I had my mates and all that, but I always felt like an outsider. But when I met Niamh, it was different. We just got each other, clicked, know what I mean?"

Charley nods unconvincingly and lets him continue his monologue.

"And I was desperate to be an actor... really desperate. I'd been in a lunchtime medical soap in my mid-teens, *Patients*, you might know it?"

"No, sorry."

"Ah well, I'm not sure they ever showed it over here actually." He laughs at himself before continuing. "But I got the bug from that. Never wanted to be anything other than an actor from then on. But I wasn't getting any more roles. I would audition, but they just never worked out. So I did a teacher training course, because my parents thought I had to do something, and that's where I met Niamh, and it was just so right, know what I mean?"

"No, sorry." She doesn't pretend this time.

"Aah sorry, Charley, I didn't mean to, you know..."

"It's fine, Finn, really... please carry on."

"Thanks, you're kind, Charley... so we got married young, twenty to be precise, but I still wasn't getting any roles so we decided, both of us mind, to move to LA, give it a go there. We were young enough then, had no ties, and nothing to lose, you know. And for a while, it went OK, not spectacularly, but OK. I got a few small TV roles and the odd advert. It wasn't amazing but, with Niamh picking up some supply teaching work and a few other bits and pieces, it gave us enough to get by. And then Johnson came along very quickly, and Martha three years later, and suddenly we had responsibilities. We were still in our mid-twenties, but we had two small kids, my work was drying up, and we only really had Niamh's unpredictable income to rely on. It wasn't fair on her, I know that now... I probably knew that then really, I was just so obsessed with following my dream, I guess I just brushed it aside." Finn stops for a second and closes his eyes. "I wish I could go back, Charley, I really do. Things could have been so different if I'd just..." His voice trails off and Charley gives his shoulder a reassuring squeeze.

"It's OK, Finn, don't beat yourself up."

"But I do, Charley, every day. I knew Niamh wasn't happy. She didn't hide it. She told me. She hated the lifestyle of struggling for every penny in a place where she didn't trust anyone and couldn't have real friends. But I kept chasing my dream. And the more I chased, the further away it seemed to be, but I kept chasing it, and ignoring what was right in front of me... then one night, we had a big argument about it... one of those real shouting-at-each-other-not-listening-to-a-word-the-other-person-says ones, the really pointless ones where no one comes out feeling any better... we'd never had one like that before. We still loved each other so much, we really did, and we always made up... it was our mantra 'never go to sleep on an argument', and we never had until that evening. I stormed out, went to a bar, and stayed out all night, drinking for a couple of hours, then just walking round town, thinking what to do, how to make our world right again... And when I got back in the morning, it was eighteen minutes past eleven, I remember it exactly because I saw the time on the clock by our bed when I found her..." His voice trails off again.

"I'm so sorry, Finn."

"She'd got up, taken the kids to school as usual, then gone home and, well, you know... and it was all my fault."

"No, Finn, it wasn't. Don't blame yourself."

"Thanks. That's kind." He doesn't believe her. And he still does blame himself.

"No really, Finn, it wasn't. That's so awful. I'm so sorry."

"And all the time I know that her last memory of me is going to be the hatred she had for me after that argument, not the love we had the rest of our time together."

"You mustn't think like that." But Charley thinks exactly like that herself. She absolutely recognises that feeling. She's felt it a lot since Art left after their argument. She can't bear the thought of him hating her. She squeezes Finn's shoulder again, and he fakes a stoic grin.

"See, I told you that you wouldn't want to hear me moaning!" The light-hearted tone is at odds with the story he's just told, and it fools neither of them.

"Oh Finn, don't, please. I'm so sorry."

He exhales heavily, puffs out his cheeks and puts his hand in his pocket to pull out his phone.

"That's enough about me. Come on, let's find Art." He smiles the resigned smile of someone fighting a constant battle to move on, and rings Martha.

The late afternoon sun is briefly gaining the upper hand in its battle with the threatening June clouds over Sonnley, as Priya wanders back from school across Marsh Park, though it looks like it'll only be a temporary victory. She can see the darker clouds in the distance threatening to blow in from the West and engulf them all in a dark storm. At least she should be safely back home by then if she keeps up a good pace.

Priya walks past St Luke's Church, just as a figure with a rucksack jogs awkwardly away from the cemetery. He's too far away to see clearly, but there's something strange about the way he's hurrying away. She hopes that he hasn't been defacing headstones or stealing the flowers, then stops in her tracks. That's not like her. She always sees the best in people, she's an optimist. Maybe she unlocked something when she opened up to Finn. She hopes not.

Some people never complain. They know that if they ever start, they will never be able to stop. There is too much for them to complain about. Priya hopes that's not what is happening to her. She glances admiringly at the beauty of the imposing church which dominates the landscape. That building has seen so much: the unadulterated happiness of couples embarking on their lives together; the joyous christenings to mark those people creating new lives; the sad farewells as those people finally leave the world.

She walks hurriedly on past the football pitch where Tommy used to play on Sundays in the early days of their marriage, and where a group of young children are currently taking their first steps down a footballing route, which will grip them for life. The little clubhouse beside it looks very rundown now, as though the years have taken their toll and drained all the vibrancy and energy out of it. Much like Tommy. Priya continues towards the cafe with the *No one else feels like this* graffiti on the side. She wants to miss the impending rain, else she would stop to enjoy the artwork. She likes it. She likes everything about this park. It's the heartbeat of Sonnley. It needs to be saved.

As she walks on, she hears shouting from the playground up ahead, so she heads straight towards it. There are three men, probably in their early thirties, with pushchairs and buggies, screaming at a large young man on a swing. Priya gets closer, and changes to a run. She swings open the gate, and rushes over towards the commotion.

"Leave him alone." She speaks as calmly as she can. She smiles at Marshall Roberts rocking back and forward on one of the swings. He is humming loudly, trying to block out the noise of the men shouting at him. Priya knows that's what he does when he's agitated. She's never witnessed it herself, but Faith has told her.

"He's a fucking pervert! This is for kids, not fucking weirdo perverts!" The smallest of the men is shouting the loudest and the largest one is moving towards Marshall to drag him off the swing.

"Don't touch him." Priya doesn't speak so calmly this time. She throws her body between the large man and Marshall, and holds both her hands up palms forward in front of her. "It's OK. I've got this. Back off."

"You telling us to back off? You'll get a slap yourself if you're not fucking careful."

Priya ignores the threat and turns to Marshall. She can hear the humming getting louder and she knows she mustn't touch him.

"It's OK, Marshall. Everything's fine. It's all OK." She speaks slowly, smiling at her friend's son and spreading her arms out sideways now to block any attempts to get past her from the men behind. After a few seconds, he gets down from the swing and starts running towards the playground exit. Priya runs alongside him, keeping herself between him and the group of men, until they are safely outside in the sanctuary of the main park.

"It's all OK, Marshall." She keeps a couple of feet away from him, and tries to reassure him, but he's not hanging about to listen. He continues running out of the park in the direction of the safety of home. Priya knows Marshall has been coming to this playground since he was a baby. It's his favourite place, his safe place. He always sits on the same swing, the one on the near right side, and he rocks gently back and forward smiling in a way that he never does anywhere else. But he never will again. Everything has changed in an instant. Marshall Roberts will never come back to the playground.

Priya looks back at the three men in the playground. They are laughing now and lifting their children onto the swings. She catches the eye of the smallest one.

"Fucking perverts" he shouts.

She looks at the man's children playing happily. One day she will probably be teaching them. He's teaching them now.

Chapter Fourteen

Gillian Mann has not been to church for over twenty years, other than for weddings, christenings, funerals, Christmas and Easter of course. But they don't count really, they are special occasions. She used to go when she was a child and when she first got married to Arthur, but then things got rather busy, what with the children and... well mainly what with the children. It wasn't an intentional neglect, more of a drift towards other things, and by the time she realised what had happened and felt guilty, it would have been too awkward to go back. People would have questioned her, criticised her priorities, looked down on her, and she couldn't face that. Admittedly that didn't seem to have happened on the special occasions she had been back, but that was different, they were special occasions, so people behave differently.

As she walks up to the entrance to St Luke's Church, she is overwhelmed with a sense of trepidation. She can feel her breath shortening and speeding up, and a strange tensing of all the muscles in her upper body. The sort of feeling she used to get when she went to those quarterly dinners with the other officers in Arthur's regiment and their glamorous, always immaculate, wives. She's not entirely sure why she's come, in all honesty. Her mind has been a bit all over the place since the unexpected visit of her eldest grandson, and then the coffee with Charlotte. Even if Charlotte didn't strictly speaking have a coffee, it still feels like the correct way to describe the meeting.

Gillian knows that there is no service nor any other event on in the church at the moment. Before coming, she checked in the church newsletter she still subscribes to. That's why it's the right time. She also learned that Reverend Duncan McHugh has also retired recently, which seemed very surprising. He always seemed so young! It's a pity he's gone. She's got many fond memories of him christening Amanda, James and finally Charlotte. In that case, he can't be that young any more come to think of it, can he? Where has all the time gone?

She pushes the left one of the two enormous doors which welcome people into the church, and is glad to see it is empty. She looks around the vast interior. She knows it very well after all these years of special occasions of course, but it still impresses her as much as the first time she walked in: the beautiful, moving painting of the crucifixion above the font; the amazing detailed stained glass windows and wonderful high walls which seem to almost reach the heavens themselves, and must have required a construction miracle to complete all those centuries ago when the church was built without modern day equipment; but most of all it's the peace which always overwhelms her, the feeling that whatever else is happening in the world, this place is a haven of serene tranquility and calmness. And if there's one thing that Gillian needs now, it is a bit of peace.

She walks down the central aisle of the church and sits down on an empty pew near the front, at the end of which a small candle is flickering. She stares at the candle for a while, captivated by the manner in which the flame keeps fading and looking as though it is about to go out completely, but then somehow bursts back into life. It never gives up.

There is no real plan to Gillian's visit, which is quite frankly highly unusual for her. She wonders whether or not she should say a prayer, and feels it would be the right thing to do. But first she just sits in silence, studying the candle, trying to clear all the thoughts out of her mind, absorbing the peace all around her.

"Hi." Gillian turns round to see a short, and though she shouldn't say it, quite rotund lady, probably aged about sixty, smiling kindly as she limps confidently down the aisle with the aid of a stick. She is wearing silver-rimmed glasses on her small nose, carrying a bible in her right hand, and has the gentle, caring look of someone who has learnt a lot from life and is not going to judge others. Or is that just wishful thinking?

"Oh hello. I'm so sorry, I didn't hear you." Gillian stands up and offers her hand out to shake, which the lady happily does once she has shifted the bible to her other hand. It seems to be called the *World English Bible*, not a version of the bible which Gillian has ever heard of, but everything seems to change so quickly these days it's hard to keep pace.

"Sorry, I didn't mean to shock you. I'm Faith Roberts. I'm a lay preacher here... well some of the time!" She laughs before she carries on. "So good to have you here. Such a lovely time to come, when it's quiet and you can breathe in the peace, savour a bit of quiet reflection." She laughs again. "At least you could have done if I hadn't rudely interrupted you. I'm sorry. Me and my big mouth as always!"

Gillian knows that name. She racks her brain trying to locate it. It's very embarrassing not being able to locate someone, and not like Gillian at all.

"No, please don't apologise. It's very kind of you to say hello. I'm Gillian." She's got it now. Faith Roberts won the council election in their ward. They didn't vote for her. Nothing personal of course. It's just Gillian and Arthur have always voted the same way and there's no reason to change. You know where you are like that, and don't need to bother reading through the mountains of unwanted junk which pour through the letter box every election cycle. It's a bit awkward nonetheless being face to face with someone she didn't vote for, especially when she seems so friendly. Gillian has never been so thankful for secret ballots.

"Well thank you, Gillian, and welcome to our humble church." Faith chuckles. The church is anything but humble. It brings a faint smile to Gillian's lips. That hasn't happened for quite a while now. "Now I don't want to intrude on your chance for a bit of peace, reflection and prayer, but if there's anything you need or you want to talk, anything really, I'll be over there, sorting those." She points over to the left side of the church, where there is a table with a mound of leaflets.

"Thank you, Faith. That's very kind." Gillian sits back down, and thinks about what Faith has just said. Did she mean it or was she just being polite? Gillian knows now that she does want to talk, she needs to offload. That must be why she came to church. She needed a place where she could sit in peace and unburden herself of all the problems that have engulfed her over the years, filling every available space in her mind until there is no room for anything else until she unloads some. What she is about to do is totally out of character. She simply doesn't do this sort of thing. It's quite exhilarating in a strange sort of way in truth. She stands up and calls over.

"Actually, Faith, it might be nice to talk if it's not too much trouble."

"No trouble at all, Gillian. My pleasure." Faith walks back over, waits for Gillian to shuffle along the pew, then sits down next to her. There are a few seconds of silence whilst Gillian considers changing her mind. She really doesn't do this sort of thing. Maybe it's going to be easier opening up to a stranger than to the people she knows. She hopes so, else there won't be much talking going on.

"It's a bit embarrassing to be honest, Faith... I seem to have got my life into a bit of a pickle." That was easier to say than she'd expected, and once she has started it is as if someone has finally fixed a jammed tap on a water butt which has been collecting rain for years, but never been emptied.

She tells Faith about how she met Arthur when he was a dashing young officer, their courtship, marriage, three children, and the wonderful life they had as the children grew up. At least she thinks it was wonderful as that was what she had always been told a wonderful life would be like, and she has nothing to compare it with, so she can't really disagree. She explains the problems they had had with Charlotte, her drug taking and making money from, well you know she didn't need to spell it out, and finally, inevitably perhaps, her falling pregnant. And she describes how Arthur and Charlotte's once impeccable relationship, which she had always been slightly envious of if she's honest, had deteriorated and culminated in him issuing his daughter with the ultimatum that if she left the house, she would never be allowed back.

Gillian confesses how she chose to stay with her husband on the understanding that she must never see her daughter; how she missed her with all her heart; how she wrote to her every week, but never sent the letters; and how she hated herself every second of every day for it, and sometimes even began to hate Arthur for it too.

She leads Faith all the way to the current situation where Charlotte's son Arthur, although he likes to be called Art apparently, unexpectedly arrived on her doorstep looking for money, and she subsequently had a not-entirely-successful meeting over coffee with her long-lost daughter. And she explains to Faith how she can never forgive herself for what she has done, and she knows she has ruined everything irreparably forever.

Then she puts her guard back up.

"I'm so sorry, Faith. This really isn't like me at all. I'm not really the sort of person who talks like this. What must you think?"

Faith takes each of Gillian's hands in one of her own. She notices the feel of hands which her mother would have said had never seen a proper day's work in their life. They feel cold now, as if the stories Gillian has just been telling have sent a shiver through her entire body.

"I think you're a brave woman, Gillian. That I do."

"Brave? That's awfully kind of you, Faith, but I think that brave is probably the last word I would use to describe me."

"You are brave, you really are. You've made mistakes in the past, we all have, but you want to make them right. And that takes bravery, believe me."

"But it's too late, Faith. They were not just mistakes, they were irrevocable life-changing decisions which were heartless, cruel and downright wrong. And I must suffer the consequences. I deserve to... Do you know, Faith, when the children were young and did something wrong, we'd punish them, usually just stopping pocket money or grounding them or the like, and I would always say to them 'you made your bed, you've got to lie in it'. And I'm lying in my bed now. It's what I deserve."

"Can I show you something, Gillian?" Faith picks up the bible which she had placed on her lap when she had taken her new friend's hands, and starts flicking through it. "You'd think I'd know it by heart being a preacher and all that!" She chuckles and keeps turning pages until she finally finds what she's looking for. "Here we go. Will you read that, Gillian? Luke Chapter 6 Verse 37." She points at a passage in the open book and passes it over.

"*Don't judge, and you won't be judged. Don't condemn, and you won't be condemned. Set free, and you will be set free...* That may be so, Faith, but I have judged, I have condemned, so I deserve to be judged, I deserved to be condemned."

"Do you forgive your husband?"

"For what?"

"For the dispute which led to you losing your daughter from your life."

Gillian thinks about this for a while.

"Yes. Yes, I think I do... I do blame him sometimes, not out loud of course, but he's not a bad man. He's just... well he's just Arthur! Everything is black or white to him, there are no grey areas. And that can have terrible consequences, as I know only too well."

"And do you forgive yourself?"

She doesn't need to think about this answer so long.

"No... No, Faith, I can't. I don't deserve it."

"You know what, Gillian? Twenty years ago, I knew a woman who everyone thought was strong, who everyone thought could handle anything, so no one worried about. But they were wrong. She had her struggles like everyone else, she just didn't share them. And one day she had had a particularly tough day looking after her five young children and just needed something to calm her down, get her away from it all. So she decided to go for a drive... nowhere in particular, she just needed to get out. She wanted to be alone, but it just wasn't possible with her youngest son. He was very clingy, and started screaming uncontrollably when she tried to go out, so she put him in the back of the car and took him too. He calmed down for a few minutes as they drove, then suddenly started screaming again, even louder and more piercingly than before. He wasn't a very verbal boy, so she turned back to see what was wrong and noticed that he had dropped the little plastic dinosaur which he liked... no... needed to hold at all times. She reached her arm back into to the footwell behind her, desperately feeling for the dinosaur, desperately trying to calm her son." Faith pauses momentarily and adjusts her glasses for a few seconds so that Gillian does not see her close her eyes before continuing.

"But this woman hadn't stopped driving, she had just stopped looking... so the car careered off the road, over the pavement and crashed straight into a tree."

"Oh no, I'm so sorry. Was she OK? And her son?"

"Her son was fine thankfully, and she was a lot luckier than she might have been. She received some serious injuries, but after a few months in and out of hospital, the only lasting physical damage was to her right knee. But it was the damage to her mind which haunted her... every day she blamed herself for her stupidity. Why did she drive when she was so wound up? What was wrong with her that she could even get so wound up looking after the children she loves? How could she have been so reckless with her four-and-a-half-year-old son in the back? And she tortured herself about what could have happened. Her son could have been seriously injured... or worse." Faith closes her eyes, without covering them this time. "And what would have happened if she'd hit some poor innocent pedestrian?"

"I'm sorry, Faith."

"And one evening, about a year after the accident, it all got too much for her. She went out for a walk and broke down, simple as that. She lay down in an alleyway, collapsed and cried uncontrollably, screaming hysterically, pleading for help. But no one helped. For twenty minutes, people walked past, tutting at her, either thinking she was drunk or just being scared of how she might react." Faith pauses for a second, reaches over to touch Gillian lightly on the arm and speaks the next sentence very slowly, emphasising every word. "But not one single person tried to help her... not one, Gillian... Until, finally, a young man in his early twenties stopped to check if she was OK. He was on his way to a first date, but he stopped to help the woman, and sat with her, listening, calming her down. He called his date to explain, and she joined them too, and between them they took the woman home to her family, and helped find organisations to give her the help she needed... And with that help she learned how to turn her life round, Gillian: she stopped torturing herself about things that hadn't happened; she stopped hating herself for the accident and for the occasional times she would wish that her youngest son wasn't autistic; and she stopped putting pressure on herself to be perfect, to be the answer to everyone's questions. She knows now that only the good Lord can be that."

"And what happened to her, Faith?"

"You're talking to her, Gillian. And the couple who were on their first date, Tommy and Priya, are now married with three kids of their own and are two of her dearest friends."

"I'm sorry you went through that, Faith."

"Please, don't be sorry. Everything has a purpose. The point is that I was being too hard on myself, and had to learn how not to be, and that we all need to forgive others and, just as importantly, forgive ourselves. If I can do it, Gillian, you can too. Believe me, it's not easy, and you may often fail like I still do loads of the time, but we've got to try, and just keep trying. What's the alternative?"

She doesn't expect an answer. They both know the alternative. They have lived it.

Faith takes the bible back and reads the words again. "*Set free, and you will be set free.* You deserve to set yourself free, Gillian. You forgive your husband, so you can forgive yourself too. You can be forgiven, Gillian." She says the last sentence with a powerful certainty.

The two women continue their conversation for several more minutes. Gillian is still not sure that she can forgive herself, but there is some clarity returning to her thoughts. She likes that. A clear mind is a productive mind. Maybe there is hope?

Had it not been for Faith's phone ringing, they may well have stayed on that pew until the following morning. But it did, so they didn't.

"Hi Priya... you OK? You sound kind of... Marshall? What? When?... The bast... Where is he now? OK. Thanks, Priya. I'm on my way."

"Is everything OK, Faith?" Gillian can hear the alarm in the preacher's voice.

"Sorry Gillian. I've got to go." The alarm is veering towards anger now as she continues. "It's my son... sounds like some... sorry, no I won't say the word I'm thinking, not in here... just someone's been picking on him... he's OK, but I need to go. He needs me." Faith pauses, closes her eyes and breathes in slowly whilst tilting her head heavenwards, before opening them again and smiling not altogether convincingly at her new friend. "Sorry, Gillian, I shouldn't have got so... well, you know."

"Please don't apologise, Faith."

"Thanks, Gillian. It's been so lovely to meet you. You will come again, won't you?" She sounds a bit calmer now, as though she is used to people picking on her son, which she is. It doesn't get any easier, but the panic doesn't set in in the same way. The anger still does though, however hard she tries.

"I will, Faith, I certainly will. Thank you so much. You can't know what good you've done me." Gillian thinks about hugging Faith, but opts against it. She doesn't do that sort of thing. So she shakes her hand, then waves her on her way. "Go on, off you go, your son needs you." She watches as Faith picks up her stick and scuttles down the aisle and out of the church doors. That's what parents do when their children need them. She wishes she had done it.

Gillian sits on her own for a couple more minutes, then slowly exits the church. As she steps outside, she has to take evasive action to avoid being knocked over by a teenage girl who is running out of the graveyard holding two plastic bags. The girl squeals an apology and keeps running. Gillian likes that. Manners are so important, and they cost nothing.

As Ray Hope makes the short familiar drive back from Heathrow Airport to Sonnley he reflects on a week well done. He had an enjoyable evening at the Monte Carlo casino, winning some money he doesn't need. But that's not the point, the point is he won. He doesn't go to casinos by choice, but his clients often seem to like it, so needs must. It was a fitting end to an evening entertaining the leadership team of an American-owned insurance company, with whom he had agreed a new contract to provide a bespoke version of the AllRays Software motor insurance module across their multi-national portfolio. The implementation alone will last years, let alone future support and enhancements. He's going to need to speak to HR about another recruitment drive.

He hadn't been planning to come back to the UK just yet, but when he got a call saying that Laura had found that missing kid, he thought it would be kind to be around, support a friend. In fact, come to think of it, if Charlotte's got her son back, maybe she'll be up for... no it's probably too soon. He chuckles to himself for having the thought. Clinching big new contracts always has a strange, aphrodisiacal effect on him.

He doesn't really need to go into the office today, and he can see there's a storm heading for Sonnley, which makes it even less appealing, but he thinks he might as well pop in. It won't take long, and most people will be finishing their working days anyway, happy to leave promptly while the boss is away. So that makes it even more worthwhile. It's always good to show your face, tell a few people what a good job they're doing, maybe tear someone off a strip in front of others. Whatever the situation warrants to get the best out of people. He's done lots of courses about motivating people over the years. Initially he was very sceptical, but it sets a good example to everyone else if he's seen to be actively participating in the same sort of nonsense that they are. Although some of them were actually quite useful. It's strange how different people are: how you get the best out of some of them by being kind and understanding and pretending that their mistakes are learning points; how some need a rocket up their arse just to get them to do the job they're paid to do; how others seem to feel constantly in fear of being humiliated or sacked, and that fear is enough to get the best out of them.

The more courses he attends, the more people he meets, the more Ray Hope realises that he doesn't need them. Obviously he needs them as employees or clients or contractors, of course, but that's as far as it goes. People are needy, and Ray Hope doesn't need needy people. He's got all he wants himself for his happiness, and when he has other needs, well, he can just pay someone to meet them. It's a win-win situation.

As he turns into the AllRays Software car park, the dark clouds begin to dominate the skyline and a heavy deluge threatens to engulf the town. Ray peers through the first smattering of raindrops on his windscreen and notices a youth with a small green rucksack loitering around the entrance, and staring straight at him. Software developers can be a strange lot, Ray knows that, but this kid looks too young to work there. Maybe he's on a work placement? It's good to give back to the community by encouraging things like that. The VP of HR has reminded him of that as many times as he has given back.

Nonetheless he makes a mental note to get security to check this kid out. Just in case.

Martha can't get much speed up as she runs back towards Marsh Park past St Luke's. The two plastic bags aren't heavy, but they make running awkward. She needs to stop Art before it's too late. She doesn't know how. She shouldn't be having to deal with this sort of shit at her age. Yet she seems to have had to more times in her sixteen years than most people do in a lifetime.

As she reaches the main fields of Marsh Park, she feels the first few drops of rain splattering down on her hair. The sunshine of just a few minutes previously, when she last saw Art, has disappeared, the sky is darkening rapidly and it's clear what's coming. Martha is not dressed for this, but she's got no choice. She stops for a moment, puts down the bags and picks up her phone. She needs help.

"Sorry, the person you are calling is on another line at the moment. Please leave a message after the tone." The automated voice sounds smug like it's mocking her for the mess she's in, the mess she created when she told Art to blame the men instead of his mum. She hadn't thought for a second he would react like this. Why does she always end up with immature, emotional wrecks as boyfriends? Maybe all boys are like that? Or maybe they are the ones she relates to?

Martha hangs up without leaving a message. Her dad never uses his phone for calls. Who's he talking to now? He should be there when she needs him. She puts the phone back in her pocket, picks up the plastic bags and starts trying to run again. There is no sound when her phone rings in her pocket, when a voicemail alert triggers, when the messages start coming in. Silent means silent.

The rain is getting heavier now, beginning to weigh down her clothes and make the running even harder. She's tired. She wants to be at home in the warmth, not chasing after a boy who's clearly intent on killing someone. She sees a familiar face leaving the park just beyond the playground, and makes a desperate sprint in her direction.

"Mrs Moore... Please... Mrs Moore." Martha shouts as loudly as her exhaustion will allow, and finally she sees her teacher stop, turn round and scan the park trying to locate the voice through the rain.

"Martha... is that you? What's up? Are you OK?" Priya is still thinking about Marshall Roberts. She hopes those men haven't been threatening Martha too, and the concern shows in her voice.

"It's... it's Art." Martha's panting means that she shoots out the words staccato style, as if they are being fired from a gun and she has to reload between each word.

"Art? What? Have you found him?"

"It's... a long... story... but we've... we've got... we've got to find him... I'm worried he's about to do something stupid?" As her breathing calms down, the reloading isn't needed so often.

"What do you mean? Is he in trouble? Where is he?"

"He's looking for Ray Hope? I think he wants to kill him."

"What?" None of this makes any sense to Priya. She wants to get home, get out of the rain, avoid the worst of the impending storm. She can feel it closing in. She can feel the whole world closing in.

She listens patiently as Martha explains as little as she needs to in as short a time as she can. It raises all sorts of questions? Why was Martha with Art? How long has she known where he is? Did she really just happen to bump into him a few minutes ago like she claimed? Has she told anyone else? Where did Art get the knife? But they will all have to wait for another day.

"So where has he gone, Martha?"

"I don't know... I wish I did... I just know he's going to find Ray Hope."

"OK, OK... let's stay calm... let's think." Priya feels anything but calm at the moment, but she knows she needs to try to be because Martha certainly isn't. "Where would you go if you were looking for Ray Hope, Martha?" Priya asks the question rhetorically really. She's not expecting any more of an answer than the shrug and the headshake she gets, which sends a shower of raindrops flying towards her from Martha's hair. So Priya answers it herself.

"Well, if it were me, I'd either go to his house or his work... does that make sense?"

"Yeah, I guess."

"And it's office hours and we've no idea if Art even knows where Ray Hope lives... but he'll know where his offices are. Everyone knows that!"

"OK... so what do we do?"

"We go there... we've got no choice. Come on." The two of them start running through the increasing downpour in the direction of AllRays Software. It's only about a mile from Marsh Park to the modern, predominantly glass building which dominates the industrial estate on which it resides. In normal circumstances it would be a dull, but not too taxing, jog through the streets of Sonnley. But these are not normal circumstances: their clothes are heavy with rain; the pavements are becoming slippery and covered in sudden puddles; the beating of thunder drowns out the sounds of their breathless puffing, pounding hearts and the two plastic bags crashing time and again against Martha's legs; and the thought of what they might find fills them with terror.

They turn into the industrial estate and run up towards the entrance to the car park. There's a barrier with some sort of electronic fob entry system for cars, but nothing to stop pedestrians entering. Martha doesn't want to run anymore. She's had enough of running. She's not sporty like her brother, she's an artist: she sings, writes songs, acts. Yet today, she has covered more miles than he probably covers in a month of daily tennis matches.

Martha spots him first. His slim frame looks positively scrawny under the weight of the drenched clothes sagging in the rain. He looks bedraggled and lost. Martha just wants to run over and hug him, tell him everything is going to be alright. But she doesn't even believe that herself. She never does really, whatever she says.

She accelerates alongside Priya, taps her on the shoulder, and points at Art. He hasn't seen them yet. He is standing on the edge of the car park looking at the building. Martha wonders what he's thinking. She can't tell. But then again, she never can, no one can.

Looking ahead, they notice two big men in hi-vis jackets coming out of the main building and scouring the car park as if they are looking for someone. They look like security. They might be looking for Art. Martha doesn't know that of course, but she knows that she has to get to Art before they do. If they find him carrying a knife, she doesn't know what they will do. And she doesn't know what Art will do.

Priya and Martha move as quickly and quietly as possible towards him. When they are within five metres, he spins round, sensing the approach.

"What are you doing here?" He sounds as matter of fact as if he were making smalltalk with someone he's bumped into in a shopping centre cafe. Except Art doesn't do smalltalk. Or go to shopping centres.

"Oh, Art... it's going to be OK." Priya talks first, using the patient, calming voice which has benefitted both her parenting and teaching effectiveness. It's kind and warm, just as she always seems to be.

"Is it?"

"Yes Art." Priya smiles. Over Art's shoulder she can see the two men walking towards her. They don't look in a hurry, more fed up that they've been sent out in the rain than anything. "Can you give me the knife please, Art? It's not going to help anyone if you use it, you know?"

Art does know that. That's why he is still standing on the edge of the car park and hasn't followed Ray Hope into the building. He knows what he had hoped: he had hoped that it would get justice for his mum; he had hoped that she would be proud of him; he had hoped he would feel better. But he knows that none of that is correct.

He says nothing, but dips his hand into the side pocket of his rucksack, pulls out the kitchen knife, and drops it on the ground in front of him. Priya picks it up and asks Martha if there is anything in her plastic bags which she doesn't need, then wraps the knife up in the T-shirt which she is handed in return.

"Your mum misses you so much, you know Art." He doesn't know. He's not seen her, remember? He doesn't say that though. Teachers don't like those sort of answers. He's learnt that the hard way.

"I would never have done it. Believe me."

"I know." Priya moves closer to Art and puts her right arm over his shoulders, causing him instinctively to shrug it off again. She can see the two security guards getting closer. "Come on, let's go."

They quickly walk back out away from the car park down and out of the industrial estate into the roads back into town. The security guards lose interest once they leave the car park, so they can resume a more sedate pace. The rain continues to lash down around them, obscuring the tears which are rolling down Art's face. That's not like him. He's glad no one can see them.

"Shall we take you home, Art, eh? Your mother wants that more than anything." Priya's voice is sympathetic and reassuring.

"Yeah, it's time, Art." Martha agrees. She's been quiet since they found Art, and largely kept away from him. She doesn't want Mrs Moore getting the right idea.

"Maybe." They walk on in silence in the direction of Marsh Park and the short walk back to Art's house. The rain stops as quickly as it started, and is replaced by a warm sunshine, which throws dazzling reflections of light off the assorted puddles. He drops back from the others and they see him bend down as if to do his shoelaces up.

Art would love to go home. He wants to, more than he can admit, even to himself. He wants to be home in his bed; he wants to chat to Llama; he wants to see his mum. But it's not his fault that he was forced to run away, is it? And the reasons haven't gone away, so it's an impossible choice really.

Walking ahead, Martha is begging Mrs Moore not to mention the knife to anyone, seeing as how Art never used it, and never even intended to. It seems to be working. But she knows that Mrs Moore is going to want answers about what has been going on. Martha wishes it could just be Art and her alone in their own little private world like it used to be. But it never can be again. She wonders if he is thinking the same. She wants to hug him, cuddle him, lie on the floor of Rosa's Kitchen, just the two of them in their exciting, forbidden secret existence. But she can't even hold his hand now, with Mrs Moore there. She feels like a child trying to live in an adult's world, but getting it all wrong. Maybe she is. She turns round to look at Art: his innocent, puppy face, his slightly uncertain steps, his lost, searching eyes, all of which demand reassurance and love. At least no one can stop her doing that.

She is wrong. They can. Art has gone.

Chapter Fifteen

Martha:

How can you wake up some days feeling invincible, like it's the most exhilarating day ever, and it belongs to you? You can do whatever you want and you want to do everything. The whole world is yours, never mind just Sonnley. You are bursting with energy, ideas and imagination and your mind races from one thrilling brainwave to the next without so much as a pause to catch breath. It is so exciting, so amazing, so unbelievably electrifying.

But on other days, you can't even face getting out of bed. You are so utterly incapacitatingly exhausted and so overwhelmingly terrified of the day ahead. You think you have no right to feel like that, no reason, no excuse. But you do feel like that. And you hate yourself for it. You tell yourself that you are worthless, you must be, and it is all your fault.

So you don't tell anyone how you feel.

If only you would. They will listen, and they will help. But you don't.

Martha gets to the graveyard at twenty past six. She knows she's early, but she's no idea if Art is going to turn up, so she can't risk missing him. It's barely an hour since she last saw him, but it feels like a lot longer. The early evening sunshine has made some inroads into drying her clothes after the storm, but she still feels cold and uncertain. She checks the two plastic bags which she is carrying. The clothes at the bottom of the bag are still dry. That's good. Art will need them. If he turns up.

She looks at her phone. There are seven missed calls from her dad, and a series of messages. She wonders what is so urgent and why she didn't hear the calls. She notices that her phone is in silent mode. That's odd. She never puts it on silent. Unless she is fleeing Rosa's Kitchen of course and doesn't want to be heard. She remembers now.

Martha listens to the voicemails and reads the messages. Her dad sounds a bit angry, but most of all he sounds increasingly worried. He's trying not to, but she knows his voice, and knows his tone. He's found out that she's been meeting Art, and he wants to talk urgently. But the first messages are from before she met Mrs Moore. How did he know then? Maybe he did see them escaping the restaurant? Maybe he's found the bin bag full of letters? He'd better not have done. He'd have had to go into her room without her permission to do that, and that would be a violation of her privacy. Either way, she doesn't want to talk to him now. She sends a brief message back saying she's OK and she'll be back later.

Martha wanders round the graveyard looking for signs of Art and pausing to read some of the inscriptions on the gravestones. She needs something to occupy her mind. The fourth one she reads grabs her attention.

Sarah Lydia Peters
April 12th 1981 – July 15th 2018.
Devoted mother, daughter and wife.
You loved everyone else before yourself, and never knew how much you were loved.
You were always too kind, too sensitive, too special for this world.
Gone to a place which will ease your pain and bring you the peace you deserve.

Martha reads the inscription a couple of times and does the maths. Sarah Lydia Peters died at thirty-seven, the same age as her own mum, and possibly in a similar way. She looks at the flowers on the grave. They are fresh, colourful, radiating joy. They don't really seem to fit. She bites her bottom lip and looks up to the sky, wondering where her mum is now, wishing she could tell her how much she was loved; how much she still is loved; how much she is missed. Martha wonders if there is a place which is easing her mum's pain and bringing her peace. She hopes so. She wants to see her mum again.

"Hello. What are you doing?" She turns round to see Art looking slightly drier, but as bedraggled as when she last saw him, and moves straight over to embrace him.

"Just reading the gravestones."

"Why?"

"I had to do something till you got here, didn't I?"

"You said six thirtyish. I'm not late." It's now six thirty-five, so he is correct.

"I know. I just got here early. I needed to think."

"Think about what?" Martha gently pulls back from Art so that she can look straight at him. He is staring at the gravestone she was reading.

"Can't you see, Art, everything has changed?"

"What do you mean?"

"It's not just us anymore. We can't go to Rosa's. It's all changed. They know about us."

"So what? Why does it matter?"

Martha pauses for a moment to consider the question. She doesn't know why it matters. It just does.

"Er no... I guess it doesn't matter... just means it's going to be different now... you know, like the honeymoon's over."

"We're not married."

She half smiles and puts her hands over her eyes. It doesn't surprise her any more when he takes everything she says so literally. It's not the same. "It's just an expression, Art."

"So what are you trying to say?"

"That's it, Art... I don't know... I guess things are going to be different now, and that's fine... just we need to do things differently too."

"What things?"

"We've got to stop hiding, we're out in the open now... you've got to go home."

"I can't."

"You've got to, Art. It's time. You can't keep hiding forever. We're out in the open, we need to be a proper couple now... you want that, don't you?"

Art looks up from the gravestone and, fleetingly, Martha stares straight into his eyes. She can see the honesty; she can see the fear; she can see that he doesn't fit in. She understands them all. They're what attracted her to him in the first place.

"Yes. Do you?"

"Yes, Art. That's what I'm saying. We need to move on to the next stage now."

"But I can't go home. Nothing has changed."

"Everything has changed, Art. Everything! And it's not just us. Your mum needs you. You've made your point."

Art hadn't been making a point. He had done what he had to. And the reasons he left are as valid as the day he left.

"I wasn't making a point. I left because I had to."

"And now you have to go back... make up with your mum... show her the letters from her mum. She deserves that." Martha had been in two minds as to whether or not to mention the letters. But sometimes you have to do what is right and suffer the consequences.

Art's face erupts as quickly as the earlier storm, but without the menace.

"You got them out of the bin?" He is angry, but in a way which makes Martha want to hug him and tell him everything is going to be OK, like a small child who is raging against the world because their favourite toy has been stepped on and broken by a careless parent.

"Yes."

"You said you wouldn't! You lied! You're as bad as the rest."

"I'm sorry, Art. But I'm glad I did. Your mum needs to see them... they could help her make up with her own mum."

"But you lied! You said you wouldn't!" Art is shaking his head furiously from side to side, as though the movement will stop what he has heard from settling in his brain and becoming real.

"Come on, Art. You must have lied sometimes too."

"No."

"So what did you say to your gran when she gave you those letters, eh?"

"That's different."

"It's not different, Art... you told her you'd give them to your mum, I bet, didn't you?"

"That's different." Art repeats the words with greater volume. The louder he gets, the more desperate and sad he seems.

"Just accept it, Art. We both just did what we thought was right."

"I knew I was right." The words trigger something in Martha. She has had enough. She dumps the two plastic bags on the ground in front of Art.

"You know what. I'm done with this, Art... I used to think you were funny, used to..."

"I was never funny."

That almost stops Martha in her tracks. Maybe he wasn't? Maybe she saw something which wasn't there? She continues in a calmer voice.

"Look Art, do you want to know how I feel? Can I tell you?"

There are two questions there, probably with different answers. Art ponders how to phrase his response, but doesn't get the chance.

"Well, I'm going to tell you anyway, Arty boy. It feels to me like all I do now is run round after you the whole time. Like you don't want a girlfriend, you want a mother."

"I've got a mother."

"Well stop treating her like a piece of shit then!"

"Are you upset?" The swearing shows her inability to express clearly what she is feeling, so Art tries to vocalise it for her. His mum used to say that he wasn't good at picking up on people's emotions. She was wrong.

"Yes, Art. I am fucking upset. I've had enough of this shit... you don't listen to anything I say. You just do your own thing whatever."

"I do."

"Do what?"

"Listen to you. I heard you say that."

"'Heard' Art! Exactly! You 'heard' me, but you don't fucking listen... there's a difference, you know." He does know. Heard is the past tense, and listen is the present tense. He thinks it not wise to mention it though, because he is good at thinking about the impact on others. So he says nothing and waits for Martha to continue.

"I'm sorry, Art... I really am... but I just can't do this shit any more?" She has started crying. It is just as well he was thoughtful enough to have kept quiet.

"Do what?"

"Us! I can't do us anymore, Art... it's just... I don't know... I've had it."

'Do us' is not an expression he knows. Again, he is tactful enough not to criticise it though.

"Are you dumping me?"

Martha leans forward, puts one hand on either of Art's cheeks, and kisses him on the forehead.

"I'm sorry, Art... I don't know... it's just too much for me right now... Like I say, I just can't handle this shit any more."

"I'm sorry. I don't mean to upset you." Art doesn't usually say sorry. It's not easy for him, and he doesn't know what he's done.

Martha stares at him. She can see the sadness. He is lost. But she can't help him find his way. She knows that now. She points at the two plastic bags on the ground.

"The clothes at the bottom are still dry. You'll need those. Don't want you catching a chill in that wet stuff." She even sounds like his mother now. As long as his mother is sobbing and hurting, which she has been a lot recently.

"Thanks."

"Are you going to be OK, Art?"

"I hope so." He wants to say yes, but he can't be one hundred per cent sure.

"Where will you go?"

"I don't know. Why do you care?" His answer is not bitter, just interested.

"Because I do care, Art. I really do. From the moment I met you I knew we shared something. I could see you were different to everyone else, just like I am."

"Well, I can't be different if I'm like you, can I?"

"Stop it, Art. I'm being serious."

"Me too."

Martha closes her eyes and lets out the sort of patient half-laughing snort which her mother used to give her when she was little and said something funny without realising.

"Yeah, I know you are... Maybe we're just like different kinds of different, eh? Look, I'm sorry, Art... take care. Please go home." Martha doesn't know what else to say. She can barely speak now.

"I'm sorry, Martha. I don't mean to upset you." Art doesn't like seeing people cry. He watches as she turns and walks out of the cemetery, without reading any more gravestones this time.

She walks on past St Luke's and back into Marsh Park. It's a beautiful evening now, the calm after the storm settling over the whole of Sonnley. She doesn't want to go home yet. She can't face the awkward conversation with her dad. It never used to be like that. Martha can't talk to him these days, and now she can't talk to Art either.

She passes the park cafe and looks at the *No one else feels like this* graffiti. She knows that is true.

"Oh good, you're back." There is a mixture of relief and anger in Finn's voice when he hears his daughter open the front door. He doesn't mean to sound angry, but he can't help it. It's dark outside now, and the clear night sky means it's getting colder very rapidly. She's let him worry until quarter past ten, not answering calls or messages since a brief message about six thirty. Why would she do that? What's happened to their relationship? He is angry: angry with Martha, but most of all angry with himself. His children are the most important thing in his life. In truth they're the only important thing. Nothing else really matters these days.

"Are you OK, Martha? Where have you been?" He wants to give her a hug, welcome her back with open arms, but he doesn't want to be pushed away. It's better not to get hurt than to take the risk.

"Out... walking... thinking." That's pretty much true. She's walked miles in the three and half hours since she left Art. Partly she needed to think, but mainly she was putting off going home.

"I was worried, Martha. It's getting late. I didn't know where you were?"

"I sent you a message, told you was I fine, didn't I? What more do you bloody want?" Finn wants her to talk to him, be happy when he's about, that's what more he bloody wants.

"I was worried, that's all. I'm your dad, remember? That's what dads do!" He tries unsuccessfully to lighten the mood, and she brushes past him and starts towards the stairs. "Where are you off to?"

"I'm going to bed. It's getting late, remember?" The echoed 'remember' arrows like a poison dart and hits its target.

"Just a minute, Martha, I need to speak to you." Finn doesn't want to have this conversation, but he knows he has to. He owes it to Charley, he owes it to himself, he owes it to Martha even. But most of all he owes it his wife. He's promised her so many times that he'll do the best for the kids. Whether she can hear him or not he doesn't know, but he needs to keep the promise to her either way.

"What?" Martha stops halfway up the stairs and looks down on her dad. She knows exactly what he wants to talk about. Mrs Moore will have been straight on the phone to him. Teachers stick together, their first loyalty is always to each other.

She's right about the topic, but wrong about the reason. Finn dips his hand in his pocket and pulls out the nose ring with the 'N' on it. He doesn't say anything, just waves it in the direction of his daughter.

"Where d'you get that? You like been snooping in my room again? I told you..." He doesn't let her finish the sentence.

"Rosa's Kitchen. The restaurant where Art was hiding... with you by the looks of the things."

"Yeah, well, so what?"

"So what? So what, Martha?! Listen to yourself, please. Art's mum is out of her mind with worry, and you're meeting him in secret. What the hell's going on?"

"That's mine, give it to me." She takes a couple of steps down the stairs and reaches out to take the ring from her dad. He drops it into her hand.

"Please, Martha. What's happening? Why are you being like this? This isn't you. Where's Art?"

"I don't know."

"But you've seen him, right?"

"Yeah."

"Why didn't you say something?"

"He didn't want me to." She was right. It can never be special again. Everyone wants a piece of it now.

"But what about the people who did want you to? What about me, what about his mum?"

"I told you, he didn't want me to."

"But you don't know where he is now, right? When are you next seeing him?"

"It's none of your business, but if it gets me off your back, I'll tell you... I'm not seeing him again. We're not friends any more." Finn can see his daughter's bottom lip quiver almost imperceptibly as she says this, but he can also see the steely determination in her eyes not to seem bothered. He knows where that comes from.

"I'm sorry... what happened?"

"I told you it's none of your business."

"Is he OK?" Finn tries to keep as calm as his maelstrom of emotions will allow. He knows he needs to.

Martha shrugs. "Dunno." She hopes so, but she doesn't know. She's never known if Art's OK really. He's just Art.

"Oh Martha, what are we going to do with you?" Finn smiles and decides to take the risk this time. He takes a step up the stairs towards his daughter and reaches out with both arms for a hug. She's too quick for him though. She turns away and races up the stairs, then opens her bedroom door, and slams it for added impact. Not that any was needed.

Finn sits down on the stairs, and stares back down at the front door, which has always been their protection from the cruelties of the outside world. It's too late now. They've got inside. He goes back upstairs and calls through the door.

"Night Martha, I love you. Please never forget that." He doesn't want to go to bed on an argument. He's made that mistake before.

He gets no reply so wanders back down, and sits on the stairs again, with his eyes closed this time, and his head in his hands. Sometimes the things people don't say hurt more than the things they do.

On the other side of the door, Martha is lying with her head under the duvet still wearing the slightly damp clothes which the storm had drenched. It's been a crap day. She wishes she were hugging Art. She wishes she were hugging her mum, talking it all through with her. But she isn't and she can't.

It's tough sometimes trying to seem tough.

"Would you recognise them? I'm going to track them down and make them fucking sorry for threatening you and Marshall."

Priya has just gently interrupted her husband's breakfast to tell him about yesterday's incident in the playground with the three young dads, and listens as he rants and screams about the revenge he's planning. She knows he won't carry any of it out. They both know. It's not even about the incident really. It's just the rage of a man who feels he has failed to look after his family; failed to be the husband and father he had always wanted to be; failed to make the most of the wonderful opportunity of life he has been given. Tommy is ranting at himself not the men who threatened her.

"Thanks, Tommy, but there's no need. I'm fine, we're both fine… I just mentioned it, because I thought you'd want to know, and it upset me a bit at the time, but I'm over it." She sits down next to him at the kitchen table where, before his outburst, he had been eating a piece of toast and reading about the latest global catastrophes on his iPad. The kids are all still in bed, so it's one of the few opportunities they can get to speak.

"Well, I'm not fine. I'm going to…"

"Tommy, please stop it! This isn't about you. This one's about me!" She knows her husband. He's not a violent man. He would never hurt anyone deliberately. If anything, he goes out of his way to be kind to everyone: he's always a shoulder to cry on for any friend in need; he messages any acquaintance who is ill or injured to check how they are and if they need anything; and he takes news of tragedies he reads about personally and frets over the victims he never knew and the impact on their loved ones who he will never meet.

But he seems intent on hurting himself. And that hurts Priya.

They sit in silence for a few seconds, him staring back at his iPad, and her looking at the side of his head. His once thick brown hair is rapidly being overtaken by an avalanche of grey. It seems to be the dominant colour in his life these days. Priya softens her tone and absent-mindedly starts playing with the wedding and engagement rings on her left hand.

"Maybe, Tommy... maybe we both need to try to get a bit better at listening to each other, eh?"

Tommy knows exactly what that means. She might as well have said "you need to get better at listening to me." But it wouldn't have sounded so acceptable. He diverts his gaze back from the iPad to his wife, looking directly into the eyes which had overwhelmed him with their vitality all those years ago. They are still so alive, and just looking into them, Tommy can sense the joy and excitement she has for life. He never wants her to lose that, and worries that he can see a few traces of tiredness and sadness creeping in. He knows what's causing that.

"I'm sorry." He leans over and rests his head on her shoulder, nestling his face into the side of her neck. Under her left ear he can see the small birthmark which looks like she has shrunk a fifty pence piece and tucked it behind her ear just in case she ever needs it for a parking meter. Though that's not the sort of situation she would ever worry about of course, not like him. He feels her pulse drumming into his cheeks, and smells the sweet, peachy aroma of her hair, comforting him and taking his mind back to a happier world.

"I'm sorry, Priya," he repeats, "I'm just struggling." She pulls her right hand away from her rings and strokes his hair. She can't see the tears, but she notices the gentle shaking movement of his head on her shoulder.

"It's OK, love, I know."

"I just... it's like everything is just hassle, hassle, hassle.... Nothing is fun anymore... I just want things to be like they were... I want to feel like I used to feel... I want to stop being scared of everything, stop seeing catastrophes everywhere... I want to have a mind which doesn't hate me."

"I know, love, I know. There is help out there. It could make a massive difference." Priya speaks cautiously. She's been down this route before. It doesn't usually work.

"I don't need that sort of help. I just need things to be like they were."

"They can't be though, can they love? But that doesn't have to be a bad thing, does it? Things have changed: we've got kids, we've got responsibilities, we've moved on in our lives, and we've changed. I've changed, and you've certainly changed."

"I just want to change back. I want to be happy again. Can you understand?"

Priya can understand that. She wants Tommy to be happy, maybe even more than she wants her own happiness. But she can't understand how he's feeling. She used to think she could, but she was wrong. She can sympathise and help as best she can, but she now knows that she can't truly understand what is going on in her husband's mind, any more than she could understand what bereavement felt like before her brother died.

"Please get some help, Tommy, please. For me, for the kids, and most of all, for you. It could make all the difference, it really could. You know I've looked into it all before. You can start with the doctor or there are lots of other places out there where you can get help if you prefer. I've bookmarked a load on the computer... All it needs is you to want to do it... I'll kick things off and ring them if that's easier for you."

"Thanks. Yeah, maybe... I'll think about it." Priya knows what that means. They've been here many times before. Life carries on. For now.

Priya doesn't push it. She's tried that before. She carries on stroking his head for a little longer, then gently edges away.

"I'd better get on now, love. Nina's football training this morning, then a full dress rehearsal of the play this afternoon. Busy day!... You don't fancy coming along to football training, do you?" She asks the question cautiously. Coaching Nina's team was meant to be their thing, something they could enjoy together. But Tommy rarely comes these days. It's always a risk asking him. She knows it makes him feel guilty and hate himself more when he says no. But she knows she needs to keep encouraging him, keep including him else he may give up altogether.

"No thanks... not today... stuff to do, you know."

She thinks better of asking Tommy what that stuff is. It's a bright, warm June morning, ideal for getting out, making the most of the day, He will be inside, sitting on the sofa, flicking between sports on TV, watching anything to stop him thinking. Maybe he'll even take note of the laminated card she gave him. She doubts it.

It's not really in Art's nature to do spontaneous things. He likes to plan, needs to get used to the idea of what's going to happen before it does. So, after an uncomfortable night spent back in the shed in his own garden, awake and thinking what to do next, the journey he is now on is probably as spontaneous as he gets.

Before he had embarked on it, he had peered through the tiny shed window for several minutes, watching his mum pottering about in the kitchen as though nothing has changed. She was probably happy, though it's not easy to tell if people are happy or not. Art knows that. It's a very difficult skill to learn, if anyone ever does.

He rings on the doorbell of the immaculate cream door which he has seen once before, and waits. He knows his grandmother will be out. Sunday mornings were included in the times she told him she 'had commitments' whatever that means. He doesn't wonder what those commitments are. He just stands on the doorstep waiting to see the man who wanted to kill him.

He hears some shuffling noises from inside, and slowly, very slowly, the door is opened. This isn't what he had expected. His grandfather is supposed to be an ex-army something or other. He should be big, strong, powerful, not frail and painfully thin, with blotchy skin and wearing a green baseball cap with the words *Sunset Valley Golf Club, Antigua* emblazoned on it. Art doesn't normally notice this sort of thing, but the man is so strikingly feeble, that even he can't help but see it.

"Don't waste your breath, boy. I'm not buying anything." The voice is a bit breathless, but he snaps the words with a force which is much more in keeping with expectations, and moves to close the door again. Everything seems to be in slow motion with him, so Art manages to step forward into the doorway to prevent it from closing. He knows he hasn't got much time.

"Why did you want me killed?"

"What?" His grandfather's voice loses nothing of its impatience, but he opens the door slightly, and stares at Art, racking his brains for some sort of recognition of why he would have wanted to kill this boy. Deliberately targeting children was not something he would ever have considered in the army or in his private life for that matter.

"You told my mum to kill me before I was born."

It makes sense now. The old man's irritated expression doesn't change. He studies Art for a couple of seconds, then opens the door fully again and nods inside.

"You'd better come in, boy."

Art follows the old man through the shipshape porch with the two pairs of shoes on the shoe rack next to the umbrella stand, and through to the impeccable living room he sat in last time. It takes longer than it should. His grandfather is painfully slow. It annoys Art. He doesn't want to be here too long. He's not entirely sure what he does want, come to think of it. When he was planning in the shed overnight, he just knew he had to see the man who wanted to kill him, let him know that he failed, that Art is alive and well and thriving. Not like his grandfather it seems. That serves him right.

Without being invited, Art sits down on one of the beige sofas, next to an open letter, which his grandfather must have been in the middle of studying when he arrived. Art doesn't notice it. He looks over at the photograph of his seven-year-old mum sitting on the lap of the old man now taking a seat on the other sofa. It is difficult to make the connection between the two men. Art had never thought about getting old before. Maybe it's not such a good idea.

"So what do you want, boy? I hope you're not going to waste my time."

"I want to know why you wanted me killed?"

The old man snorts a laugh reserved for people who ask stupid questions.

"Is that it? Are you serious?"

"Yes. Why did you want me to..."

"I heard the first time, boy." His grandfather raises a hand for silence and surveys Art up and down, as though carrying out a parade inspection. "You're darker than I would have imagined... a bit scrawny too. You don't look like a Mann."

Art doesn't like being inspected. He also doesn't like being told he doesn't look like a man. Or is it a Mann? He can't be sure. It was a very unclear statement. He searches around for something else to look at to avoid the stare of the intimidating, frail old man on the other sofa, and rests his eyes on the letter beside him. It's from the Oncology Department at Sonnley General. He knows what that means.

His grandfather continues to talk at him. "You're called Arthur, aren't you? Named after me of course... pass me that glass of water, boy." Art wonders why he doesn't use his name if he knows it.

"Yes. I suppose I was." He picks up the glass of water from the coffee table next to him and carries it over to his grandfather before returning to his sofa.

The old man shakily lifts the glass to his mouth, then pauses for a couple of long breaths, as though the exertion of drinking has exhausted him.

"That's one nice thing Charlotte's done then."

"She does lots of nice things."

His grandfather grunts the same disparaging laugh as before.

"So you want to know why 'I wanted you killed' as you put it? Right?"

"Yes."

"Why do you think I did, boy?" Art knows what his grandmother told him. He also knows that he needs to hear it from his grandfather. It's not a question he should have to answer.

"It doesn't matter what I think, it matters why you did. And you need to tell me."

"You've got your mother's directness, I'll give you that!" The laugh sounds a little more genuine this time. "OK... I'll tell you. It's simple. I wanted to save my daughter's life. There, I told you it was simple."

"By telling her to kill her child and kicking her out of her home? How is that saving her life?"

"Is she still alive?"

"What?"

"You heard me, boy. Is she still alive?" The words are spat out as venomously as his fragile condition will allow.

"Yes."

"Well, it worked then, didn't it?"

"Not entirely. I'm still alive too."

"And bully for you!... This was never about you. This was about saving your mother. Any idiot must realise that. You weren't even born. You weren't part of the equation... sometimes there is collateral damage when you fight to save something that needs to be saved. That's just the way the world goes, boy."

"So are you pleased I wasn't killed?"

Art's grandfather pauses for a moment and takes another sip of water.

"It's not a question I've ever thought about, boy. I'm pleased for Charlotte if you make her happy. And I'm pleased for you too. It was a long time ago." For Art it was a lifetime ago. Almost a lifetime he didn't have.

"Are you pleased you abandoned your daughter and kicked her out?" The old man flinches momentarily, but Art doesn't notice.

"I just did what I had to do, boy. If I hadn't done it, your mother would be dead now, and you... well you might be dead too. I saved her life. Maybe I saved yours too." That makes no sense to Art, but his grandfather seems to believe it. Maybe he has to.

"But..."

"No buts, boy." There is a no-nonsense dominance bursting through the brittle tones now. "Life is not easy. It's as simple as that, boy. The easy decision is not always the correct one, and I believe in correct decisions."

"But..."

"That is the end of this discussion, boy. You've got your answer... now it's my turn."

"What?"

"How is Charlotte? Is she happy?"

"I don't know. I've never asked her."

"Is there anyone looking after her now?"

"It's just the two of us. That's all we need."

The mocking laugh briefly raises its head again. "Come on, boy, I'm not stupid. I know what's going on. I know you've run away. You question me for abandoning her when I saved her life, but you're quite happy to abandon her yourself... I can't tolerate hypocrisy."

"It's different."

"Ha... it always is! Typical. Never any responsibility these days." He shakes his head slowly at Art. "And what is your mother doing with life? Is she working?"

"She's an escort."

"A what?!"

Art assumes this is a question he is meant to answer.

"Rich men pay to take her out for the evening and then pay more to have sex with her. Sometimes."

Art watches as his grandfather gets up from the sofa and turns to look out of the window. From behind he looks even smaller and frailer than from the front. He seems to be struggling to speak, but slowly he forms a sentence, with each word punctuated by a deep breath and a long pause.

"I... think... we're... done... here... now .... boy." He turns back towards his grandson and gestures towards the door. Art gets up and follows him. As they reach the hallway his grandfather's tone softens momentarily.

"You look after her, boy, won't you?" Art thinks about it. He will. He doesn't reply, so his grandfather continues. "I still care about her... deeply." He closes his eyes as though he is about to make a confession that will deeply embarrass him. "Let her know that I think about her every day if you ever go home, won't you?" Art won't.

They walk slowly in silence into the porch before Art asks a final question.

"Are you dying?"

"What?"

"Are you dying?"

"I heard what you said. Why on earth do you ask that?"

"I saw the letter on the sofa."

"How dare you read my private letters!"

"I didn't read it. I just saw it was from the cancer department."

"It's none of your business. I told you before. We're done here." He pushes his grandson lightly in the back to speed him toward the front door. Art barely notices it.

"Don't you want to see your daughter again before you die?"

"You've got a nerve, boy! You're in no position to tell anyone what to do... come on... Out!"

Art heads out of the front door without a goodbye and hears it slowly close behind him. He wasn't telling anyone what to do. He was asking a question.

Chapter Sixteen

Finn should be buzzing after the dress rehearsal of the play, but he's not. It went much better than he could have hoped for. Everyone performed well, the complicated scenery changes and special effects were all carried out seamlessly, and Martha even knew her lines. That saved him from an encounter he'd been dreading.

But as he walks up to the door of Charley's house, he is certainly not buzzing. Far from it. And he knows why now. Priya had been gushing with her praise of Martha's performance, and had said that the sadness and vulnerability she brought to her portrayal of Reagan had added a "beautiful, unexpected twist to a character often portrayed as confident, gung-ho and jingoistic." She was right. Martha was excellent, moving even. But the sadness was more than an act. Finn could tell that, and it worries him.

He knocks on Charley's door and she answers whilst talking on her mobile. She looks happier than he's seen her before. He's pleased to see that. It makes him realise how much he's been looking forward to "popping round for a cuppa" as she'd said in her message. She holds up her index finger to indicate she'll only be a minute and waves him inside.

"That's crazy... typical Art... uh huh... Thanks so much, Laura... no, no, I mean it, that's great... thanks." She talks as they walk through to the kitchen, then puts her phone in her pocket and instinctively launches towards Finn and embraces him. They both hold the pose for a few seconds in silence, neither fully aware how much they both need the reassurance of human contact, of knowing someone cares, of being close.

"Sorry... I couldn't help myself, Finn... I just... I'm just so relieved." She gently lets go, and takes both his hands in her own, waving them up and down in her excitement. "That was the P.I. She's found him again, Finn."

"Fantastic! I'm chuffed for you, Charley, I really am. Where is he? Let's go get him." Finn means it all, but he also wants to let this moment spread out for as long as possible. He wonders if it means so much because it's been so long since he's felt any closeness or if it's because it's Charley.

"No, Finn. We do nothing. I made that mistake last time."

"Eh? Sorry... I don't get it."

"I made us rush after him, so he disappeared... I should have known, I really should. Art has to do things on his own terms. You can't force him into anything he doesn't want to do... Believe me, I've tried." She is almost dancing now, lets go of Finn's hands and skips over to take a few things out of the fridge.

"Where is he?"

"You're not going to believe this, Finn, but he's sleeping in our shed now! He's almost home!"

"You're joking me? Just out there?" He turns his head to peer out into the garden.

"Yep!"

"So what do we do? We could just go out and get him now, couldn't we?... We can't just leave him, surely?" A lot of things are confusing him now.

"That's exactly what we do, Finn. I scared him away last time. I'm not doing that again. This time I'm going to make him want to come back... make him think it's his own decision... no, that's not fair on Art... make it his own decision." She puts a big casserole dish on the cooker and drizzles some olive oil in it, before chopping some onions, carrots, thyme and celery and throwing them all in.

"But..." Finn doesn't get the chance to finish his sentence.

"Do me a favour please... there's a pack of chicken thighs in the fridge... second shelf down, I think... might be the third though... could you get them out for me?"

Finn does as he's asked and manages to speak this time.

"I'm sorry, Charley. You've lost me." He feels like he's been asked to complete a particularly tough cryptic crossword without even knowing how many letters are in the answers. Not that he ever does cryptic crosswords. He's got neither the time nor the inclination. Maybe when he's older.

"No, no. I'm sorry, Finn. I know I'm probably making no sense, but it's clear to me now." She grabs a couple of cans of haricot beans out of a floor-level cupboard to the side of the cooker and carries on shooting rapid-fire explanations as she opens them. "I know where Art is now. I know he's near and I know he's safe. So I know I need to keep him there... there where he's safe." She pauses from opening the cans to stir the casserole dish and look at Finn. The little scar on his left cheek reminds her of the pain he's been going through in the last few years, though it's not responsible for any of it.

"Oooo...Kaaay. I sort of get it, Charley." The way he drags the words out makes it clear he needs more.

"I drove him away last time by going after him... I put him at more risk of harm, didn't I?"

"Well, it wasn't your..."

"It's OK, Finn, you don't need to." She holds a palm upwards to stop him. "I should have known that would happen. But I've got another chance, and it's even better. He's right here, so I'm not going to blow it this time. I'm going to let him think we don't know where he is, so he stays there until he's ready to come home... and in the meantime I'm going to make sure he's got what he needs to keep going?" She smiles and points at the casserole simmering away on the cooker. Finn had wondered why she was cooking so much. It seemed unlikely she would have a dinner party in the present circumstances. In reality, she never has dinner parties in any circumstances.

"How do you know he'll come back for that?"

"It's his favourite, chicken casserole is. But it's not just that, I know he's been back a few times, Finn. He thinks I don't, but I do... bless him, but Art is not the tidiest, most subtle person. He always leaves clues... footprints on the carpet, goldfish food put back in a different place, that sort of thing, so I always know. It's been my lifeline in all honesty."

"You're smart, Charley."

She blushes slightly and laughs. "I don't think you have to be smart to spot where Art has been! He can't help it... so if I make way too much casserole, I know he'll come back and have some, thinking that I won't notice any has gone. And most importantly I'll know he's getting fed properly until he comes back for good. Simple!"

"Definitely more like smart if you ask me!" He smiles, but only momentarily. "But how... no, don't worry."

"Go on, Finn. What were you going to say?"

"Well, I just... I don't really know how to say this."

"It's fine, I'd rather hear it."

"Well, how do you know he will come back for good? Sorry."

"No, that's fine, Finn. Good question... I know Art. I know that he always calms down eventually, whatever it is. This one may take longer than usual, but he will calm down eventually... But he'll never back down. He can't be wrong. It's just the way he is. So he'll wait until he finds a justification in his own mind, and then he'll come back."

"Wow!"

"I've had a lot of time to think about this since he left, and I've been up, down, all over the place. But I think I realised quite early on that he'd come back eventually, as long as nothing terrible happened to him... that was my biggest fear, Finn... that something..." she shivers her shoulders and shakes her head, "well, you know, something awful would happen to him and I'd never see him again... so now I know he's in our garden, I know he's safe. He's almost home, Finn." She walks over to him, plants a kiss on his forehead, then turns back to stir the casserole. "Tell you what, Finn, when this is ready, I don't suppose you'd want to go out for a quick drink or something?... give Art a chance to come in and eat."

"Sure. I'd love to."

Why is Mr James there? What's he doing in their house on a Sunday evening? Art peers through the little window in the garden shed and, even though it's beginning to get dark, the kitchen light is on so he can see exactly what's happening. He doesn't like it. Sunday evening has always been their time: him and his mum, sitting down watching a film with their dinners on their laps. It's the only time they eat in front of the TV, and he loves it.

They are hugging now. That's pathetic, embarrassing even. How old are they? They look like a couple of lovestruck teenagers. Don't they know that he is still missing? Don't they care?

Now she's holding his hands and they look like they're dancing. Who dances in their kitchen with a teacher? Especially a teacher whose daughter dumps people for no good reason. It's excruciating to watch. Maybe she's drinking again and doesn't know what she's doing? That wouldn't be surprising. It seems like the first thing she did when Art went away, was buy a bottle of vodka to celebrate. And it looks like she's not stopped. Maybe she's happier without him? He knows he's not happier without her.

She's got the massive pan out now, the one she only she gets out when Aunt Amanda and her family come round and she's cooking for loads of people. She must be having a party. How could she? Art is still missing and she's celebrating. It's horrible. She's changed. Or maybe she hasn't changed, she just used to lie about liking having Art around. It wouldn't be surprising, she's lied to him before.

She's put some chicken in the big pan now. Is she making chicken casserole? That's his dish, the one she makes on special occasions, like his birthday, her birthday, first day of the holidays, last day of the holidays, Christmas Day (Art prefers it to turkey), New Year's Day,

Easter, the May and August Bank Holidays and the days she feels guilty about something and wants to make him like her. She's asked him lots of times if he'd like to have something else for a change, but he doesn't. Chicken casserole is his favourite. Why would he want anything else?

But now she's making it for other people, lots of people, like it's not his special dish. There's loads in there. She must be having a party. Her son is missing and she's having a party. How could she? Is she some sort of monster?

She's laughing now. They both are... Oh no, she's just kissed him. That's disgusting. He's a teacher. You don't kiss teachers. Especially not when your only son is still missing.

Art can't watch any more. He sits on the floor of the shed looking up at the window where all he can see is the sky beginning to disappear into the night, and the reflection of the kitchen light on the shed window. After a while the light goes out, and he quietly opens the door, leaves the shed, and creeps up to the house for a closer look. No lights have come on upstairs, so he listens for noise from inside for a few minutes and calculates that they've gone out, before opening the back door and going into the kitchen.

She must be making the casserole in advance. The party must be another day. He takes one of the many plastic takeaway containers out of the cupboard above the bread bin, and starts ladling spoonfuls of chicken casserole into it with one of those big spoons that would make a good cereal spoon for a giant, but his mum uses to serve casserole or soup or any other dish with juice in. There's so much there, she won't notice a little bit has gone. She might spot the slops of liquid he spills on the cooker as he fills the container, but he doesn't. He cleverly rinses the massive spoon under the tap, dries it and puts it back in the drawer where he found it.

Leaving his food on the side, Art nips up to his room, turns on the light, feeds Llama, and says a few words.

"I can't stop, Llama. She could be back any minute, and my dinner'll get cold. I hope you're OK. I miss you. I still can't take you with me yet, I'm afraid, but hang in there, it won't be long, I hope. Will you keep an eye on mum for me please? She's doing some really odd things at the moment. I don't like it. Thanks. I'll be back soon. I'm nearby now, so it's much easier. Bye." Art knows that Llama will remember this. He's read that scientific research has proven that goldfish have much longer memories than the few seconds which people attribute to them. Most people don't know that though. They just believe what they're told. It's ridiculous how gullible some people are.

He heads downstairs, takes a knife and fork out the cutlery drawer, picks up the takeaway dish and heads back to his new home in the garden for dinner.

He deserves a proper hot meal. It's been a tough few days.

The freshly painted wall which supports the entrance gates to Sonnley AllRays Academy is the perfect spot for a painting. It's about seven feet high, seemingly designed to stop the students escaping or even being able to see that there is another world out there. And it's got a ready-made captive audience to view it every day, or every schoolday at least.

It's dark enough for the artist to be confident that they won't be spotted by people in the nearby houses, and it's Sunday evening so no one will be in the school, but it's still wise to act quickly. They've done this so much recently that they pride themselves on the speed at which they work, much like the people who change the tyres in a motor racing pit stop in more or less the time it takes the artist to decide which other TV channel they would rather be watching. But the artist works alone, so it's not that fast of course, and you wouldn't want to watch anything else if you saw it.

They open the large sports bag, take out all the tools they will need, and attach the first stencils to the wall. Then the spraying begins. They still have to be careful, it's a tricky job. Everything has to be done exactly right, the colours sprayed in the correct order using the relevant stencils. There's nothing worse for an artist's reputation than a botched painting and, unlike a canvas, they can't just throw it away and start again.

The artist finishes their work, packs away their materials back in the bag, and peers through their balaclava to check the results: Five schoolchildren in Sonnley AllRays Academy uniform are all grinning with uncontrollable joy as they stand in a hot air balloon surveying the world beneath. The balloon is a beautiful, vibrant, explosion of colours, skilfully emphasising the delight and excitement of the children on board. On the ground, a plump, balding middle-aged man in a tuxedo and a black bow tie is holding a bow and looking smug. The arrow he has fired is about to make contact with the balloon, and the audience's imagination can do the rest. The caption *Everything can change in an instant* is written underneath the balloon with the usual Neola signature below it.

"Oi, you little fucking toe rag, I've gotcha now." The anger in the man's voice is matched by the force with which he grabs the artist round the neck from behind. He moved his family to Sonnley so that his son, Dan, could get a good education at what was supposed to be one of the country's best state schools. He didn't give up the trappings of London life for a town where hooligans vandalise property with no consequences; where councillors ignore his complaints about wasting money on homes for the mentally handicapped; where some teacher's daughter gives his son ridiculous unrealistic dreams of believing he can be a rock star, which he never will be.

All the disappointment and rage at the decision to uproot are channelled into this moment. He can see that the toe rag is a bit taller than him, and certainly a lot younger. But he's got the advantage. He's attacked him from behind. With his arm round the toe rag's neck, the man drags him backwards so that he topples to the ground where the man sits on top of him and starts punching him in the face.

The artist is not a toe rag. But he has a rage of his own too, and he is stronger than the man. It is the first time in his life that he has realised that he can fight back against adults with an equal, let alone superior strength. He grabs the man's arms and pushes him off, then hits him several times in the face with a force that can only come from years of repressed anger.

The man lies on the floor, his eyes swelling already, and blood oozing from both his nose and his mouth. The artist stops punching and stares at the man on the ground next to him, listening to his weird wheezing, moaning sound, wondering how it came to this. Maybe no one else ever really knows why people end up like they are, but there is usually a reason. There certainly is for both the artist and the man.

The artist turns away to get up and leave the scene, only to feel the sharp fingernails of the man digging into the side of his face and tugging at the balaclava. Before he can react, his disguise has been pulled off, and the artist and the man are staring face-to-face into each other's eyes.

"No... no, it can't be... no fucking way." The man's voice is simultaneously enraged and defeated, like his whole existence.

Chapter Seventeen

We are taught to feel lucky if we have a job: appreciate the fact that we are able to earn money, buy food, pay for trips out, look after our family if we have one; understand that there are millions, no billions, of people around the world who can't even access the bare essentials which we take for granted; enjoy the luxuries which our salaries allow us to do. And that is all true, of course. But what happens when that job saps the soul which is the very core of our existence, and drains the energy and joy which make life fun and worth living?

We feel guilty and ungrateful. That's what happens. And Tommy Moore knows that better than anyone. He has just got back from another day he has hated at AllRays Software. It's a Monday, so he knows there are four more days to dread this week. He knows he shouldn't feel like that. He knows he is lucky. He knows that there are so many people worse off than him. So he just feels guilty, and ungrateful.

He sits down on the sofa in the empty living room. Priya is still at school, probably another play rehearsal or something, and the kids are doing whatever they do in their rooms. He is exhausted. The mental effort of eight hours pretending to be happy, faking an interest in work that he despises, and handling the stresses of the actual work itself have all taken their toll. Like they do every day. He wants to have a drink. He knows he shouldn't, it's only Monday. He picks up his iPad searching for something to distract his mind from the guilt and self-hatred which is overwhelming him, but is only seconds in when the doorbell rings. He waits for one of the kids to answer it. They don't. It rings again, so he has to get up this time.

"Tommy... please... Rosa's gone off again." Mel looks even more drained than him, like she has not just reached the end of her tether, but has got it wrapped round her neck and it is slowly wringing the last vestiges of life out of her.

"It's OK, Mel. Please, don't worry. We'll find her." Tommy smiles as kindly as his own exhaustion and desire to go back and sit on the sofa will allow. He puts on some shoes, shouts upstairs to the children, who aren't listening, to let them know he's going out and steps out into the early evening sunshine with his neighbour.

"How long has she been gone?"

"I don't know, Tommy... I was doing a bit of gardening. She was happy in the front room, listening to some music, and when I came in, she was gone." The panic in Mel's tone betrays her belief that this is all her fault.

"It's OK, Mel. We'll find her. How about I head off towards the park and you go towards the shops?"

"OK... thanks, Tommy... I'm sorry... You're kind." That is the last thing Tommy thinks he is, but he's always been good at pretending. Once, when Tommy had dressed up as a clown and put on a show at Mia's 5th birthday party, Priya had hugged him, squeezed his clown's nose and told him he should have been an actor. He is.

Tommy and Mel head off in different directions, and he jogs up the leafy roads heading towards Marsh Park, diverting down each side road as he encounters it, and calling Rosa's name. A couple of people stop to ask him if he has lost his dog, and seem less interested when he explains the truth.

After barely five minutes, he spots her about fifty yards away. She is standing outside a front garden with some freshly-picked flowers in her hand being shouted at by a man of about Tommy's age. Tommy starts running towards the scene.

Up ahead, Rosa is holding the flowers in her right hand. They are beautiful flowers, which she has just picked herself from this wonderful garden. Her lovely Mel will be so pleased. She deserves them. She is so special, and Rosa loves her so much.

But this man is shouting and being rude and cruel. Why is he doing that? She is only picking flowers for her wife. Doesn't he ever pick flowers for his partner? Probably not. He probably hasn't even got a partner. Who would want a nasty man who screams and shouts like he does as a partner?

Rosa can't wait to take the flowers home and give them to Mel. The colours are wonderful: red, yellow, and some small purple ones. It will light up Mel's day, let her know how much her little Rosa loves her. But she can't get away. The shouty man is trying to block her way. He's horrible. He should go and pick his own flowers if he wants them.

And now another man is running towards them. Is he going to shout at her too? This is too much for Rosa. She pushes past the first man and runs as best she can in the other direction across the road, away from the shouty man and the other man running towards them.

As Tommy nears the scene, he sees Rosa run into the road, just as a small red car comes careering away from the park, clearly doing over the thirty miles per hour speed limit. There is nothing Tommy can do. He hears the noise first, the desperate screeching of the brakes to no avail, followed by the sickening thud of impact, the brief ear-shattering scream which will haunt him forever, and then the silence. Probably only a couple of seconds or so, but the silence overwhelms everything and reverberates around the entire town. The birds seem to have stopped singing out of respect for Rosa. They remember her as she used to be, so full of life, love and joy: all the things which Tommy wishes he was full of.

By the time he reaches the accident, the man who was shouting is on his phone calling an ambulance, and the driver is out of the car screaming hysterically. She is probably only in her early twenties, and has certainly never killed anyone before.

Tommy crouches down on the road next to Rosa and holds her hand. It is still warm, though he knows it won't be for long.

"Mel loves you so much, Rosa. We all do. You show us how life can be. Thank you... thank you... thank you." She can't hear him, but he needs to say it.

Tommy blames himself. If he hadn't sprinted towards Rosa, she wouldn't have run into the road. He hates himself for it. But this isn't about him. It's about Rosa. It's about Mel. Poor Mel. She needs to know. She needs to see her little Rosa one last time, say goodbye.

Tommy picks up his phone and dials.

The light is fading fast over Sonnley, as though a shining beacon has finally been extinguished, and a shroud of gloom has engulfed the town. Maybe it has. Art sits on a swing in the Marsh Park playground thinking. There is no one else around, the noisy children who ruin the park in the day should all be safely tucked up in bed by now. He wishes he were too. Running away is tiring, and after a while it gets boring, lonely even. Art's had enough of it. He wants to go home, but he can't, can he? Nothing has changed. He rocks gently back and forward, building up a repetitive rhythm: what to do? what to do?

"Well, well, well, who have we got here then? If it isn't the missing Arf a Mann!" It's difficult to tell which comes first, the familiar threatening tone or the first big push in the arch of his back which propels Art out of his comfort zone, higher than he ever goes. But it doesn't really matter, either way he knows this spells trouble.

What kind of a phrase is 'if it isn't'? If he weren't so scared, he would be challenging it. What's wrong with 'it is'? It's a much simpler way of saying the same thing. No one would ever say 'if it isn't a much simpler way of saying the same thing'.

Art wants to slow down, he wants to get off, he wants to be back home, safe. But as the shoving continues and he soars skywards, he can't even turn round to see his pusher. Not that he needs to, or even wants to.

"I'm sorry, Mek. I... I didn't mean to hurt you." He wouldn't usually lie, but he's not stupid, whatever the teachers think.

"Do these things go all the way round?" It's actually a question Art has asked himself many a time before, but he doesn't want to find out the answer now. He grips tightly to the side chains which are keeping him in place, until his knuckles are as white as the moon he sees directly above him on the upward motions. A children's swing is meant to be a safe place, not somewhere he should fear for his life.

He expects to see the key moments of his sixteen years flashing before him in his mind. That's what happens when people are dying apparently: the time he was pushed over in playgroup for not wanting to kick a ball with another boy; the first day at school, feeling abandoned, when all he wanted to do was go home; when his primary school teacher told him to stop rocking on his chair and sit still, and everyone laughed at him at the end of the lesson when he didn't get up to leave; the day the first Llama came home; the first time he was told off for a history essay; the day the second Llama came home; the day he found out about his mum and she ruined his life.

But none of them do. All that happens is the swing starts slowing down, until it is barely moving and Art is face-to-face with Mek, who has walked round to the front. If anything, this is more terrifying than the thought of the swing going all the way round. He looks down at the playground floor, which is supposedly designed to stop children hurting themselves when they fall over. It doesn't look that comfortable. He doesn't want to end up lying on it any time soon.

"No one's ever hit me before, have they?" It's a ridiculous question, which Art obviously does not know the answer to.

"Sorry.... Er I mean, I'm not sorry that no one has ever hit you before... that's good. I'm sorry that I hit you." Art is relieved he clarified, though Mek makes no reference to it.

"I'm the one who hits other people, right?"

"Right." That is certainly true.

"Why do you always look at your feet?" Art is actually looking at the ground, not his feet.

"I'm not always... sometimes maybe, but not always." The clarification is important. People often make sweeping generalised statements which are not true. It's annoying.

Art looks up from the ground and raises his head as far as Mek's chest. He doesn't want to go further. That is frightening enough.

"You going to get off that thing then?"

"Er... yes, OK." Art waits for the swing to stop completely, then steps off so that the difference in size is clear. At five foot eleven and a quarter inches, he's not small for his age, but it's like a flyweight boxer being thrown into a ring with the heavyweight world champion.

"Are you scared?"

"Yes."

Mek starts laughing. Why is it funny to be scared?

"Why?" It should be obvious, but Art spells it out anyway.

"Because I think you might hurt me."

"Why would I do that?"

"Because I hit you."

"Yes, you did, didn't you?" He is still laughing. It is difficult to see what the joke might be. "Are you a tough man, Arfa?"

"No."

"So was it a good idea to hit me?"

"No."

"Are you going to look at me, in the eyes, like a man?" The laughing has stopped now. Art lifts his head a bit further so that he is looking at Mek's chin. Even that looks strong and menacing, and is covered in black stubble which makes him look much older than he is.

"Sorry."

"I said look at me... in the eyes." The words are louder this time. There is no choice. Art peers up at the boy mountain's eyes and has time to notice they are blue before he has to look away again. Mek laughs again, shakes his head from side to side, and carries on.

"You're a fucking weirdo, Arfa... two pisses short of a bog flush." Art has no idea what that means, but doesn't get the chance to ask. "You told anyone what happened?"

"No."

"Good."

"Well, sorry, actually I did tell my mum, but no one else, honestly."

"Your mum, eh? How is she? Oh no, you don't know, do you? You've run away, haven't you?"

"Yes." Art can smell the aftershave as Mek lowers his head towards his. Why does he wear aftershave if he doesn't seem to shave? It makes no sense. In fact, the only thing which makes sense is that Art is scared and is shaking as a result. He doesn't want to be here. He doesn't want to get killed. He wants his old life back, where the likes of Mek didn't even know who he was.

"My mum's Italian, well her parents were, you know?" Art could not possibly know this, so lets Mek carry on. "And if anyone slagged her off, I'd do what you did, wouldn't I?"

"Yes." While he couldn't know that for sure, he would certainly have guessed it.

Mek pulls his head away and smiles, though Art doesn't see it.

"I like you, Arfa... OK, you're a fucked-up weirdo, but I like you, don't I? Coz you're the only person who's ever hit me, and that takes guts, doesn't it? You were protecting your mum, and I like that, don't I?"

"It sounds like it."

"So we're good now, aren't we? As long as you keep your gob shut about it to everyone else, eh?"

"Yes. Of course." Art is not sure if he is meant to keep quiet about what really happened when he hit Mek, or the fact that they are 'good'. He'll do both, just in case, if it means that he won't have to experience the overwhelming terror of the last few minutes. He won't even ask what it is that they are both good at. If he doesn't know then he is unlikely ever to say anything about it to anyone by accident.

"Go on then, aren't you going to fuck off?" Mek nods his head in the direction of the playground exit, then sits down on the swing himself.

"Yes... thanks." Art starts walking towards the exit. He wants to run, but is not sure exactly what pace "fuck off" needs, so plays it safe.

"One more thing, Arfa, eh?" Art has only taken about five paces, when the call comes. He turns round and looks at the ground below the swing. "You wrote that weirdo play, didn't you?"

"Sort of... I wrote the story it is based on, not the actual play itself." If it's a weirdo play, it's because they've taken liberties with his story.

"Well, it's good, isn't it?"

The words should probably mean more if a history teacher had said them. But they wouldn't.

People like to have someone to blame. It makes things easier to understand. The thought that something terrible might just have happened is too difficult to deal with. And Mel blames herself. She is staring at the floral tributes to her wife, which have already appeared at the scene. Faith is at her side with her arm clasped firmly round Mel's shoulders, as if it is the only thing stopping her collapsing in a heap on the pavement. Maybe it is? The morning sky is dark, in stark contrast to the sunshine of the past few days. They barely notice the light constant drizzle which is much wetter than it would look through a window.

Why did she leave her little Rosa alone in the house for so long while she was gardening? Why wasn't she there to protect her when the man shouted at her? Why did she love flowers so much that, even in her confused state, Rosa was picking some for her? Why did she resent the way Rosa had changed with the illness? Why does she feel such a sense of relief that Rosa has gone? Why did she see a bit of time on her own in the garden as a well-earned break from caring for the love of her life when she needed her? How could she ever have had those fleeting thoughts that life would be easier and better for them both when Rosa had passed? What is wrong with her? Nothing could be worse or harder than this.

Mel looks at the cards and the flowers in front of her. She can't face reading any of the tributes. Not today. It's too soon. As the splatters of rain wash away the words, and soften the cards, it will soon be too late. The flowers are a beautiful, vivid explosion of colour, just like Rosa herself. They all look grey.

"She was my life, you know?"

"I know." Faith pulls her friend in tighter and squeezes her shoulder.

"What am I going to do without her? I've got nothing, Faith, nothing without my little Rosa."

They stand in silence for a few seconds, the drizzle falling off their hair and tracking its way down their faces before tumbling to the ground, where it will rest for a while until it evaporates back into the atmosphere to be turned back into a cloud and the cycle will start again.

"*Don't be anxious for tomorrow, for tomorrow will be anxious for itself. Each day's own evil is sufficient.*" Faith speaks slowly, not preaching, just trying to help.

"Bible?"

"Matthew Chapter six Verse thirty four... it says it better than I ever could. Don't worry about the future, Mel, allow yourself to grieve, let yourself deal with that for now. The future will take care of itself." She gently lifts her other hand and wipes some of the water away from Mel's eyes.

"Rosa used to love your bible quotes, you know? She used to say 'I bet Faith's got a quote for that', whenever something would happen, good or bad... she didn't mean it in a bad way, wasn't being nasty, she was just... she was just being Rosa."

"I know, Mel, I know. She was probably right, mind!" Faith watches a faint smile briefly creep across her friend's face. It's a start.

"She loved you, Faith, you know that, don't you?"

"Of course I do. She loved everyone... well, except the ones she hated of course!" There's a little chuckle this time, short but clearly audible.

"I wish she could see all this, Faith." Mel waves an arm in the direction of the flowers and the sogging cards. "She'd love the fuss, relish every single one of them!"

"She surely would!"

They stare in silence at the tributes for a few seconds more.

"I should have been there for her, Faith. I can't bear the thought of her being shouted at, terrified, confused."

"You were always there for her, Mel, and her for you. That's why you're so special together."

"Thanks." Faith feels an involuntary shudder whistle across Mel's shoulders.

"It's wet and cold... how about we go back and have a cuppa, eh?"

"OK. Thanks, Faith."

They walk back towards Mel's house, which is only Mel's house now. It feels so empty already.

As she opens the door into the living room, Mel longs to see the welcoming face of her wife, grinning crazily and leaping up to welcome her home. But she doesn't. As she stares at the empty sofa, where Rosa would sit, all she can picture is the confused, sometimes anxious old woman which the illness had created, asking her 'where's Mel?' And she feels an overwhelming wave of relief surge over her, pierced only by the sharp arrows of guilt.

Faith goes into the kitchen to make the tea, so Mel crouches down facing Rosa's seat on the sofa, and buries her face in the cushion which she always had tucked in behind her.

"Where's my little Rosa?" she whispers.

Chapter Eighteen

Song:

*All of my life I've wanted
To belong
I wanted to be right sometimes but
I was always wrong.*

*When the sun went out,
When the stars refused to shine,
When the nights were dark and the days were too
And there was nothing left to look forward to,
I was out of time, I was out of time.*

*All the dreams that I used to have
Have drifted away.
Fear and dread from the moment I wake
Are all I've got these days.*

*When the sun went out,
When the stars refused to shine,
When the nights were dark and the days were too
And there was nothing left to look forward to,
I was out of time, I was out of time.*

And when the light goes out on me
I will rue this missed opportunity.
But I never worked out how to play the game
And when I reached a point when every day was pain,
I was out of time, I was out of time.

Martha's excitement as she walks over to Dan's house surprises her. Not because she doesn't get excited, but because it's only been six days since she split from Art, and she still feels there was a special connection there. She misses him. But today she's focused on her new song, and she's singing it to herself as she makes the short walk in the late afternoon Sonnley sunshine. She wrote it a few weeks ago, on one of those days when everything seems too much and all she can see is the pain and despair which overwhelms her. She's no idea where they come from or where they go, but they haven't come today, so she can be excited.

She's looking forward to telling Dan about the *everything can change in an instant* graffiti on the school walls too. He won't have seen it yet, as he's been off all week, and he tries to keep away from social media these days after the pain it's caused him. So she'll be the one to break it to him, and that always feels good. It's like telling your friends about a bit of a gossip or a celebrity death before they have heard. It shouldn't matter that you knew before them, but it does.

The new graffiti has been the main conversation piece at school this week, relishing the defiance, trying to guess who did it. And for Martha, it has become a bit of an obsession. It has to be someone close to her, she knows that, and that adds to the excitement. It's her family's phrase, and she's only ever spoken of it with a couple of other people. Her dad wouldn't do it, surely? No, he must think Martha did it, but he'd never challenge her about it. And Johnson, well he's kept his artistic talents superbly hidden a whole lifetime if it is, not to mention discovering a rebellious streak which she thought was hers alone in the James family. She hopes it is Johnson, in truth. She would love to see him sticking two fingers up at the status quo, stop being the golden boy for a while.

After school, Martha had popped home, grabbed her guitar and the bin bag full of letters. At the time she hadn't been sure if she should dump them back in a bin or drop them off at Art's mum's house. The first option would be easier, the second kinder. She had taken a detour past the house still undecided, hoping that it would somehow help her decide. And it had. She had seen the front window plastered with the posters begging for news of Art, and had dumped the bin bag on the doorstep. She wouldn't be seeing Art again, so he wouldn't get the chance to have a go at her about it. It wasn't much of a consolation.

"What the fuck's happened to you? That's why you haven't been in school this week, right?" As Dan opens the door, it's impossible to miss the swollen lip and the cut under his left eye. Or maybe not impossible. Art would have done. She knows that.

Dan holds his left index finger to his mouth to silence her and marches them both quickly up to his room. Once inside he closes the door, and they both sit down on his bed.

"Well, Danny boy, go on... what happened?" Martha is laughing. This could be good.

"Aah it's nothing... just got in a bit of scrap... nothing much... you said you had a new song. You going to play..."

"Whoah. Stop right there! I need more info than that! Who was it?"

"Nah, it was nothing. Seriously." He starts to open her guitar bag and pulls out the second-hand acoustic which her dad had bought her as a present when they had first moved to Sonnley.

"Come on... like spit it out. I need details!"

"Nah, really, Mar... nothing to say." He tries to hand her the guitar, but she pulls both hands behind her back.

"I'm not playing until I get some details. Come on Danny boy!"

"OK... but you don't tell anyone, right?"

"Yeah. Sure... go on."

"It was my dad."

"What the fuck?!" Martha reaches into her pocket for her phone. "I'm calling the police."

"No, Mar, it's not like that... I hit him too."

"You hit your dad!! Fucking legend!" Martha laughs. She's never liked Dan's dad.

"I don't feel like a fucking legend."

"What happened? Why?"

"It was nothing really. I was doing something he didn't like and it just kind of kicked off... you know." Martha can't imagine hitting her own dad. He would back down before it ever got to that.

"What were you doing?"

"Just... oh it doesn't matter, let's get on."

"No Dan. It does matter. What were you doing?"

"Oh... just doing something in a place he didn't like."

"You might as well tell me straight, Dan. You know I'll get it out of you in the end!"

He takes a deep breath and stares straight at his ex.

"OK. I painted something he didn't like in a place he thought I shouldn't. OK!" He raises his voice, trying to end the conversation. It all makes sense to Martha now.

"No fucking way... Woah! You're fucking Neola, aren't you? I didn't even know you could draw a stickman!"

"Shh." He doesn't need to say that. No one is going to hear. He's at the top of the house, the windows are closed. He hasn't been near his dad since it happened, and has only seen his mum when she's popped meals up to him when it's just been the two of them in the house.

"You really are a fucking legend, Dan!" Martha is rocking back and forward with laughter now.

"It's not funny, Mar. I'm screwed."

"I can't get over it... you're Neola! Wow! Nice one, Dan!... I'm just... wow... what made you start doing that?"

"I just needed to, Mar... simple as that. You've got your music, and you're great at that, you really are. But, let's not kid ourselves, I'm shit at it. I'm not going to be a musician. I know that. We both know that."

"No, that's not..."

"Come on, Mar. We both know why I want to keep the band going. Let's not mess about."

"Eh?"

'It's the only way I get to see you, isn't it? So I've got to keep doing it."

Martha doesn't know what to say. She picks up her guitar and plays her new song, *Out of Time*, wondering if you can ever really know anyone as much as you think you do. Dan sits beside her on the bed, watching the fingers of her left hand effortlessly shifting between the chords, the pain of his injuries overshadowed by the pain in his heart.

"That was great, Mar, really great."

"Thanks, Dan."

"It says exactly how I feel too, you know." Martha does know. She knows that Dan is hurting. He always is. But she doesn't want to go down this route: the "we're different from everyone else", "we're two of a kind", "we share something that no one else can ever understand" route. She knows where that ends up.

"Your paintings are special, Dan. I wish you realised how good you are."

"Thanks, Mar." He turns his head away from her and buries it in his hands, so that all she can see is his long blond hair tumbling down over his face, trying to give him the protection he's always desperately needed. "Listen... I'm sorry, Mar."

"Sorry? Why? What's up?"

"I've treated you like shit... screamed at you when you've said you wouldn't get back together, all that kind of stuff... I'm so sorry... it won't happen again, I promise."

Martha feels the muscles in her arms tightening, as if bracing for an incoming onslaught. She hears his words, and she knows that's what people say. She also knows that it's not usually true. He may mean it now, but it won't stop it happening again. It's all clear now. She's not scared of Dan, she never has been. He's weak, pathetic and powerless. She doesn't hate him, she feels sorry for him. He's lost, lonely and scared too. Maybe that's what drew her to him in the first place? She doesn't know. But she knows it doesn't draw her to him now.

She picks up her guitar and puts it back in its brown travel bag. Dan is still beside her on the bed, with his head in his hands. He knows it's over now. They both do.

"Keep going with the art, eh, Dan? You're good, I mean it, really good." She gets up from the bed and walks over to the door.

"Bye, Mar, sorry."

"Yeah, bye, Dan. Take care. Maybe see you around sometime?" They both know she doesn't mean it.

"What's wrong with me, Finn?" Charley Mann looks up from the glass of sparkling water she has just taken a sip from. It's a beautiful early evening, as though Sonnley were now on a completely different continent to the one with the cold, grey drizzle of yesterday. She has spent most of the day sat inside reading her way through the hundreds of letters and cards in the bin bag she found on her doorstep. She would have gone in the garden, but that would have left Art with no escape route from the shed, and she doesn't want him feeling cornered.

"What are you talking about? There's nothing wrong with you, Charley! You're wonderful." Finn's response is more open than he'd intended, but he couldn't stop it. He shifts his head slightly so as not to catch her eyes, and looks over at the bridge which links Sonnley residents to a world of possibilities. The Boathouse pub is busy, as it always is on a warm summer evening, but they still managed to find a garden table which they don't have to share with anyone else.

"You're kind, Finn, you really are. But let's face it, I just seem to drive people away."

"You don't!"

"I do, Finn. I've been reading the letters from my mum I told you about, and it's all clear now."

"What's clear?"

"Well... first of all I was angry, thinking what's she doing writing all these letters and not sending them... All she had to do was reach out to me, her daughter... I don't know, come round, whatever. But she didn't. She just wrote these letters saying how much she loves me and Art and thinks of us all the time. And then didn't even send them."

"But that's not your fault."

"No Finn, it's not... but would you ever do that to one of your children? Cut them out of your life." Charley drums her fingers on the table, the rhythm helping her thoughts march in orderly, flowing steps to the conclusion they have reached.

"Of course not, Charley... but that doesn't make it your fault."

She takes another sip of her water, more through habit than need.

"So what is it about me that makes my own parents abandon me?... and makes my son run away?... I've never even had a proper boyfriend, Finn... well not since I was fourteen, and you can't count that."

"It's not you, Charley, it really isn't, believe me." He pushes his right hand forward across the table so that it rests on top of her left one and looks straight into her eyes this time.

"Thanks, Finn, but you don't have to say it. I drive people away... I don't mean to, but I do. There's something wrong with me."

"Please Charley, enough of this. Please! You don't drive people away... Look I'm here, aren't I?" He instantly knows that was a very poor attempt to lighten the mood, but she squeezes his hand anyway.

"Thanks, Finn, you're kind. You just don't know me well enough to be driven away yet, I guess!" The flippancy only accentuates her sense of isolation.

"I'd like to." He takes her right hand in his other, "I really would."

"But would you, Finn? Would you really?"

"Yes."

"I'd like that too, but it wouldn't work."

"Why not, Charley. You can't not try things because you think you'll fail. Believe me, I know."

"You know how I earn a living, don't you?" Her face reveals everything: a collage of hope, weary resignation and level-headed pragmatism.

"Yeah, of course I do... that's... that's not a problem." The slight hesitation in his voice seems to say otherwise.

"Isn't it, Finn? Are you sure? In my experience the most liberal people are only liberal when it doesn't directly affect them... you must have seen it... the open-minded, kind people who fight for more help and better facilities for drug addicts or ex-prisoners, until they start housing them next door."

"I'm not like that, Charley."

"I know, Finn. I'm not saying you are. But you haven't lived the reality of it yet. You don't know how you'd react."

"We can try... surely, we can give it a go, can't we? Please."

"I like you, Finn, I really do. I'd love us to... but could you... how shall I put this... whatever you think now, could you really put up with going out with someone who sleeps with other men for money?"

Finn looks down at the half-empty pint glass on the table in front of him.

"Er... sure... yeah... I could." He looks up triumphantly like someone who has just solved a Rubik's Cube for the first time. "Or I'm sure we could make do with my wage for a bit until you find something else you want to do."

Charley squeezes his hands again, and exhales slowly.

"I think you've answered my question, Finn. I don't want to live off your wages; I don't want to find a new job. Why should I?... I get it now. Everyone always wants to change me. It's their problem, not mine. There's nothing wrong with me."

"I'm sorry, Charley... you're right, I'm sorry. I wasn't thinking."

"Sadly, that's exactly what you were doing." She gently lifts up her right hand, which is still holding his left, and kisses the back of his one. "I'm not angry, Finn... it's just the way it is."

Art has pretty much perfected the skill of knowing when his mum goes out now. He enters through the back door as usual, carries out the normal checks to ensure he's alone and walks up to his bedroom to feed his goldfish. He is holding the little notebook his mum had given him all those years ago to record his feelings, and which now contains his grandparents' address but nothing else.

"I don't like this, Llama. It's not comfortable in the shed, and it's boring. I wish I could come home, but I can't, can I? I'm not angry with mum any more... well not as angry anyway. But that doesn't mean I can come home, does it? It'll look like I was wrong if I do, won't it?" He watches the fish, oblivious to the worries of the world, just focusing on the moment, happily pecking away at the food Art has just sprinkled into the bowl. If only life were that simple.

Art looks at his greatest inventions poster. Charles Macintosh invented the mackintosh waterproof fabric in 1823. It's no surprise that he was British. Art could have done with some of his waterproof fabric whilst he's been away. It must be fun being an inventor. No one thinks inventors are stupid. Even William Congreve, Samuel

Colt and Hiram Maxim, who are on the poster for inventing the military rocket, the revolver and the automatic machine gun.

He picks up a pen from beside the goldfish bowl, then tears a blank page out of his notebook, and sits down on his bed, using the notebook to support the single piece of paper while he writes on it.

Hi mum. I am OK and I hope you are doing OK too. I know that the play of my history essay is on this weekend, so I hope you will enjoy it and be proud of me. Love Art.

He walks out to his mum's room and puts the note on his mother's pillow, before returning to his own room. The bed looks so comfy. He lies down for a few seconds to feel the cosiness of the pillow and breathe in the familiar smell of the freshly-washed sheets. He's missed these. He has never had any trouble getting to sleep on this bed, it's so snug and relaxing. And he doesn't today.

It's only the sound of the front door opening that wakes him up. For a few seconds Art surveys the surroundings he knows so well, content in his peace. But only for a few seconds. He knows he needs to get out before she spots him. He hears her walking up the stairs, into the bathroom and closing the door behind her. This is his chance. He races as quickly as he can out of the room, downstairs, and out of the back door back to the discomfort of the shed. It is dark and getting cold now, not like his bedroom.

Art's mum hears the unmistakable reassuring noise she has often compared to an elephant jumping off a wall. She knows that there is only one person who can make it when they go downstairs. And she knows that he's gone again. But she knows he's been back and that's another small step. Hopefully it won't be long now till he stays.

She heads downstairs, locks the back door which he had left open, and pours herself a glass of tap water, which she takes up to her bedroom. She finds the note on her pillow and reads it over and over. She lies down on her back and stares up at the white ceiling above, until her tears turn it into a misty white blur. Art says he hopes that she's OK. She's relieved, she's sad, she's tired, she's angry even. But is she OK? It's getting difficult to tell.

Chapter Nineteen

"Showtime!" Priya tries a poor American accent as she walks into the kitchen where her husband and oldest child are sitting in silence at the table, Nina looking at her phone and working her way through a bowl of cereal, Tommy eating a piece of toast and staring at his iPad. Nina doesn't look up but shakes her head, in the way that only teenagers can, to highlight how embarrassing their parents are.

"I've got a very good feeling today, Nina. We're going to win, the play's going to be a success, Marsh Park is going to be saved!"

"Sure, mum, whatever." Nina takes her last mouthful of cereal, then gets up, leaving her bowl on the table. "You're right about the football bit, though. We're going to win." She clenches her fist in a victory celebration and waves it at her mum as she heads out of the room.

"We need to leave in half an hour, right, Nee?"

"Sure."

Priya picks the empty bowl off the table and puts it in the dishwasher.

"Are you going to come along, love?" She wishes she could detect the same sort of belief in her husband.

"Er... I'm not sure... I'm..."

"Come on, Tommy. This is Nina's big day! Biggest game of the season. It'll mean a lot to her if you're there."

"I doubt it."

"Tommy, stop it. You know it will."

He doesn't know that. He just knows that the idea of standing on the side of a football pitch making smalltalk with other parents, pretending everything is great, is too much to contemplate at the moment.

"I want to, Pri... more than I can say, I want to be there."

"Good. Thanks."

"Hang on, I've not finished. I want to be there, I just... I just don't know if I can face it." He gets up from the table and puts his plate in the dishwasher, rearranging the other contents as he does so. Priya always puts the bowls on the top level, where the glasses are meant to go, as if it's not important.

"Come on, Tommy. You can't just opt out of everything. It's no good for you, and it's not fair on Nina."

He often wishes he could opt out of everything, once and for all. Maybe they would all be better off.

"I said I want to be there, Pri, more than anything... It's just been such a crap week at work, I'm tired, I'm not sure I can do it."

"You can't just keep making excuses, Tommy. If you won't get help, you won't get better, so is this it forever?" Priya doesn't mean to sound as irritated as she does. It never helps. But it's not always easy to hide. She picks up the half full glass of orange juice which Nina has abandoned, drains it so as not to waste anything, then puts it on the bottom shelf of the dishwasher.

"You don't understand, Pri. It's OK for you. You don't feel like this." He moves the glass to the top level, and faces his wife. Priya knows this look well. His bottom lip quivers, and his eyes are defeated and pleading, searching for something to drag him out of his pain. She wants to hug him, let him know that everything is going to be alright. But there's no point. She's tried that so many times before, and it doesn't work.

"You're right, Tommy. I don't understand, I don't feel like you do. I'm glad I don't, and I wish you didn't, with all my heart. But I do understand what it would mean to Nina to have her dad watching her for the biggest game of her footballing life. She wants you there, I want you there, come on Tommy."

He plucks an enamel pan, which should never have been in there, out of the dishwasher and starts washing it up in the sink.

"Like I say, you don't understand. You don't feel like this. No one else does."

"What's the point, JJ?"

Johnson looks up from the frying pan as his sister walks into the kitchen wearing one of her dad's old white t-shirts with the fading words *Dance till you're dad* emblazoned across the front. She has no idea he was given it by her mum when they first found out they'd be parents.

"Like the point of life, everything. This, us, everything." She gestures around the kitchen then points at her brother.

"Is that another line from your play?"

"No."

"Holy shit, sis. What the fuck?!" Johnson flips a couple of pieces of bacon in the pan. It was a heavy night last night, he could have done with the restorative powers of a fry up before having to deal with this. He pats his right hand on the side of Martha's left arm. "Are you OK? What's up? Is it pre-performance nerves?"

"No, JJ. I've just been thinking. What's the point of it all?"

"That's heavy shit, you know, sis! What's up? What's happened?"

"It's just a question, that's all. I want to know what you think." Her voice is quiet and monotone. It doesn't sound like she's messing about.

"You want to know what I think? Wow, that's a first!" He tries to lighten the tone, bring back the usual bickering little sister he likes.

"I'm serious, JJ. What do you think?"

Johnson gently nudges some mushrooms in the pan with a plastic fish slice to make space for the egg which he cracks into the vacant area.

"OK... I think it's about who we are, how we live, making the most of everything we do... relishing the moment, I guess. It's about the big things, you know, the tennis tournaments for me, the music, the play for you... and it's also about all the little things, the drinks with friends, the songs which make us feel alive, the people we meet, the places we go, the fun we have." He points with the fish slice at the frying pan. "And most of all at the moment, it's about stuffing this lot in my face and loving every fucking moment of it!"

"Do you want to be a tennis coach all your life then, JJ?"

He starts flipping the food out of the pan onto the plate he's got ready beside it.

"No, you know I don't."

"So what do want to do then?"

"I want to sit down and eat my breakfast!" He sees that Martha doesn't find the answer as funny as he does, so turns off the gas under the pan, stops serving and looks directly at her as he continues. "Look, sis, I'm nineteen, you're sixteen. We don't need to have a fucking life plan. The future may be a second away, but it is also years away. Don't worry about it now. You can do whatever you want, you know?" He takes both her hands in his and squeezes them reassuringly.

"Can I?"

"Of course you can, sis. Look, I used to dream of being a tennis star, right?"

"Yeah."

"Well, that's not going to happen now, is it? And that's cool... sure it was a bit tough at first, but it's fine. Other things will crop up. We don't know what's going to happen in future, and that's what makes it all so exciting." Johnson smiles and winks at his sister before continuing. "I hate to say this, of course, but you've got everything going for you. You're intelligent, you can act, you can sing, like I say you can do whatever you want... but for now we just need to enjoy ourselves, make the most of every minute, live the moment. Just have fun!"

"Is that enough?"

"It is for me. Isn't it for you?"

"I don't know." Martha pulls her right hand out of her brother's grasp, leans forward, grabs a piece of bacon off the partially filled plate, and puts it in her mouth before he can react.

"Hey, what the fuck?!" They are both smiling now. That's a start.

"Thanks, JJ."

"Seriously, sis. You've got the play this evening. That'll be great. Enjoy it. Make the most of every second of it. And watch out for the guy in the front row trying to put you off."

"You'd better not!"

"Just wait and see!" Johnson moves his plate further away from his sister and fills it with the rest of the contents from the pan. As he carries it over to the table, he pauses to look back at Martha.

"Don't worry, sis. You'll be amazing, like you always are."

"Yeah, hopefully." Martha half smiles back at her brother. She certainly doesn't feel amazing.

When a person steps on an ant they usually don't notice and it means nothing to them. To the ant it is the end of everything. The words are written in large red letters underneath the enormous *Save Marsh Park* banners which welcome visitors to the annual summer fair. The event first happened in 1946, as a post-World War II celebration of freedom, and today could be the last one if the park becomes a supermarket. At every stall, every temporary food outlet, every fairground ride, someone is standing with a bucket for donations to raise the money to save the park. It may not be enough, but it's all they can do.

Priya gathers the girls round her for one last pep talk. It's one minute to three; one minute to the game that means so much not just to those who are playing, but to all the people who have been told they're not good enough. At least, all those who have been told they are not good enough and know that the game is happening. Judging by the crowd who are gathered two deep round the pitch, there are quite a few of those. As usual, Sonnley Town have won the previous three matches of the day comfortably with the six-two defeat for the Marsh Park Rovers Under Fifteen boys being the closest contest. But this is the one the home team chose to put on last. This is the one they believe they can win.

"OK, girls. This is it. Trust yourselves, trust each other. Everything you do, you do together. You are talented. You are strong. And, most of all, you are together. You are a team, and you are going to make history. Let's do it." Priya knows it sounds corny, exaggerated even, but she doesn't care. At this moment, there is nothing she wants more in her life than for Nina's team to win. For ninety minutes (forty in each half, plus a ten minute half time for this age group), she can forget everything else. She walks away from the pitch, leaving the team in their yellow shirts and black shorts, grouped in a circular huddle with their arms over each others' shoulders, looking like a nest of bees ready to play their crucial part in keeping the world going.

Priya glances round the crowd looking for signs of her family. She spots Mia with a couple of her friends chatting behind one of the goals. Kian is standing next to them, staring at his phone, looking every inch like the bored younger brother who has been forced to tag alone with one of his sisters and watch the other play football against his will. He's not quite at the age to refuse yet thankfully.

There is no sign of Tommy. His loss.

The first twenty minutes are a cagey affair, as both teams are more concerned with not making mistakes than with trying to make anything positive happen. Priya doesn't mind that at this stage. They're feeling their way into the game. But as the half continues,

Marsh Park Rovers start to dominate, inspired by a tall girl in midfield known as Tarra. She's the only player in the team to have played for the county, the only one to have scored twenty goals this season, the one who is clearly better than all the rest. And she knows it. That's what worries Priya. She needs a team today.

With three minutes to go before half time, Tarra receives the ball in the centre circle facing her own goal, turns without appearing to move, leaving her marker in her wake and sprays the ball out to the left wing where Nina is sprinting. She may not be the greatest player, but she is certainly one of the fastest, and that is an asset not to be overlooked. She outruns the defender, reaches the ball then pulls it back towards the edge of the penalty area just as Tarra arrives and strikes it first time into the top left hand corner of the Sonnley Town net. One-nil. Priya leaps in the air, hugs another of the coaches, then glances at the jubilant players, checking for any signs of surprise. They need to believe.

Half time arrives without any further chances, and she gathers the team round, encouraging them to rehydrate, making sure no one is injured or too tired to carry on, and reiterating the messages of togetherness which can help them beat their rivals. It's ten minutes, but it seems to disappear in a moment before she's had a chance for a quick individual word with each player as she likes to.

After the break, the tempo of the game ups dramatically, and the caginess of the first half is replaced by an open end-to-end game as Sonnley Town aim to get back into the match, and leave themselves open to counter-attack as a result. Tarra hits the post for Marsh Park Rovers with a free kick, and their opponents have two efforts cleared off the line in separate goalmouth scrambles after corners. It doesn't look like a game that is going to finish one-nil. And it doesn't.

With seven minutes to go, a Sonnley Town defender aimlessly hoofs the ball upfield, more in tired desperation than expectation. It is easily collected by Twitch, the quicker of the two Marsh Park Rovers central defenders, who gained her nickname from a not particularly useful ability to move her left ear back and forward without any manual intervention. Twitch does what she has always been taught and plays in the direction she is facing which, as the ball was behind her when she got it, means passing back to her goalkeeper. But she hasn't noticed the approaching Sonnley Town forward, and she doesn't put enough pace on the ball. The opposition striker intercepts, easily rounds Hannah "Hands" Henderson in goal, and slots the ball into the empty net.

"You fucking moron, Twitch. What the fuck are you doing? You're useless." Priya hears the words being screamed on the pitch at the broken defender, whose bottom lip is twitching more than her ear ever does, and who is staring at the ground. She watches as Tarra runs up to Twitch continuing the rant, increasing the abuse. The poor defender looks beaten. The day she thought would be the happiest of her life so far has fallen in on itself and buried her in its rubble.

Priya looks at the defeated girl who can wiggle her left ear on demand, and gestures to the referee that she wants to make a substitution, then calls over one of the two substitutes who have been warming up for five minutes.

"OK, I'm making a change" she calls from the touchline. "Tarra, you're coming off." She sees the looks of incredulity sweep across the faces of all her team, and feels the contemptuous glare of Tarra, standing her ground next to Twitch, not moving, but not screaming at her team mate any more either.

"No way... you're joking, right? You can't take me off."

"Tarra... Off. NOW!" Priya shouts the last word with a force which Nina has never heard before, and watches as the referee ushers Marsh Park Rovers' best player off the pitch.

"What the..."

"Get yourself warmed down, Tarra."

"What are you doing? They won't win without me."

"We're a team, Tarra. That comes above everything." Priya looks back at the action on the pitch as the substituted girl picks up a water bottle, throws it to the ground and kicks it back in the direction of the coach who has taken her off. It catches the back of Priya's shoe, splashing the back of her calf with water, which she ignores and carries on focusing on the match as it heads into its final stages.

Sonnley Town press, searching for the winner, the momentum of their goal giving them extra reserves of energy and belief which were unimaginable only minutes ago. They win four corners in the last three minutes, culminating in a final one, as the referee glances at her watch, and observes that the match is entering the single minute of injury time to be added.

The ball is flighted into the penalty area over the outstretched arms of the Marsh Park Rovers goalkeeper towards the head of the largest Sonnley Town defender, who has made a rare excursion upfield in search of the winning goal. She outjumps the despairing Marsh Park Rovers defenders and meets the ball perfectly, propelling her head forwards with all the power that her neck muscles can muster, so that it fires down towards the goal.

"Noooo." Priya can't help herself. She screams with an agony she hadn't realised was there as the ball heads to the goal where the goalkeeper no longer is. But her pain is short-lived. Twitch hurls herself feet first across the goal line, and meets the ball with her flailing right leg and a force which propels it out of the penalty area towards the left hand flank.

"Go Nina, go." Priya knows that voice better than she knows her own. She can't look to see where it's coming from as she needs to watch the action, but she knows Tommy is here. He is yelling encouragement with an enthusiasm she has not heard in too-long-to-remember as their daughter races down the left touchline with the ball, which seconds ago looked destined to break her heart. She kicks it forward into the opposition half, and races after it with as much speed as eighty minutes of football have left in her legs. She catches up with the ball, knocks it past the Sonnley Town right back, uses her pace to get past her, and cuts back inside towards the penalty area. She looks up, into the space where she knows Tarra would usually be arriving, but no one is there. There is only one option. Nina darts inside to the edge of the penalty area before switching back the other way so that she can shoot with her favoured left foot. She strikes it powerfully and uppishly in the direction of the far top corner of the goal. It seems like the whole of Marsh Park, the whole of Sonnley even, has started moving in slow motion as the ball fires towards its target, past the despairing dive of the goalkeeper, arrowing its way towards the top corner.

The ball strikes the inside of the junction where the post meets the crossbar and fires back downwards, bouncing on the ground just in front of the goal line and escaping back in the direction whence it came, where it is gratefully received by a Sonnley Town defender who, without considering other options, boots it as far as they can out of play for a throw in by the half way line.

The smallest of margins can make the biggest differences.

"Great effort, Nina. So unlucky!" Priya closes her eyes for a second and listens to her husband calling his words of comfort to their daughter.

The referee blows her whistle to end the match. A draw. The girls have shown they can compete with anyone. They will be disappointed, Priya knows that, but they shouldn't be. That's her job to let them know that, make them feel proud of how much it means to show that Marsh Park Rovers are a match for anyone; that they can achieve amazing things with belief; that no one is better than them.

But they may not get the chance again. This may be the last game that Marsh Park Rovers ever play. This may be the last time that Marsh Park hosts any football matches for that matter.

However, there is still a last chance to raise more money today and Priya needs to be there. She calls the girls over, runs them through some warm down exercises, and watches as Tarra puts an arm round Twitch, and says something which is hopefully an apology. She then gathers them in a huddle, lets them know what they have achieved, and savours the moments as they all walk away slightly taller, with their heads held high, in the direction of their families and friends.

Priya can't do that. She has to get to the play. It's going to be a long day, but it's the sort of day she lives for. She knows that. She walks down the side of the pitch, and spots Tommy and Nina by the centre circle, kicking a ball back and forwards to each other, juggling it and trying to stop it hitting the ground. They both laugh as Tommy slips when making a desperate lunge for a pass just out of his reach and ends up lying on his back on the grass. This is even more the sort of day she lives for than she had realised.

Chapter Twenty

Finn takes his seat in the front row next to Priya and looks behind at the chattering audience filling the *Ray Hope Centre for Performing Arts*. This is just an evening out for them, an unwanted duty probably in some cases. But for him, it is so much more. He spots a lot faces he recognises, including teachers, pupils, neighbours, and finally the person he was looking for. Charley is sitting towards the edge about halfway back, next to a couple of people she's doesn't appear to know, judging by the way she is not interacting with them. Or maybe that means she does know them. Either way, Finn waves in her direction, unable to tell if she hasn't noticed or is ignoring him.

This is it: the moment he has been waiting for; the last push for the fundraising to save Marsh Park; the chance maybe to enthuse a few students that acting is the dream they can follow. Though he is in two minds about that. He knows the downside that can come with that.

Finn feels a little rumble echo around his stomach, either through the lack of food he's had a chance to grab today or the nervous anticipation about what is about to unfold. He hopes no one else hears it. There's nothing he can do now. It's down to the students. It's out of his hands. That's scary. He's a teacher, he likes to be in control. His mind is darting all over the place: hoping no one freezes or forgets their lines; wondering whether or not he should confront Martha about the *Everything can change in an instant* graffiti at the entrance to the school grounds; worrying that what he thought was a great idea for a play will be hated or, worse still, mocked by the assembled audience.

"It's going to be great, Finn." He turns to his left, where Priya is wearing the smile of a mother whose baby has just said 'Mama' for the first time. How can she be so relaxed? How can she be enjoying these moments? How can he not?

"Yeah. Too right." He sounds a lot more confident than he feels. But, then again, he usually does these days. This is more than just a fundraising school play. This is a chance to prove to himself that he has got something to offer; a chance to believe.

The lights in the auditorium are lowered, the murmuring crowd fall silent, and for a few seconds everything goes dark.

It's a sensation Finn knows all too well.

Gillian Mann would not usually be late for anything. Absolutely not. Tardiness is a telltale sign of a weak, disorganised mind, and she has not got a weak, disorganised mind. At least, not a disorganised mind. She's not so sure about the weak bit any more.

But today is different. She's thinking of her daughter. She doesn't want to make a scene or upset Charlotte's pride and enjoyment at watching her son's story come to life. So she has entered the *Ray Hope Centre for Performing Arts* just as the lights are lowered for the performance to start. She is standing behind one of two large curtains which have been pulled across the back of the hall, and is peering round so that she can see the play, safely out of view of everyone else. Everyone else except one person it seems.

She spots the figure peering round the other end of the curtain, and wonders if it is someone assigned to inspect tickets and stop the unwanted freeloaders who seem to be everywhere these days and expect something for nothing. Gillian is not one of those, and she needs to ensure the figure realises that. She edges along behind the curtain until she reaches the figure then pulls out her ticket and whispers through the darkness.

"Here's my ticket, though I'd rather stand and watch from back here if you don't mind."

The figure says nothing and continues to stare past the edge of the curtain towards the stage. How rude!

As Gillian's eyes adjust to the darkness, she makes out that the figure is a young man, probably a teenager. He is about six feet tall, slim and standing slightly awkwardly, shuffling his body from side to side as he shifts his weight from one foot to another.

"Arthur, sorry, Art? It's you, isn't it?" She keeps her voice as hushed as her surprise will allow and taps him on the shoulder.

"What do you want?" Art is noisier than the situation demands. Volume control is not his strength, though he does move his face further behind the curtain, so that his mouth is behind it and only his eyes and above are peering round the edge.

"I just want to see the wonderful play you've written."

"I didn't write the play, I wrote the history essay it's based on." He is still looking directly forward at the performance.

"Yes, yes, of course, I know."

They stand beside each other in silence for a couple of minutes, before Gillian whispers again.

"You should be out there, up front Art, getting the praise you deserve, making your mother proud."

"I can't."

A further few seconds of quiet follows, punctuated only by the voices on stage, until Art's grandmother continues in hushed tones.

"Listen, Art. I know you don't care what I think, and why would you? I've not been a part of your life, and I apologise deeply for that." She pauses for a moment, wondering how best to phrase it. "But I've made a terrible mistake, I've failed to see what really matters, I've failed to know when to let go and move on, and it's cost me my daughter and my grandson."

"So? Your choice."

"Yes, it was my choice, Art. And it was the worst choice I have ever made. It's too late for me to fix it, but it's not too late for you."

"Why should I fix your mistake?"

"I'm not asking you too, Art. I'm asking you not to make the same mistake. It's not an admission of failure or fault if you go back home. In fact, it's the opposite."

"How?"

"It shows that you are selfless, that you are a special person, who can forgive and let go, and do something for the good of someone else... someone you really care about, like your mother... it's not easy, but it'll make you both much happier. Believe me, I know."

"I'll think about it."

"She's really struggling, Art, this situation is awful for her. You can do it for her, can't you?"

"Like I said, I'll think about it."

Art knows he is a special person. His mum has told him that before many times. He also knows he can not let go of what has happened. Actions have consequences. But can he do something he thinks is wrong purely for someone else's sake? He'll think about it. He can see his mum, sitting on the edge of the audience about halfway up the hall. She doesn't look like she's struggling. She looks like she's happily watching a play without a care in the world.

"Thank you." Gillian smiles and squeezes her grandson's left forearm for a split second before he pulls it away. "May I stay here and watch the play with you?"

"No."

"You gotta beat the crap out of them and kick their butts, Maggie."

"That is precisely my intention in giving them Liverpool, Ronald. They won't know what's hit them." In his blue suit and coiffured wig, Mek is not exactly the spitting image of Mrs Thatcher, but he's doing a very passable impression.

"No, Maggie, that's not enough. You need to really hurt them too. Let me tell you a story... You know our beautiful island of Hawaii, right?"

"Of course, Ronald."

Martha is about to embark on one of the longest passages that she has in the play. She hopes she can remember it. Almost as much as her dad does. It's the closing scene, and it's the final memory the audience will have of the performance.

"Well, Maggie, Hawaii used to be part of the mainland, you know, till those damn Russkis came along and tried to steal it. They brought their best fleet... thousands of large ships, submarines, jet propelled tugboats." Martha pauses for a moment. Jet propelled tugboats sounds wrong. She looks at the audience. No one seems to have noticed. Maybe they're not listening. Oh well, carry on, carry on.

"Wow, Ronald! What did you do?" Mek adlibs to buy his co-star a bit of time, and Martha finds her way back.

"Well, we weren't going to buy it off them like we did Alaska, that's for sure. No doggone way. So we kicked their Commie butts, Maggie, that's what we did. And we kept kicking them, so damn hard, that they went away with their goddamn red tails so far between their legs that they could barely walk." Again, not quite right, but it will do.

"Well done, Ronald."

"And do you know what the lesson is, Maggie?" Martha needs a second to remember the lesson. She can see her dad silently mouthing something in the front row, but it's hard to make it out with him sat in the darkness.

"I'd certainly like to, Ronald." Mek is not sure he's going to find out. He prepares himself to step in and say the lines himself, just in case.

"Well, Maggie, er ..." the pause echoes round the room, as if expertly crafted to build the expectation, instead of just being a byproduct of Martha scanning her memory desperately for the lines.

"Did you forgive them, Ronald?" Mek throws in a prompt.

"No, Maggie, no goddamn way. Never forgive and never forget, that's the lesson. If someone steals a cent from you, you don't just take your cent back from them. You go back every day for the rest of their doggone life and take every darn thing they've got each time."

With that, the hall curtain slowly lowers in front of the two performers on stage, and some words are projected on it, in a vibrant white light which contrasts with the message.

The population of the Falklands/Malvinas at the time of the war was 1,847. Over 900 people were killed in the war. Many were British, even more were Argentinian. They were all sons or daughters or brothers or sisters or fathers or mothers.

After a few seconds of sombre silence, the lights go on, and the curtain rises again to reveal the performers lined up on stage, arms around the shoulders of the person next to them, awaiting a reaction.

They don't have to wait long. It starts with a few murmurs of irritation at the political nature and historical inaccuracy of the play. Finn sits in his seat unable to turn and face the watching public behind him. Then the atmosphere changes. The majority of the assembled audience overrule the naysayers and showcase the acoustics of the *Ray Hope Centre for Performing Arts* with enthusiastic applause and screams of support, forcing the curtain to be lowered and raised three times as they call the cast back for three encores.

Finn walks onto the stage. He needs to say something before everyone leaves. "Thank you everyone. Thank you so much for coming. Thank you so much for your support. I can't tell you how much it means to all the fantastic cast, to me, to Mrs Moore, to Sonnley in fact. But we mustn't forget why we're here... what this is all about. We need to save Marsh Park. It's our history, it's our present, it's our future. Please, please, please give as generously as you can to the appeal. Today is our last chance."

As he speaks, he notices a short, angular balding man wandering up to the stage below him. Finn knows who he is. Everyone in Sonnley does.

"One second..." Finn pauses his appeal and leans down from the front of the stage to speak to the man in hushed tones, before returning to his speech, grinning.

"Wow! We've done it! Ladies and Gentlemen... I... I...Excuse me a moment." Finn leans away from the microphone, closes his eyes and takes a long breath, trying to come to terms with the unfamiliar, overwhelming emotion of a dream fulfilled. The smile which engulfs him as he starts talking again says more than the words which come out. "A round of applause please for Mr Ray Hope, who has pledged to make up any shortfall in the Marsh Park appeal fund and ensure that we raise the total required to buy the park for the people of Sonnley."

The audience erupts again. To some of them, this means a lot. To others, it just means a few more minutes stuck in a performing arts centre instead of doing what they would much rather be doing on a Saturday evening in June.

About halfway back, in a seat to the side of the hall, Charley smiles to herself. So that's his game. She remembers Ray saying that people need to show how much they want it, do something for themselves. They've done enough now. She can see the mass of contradictions in Ray: someone whose raison d'être is making money, but has no one to spend it on; a fearless businessman who is terrified of being close to anyone; someone who seems to have everything in the world, yet nothing at all.

Finn notices her smile from the stage. He hopes it's for him and smiles back. As the applause dies down, he notices a few people fidgeting in their seats, ready to leave. He's not stupid. He knows this doesn't mean as much to everyone as it does to him.

"I'll try not to keep you much longer, but I just want to say a final thank you to the person who made this play possible, the one who enabled us to raise the funds, the boy who literally rewrote history... Art Mann."

At the back of the hall, Gillian has manoeuvred herself back next to her grandson behind the curtain. She doesn't do this sort of thing. Not at all. But this time she has to. She shoves him in the back so that he goes tumbling through the curtain into the main auditorium, and falls into the chair of someone seated near the back. She waits long enough to see everyone turn to see what the commotion is all about, and Art get to his feet and start walking awkwardly towards his mother's seat, with his eyes fixed firmly on the ground in front of him. Then Gillian disappears into the dimming evening warmth.

In so doing, she misses seeing her daughter happier than she's been since her childhood, and maybe even happier than that, hugging the boy who can rewrite history but can't face being hugged. She misses the emotional, heart-wrenching reconciliation of a mother with her long-lost child: the relief, the happiness, the elation that only a family bond can bring; the feeling that a lost life is worth living again; the joy that comes from forgiving and moving on before it is too late.

And Gillian will always miss it. She knows that, for her, it is already too late.

Chapter Twenty-One

The person who jumps:

So the longest day of the year is here. And for you it's the final day of the year, the final day of forever. No one else knows that yet, but they will. And, for some of them, the pain it will cause will slash like the sharpest blade at their lives, destroying all their happiness until they too reach their final day.

You don't know that of course. You don't want to hurt anyone. All you know is that your pain must stop, and that is all-consuming. It feels like there is no space to think of others, no room to talk to someone about how you feel and get help that maybe could save you. If only you could find that room, everything could still be so different.

You are sure that there is something wrong with you. You're ashamed. You couldn't tell anyone how you feel: the dread which batters at your mind, drilling a hole into your brain that you must fall into, falling, falling, falling; the self-loathing which tortures you, dripping its poisonous bile about how useless and ungrateful you are until the incessant repetitive rhythm of the drips explodes your head; the excruciating loneliness of thinking that you are a freak, that you will never fit in, never be like everyone else.

No one else feels like this. You know that. But you are wrong.

If the longest day of the year is meant to be the day with the most sunshine, it would surely not be today. It's been drizzling on and off, though more on, all day, and there's a biting chill in the air as if it knows what is about to happen. Whereas the sun gloriously celebrated the Marsh Park Fair yesterday, it is now taking a well-earned day off to make amends. It's a frustrating waste of a day, where the rain hasn't quite got the energy to pour or to stop altogether, almost like someone were trying to fill a bath with a dripping tap. Many sensible folk will just be staying at home, doing as little they can, possibly getting a bit bored and irritable, and hoping that tomorrow will be better.

But, as the rain continues to dribble down intermittently into the late afternoon, doors are opening all over Sonnley, as people head out to their evening destinations: there are friends to meet and friends to help; pasts to reflect on and futures to hope for; bridges to be built and bridges to make final shattering decisions on.

Ray Hope gets in his car and drives away from the office feeling justified for having popped in. It's always good to know that some people have been working on a Sunday, putting their careers ahead of their private lives. Of course he had made sure that he had said hello to each of them individually, passed on his thanks, made them feel valued and that their work is appreciated. It's important to do that. It costs him nothing and it means they are more likely to give up their weekends for his business again.

It's been a good weekend for Ray, what with saving the park that everyone seems to make such a fuss of. Successful people like him often get such a bad press, despite providing employment for hundreds of people and bringing money and investment into the town on a scale that no one has ever thought to measure, let alone thank him for. But they all want to thank him now, for giving a few quid to save a park. It's crazy. But Ray's not stupid, he knows that their jealousy will be back soon. Still, it was quite fun last night having all those people he'd never wanted to meet tell him how great and generous he is. That's not why he did it of course. He helped because he could. As Tommy Moore had said to him all those years ago after saving Ray's life "why wouldn't I?" Those kinds of things stick with Ray.

Tommy had been one of the ones to thank him yesterday, in fact. He had looked so proud of Priya for sorting the play. It's good to see him happy. He deserves it. No need for him to say thank you though, ever.

Ray had even got a thank you message this morning from Charlotte. He liked that. It was short and to the point, but certainly encouraging for the chances of them meeting up again in a more fun manner when he next comes back. *Thanks so much for all your help, Ray. You'll never know how much it means x.* The message didn't actually clarify if she was thanking him for saving the park or for helping her reunite with her son who wrote that weird, largely tedious, play, which Ray had felt compelled to watch prior to saving the park. It's not like Ray to make a mistake like that. It would have been much less painful just to show up at the end, and not watch the thing. Oh well, like he often says, we learn the most from the bad decisions.

As he drives through Sonnley on his way out to Heathrow, and the sanity of Monaco, Ray stops at the zebra crossing by the Boathouse Pub just before the bridge to let a slim short-haired blonde woman cross. She holds up her hand in gratitude, but it looks more like an automatic response than a considered one. Not that it really matters. He studies her for the few seconds that she walks in front of him. Slung over her shoulder is a large tote bag adorned with the words *Planet first, No second chance*, and she looks cold and wet. She is probably fifteen or twenty years older than Ray, but has that ageless beauty which immediately makes him wonder how stunning she must have been when she was younger, her skin was smoother and, hopefully, her eyes were not so clouded by heartbreak. Ray would have liked to have got to know her then, for sure. But he wouldn't say that to anyone, of course. He knows it's sexist and a totally inappropriate way to speak about women. So he just thinks it instead, and only for a few seconds. As soon as she steps on to the pavement and he drives off, Ray files the idea away in the *transient thoughts not worth revisiting* section of his brain, and never thinks of her again.

Mel Jarvis's memories of the man in the expensive car who stops at the crossing for her will last even less time. They won't even start. She doesn't notice Sonnley's richest man; she doesn't notice the rain; she doesn't notice the cold. She just walks, taking in all the sites which made her life with Rosa so special, and heading towards her destination. Sonnley Bridge looms large in front of her now. Not long till she's there.

She hears Rosa's familiar howling laughter and, just for a moment, she feels her wife right back there with her by her side. Rosa used to like being a ringtone. She said they were noisy, irritating and would always pop up at the most inconvenient times, just like her. Mel used to laugh and say that they also show someone cares enough to want to chat.

She gropes in her bag for her phone, pulls it out and looks at the screen. It's Faith again. Mel does exactly what she has done with her previous three calls and the two from Priya, she diverts them straight to voicemail. But this time she decides to turn the phone off completely too. There's no point having it on. She's not going to answer.

Faith puts her phone back in her bag and pauses to say a short prayer. She wants to find her friend. She had popped round to Mel's house to check how she was doing before church this morning, again in the afternoon, and once again after the late afternoon service, but with no answer any time. That's not like Mel. Neither is her not answering her phone. So Faith had rung Priya and the two of them have been out separately searching Sonnley for the last hour or so: Marsh Park, where Mel loved to walk; the coffee shops she used to go to; the site of Rosa's tragic death with its glowing floral tributes. But no sign of their beloved neighbour anywhere.

Faith gets her phone out again and rings Priya for an update. Maybe she's making better progress.

She isn't.

When Priya finishes the call with Faith, she tries Mel again. It's more hope than expectation, and expectation wins. It goes straight to voicemail this time, without even ringing first.

"Damn." She mutters to herself and puts her phone back in the pocket of her waterproof jacket. Priya is worried and angry with herself. She's been so busy with the fair, the football and the play this weekend that she hasn't given enough time to her grieving friend. All the time that she has been revelling in the successes of the past thirty-six hours, poor Mel has been struggling alone.

Before going out searching, Priya had told Tommy about Mel being missing and explained her guilt for putting her own selfish enjoyment ahead of looking after her friend. He had been sunk in his armchair half-watching some football match on the television with that look on his face which she knows so well and dreads: the look which says his mind is in overdrive, he's given up, and he's not going to do anything. And all he had said was "I know a lot about that kind of selfishness."

It hadn't been what Priya wanted to hear. She had wanted him to reassure her, tell her not to feel guilty, not to blame herself, like any supportive partner would. But all he had said was that he is used to her selfishness. She hadn't answered. There was no point. She had walked out of the room, put on her jacket and shouted "Well, fuck you then" as she had slammed the front door and headed out to look for Mel.

Tommy walks across Marsh Park in the direction of Sonnley Bridge. He hasn't made his mind up yet. His wife hates him. He knows that. She had screamed at him and stormed out when he had tried to console her in her guilt by letting her know that he feels selfish and guilty the whole time: that when he can't face going out, can't face talking to people, can't face spending time with his own kids even, he feels guilty and selfish beyond words. And he hates himself for it. But when he had tried to tell Priya, all she had done was raged and marched out on him. If even she has given up on him now, who is left? He doesn't blame her. He blames himself. She's begged him so many times to get help, talk to someone. Why hasn't he? He can't answer that in any way that she will understand. So he tries not to think about it.

When Priya had stormed out, Tommy had called his mum and asked her to come round to be with the children for a few hours. Once she had arrived, he had thanked her for everything, grabbed his waterproof and headed out into the drizzle.

Which is why he is now approaching the bridge and can hear a lot of noise coming from the garden of the Boathouse pub, triggering him to look over. There is a large group of older teenagers, laughing, playing drinking games, just enjoying themselves, at a couple of tables at the back of the pub under the large awning, which primarily serves as protection from any rain for outcast smokers. Tommy knows how it feels to be an outcast: to feel different to everyone else; to be unable to enjoy anything like other people do; to detest the things that the whole world loves. He wants to be having fun like those people in the pub garden, like he used to do when he was younger in fact. He watches the group, even wishing he could be the young man who has obviously lost the latest game and is drinking down in one a cloudy concoction which has been created from a sample of each of his friends' drinks.

Johnson James slams the empty pint glass back down on table, makes a loud gagging sound and laughs. "It wasn't that bad actually."

"Have another then!"

"Yeah... maybe not!"

Johnson doesn't need to look beyond this moment. He's having fun surrounded by friends, that's all he needs right now. The future will happen when it happens, and the past, well he can't change the past, so he won't dwell on it. That can't be said for all his family.

The James home feels empty with both children out this evening. Finn pours himself a large glass of Malbec and sits down on the sofa, trying to bring some order to his thoughts. The play couldn't have gone better and Marsh Park has been saved. Everything he's been working towards has worked out as he'd hoped. He should feel joyous, elated, pleased with himself even. But he doesn't. And he knows why now. The cliche says that a problem shared is a problem halved, well the reverse is true too. Happiness shared is happiness doubled. Finn needs someone to share it with.

If only Niamh were here, she would love this. She would love seeing the play a success; she would love being part of the community they are now so embedded in; and most of all she would love seeing the people that their children have grown into. Niamh would have been a great mum. She would have understood what Martha's going through, helped Finn communicate with her properly again, helped her negotiate the path to adulthood with a calm, consistent approach, which he knows he is too scared to try in case he alienates his daughter further.

But Niamh is not here and she never will be. It's just Johnson, Martha and him, and they are both out this evening anyway, so it's just him. It's going to be more and more like that over the next few years until finally it will be just him every day. Finn doesn't want that. He wants to build a future. He hasn't realised that before, because everything has always been about surviving, trying to give the children stability and hopeful lives, and then surviving again. But he knows that now. Meeting Charley has de-misted the fog in his brain so that he knows what future he wants, yet he's driven her away too.

He drains his wine, and another, until he thinks he can see things more clearly, then grabs a coat, and heads out. He's decided what he's going to do.

Charley steers the car over Sonnley Bridge and switches the windscreen wipers back to intermittent. It's the sort of weather where they start making an annoying scraping sound if left on the whole time, but don't clear the rain away quickly enough if left on intermittent. It's only a short journey to her sister's, but this rain has given her an easy excuse to drive and she wants to be able to get away quickly if needs be in any case. This is not something she ever thought she could do, but she's pictured it more times than she can remember. She knows how hard it must have been for her son to back down and come home, though she would never call it backing down to him of course. But if he can do it, surely she can? It's still just a question, she doesn't know the answer yet. She glances over to her left where Art is sitting in the passenger's seat, playing a game on the phone he has missed for several weeks. He doesn't want to go to her sister's, he has made that abundantly clear. But he did agree in the end, that's something, she supposes. He looks different now, older somehow, as though he will never be just her child again. It's good, she knows that. But that doesn't make it easy. He's all that she has had, all that she has needed for so long now.

Art doesn't want to go to Aunt Amanda's. It's not that he doesn't like her or Uncle Matt, or their kids even, although they can be very irritating and childish at times. He had once said to his mum that he hoped he hadn't been like that when he was their ages and she had replied that he hadn't, and that he hadn't been like any children of those ages she'd ever met in fact. That's a relief.

But he knows that Aunt Amanda will be cooking a traditional Sunday roast. There's nothing wrong with that of course, but it's not chicken casserole. And when you've been away for as long as he is, the first full day back should surely be marked by chicken casserole if you mean as much to someone as his mum claims he does to her. Worse still, she has told him who else will be there, and he certainly doesn't want to see them again. They tried to kill him.

It's lucky that Art is so good at thinking about the impact on others, and not just saying exactly what he thinks, else it would have been a bad start to being back home. OK, so he had said he wouldn't come three times when his mum had told him where they were going and who would be there, but once she had started crying and said "please, this is hard enough for me as it is", he had agreed to go. She hadn't smiled, but she had thanked him and stopped crying, which was good. He still wishes they weren't going though. It's his own fault. He thinks of others too much probably. He had thought that his mum would want to know that her would-be murderer of a father had cancer and it would serve him right if he died. Art would never have mentioned it if he had known it would lead to this.

As they reach the other side of Sonnley Bridge, Art glances up from his phone and out of the passenger side window towards the tennis club which Johnson doesn't own, and the backstreets where he stayed in that cold, dirty rundown old restaurant. It's much nicer being home, having his familiar things around him and Llama to chat to. But he liked Martha. He wishes she hadn't got all weird and dumped him just because she didn't think he knew the difference between 'heard' and 'listen', when he knew they were clearly different tenses, but was so good at thinking of the impact on others that he hadn't said anything. But she had dumped him, and he's home now. Or at least he will be home again after this trip to Aunt Amanda's which he doesn't want.

Martha is much too warm as she walks through the park she helped save. Her coat is far too thick for June, but it's the only one she's got which is waterproof, so she had to make a decision about what was more important and then make do. That seems to be the way with life. You can't have everything. You just have to make do. Johnson would probably say it's not making do, it's making the best of it, but at this moment it definitely feels like making do to Martha. And she's not making do very well today.

She had woken up this morning expecting to feel the glow of adulation and the beat of the applause from last night's performance echoing through her mind. But it hadn't been. The buzz which had given her last night's highs had been replaced by a dull, pounding emptiness, like the pain of a terrible hangover leaving its curse, so that the body aches from the hammering head down to the aching legs. But it was nothing to do with alcohol. There doesn't tend to be much of that around in schools for students when teachers are around, even after a play, and she hadn't needed it then anyway.

After spending all day in her room, Martha had needed to get out. She had heard Johnson cheerily shouting goodbye to any interested parties, and had gone out herself about twenty minutes later without a word. She knows where she's going. She walks through Marsh Park, unnoticed by any of the few people who are braving the rain. She might as well not be there. Everything is back to normal. Why do the lows always seem to outweigh the highs?

There's been a lot for Martha to think about recently, what with the play, Art, Dan, the band falling apart. But she knows that none of those explain why she's been carrying the crushing weight of unbearable misery and fear with her all day. Usually she would cope with all of those things. But today, she can't cope with anything at all. She just seems to get days like this: no warning, no reason, seemingly no way out of them. And they're becoming more and more frequent. She feels like she's stuck in the middle of a dense, heavy cloud where all she can see is the pain and the fear right in front of her, mocking her every movement.

So she doesn't see the person on the footpath walking towards the bridge as she reaches it on the road above.

As Dan nears Sonnley Bridge, he pauses and pulls the hood up on his coat. He doesn't want anyone to see him. He has to do this alone, he knows that. But two people are standing directly under the bridge, blocking his route along the footpath. They probably won't notice him, because they are too interested in each other, kissing, caressing, exploring each other with a fervour that he wishes someone would feel for him. If they weren't so closely entwined it would look like one of them was a lot nearer to Dan than the other, given the massive difference in sizes of the couple. He recognises the large one and certainly doesn't want to antagonise him, so he turns back down the towpath until he is out of sight, but will still be able to see when they have gone, so that he can return to his mission.

Mek momentarily pulls back from the Sonnley High girl he is kissing under the bridge.

"You know I like you, really like you, don't you?"

"Sure, Mek. Me too."

"Do you wanna... you know?"

"What? Here?"

"No... somewhere else?"

"Where?"

"Yours?"

The girl laughs. It's a laugh reserved for ridiculous suggestions.

"I don't think you're quite the sort of boyfriend my parents would expect me to bring home!"

"What do you mean?"

"Oh, come on, Mek. I like you. I really do. We have fun together. But we're not... how do I put this? ... We've not got a lot in common, have we?"

"You saying I'm not good enough for you?" Mek pulls completely away from the girl, and shrugs her off as she reaches out to grab his arm.

"No, Mek. Come on. Don't be stupid. We're just very different, that's all. I'm not better than you, you're not better than me. We're just from different worlds. Fact. That's all."

"I get it, I'm not stupid, am I?" He hunches over, his usually enormous frame shrinking with her every word.

"Come on, Mek. This is crazy. You're overreacting. Let's just have some fun."

She leans towards him again, but he flinches out of the way, causing her tone to harden as she carries on. "Last chance, Mek, I'm warning you. I'm not playing childish games. Do you want us to carry on or not?"

Mek shakes his head and spits on the ground in front of him. It's probably what she would expect him to do.

"What's the point in carrying on."

"You said it."

Chapter Twenty-Two

The person who jumps:

You are overwhelmed by a feeling that you just can't go on. It's not the first time you've suffered it, but it's the first time it will win. You feel you can't fight it, even if you had the energy to do so. All you can do is let the despair swallow you up, the pain batter every sliver of your soul, and your mind stab at your existence, torturing you until you can't take any more. You need the unbearable agony to stop, and you can see only one way.

Except there is not only one way, it's just you can't see that through the fog in your head. All you can see is what is overwhelming you at the moment. And that is too painful, too terrifying, too lonely to put up with any longer. There is no future if this is the future.

But this needn't be the future. For you, it will be, but it needn't be. No, more than that, it absolutely shouldn't be the future and could be avoided. People would help, if only they knew.

But, by the time anyone realises, it will be too late. Too heartbreakingly, avoidably, tragically late.

With some people it is easy to see that their lives are utterly overshadowed by some unspeakable sadness: the despair in their eyes is so heartbreaking, you need to avert your gaze almost instantly.

With others it is not so easy: the pain is hidden underneath several protective layers of false joy, designed to keep their innermost hurt as a secret known only to themselves. And when those layers start to crack and fall away, which they inevitably do, it is often too late.

Mel most definitely fits into the first category. She stands on Sonnley Bridge staring at the water below, accelerating before crashing into the weir fifty yards away. It is a dangerous but intoxicating view, and that's why Rosa used to love it so much. They would stand here in silence together, transfixed by the irresistible power of nature, simultaneously both beautiful and terrifying, much like a combination of Mel and her beloved wife. There is a relentless, unpredictable majesty to the flow. It will continue regardless, whatever is thrown at it, forever swallowing the secrets and the pain of the few who have accidentally toppled into it from the towpath after a drunken night at the Boathouse pub or who have intentionally chosen it as their final destination from the bridge. There haven't been many, but there must have been a handful in the thirty-seven years since they left London to start their new life together. Mel doesn't remember any of the names, but she thinks of them and their pain nonetheless as she stares at the water below. It seems oblivious to its own natural power and is focused only on its determined never-ending duty to keep rolling. Everything seems so insignificant in the face of such a mighty, energetic force. Maybe everything is.

On the footpath below, Dan is studying the abutment which holds up the bridge on the Sonnley town side. With Mek gone, he is now safe to plan his next move. It's too early and too light to do it now, as anyone in the Boathouse pub garden could easily see him, but he can take the measurements, visualise the result. He has the design planned out in his mind already. This is the right place for it.

With his hands, he traces a tree arching out over a crocodile-infested river so that its branches hang directly above the open jaws of the hungry reptiles below. A young woman in a simple white dress is desperately clinging on to the end of one of the overhanging branches. At the base of the tree stands a chubby, balding middle-aged man in a tuxedo and black bow tie. He is laughing and using a saw to cut through the wood and topple it. Dan already knows what words he will write underneath the picture: *What happens when the support is gone?*

He turns away from the base of the bridge and stares down at the water below, tearing past towards the weir, so chaotic and yet so peaceful at the same time, calling out to him like the only one who cares. Instinctively he takes a step back and reaches out for something to grab on to. There is nothing there, no one to grasp, no branch to clutch to.

"Are you Neola then?" Dan recognises the voice and is not pleased to hear it.

"Eh?"

"I've been watching you, haven't I? D'you reckon I couldn't see you marking out your next drawing on the bridge? You're Neola, right?"

"Er, sorry, Mek. I didn't see you there."

"I wasn't planning to watch, was I? I just looked back, and you looked weird, didn't you? Why d'you do that graffiti shit then?"

"Sorry... er I don't want any trouble." Dan takes another step back to be further away from the much larger boy. He may have finally stood up to his dad, but this is a fight he knows he would never win.

"Nah, you're alright, I like them, don't I? Why d'you do them?"

"I don't know... I guess they're the only way I know how to express myself. I always get it wrong when I say anything. All I do is let people down and hurt them... and hurt myself."

"You're not the only one who does that."

"Why? Do you?"

Mek avoids the question with one of his own.

"Why don't you try doing a happier one?"

"Like what?"

"I dunno..." Mek pulls at his bottom lip and stares at the bridge for a few seconds before continuing. "How about you start with that posh old bloke in the dodgy suit... you know, the bald, fat geezer you always do... looking sad and fucked off in the dark, and then... I don't know... you follow it up with another picture on the right of one of the younger ones you do pulling him towards the sunrise and the old bloke looking happy or something?"

"What, like a sort of comic strip?"

"I don't know, do it how you want, I'm not the artist, am I?"

Dan nods slowly, trying to think of a way to say he doesn't get it, without causing offence. He fails, so plays it safe.

"Yeah, it could be good. Would you put any words with it?"

"Yeah, of course... how about 'It is always darkest just before the day dawns'?"

Dan gets it now and he likes the hope it offers, not just for the chubby, balding man in the tuxedo, but for his young characters too. He grins and nods faster.

"That's good, I like it. Did you make that line up?"

Mek lightly taps the side of Dan's head with his index finger.

"Think, Neola... do I look like I can make lines like that up? It's an old, traditional saying, been around hundreds of years, ain't it?"

Dan tries to hide his laugh with a cough, but with no success.

"Sorry, Mek. I didn't mean..."

"Don't you like it then?"

"Yeah, I do, it's great, honest... I guess I... er... I just like didn't think you'd be into old, traditional sayings!"

"There's loads of shit that people think and don't think about me which are wrong, ain't there?"

"Yeah, sorry Mek." Dan looks over at the bridge and starts to paint the scene in his mind. He likes what he sees. After a few seconds, he turns his head back and looks up properly at the bigger boy's face for the first time. It's not what he expected to see. Mek's jaw is quivering slightly with a nervous energy that shows this means a lot to him.

"Well... you going to do it, Neola?"

"Yeah, it's brilliant. I love it... and it gives hope. You're good at this."

Mek's jaw stops trembling and his face lights up with the sort of smile that a small child beams when a loving parent tells them they've done something good. It's not a smile that Dan recognises.

"Isn't Neola a girl's name?

"It's an anagram."

Mek thinks for a couple of seconds, then nods approvingly.

"Oh right, that's clever shit, eh?... So does that mean you don't want someone to work with you then... I don't know, keep a lookout, whatever?"

"What, d'you mean you, Mek?" Dan's voice can't hide his surprise. His smile can't hide his delight.

"Can you see anyone else talking?"

"No, yeah, thanks, Mek... thanks... thanks."

Finn knocks on the door and waits. He hopes Charley is in, and he hopes she'll speak to him if she is. He's let her down. He didn't mean to, but he has let her down. He knows that. He thought he was open-minded, but it seems he's not. He thinks of Martha. Maybe that's why she doesn't seem to like him these days? Has he let her down too? He wants to be the support she needs but he clearly isn't. He doesn't know what to do. Niamh would have known, but she's not here.

The lights are off in the house, and there is no movement from within. She's not there. Finn knocks again, but it is only a half-hearted, just in case, knock. Maybe Charley saw him approaching and is pretending not to be in, like someone trying to avoid the trick-or-treaters on Halloween? He couldn't blame her.

He shouldn't have come. It was a stupid idea. He takes a final look through the front window, then pulls himself up straight, as if trying to regain some dignity, and walks back out into the dreary evening on his own.

Charley keeps three feet away and faces her father for the first time in over sixteen years. She can see that those years haven't looked after him. Where he was once athletic and upright, he is now frail and stooped; where his skin was once clear and vibrant, it is now blotchy and grey; where his eyes were once full of energy and pride, they are now dull, but still trying to cling on to that pride.

"Good evening, Charlotte. How are you?" He is sitting in an armchair, which has lost as much buoyancy as him, so that he has sunk deep into it and appears to have shrunk even more than he actually has. He speaks slowly, pausing for breath between the sentences.

"We're OK thanks. Both of us."

"You took your time, didn't you?" Charley can't tell if this is a joke or not. When she was a child she would have known instantly, but nothing makes people strangers more than time apart.

"At least I came." She stares at her father, searching for a reaction to the dig, some remorse maybe? He says nothing, but matches her stare, and leaves his wife to respond.

"Yes dear, we're all so pleased you came, aren't we, Arthur?"

It takes a while for him to answer, and it's difficult to tell if the pause is unavoidable or deliberate.

"Yes." His head nods up and down slowly, in time with the slight upturns of the corners of his mouth into a sort of faint smile, which only those who are looking carefully and really wishing for would notice. Charley's mother spots it. Charley doesn't.

"And Art too, right dad?"

The smile is more obvious this time, the sort of resigned but admiring look of a chess player who has just realised that their opponent has outplayed them and will have them in checkmate in three moves.

"You haven't changed, Charlotte."

"You have."

"On the outside, yes."

"You didn't answer."

"Answer what?"

"You're pleased to see Art too, right?"

Charley watches her father purse his lips thoughtfully and drum the fingers of his right hand on the arm of the chair as he turns to look his grandson up and down, as he would view a new recruit in his army days, weighing up if they were suitable material or not.

"He's a lot like you, Charlotte."

"Go on."

"He knows his own mind."

"Good… are you going to say it then?"

"Say what?"

"That you're pleased to see him too."

Her father stops drumming and rubs his chin with the same fingers, studying Art again as he makes the final decision.

"I'm pleased to see you, Charlotte… and your boy. He's got a good name."

Charley knows that's as good as she's going to get. Her father won't have found that easy. That's all she needs. She walks forwards, bends down over the armchair, and wraps her arms around him, nestling her face on his right shoulder and sobbing quietly into it.

"Thanks."

"I hope you're not making my sweater wet."

―――◆―――

People cry when they are happy, when they are sad, when they are moved, and when they are laughing uncontrollably even. Art knows all that, however nonsensical it may be that such polarised emotions can provoke the same response. It makes it very difficult to judge if someone is upset or joyful, and respond appropriately though. So he decides that it is best not to guess in this case, and lets the scene play out on its own.

He peers across to the other side of the room where his two younger cousins are hiding dog treats under what look like some upside-down flowerpots, then shuffling the pots round and saying "fetch" to their bemused but enthusiastic retriever, Molly. Art doesn't look too carefully though. He doesn't want them trying to involve him. They are annoying, like he never was.

There are a few different conversations going on in the room now, what with the children, Art's mum and her dad, and Aunt Amanda choosing this moment to bring in some cheese straws from the kitchen and offer them around. It's difficult for Art to focus on any particular one of them. Words become just noise when there are too many of them.

"Can Molly have one, mum?" "Anyone need a drink?" "Six months if I'm lucky."

Art stares down at his shoeless feet. Aunt Amanda has got a new carpet apparently, so all footwear is in the hall. It looks much the same as the last one, though he doesn't remember what that looked like any more than he notices this one, so maybe it doesn't. But it does help him notice that his feet look the same size today. Maybe the right one has had a growth spurt to catch up the other. Why don't they just grow at the same rate like they should do? It would be so much easier if everything did what it was meant to do and stuck to the rules.

"Art.... Art." As the various conversations are replaced by the sounds of people munching on cheese straws, he hears his mum. He looks up to see her sitting on the arm of her father's chair, smiling. There are no tears now. That's good, and much easier to read.

"Yes."

"Are you going to give your grandad a hug?"

Why has she asked him that? He hates hugging, she knows that. Though he did like the ones he had with Martha, but his mum doesn't know that and he's not going to tell her. Just as importantly, he doesn't like people who tried to kill him before he was even born, before they had even had a chance to meet him and decide that they didn't like him and that they therefore would like him dead. At least there would be logic in that conclusion.

Art looks back down at the floor, and his same-sized feet.

"No."

Martha peers over from the townside of the bridge into the garden of the Boathouse Inn. She can see Johnson and his mates. They look happy, like there is nothing more to life than fun. That's more or less what he had told her when she had asked him. Is he right? She doesn't know. It doesn't feel much fun now. She peels off the waterproof coat, which is making her too hot, and swirls it around on her right index finger, before tossing it over the side into the water below. She watches it career down the river, bobbing up and down like a drowning person desperately trying to stay above water, before it crashes into the weir, hangs momentarily to a rock in a last attempt to stay afloat, then disappears down the weir into oblivion.

"Useless fucking thing. What's the point?"

Tommy stands at the other end of the bridge, glancing up and down it, then into the water, and finally at the traffic which moves slowly on the other side of the barrier separating the pedestrians from the cars. All he can picture is Rosa leaping out in front of a car, trying to reach safety, trying to escape from him. It was Tommy's fault, he knows that. He scared his friend so much that she ran away from him and lost her life. What kind of person does that? He hates himself. His wife hates him too now. The children think he's a waste of space. They don't say it, but they don't need to. And they are right.

He scans up and down the bridge looking for Mel. This is where he would come if he were her. In fact, he has, many times. He has stood in this exact spot on several occasions, when he has decided that he can't cope any more with his mind incessantly torturing him, mocking him, despising him. He has stared at the river below, wondered how long it would take to end it, tried to guess if he would swallow too much water and drown or would have to wait until he smashed into the rocks which lie below the surface as he were hurled down the weir.

But he is still here, still in Sonnley, still alive, and still going back to the bridge. Maybe he doesn't want to die? Maybe he just wants the pain to stop, wants to be happy? How long can he wait for that though?

Priya pushes on the back door of *Rosa's Kitchen*, hoping she has guessed right. She sees a light flickering in the main restaurant area and hears a voice and some music. It feels wrong to intrude, so she stands in silence in the corridor and watches for a few moments. Mel is sitting on a picnic blanket laid out on the floor with a solitary candle shimmering in front of her and some Middle Eastern sounding music tinnily reverberating from her phone. She pours the remnants of a bottle of red wine into a glass and raises it in a toast.

"My darling little Rosa. You made my life more than I could ever have dreamed of. Thank you." She takes a sip from the wine. "You introduced me to this. Chateau Musar... Lebanese wine... I'd never heard of it, but it's the best on the planet... but then you introduced me to so much, my little Rosa, and they were always the best. I'd never known joy, real uncontrollably happy joy, never lived life like it should be lived, never known the true unstoppable waves of elation of real love until I met you. But you introduced me to them all, my darling little Rosa, and I thank you with all my heart."

Priya leans back to ensure she can't be seen. She mustn't interrupt this moment. She wonders if she should leave. This is a private occasion.

"I'm going to be fine, my little Rosa, because that's what you would want me to be. I went to the bridge a few minutes ago, the spot where we always used to go, and it all became clear. You'll always look after me and I'll always have you and all our memories with me, I know that. And, one day, we'll be back together, I promise you that. I won't let you down, I never will again. I'm going to be strong like you always told me I could be. I love you more than anyone will ever know... Cheers my darling little Rosa!" Mel lifts her glass again, then presses it against her lips before tilting it back and emptying its contents. She blows out the candle, then rises a little unsteadily to her feet, and starts to speak again as she neatly folds up the blanket and stops the music from her phone.

"Thanks for coming, Priya." She looks towards the corridor from the back door into the restaurant.

"Er sorry, Mel... I didn't mean to..."

"It's fine, it really is. Thanks for caring."

Priya walks into the dining area and places her hand under her slightly unsteady friend's elbow to support her.

"Have you seen this, Priya?" Mel sways towards her *Planet first, No second chance* tote bag and pulls out a simple white postcard, with some neat handwritten words on. Priya recognises the writing and reads it slowly out loud at her friend's encouragement.

"*Love is patient and is kind. Love doesn't envy. Love doesn't brag, is not proud, doesn't behave itself inappropriately, doesn't seek its own way, is not provoked, takes no account of evil; doesn't rejoice in unrighteousness, but rejoices with the truth; bears all things, believes all things, hopes all things, and endures all things.*"

She finishes reading and hands the card back to Mel, who lifts it to her heart and holds it there.

"Faith gave me that, you know?"

"I thought she might have done!" Priya smiles and Mel gurgles a little laugh of understanding.

"That's exactly what Rosa was like with me, you know? She loved me as love should be, Priya."

"I know, Mel. You were very lucky. And so was she."

"I don't know. I hope she was."

Priya leans over and gives her friend's left hand a squeeze.

"We're all here for you, Mel. You know that, don't you?"

"Thanks. I know you are. It's strange, you know. I used to dread the thought of it happening... thought I'd collapse or it'd be the end of me. But now she's gone, it's just this weird mix of emotions from one second to the next... one moment I'll feel I can't go on, another I'll be laughing at the happy memories, sometimes I'll feel so desperately, desperately lonely and then others I'll even feel relieved... yes, relieved, Priya... relieved that Rosa's suffering is over... relieved for me that I'm not going to be caring for her all day and all night any more and that my memories of her are not going to be any further diluted by the shell of the real Rosa she was becoming. Does that make any sense? Because it sure makes me feel guilty as hell."

"It's fine, Mel. It really is. Please don't be hard on yourself. You're going to feel all over the place at the moment. Just go with it, let yourself feel how you feel. That's OK, believe me."

Mel knows what Priya is referring to. She probably only met Priyesh a handful of times, but that was enough to see what the twins meant to each other. She hugs her friend with a strength she is beginning to feel.

"Sorry, Priya. Of course you know, you've been through it. Don't worry about me. Rosa taught me a long time ago that even the lowest moments, which can feel like they will last forever, will pass in time." Mel pauses and looks up towards the ceiling of Rosa's Kitchen, as if hoping to see her lost loved one smiling down and reassuring her. It seems to work. She takes a long, deep, breath and manages a wistful half-smile herself as she continues "and I'm hanging on to that. I'm going to be fine... Rosa wouldn't let me be anything else, would she?!" She snorts a more confident laugh this time, before resuming in a serious tone. "Are you fine though, Priya? You need to look after yourself. You're always thinking about everyone else. When are you going to put yourself first?"

Priya conjures up a memory of her lost, beloved brother in his early twenties laughing hysterically with his best friend, who is now her husband, as they tried unsuccessfully to knock a flowerpot off a table by throwing tennis balls at it. She remembers telling them both to grow up. She wouldn't have said it if she'd known what growing up would mean for them.

"It's not that simple, Mel."

Tommy looks out at the water below and thinks of something Priya once said to him: *No one ever lies on their death bed thinking 'I wish I'd spent more time worrying.'* It had been meant to help, but it hadn't. It had just made him feel more guilty, hate himself more. He worries about the children, he worries about Mel, he worries about Priya leaving him, he worries about the victims of tragedies, he worries about leaving the taps on, he worries about upsetting people, he worries about life, he worries about death, he worries about everything. And he hates himself for it. But he can't stop.

He lifts his head and looks up at the sky where the moon is beginning to be visible through the drizzle, then glances back down the bridge, where he sees another figure peering out at the water, just as he has been. He worries about them.

Martha is beginning to chill off now, as she stands in the rain without her jacket and stares at the water gushing below. It looks dangerous, but strangely appealing too, beckoning her down, promising to be the answer to all her problems. She doesn't understand how one day she can feel so full of life, so excited, so positive, and yet another day, she hates it all. It makes no sense. Nothing makes any sense. She's not like other people. No one else feels like this. They all seem so content with their lives, so well-balanced, so happy to continue as they are. But Martha doesn't want to continue as she is: she wants every day to be a happy, positive day; she wants an end to days like today when pain is all she can see and life seems to hate her; she wants to hug her mother again and feel safe.

She pulls out her phone and flicks through to a family photograph: her mum is sticking her tongue out at the camera and laughing with Martha on her knee, whilst Johnson and their dad are grinning like they know life will never be better than this. And it never has been. As the raindrops splatter down on the phone, the image becomes less and less clear, the happy memories more hazy, the reality more blurred.

Two days after that photograph, Martha's mum was dead.

Tommy pulls his wallet out of his inside pocket and fishes out the beautifully constructed handmade card from Priya. The rain glides off the laminated surface without any impact. She thinks of everything. He stares at the happy family photo and the words *Please, for all of us* on the front, then turns it over. He's always thought he'd do anything for his family.

He reads the words on the back of the card, knowing what he has to do. Priya has written a list of the names, web addresses and emergency telephone numbers of several mental health support organisations including *Samaritans*, *Mind*, *Campaign Against Living Miserably* and *National Suicide Prevention Helpline UK*.

He takes his phone from his pocket and starts on the *Samaritans* number. He's heard of them.

"Jump, jump, jump." There's just one voice at first, coming from outside the pub, but it is soon joined by three, then four more, finally settling on a chorus of about ten, mainly male, drunk, laughing voices: no harmonies, no malice, just no idea what they're doing.

Johnson walks out of the pub carrying a tray of drinks to hear his friends chanting. He glances up at the bridge, where he can see a figure standing on the edge. The sky is darkening behind the person, so he can't make out any detail, but he knows he's got to do something quickly. He slams the drinks down on the table, causing a couple of glasses to fall off the tray and shatter on the ground below, then lifts both hands in the air, and waves them urgently.

"What the fuck are you doing? Stop it! That's a person up there, you arseholes! Shut the fuck up!"

It works. They shut up, but it is too late.

Tommy has heard the chanting too, stopped dialling and is running down the bridge in the direction of the figure at the other end. He wants to save them. It's not too late. There is help they can get. Tommy knows that. He's been told often enough. He's made that decision himself now.

Martha looks down at the garden of the Boathouse pub. It is well lit, so she can see exactly what is happening. JJ is waving his arms in the air, conducting his friends as they sing for her to jump. It will be her last memory.

Everything can change in an instant. It used to be the family motto; it used to be the reason not to worry. Things can get better just like that. But they can get worse too. She wishes her mum were here, hugging her, making her know that everything will be alright, letting her know how much she loves Martha. But she's not. Her mum chose to escape life rather than hug her daughter. Or, more accurately, she didn't choose, she just couldn't see any other option through the darkness engulfing her. How much pain must she have been in to do that? A pain that stopped her seeing straight; a pain that blocked out the ability to see the good things in her life; a pain that overshadowed even the dazzling, shining love she felt for her children so that, for a few seconds, it wasn't at the forefront of her thoughts. And a few seconds were all it took.

Martha understands that and wonders if her mum felt like she does today. With all her heart she hopes not. Today is one of those bleak days when, for no obvious reason, the pain pounds her head with such force that all she can focus on is stopping it; when the future looks as dark as the water rushing down the river below towards the weir; when Martha needs someone to help her, but they won't because they don't realise how she feels. She can't explain why she feels like she does, there's no cause she can pinpoint. She just does. And today she hasn't got the strength to fight it. On a better day, she would know that Johnson, her dad, anyone would help if she spoke to them and they knew. But today is not a better day, and they don't know. She always hides it too well.

Finn knows he should never should have gone out this evening. His clothes are drenched and the rain is dripping down his face, pausing only to take a detour around the scar on his left cheek, a remnant from when he used to fight for things. Though never the right things. Who was he kidding today? Why would Charley ever be interested in him? He doesn't deserve love. He had it once. And he ruined it.

He closes the door on the miserable evening, but is unable to stop the memories flooding in of the night he will always regret. He sits down on the stairs, squeezing his head in his hands as if trying to crush the thoughts of the last time he saw Niamh, but it only serves to push them to the front of his mind. She had been angry, lashing out at him that all her problems were his fault, that she had never wanted to be in California, that she would never have felt so desperately overcome with the relentless pain of mocking, unbearable depression were it not for his insistence that they all follow his dream. And maybe she was right. Finn will never know. She had said it before, many times, usually when they had both been drinking heavily, and he had always tried to reassure her, offered to return to Ireland to set up whatever life she would like, talked her down from her threats to kill herself. And every time, they had cried together, apologised, made up, confirmed their devotion to each other and their love, which really was genuine, and gone back to the same life. He knows now that that wasn't enough. Niamh was ill, badly ill. She needed proper help, the sort that he couldn't give. But he could have helped her get it. He knows that now too, and reminds himself every day.

But that night, he had been tired. It's no excuse, but it's the only one he's ever been able to find. And it's not good enough. He hadn't been frightened by her threat to end it all, and he hadn't believed for a second that she really would. He had heard it so many times before that it no longer had an impact. So he had shouted back, opened the drawer with all her prescription and non-prescription drugs, and thrown them on to the bed. "Go on then, just fucking do it." That's all he had said, and then he had left. He hadn't meant it, of course he hadn't. He had loved her with every fibre of his body, but sometimes even love can't withstand the momentary power of rage. So he had said it, gone out, and regretted it ever since.

It was the last time he had ever seen his wife alive.

It was the last time he had ever shouted at anyone.

It was the last time he had put himself before others and, most importantly, his children, their children. They're all Finn's got left to remind him of Niamh and they're all he cares about now. If he looks after them then maybe, just maybe, she will one day look down and forgive him for what he did.

But it may be too late. It often is.

Martha hauls herself up on the side of the bridge. She can hear footsteps racing towards her, so she has to be quick. She hurls herself forward and crashes into the water below.

Tommy is probably only a couple of seconds away when he sees the girl jump. He screams "noooo", grabs his phone from his pocket and dials 999. He has thought about this so many times before, but he has always been the participant not the observer. What makes one person jump and another decide not to? Who is the brave one? Who is more selfish? He hates himself for even thinking that. He hates himself for all his thoughts in fact. How unlucky is he to have witnessed two tragedies within a few days? He shouldn't be thinking that. It's not about him, it's about the two people whose lives he has seen end, and the pain of their abandoned loved ones. But he can't control his mind, it does what it wants. Especially when it knows it will intensify his self-hatred.

Johnson sees the person tumbling down to the river and starts racing towards the water. He is going to dive in, he is going to save them, everything is going to be OK.

Except it is not. He is rugby tackled by a friend trying to save his life, and lies face down on the ground in the garden of the Boathouse pub, as his sister is dragged towards the weir, its steep descent and the rocks below.

He doesn't know it is his sister yet. But he will find out. And he will search for answers, look for the events which caused Martha to jump and the people who made her feel so lost and desperate. But he will not find them, because they are not there. All he will find is an illness he didn't know she had, and maybe she didn't know she had.

And Johnson will know that he would have done anything to get his sister the help she needed, if he'd only known how she was struggling. But she had never told him, he had never noticed, and he had never known. He will always carry that too. She could have been helped, she could have been saved, and this could have been a very different ending. But she wasn't and it isn't.

Everything can change in an instant, and everything has.

Epilogue

Tommy Moore sits at the kitchen table staring at his iPad. Priya has gone to take some meals round for poor Finn and Johnson, and Nina is out with her friends. He can hear his youngest two children roaring with laughter in the front room as they watch clips of people trying the most dangerous or disgusting ways to eat different foods. It's as though nothing has changed for them. And, in truth, nothing has really. They are just like most of the residents of Sonnley: sure, they have heard or read about a couple of tragedies, maybe felt some twinges of sadness even, but mostly they didn't directly know the people involved, so their lives continue as usual.

For Tommy and those even more directly affected, however, nothing can ever be the same again. Their lives have changed forever. How will Finn, Johnson and Mel cope with their losses? What does the future hold for them? What do they do now? Tommy has asked those questions a lot recently, but he can't answer them. He can't even say with any confidence what's next for him.

But he's hopeful, and he can't remember when he was last able to say that about himself. The day after the tragedy, when he was alone in the house, he had taken out the laminated card again and completed the call he had almost made on the bridge. It had taken a while for him to open up, but once he had, everything had tumbled out as though his whole being had been constrained by a straitjacket for years and, with its removal, he were suddenly able to breathe and feel and express himself again.

He had told the stranger on the other end of the line about his self-hatred, his anxiety, his sense of worthlessness, his catastrophizing, his inability to be the parent and husband he had always longed to be, his guilt, his overwhelming fear, his self-hatred again, his lack of enthusiasm for anything, the terror which dominates his mind, the two tragedies he has recently witnessed, the impact of his behaviour on his family, his guilt again, the horrendous thoughts which seem intent on destroying him, the times he has considered killing himself to stop his pain and make his loved ones' lives better, and the utter, crushing desperation which had led him to make the call.

It hadn't magically made everything better, of course, but the overpowering relief he had felt after unburdening had been so unexpectedly liberating, like having a dental abscess drained so that it no longer pounds incessantly at every part of your head and it stops smashing your brain with a sledgehammer force which makes clear thinking impossible. You know it hasn't solved everything and further treatment will be required to resolve the underlying problem, but this first step has taken away so much of the immediate pain that has made life unbearable. But it's different too, because everyone is affected by the attitudes of the world they live in: Tommy wouldn't have waited almost fifteen years to have a dental abscess treated.

Since the call, he has found the strength to take other steps which he would never have felt able to before, for whatever reasons. He's had an appointment with a doctor, discussed options such as counselling, medication and Cognitive Behavioural Therapy, and he's beginning to get some hope back. There's a long way to go, and the thoughts, worries and fears haven't miraculously disappeared yet, but it's a start. And where there's a start, there's a chance of an end.

Tommy looks at a comment piece on the Sonnley Gazette website by someone whose qualifications he instantly forgets. He can't seem to help himself in the two weeks since the tragedy on the bridge. He's read everything he can find online about the heartbreaking incident, secretly of course, so that no one thinks he's got a warped morbid fascination with what happened. He hasn't, at least he hopes he hasn't. He just wants to try to make sense of it all, if there is any sense to be made, that is.

He flicks through the comment piece as it reflects on how Martha's "tragic case" should be a wake-up call for the whole town, until he reaches a few sentences which he reads over and over again.

What we do know with absolute certainty is that there will be many more people everywhere in the world struggling like Martha. In some cases, it'll be obvious; in others, it'll only be visible to a few; in others still, not even the closest family and friends will spot it.

But there are ways forward: give help when we see it, ask for help when we need it and keep checking just in case. Keep listening, keep talking, keep asking.

Tommy thinks about Finn, Johnson and Mel again, and shudders at the thought of the pain they must be going through. But he makes himself stop before his mind follows its usual downward spiral into a series of what-ifs and imagined further horrors. It's not that he doesn't care, of course he does. But if he follows his mind, it's not going to help them and it's not going to help him. It's not easy, but he forces himself to get up and go over to open the door to the front room. Mia and Kian don't notice him come in. They are both rocking back and forwards, laughing hysterically as a blindfolded man tosses the contents of a can of dog food in the air and tries to catch them in his mouth. Tommy stands in silence for a few seconds and just listens to his children's uncontrolled laughter and pure, unconditional joy. He smiles, sits down on the sofa next to them and focuses on the action on screen until there is nothing else in his mind other than this moment. Then he too starts laughing.

It's a start.

Acknowledgements

Thank you to my children, Joe, Alice and Chloe for your love, support and putting up with me all your lives.

For reading and giving invaluable feedback on my novel, I thank Oscar, Jenny, Joe (again), Dave, Cath, Tom and Daf.

Thanks to Robin and Julie for your wonderful artwork, kind comments on the book and coping with my indecisiveness.

To all the family and friends who have encouraged me along the way, thank you. I am lucky to have you.

And finally, special thanks to the two people without whose generosity, support and input this book would never have happened:

My brother, Dave, thank you for your amazing help and hard work, reading and re-reading the book many times, editing, telling me honestly what did and didn't work, and giving me the opportunity to complete the book. I couldn't have done this without you.

My wife, Daf, thank you for your sacrifices, your tolerance and your belief which allowed me to focus on and complete the book. You kept me going through the writing, and you keep me going through life.

Printed in Great Britain
by Amazon